THOUGHTS BY PAULEY

STEPHEN G. PAULEY JR.

A compilation of musings, poems, phrases, peculiarities, tales, memories, and various curiosities from my mind. You can read it sequentially from start to finish or select a number and read that piece. Some entries are brief, while others are more extensive. A few might evoke memories for you, while others may paint vivid images. You might even find yourself pondering or discussing a theme or two. You may love it, dislike it, or feel indifferent about parts of it. I welcome your thoughts and feedback, as I appreciate how different people interpret these writings.

TABLE OF CONTENTS

1. I Envy You

I envy you.

I envy the person who makes more money than me.

I envy the person who makes less money than me but appreciates all that they have in life more.

I envy those who have a multitude of friends and family.

I envy those who have few friends and family but form a solid bond that lasts longer with more meaning.

I envy those who travel to beautiful, scenic, exciting, and adventurous destinations.

I envy those who cannot travel but can look out the window and appreciate the beauty in nature around them with a genuine smile.

I envy those who smile like they have no worries in the world.

I envy those who live their life in a constant struggle but can look you in the eye with a warm and gentle smile.

I envy those who always seem to be on top of the world.

I envy those who get knocked down but always come back stronger.

I envy those who have a rewarding, fulfilling career.

I envy those who awake each day and, go to work, and do the best they can with what they are given.

I envy you.

2. My Hot Tub Is My Solace

I cannot deny that my hot tub is my refuge. It serves as my sanctuary, a place where I can retreat from the chaos of the outside world and the burdens of life. Beyond the warm, enclosed waters, there exist stress, worries, and dark thoughts. Yet, within, I find warmth, relaxation, comfort, uplifting thoughts, and an unexpected sense of Zen. Caring for my old hot tub is also a way of preserving my mental clarity. It allows me to carve out moments of tranquility amid the daily demands. My hot tub embodies my peace, and the ritual of maintaining it symbolizes my commitment to my own well-being.

My son at an early age, and I in my hot tub I have kept for many years

3.   Random Acts Of Kindness

What if we were each required to carry out one random act of kindness every day? Perhaps this would lead to more smiles and fewer frowns. As we exchanged more kind gestures and shared smiles, the overall atmosphere in the world could transform. People might feel a greater sense of connection, value, and belonging.

There could also be a shift from sorrow to hope. Kindness can serve as a shield against life's difficulties. On challenging days, just knowing that someone cares enough to show kindness can offer vital hope and encouragement. Ultimately, life could become a little easier for everyone.

4.   Change Your Routine

Can you change your routine?

Can you turn off the news for a day or two?

Can you survive without social media?

Can you find something new?

Can you explore?

Can you grow?

5. A Simple Clock In My Home Is My Home's Heartbeat

I have a simple clock in my home—a battery-operated Ohio State Clock. It hangs in a somewhat awkward spot in the archway of the living room leading to the kitchen. However, if you silence the TV, your phone, and all the music, you can hear its ticking. Indeed, the ticking of my clock serves as the heartbeat of my home, its rhythmic pulse. If you linger a little longer, you might even notice my home breathing. That's just the furnace, providing warmth and life to the space. As you stroll through the hallways and various rooms, you might hear the soft creaks—are they the bones of my home, much like my own body creaks with age and arthritis? My belongings grow old and worn, and as I age, I often seek something new to revitalize myself. Sometimes, I simply change things up to feel refreshed. I look around my home, aiming to repair something old or bring in something new to enhance its ambiance. I often wonder if my home appreciates it when I clean, rearrange, or introduce something fresh. Perhaps it smiles when I tend to it, and in turn, maybe it takes care of me.

6.   You Cannot Change People

You cannot change others; each person is responsible for their own transformation. Only they have the power to take the steps necessary for change. Our role is to provide support. People may seek your support in different ways, and you can offer it simply by being present, listening without judgment, and giving them the space to share their thoughts and feelings. Ideally, they will recognize this and reach out when they need it. It's important to let those who are struggling know that you are there for them in whatever capacity they require. But is it most effective to communicate that you're available to support them in any way they might need?

7.   Birds Of A Feather Flock Together

As I continued to watch the birds gliding through the open sky, their synchronized movements evoked a sense of camaraderie and purpose. The image of that one bird struggling to keep pace sparked a deeper reflection within me. Why is it that some birds thrive in unity while others find themselves apart, searching for a place where they belong?

I imagined the solitary bird on the pond, its wings fluttering aimlessly as it splashed in the water, blissfully unaware of the vast world beyond. When the realization hit—the absence of the flock—it must feel like the ground beneath it has vanished. The water, once a playground, transforms into a cage of uncertainty. Would its calls be heard? Would they pierce through the rhythm of the flock above, or would they fade into silence?

In this moment, I contemplated my own role in this tapestry of flight. Am I the leader, confidently guiding others, ensuring that no bird lags behind? Do I take charge when the winds shift, charting a course for all to follow? Or am I the wingman, offering support, a steady presence that others can lean on in troubling times, ensuring that no one flies too far afield alone?

But could I also be the lost soul? The one searching for direction, floundering in the vastness of choices and paths? It's a troubling thought, feeling adrift in uncertainty, longing for connection but unsure where to seek it. In moments of confusion, do I cry out for help, reaching for the familiar calls of fellow travelers?

As I pondered these questions, I felt the urge to reach out, not just for myself but for the solitary bird, for anyone who has experienced wandering in circles, yearning for a place within the flock. Perhaps the true essence of flight lies in the understanding that we are all interconnected—leaders, wingmen, and lost souls alike.

And in that connection, there exists a power: the power to notice those who struggle, to glide back and extend a wing, to guide them home. After all, the beauty of the sky isn't solely in the formation of the flock but in the strength found in unity, the compassion of returning for those who need it most. So, what choice will I make today? Will I soar alone or embrace the challenge of ensuring no one is left behind?

8. Around The Bend

I have always been captivated by streams, creeks, rivers, or any flowing waterway. The water carries you along your journey, encouraging you to observe the banks for anyone or anything that might be watching. Bridges serve not only as crossings but also as reference points in your travels. You become aware of your surroundings, absorbing everything around you. Occasionally, you glance back to reflect on your origins and check for anything approaching from behind. As you look ahead, your neck twists in anticipation of the bend. Your mind fills with questions: What awaits around the curve? Could it be new adventures or perhaps an obstacle like a dam?

Even more captivating is the fork in the water—an important decision lies ahead. Which path should you take? Will it lead to a good choice? Is it quicker, safer, or filled with more excitement and opportunities? In life, we strive to move forward, sometimes aided along the way. While we enjoy the scenery, we also stay vigilant for what might be following us and what lies ahead, just as in our lives. The journeys of others intersect with ours, much like bridges we pass beneath throughout our lives.

Life is laden with choices. When faced with a fork in your path, don't dread the possibilities you may have left behind. Embrace everything that comes your way and appreciate it. Rather than ruminating on missed chances, welcome the opportunities that present themselves, both on the water and in life. This is a reminder to stay present in our experiences, to relish the beauty of each moment, and to recognize that every journey is enriched by the people and encounters we experience, each acting as a bridge connecting our stories. May you find joy in your journey, no matter how the currents may carry you.

Roaring Fork Motor Trail, Gatlinburg, Tennessee

9. The Journey Or The Summit

Reaching the summit isn't what truly matters; rather, it's the journey that leads us there. Some claim we are all meant for a specific purpose in this world, but I believe our true selves are shaped by the paths we choose. As we navigate life's highs and lows—its challenges and triumphs, successes and setbacks—it's essential to surround ourselves with supportive people who can lift us when we stumble, just as we offer them our support in return. Let us stand strong today and embrace each moment, fostering resilience as we move forward together.

10. The Sting

I'm not sure why, but I recently recalled a time from my high school football days. During warm-ups, I decided to lie on my back to stretch when suddenly, I felt a sharp pain in my back. It took me a moment to realize I had been stung by a bee. I called over a helper—who wasn't really a coach—to get some ice. He applied it to my back, and I managed to play through the entire game.

I also think back to my little Yorkshire Terrier, Winston. One day, I found him in the yard behaving oddly, biting at his back—something he never did. I brought him inside and grabbed a comb. As I started to groom him, I discovered bees tangled in his fur. Poor Winston must have stumbled upon a hive in the ground. They were stinging him and getting caught in his hair, and he was struggling so hard that he even lost a few teeth. Despite his pain, he never cried or whined, but the discomfort in his eyes spoke volumes. Animals have a remarkable ability to communicate their feelings without words.

Then, there was the time my mother got stung by a blue hornet in our backyard. Her arm swelled to twice its size, but she was tough and recovered quickly without much complaint. It's astonishing how much damage a tiny insect can inflict.

I remember playing catch with my brother once when a wild throw hit a tree branch, triggering a hornet's nest. Suddenly, my brother took off running toward the house at lightning speed, realizing too late that hornets were stinging him on the way. For some reason, he never wanted to play catch with me again after that.

I've also had my fair share of encounters with hornets. While trimming the yard near a big old dead tree, I was stung in the head and arm by a swarm of large European hornets. In a panic, I dropped everything and bolted to my neighbor's house, banging on the door. Surprisingly, they quickly offered me ice, and I asked them to keep an eye on me for a few minutes, just in case.

My friend and I devised a strategy to eliminate the hornet problem in that tree. We donned extra layers of clothing, safety glasses, and gloves to protect ourselves. Despite using various sprays and even Sevin dust, nothing seemed to work. In the end, we resorted to foam to seal the queen inside the nest. Afterward, the hornets dispersed, and the dead ones may still be trapped within the tree's hollow center. One day, I might cut apart the stump to uncover the remnants of that unsettling experience. Those colossal bugs have definitely left an impression on

European Hornet – actual picture and close up stock picture

11. The Word Of Mouth Or The Human Touch?

Which is more powerful, word of mouth or human touch? Words hold incredible power in numerous ways. They can direct our actions, shape opinions, and inspire change. They offer encouragement, praise, and joy, as well as the ability to influence decisions and disseminate information quickly. However, they can also bring pain, sadness, and anger.

In contrast, human touch establishes a unique connection that goes beyond verbal communication, creating a deep emotional bond. A simple touch, such as a hug, a pat on the back, or holding hands, conveys empathy, understanding, and support in a very real way. It brings feelings of warmth, compassion, and hope, fostering a sense of safety and belonging that can profoundly impact mental and emotional health. Often, the warmth of human connection can heal wounds that words cannot reach. The simple act of a hug is a treasured gift, as the human touch is always infused with love.

12. The Robin And It's Morning Song

Initially, I thought of the robin as a rather unique little bird. It's not the most visually striking creature, and it rarely visits bird feeders. Instead, it prefers to scurry along the ground with its head tilted, searching for unsuspecting worms. Robins don't typically associate with other bird species, although I've occasionally spotted a group perched together in a tree, seeking comfort and protection. They remind me of the way nerds congregate in a school lunchroom for camaraderie. Together, they seem to feel a greater sense of safety. However, upon further reflection, I discovered more about robins. Their distinct morning song is like an alarm clock for some people, often starting as early as 5, 4, or even 3 a.m. For light sleepers like myself, that early wake-up call doesn't always align with the schedule! Interestingly, their melody consists of a series of whistles with repeated syllables, descending in pitch but speeding up as it progresses. Some liken it to the cheerful phrase: "cheerily, cheer up, cheer up, cheer up, cheerily, cheer up." This rise and fall in pitch is delivered steadily, punctuated by brief pauses before it begins anew. Robins have nearly 100 intricate songs and phrases, though I can only identify one. They sing to establish their territory and attract mates.

There is a belief that dreaming of a robin signifies new opportunities for growth. Just like each robin, we are all unique and special in our ways. We strive to protect our homes and claim our space while also singing our own songs to seek love. We may not always be striking in appearance, but the beauty within us serves a purpose, even if it goes unrecognized by others. So, the next time you see or hear a robin, may it remind you of new possibilities, familial connections, and a sense of hope.

16

13. The 2-Minute Sunrise

At sunrise, the transition from the first glimpse of the sun's tip to its full emergence takes about two minutes. I've had the wonderful opportunity to experience a true sunrise rising from the Atlantic Ocean, and it was nothing short of magical. As I made my way to the beach, the darkness gradually receded, giving way to the gentle light awakening the day. I set up my chair on the sand, listening to the waves crash on the shore while a soothing breeze brushed my face. It felt as if I had just taken my seat in a grand concert hall.

Looking around, I noticed individuals and families arriving for the show. They each found their spots, with some choosing to stand and take it all in. Mothers held their children's hands, engrossed in playing with seashells, oblivious to the breathtaking spectacle about to unfold. A father lifted his young son into his arms, turning him toward the horizon with a beaming smile as if to say, "Just wait, son; this is worth the wait. You might not fully appreciate it now, but someday you will." An elderly couple embraced, their eyes fixed on the horizon, eagerly anticipating the conductor's signal to start the performance.

Indeed, I felt like I was in a natural symphony hall, surrounded by the sounds of a crowd buzzing with anticipation, like the instruments warming up for a concert. Then it happened. The conductor tapped his wand on the stand, and the crowd hushed, eyes directed toward the horizon, now a stage. The performance commenced as a faint orange glow began to rise. Gradually, clouds lingered above, and as the two minutes unfolded, the colors became bolder and brighter. The atmosphere crackled with excitement as the clouds parted, revealing the sun like a maestro guiding an orchestra.

Finally, the climax arrived—the sun ascended fully above the horizon, radiant in its splendor. The conductor lowered his wand and bowed. The elderly couple shared a kiss and strolled away hand in hand, while couples reunited as children resumed their playful antics in the water and with seashells. Some individuals walked away, initially cast down by despair, only to turn back and seek solace in the sun's hopeful glow.

I found myself wondering if anyone else on the beach would express their appreciation for the spectacle. As I stood and applauded, a few turned to smile and laugh at me, but many joined in the standing ovation, united in awe and reverence for the beauty of nature we had just witnessed. It was a brief performance, yet one of the most memorable experiences of my life.

Sunrise – Myrtle Beach, South Carolina

14. Wit Over Education

Some individuals possess extensive education yet may not appear particularly intelligent, while others may lack formal schooling but come across as very insightful. Education and intelligence don't always align. Personally, I find great joy in engaging with people who have wit and character. When someone with these qualities shares their stories and adventures, I'm eager to listen all day long. Those who have lived rich lives filled with diverse experiences tend to tell more engaging stories.

Wit and character can elevate a simple chat into an exciting adventure, often infused with humor and profound insights, making the conversation more compelling.

By embracing life and continually learning from our surroundings, and by infusing our discussions with humor and authenticity, we create a lasting impact. Indeed, a person who is rich in life experiences often shines brighter than any formal education could provide.

15. Unspoken Words But Being There

When my father was nearing the end of his life, I felt somewhat numb and uncertain about what to do or say. However, I recognized the importance of being present for both my mother and father. I did what I could physically—driving them around, picking up things they needed, and giving my father every chance to share his thoughts with me. I hoped he might offer some advice or express what he wanted for my future. In the end, he only asked for a final Whopper from Burger King and for assistance getting to the bathroom while he had a catheter. It was a clear sign that the end was approaching. I prioritized my father's needs over my own during that time.

Now, my approach to communication with my son has changed significantly. The experiences I went through with my father's passing have taught me to embrace a more open and heartfelt way of connecting. I truly value our one-on-one conversations, where we can share our thoughts in a personal manner. Although we can't physically support each other like we did when he was younger, we both know we're there for one another, even in silence. I hope my father knew that I was there for him during his final days.

16. Flying In Your Dream

I've had a few truly unique dreams, though I can't pinpoint what triggered them or what was on my mind at the time. This particular dream stood out as different. I found myself walking in the backyard of my childhood home when, for some reason, I began to run for a few steps. That running transformed into the motion of pedaling a bike, despite there being no actual bike—no handlebars to grip or pedals for my feet. As I pedaled faster, I suddenly lifted off the ground, gaining altitude and direction control while floating above the trees. How could I conjure such an image that I'd never witnessed while awake? What was I seeking? I distinctly felt the exhilaration of floating and the power of controlling my flight. The view from above offered a fascinating perspective, and something urged me to go higher before ending my journey. Gradually, I slowed my pedaling and descended gently back to the ground. When I landed, my pedaling transitioned into a light run, and I came to a smooth stop before waking up. After reading about potential interpretations of this dream, I found that dreams of flying often symbolize a yearning for freedom, escape, or the desire to rise above challenges and explore new perspectives. It also suggested that my questioning during the dream reflects an inner search for solutions or clarity regarding real-life situations.

17. Smiling Back To Prison

I had a dream about someone I know who was on vacation in a place where I was as well. (Dreams can be quite fragmented at times.) He was smiling and clearly happy to be experiencing a goal he had set for himself. But suddenly, he had to get into a vehicle, and the people were taking him back to prison. Remarkably, he kept smiling and seemed unconcerned about what was happening. This made me reflect on the idea that one should pursue their goals without regrets.

18. Red And Blue

Red and blue are the colors I adore;

Green and yellow may suit others more.

Black clothing seems dreary and bland,

While white comes off as plain and unplanned.

Chartreuse was the shade I chose for my fishing lure,

And pink on a man comes across as quite mature.

I prefer to embrace bright and vibrant hues,

Hoping to uplift spirits and spread good news.

Coco Chanel famously stated, "The best color in the world is the one that flatters you."

Imagine if everyone wore chartreuse; what a fresh perspective we'd pursue.

19. The Grocery Shopping Dream

I walked into a small grocery store that I thought I was familiar with, but the layout was quite different. I had a grocery cart with me and was holding a large piece of chocolate candy from an unknown brand that I had brought into the store. I worried that I might have to pay for it, and I felt like people were giving me strange looks as I moved around, partially opening the wrapper and eating while shopping. It felt like I had no taste for it, and I was trying to eat the candy quickly to avoid making a mess and to stop the stares. The store's arrangement seemed completely chaotic, and I felt like I was going in the wrong direction.

As I continued, I encountered some plates filled with food blocking the aisle. Unsure of what to do, I got down on my knees to move each plate out of the way so I could get my cart through. Suddenly, my dream shifted to a different area, and I noticed a tangle of string lying on the ground — it was part of my bracelet, all in a mess. I started to pick it up, but it was difficult to hold because the candy wrapper was still in my hand and it was hard to manage the cart at the same time. I never made it to the checkout, as my dream either changed or I woke up.

It's interesting how my dreams are often fragmented and never unfold in the way I expect. I always find myself pondering what prompts my mind to create these scenarios. I believe dreams consist of elements from the past, present, and future, all intertwining to form the strange experiences I encounter. I've read that my dream could reflect discomfort or confusion in unfamiliar settings. The candy might symbolize indulgence or temptation, illustrating behaviors during vulnerable moments. The blocked aisles could represent life's barriers and feelings of being overwhelmed by responsibilities. My instinct to get on my knees to clear the plates shows my willingness to tackle obstacles with humility, even when faced with challenges that can make me feel small.

20. The Quiet? Morning

The serene atmosphere wrapped around me like a warm and fuzzy blanket, creating a perfect sanctuary for relaxation. The gentle cadence of the birds' chirping blended harmoniously with the rhythmic ticking of the clock, lulling me deeper into tranquility. Sunlight filtered softly through the curtains, casting a warm glow that felt inviting and peaceful.

As I stirred awake, the realization of my own snoring drew a smile across my face. It was comical yet comforting to know that I wasn't alone in my Sunday slumber. The sounds of gentle snoring from another room suggested that someone else had succumbed to the soothing embrace of this lazy morning, too.

In that moment, the world outside faded away, and it struck me how Sundays seem to possess a unique magic—an unhurried pace that encourages us to slow down and savor the stillness. It's as if time itself decides to take a break, allowing everyone to embrace the soft silence and let their minds wander to rest.

With that thought, I settled back into my chair, closing my eyes for just a moment longer, knowing that the quietness of a Sunday morning is a gift we all deserve.

21. My Yard Is Not Pristine

My yard isn't pristine; it's distinctive and filled with character and imperfections, much like myself. It boasts dandelions, just like the attributes within me that some may view with disdain while others find beautiful. There are uneven patches throughout, just as my body has its own curves and contours. Some might glance at my yard and not be particularly impressed—and the same goes for how many perceive me. Yet, my yard is brimming with character. When you take a closer look, you discover all kinds of fascinating details, much like when you delve into my life and truly get to know me. Some days, I might resemble crabgrass; other days, I could be like a wild weed or even like thriving Kentucky bluegrass. There are days when my hair is long, reflecting the overgrown state of my yard, while other days, a fresh haircut leaves me feeling revitalized, just as mowing and trimming transforms my yard. Indeed, my yard is just as captivating as the intricate tapestry of my life.

22. Unicorns Vs Warm Blankets

Unicorns, dragons, stardust, moonbeams, electric seahorses—or perhaps warm blankets, sunshine, smiles, lively music, and delicious food? I truly believe that joy can flourish in our imaginations and dreams. However, nothing compares to the tangible warmth of happiness we can experience in the real world. Is true love nestled somewhere in the middle of these experiences? Perhaps finding a balance between the two is essential not only for our own happiness but also for uplifting others and making the world a better place.

When you feel a chill, wrap yourself in a cozy blanket. Relish the sensation of sunshine on your face and let it bring a smile. Dance to your favorite tunes and savor every bite of delightful food. When you're feeling low, take a moment to immerse yourself in your imagination. Picture unicorns frolicking with dragons, gliding along moonbeams with trails of stardust while electric seahorses swim alongside. Embrace the magic of both reality and fantasy to enrich your life and spread joy to those around you.

23. Poison Ivy/Sumac/Oak

Every year, it's the same story for me: I decide it's time to tackle some yard work and plan to wear a long-sleeved shirt for protection. But after a while, I take it off to take a break, grab a snack, and have a drink. I convince myself that I can finish quickly without it. A day or two later, I notice a small bump on my arm, and I think, "That's not too bad." I apply a dab of cream and move on. However, as time goes on, the rash spreads, and soon enough, it feels like a burn in the middle of the night, keeping me awake. At that point, I resort to slathering on various topical treatments and taking long hot showers to alleviate the itch. I can't help but wonder when I'll finally learn my lesson. I try to stick to wearing long sleeves while it heals, worrying it won't clear up before my appointments, holidays, and vacations. But the rash continues to spread instead. I eventually run out of ointments and start searching for other remedies. Yet, I still haven't made it to the doctor or the drugstore for cortisone and steroids. I guess it is just classic stubborn me.

I might catch this just from the picture

24. The Sound And Movement Of A Storm

As I lounged on the couch, I noticed a storm was forecasted to hit my area. Most people would have hurried to the basement, gathering candles, radios, cell phones, important documents, and laptops. But not me—I felt an urge to step outside. With the rain holding off for now, it was the perfect opportunity to soak in the atmosphere.

The low rumble of thunder echoed in various directions, both near and far. There was no sharp lightning typical of a severe storm; instead, soft rumbles hinted at the brewing tempest. For a fleeting moment, I wondered about the odds of being struck by lightning. The flashes seemed gentle and tucked away in the clouds, not reaching toward the ground.

I looked around, observing the changes in the sky. I tried to understand if the clouds were moving in different directions or growing in volume, darkness, and intensity. The storm appeared to be a subtle grey, with light, airy clouds that exhibited a bit of movement. Surprisingly, there was not a hint of dark weather on the horizon despite the warnings of impending severe conditions.

When the rain finally began, my outdoor nature show came to an end, and I retreated inside to stay dry, occasionally glancing out to check for changes. Would I venture out again in the calm before a storm? Absolutely!

25. The Gas Attendant

I remember being a young kid, nestled in the backseat of my parents' car. I can't quite remember our destination, but I vividly remember a stop at a gas station. Back then, there was an attendant who would rush out to take payment and begin filling up the tank. He took my father's money and started pumping gas. As he neared the $10 mark, he would do a playful 360 spin and tap the pump like a cowboy with a gun. Sometimes, he'd hit it right on target; other times, he'd be off by a few cents. I wonder if he ever faced repercussions for going over, but he seemed to enjoy his straightforward job too much to care. Perhaps we could all use a little spin at our own jobs now and then to lighten the day. I just hope a young child doesn't misinterpret my actions.

26. Devil's Hill

During my youth in winter, sledding was the ultimate thrill. For many, Mount Oberlin, located behind the hospital, was the go-to spot—a popular destination that, for me, lacked any real enchantment. Climbing the hill only to slide straight down felt too predictable and dull, and the throngs of kids diminished any magic the place might have offered. My friends and I, however, had our hearts and minds set on Devil's Hill, a spot we considered truly special.

The trek to our treasured hill was always a snowy adventure. We would huddle together, sometimes catching a ride on a sled from a parent, but mostly relishing the walk. Starting out on the sidewalk, we would reach a fork in the path: the old railroad tracks or the winding trail. For me, the choice was easy—the trail was more than just a route to the arboretum where Devil's Hill lay; it was an adventure through nature. Often untouched and blanketed in fresh snow, it beckoned us to forge our way through. Birds greeted us with their songs, filling the crisp, cold air with life, while the sun illuminated the white-coated trees, creating a winter wonderland that felt like a scene from a storybook.

The journey would often feel endless until we rounded a familiar bend and saw the little ridge marking the summit of Devil's Hill. The sight of the little ridge marking the summit filled us with anticipation and joy. Standing at the top, we were greeted with a breathtaking panorama, a sprawling view that invited us to scan the landscape for the best sledding paths to take. Our eyes would glare down the hill, searching for glimpses of the creek tucked away beyond the base. The thrill of potential exploration danced in our minds, but first, we checked to see if we had the place to ourselves. If the hill was empty, a wave of glee washed over us as we felt that this snowy paradise felt entirely ours. But if others were there, we formed an unspoken agreement to stick to our own paths, hoping they would soon vacate so we could take full advantage of the hill's offerings.

We loved carving new trails and building daring jumps that launched us momentarily into the air. The feeling of weightlessness was exhilarating, mingling joy with a tinge of fear as we glided down, wondering if we might land awkwardly and injure ourselves. At the bottom of the hill, we would look back up, surrounded by tall trees on three sides, as if we were in our own winter fairy tale. The creek loomed behind us, but we never worried about crashing into it, as a small ridge served as a natural barrier.

After playing games of who could go the farthest, who went first, and who had the coolest jump, we would sometimes venture to explore the creek. Occasionally, it was frozen; sometimes, it wasn't. If it was, we felt compelled to test our courage by walking on the delicate ice. One particularly memorable time, we walked along the creek until we hit a patch, and all fell in up to our chests. It sparked chaos and laughter, with our squeals echoing among the trees. Our boots squished with every step, and the fabric clung to our skin. Despite the unexpected mishap, we were happy to be together, sharing in the fun, though we were all a bit anxious about how our parents would react when we returned home. As it turned out, our parents were just relieved we were safe rather than scolding us for our adventure.

Later in life, I took my son and a neighbor to this magical place. We drove there, entering from a different direction, and I didn't realize how challenging it would be for them to navigate through the deep snow to reach the hill. When we finally got to the base, they collapsed in exhaustion, lying in the snow for a moment. After one quick run up and down the hill, they were ready to go home. They trudged back to the car, demolishing the spectacle of it all. So, what was magic to me was definitely not to them.

While Mount Oberlin might have dazzled some, I would choose the magic of Devil's Hill any day. Our experiences shape our feelings about places and activities, even when they don't live up to the grandeur of our cherished memories.

27. Rhythmic Phrases We Used To See Who Went First

The magic of childhood often lies in the little rituals we created, and nothing captured that spirit more than the phrases we'd chant in a circle before diving into a game. Gatherings marked by laughter and anticipation surrounded these rhythmic incantations, each serving to determine who would lead the fun.

One of our favorites was a classic: "Eenie, Meanie, Minnie, Moe. Catch a tiger by his tail. If he hollers, let him go. And you are not it." It felt almost like a musical countdown, a delightful prelude to whatever game came next, and the excitement in the air was infectious.

Then there was the whimsical: "Bubble gum, bubble gum, in a dish, how many pieces do you wish?" The playful exchange, where the chosen one would declare a number, initiated a countdown full of expectant giggles. "One, two, three, four…" we'd count, fingers pointing toward each hopeful participant until the final declaration of, "…and you are not it." "Engine, engine number 9, going down Chicago line," was another favorite, with its catchy rhythm that prompted responses of "yes" or "no." The anticipation built as we'd pivot our fingers to spell out our destinies: "Y, E, S," or "N, O." The thrill of being chosen—or not—was profound.

When it came to hide and seek, we'd count with fervor: "5, 10, 15, 20…" racing through the numbers, with anticipation building as we reached "100." "Apples, peaches, pumpkin pie, who's not ready holler 'I.'" Yet, humorously, no one ever did shout "I"; we seemed to enjoy the thrill of hiding more than anything else.

But my favorite of all was a line that flowed effortlessly, steeped in memories: "My mother and your mother lived across the street, and every night they have a fight, and this is what they say: Ikaboda, sodabaka, ikaboda boo, ikaboda, sodabaka, out goes you." The playful rhymes wrapped around my tongue and stuck in my head, a verbal melody that felt like a secret code shared amongst friends.

These phrases weren't just silly chants; they were the fabric of our childhood camaraderie. Each repeat carried with it laughter, creativity, and the beautiful simplicity of youth. They felt like rites of passage, passed down from one generation to the next, holding within them the essence of carefree days.

In a world often too serious, those chants are time capsules of innocence and joy. Hearing one can instantly transport us back to sun-drenched afternoons, where our greatest worries revolved around who would be "it" in the next round of tag. They encapsulate the spirit of friendship, spontaneity, and the playful language that flourished among kids as we crafted our own little worlds. As we reminisce, these phrases conjure smiles, laughter, and a profound fondness for the moments that shaped our childhood.

28. The Infamous 21st Street Bridge Jump

My father was a rather reserved man who enjoyed engaging with others through conversation. Occasionally, out of nowhere, he would share some wild anecdotes. To this day, we still aren't sure if they were genuine experiences or just elaborate fabrications designed to amuse those around him. One particular story stands out as quite remarkable. In Lorain, Ohio, there is a lengthy bridge that spans the Black River—it's called the 21st Street Lofton Henderson Memorial Bridge, named in honor of a local hero who lost his life in the Battle of Midway when he crashed his plane into a Japanese ship.

As a child, I found the bridge intimidating, with its daunting steel framework. Driving across it felt like entering a tunnel of twisted metal, casting a foreboding shadow on my mind. Then, one day, my father recounted a daring tale from his youth related to that very bridge. "I once jumped off this bridge," he announced. We all exchanged surprised glances, thinking he must be joking. Intrigued, we pressed him for more details. He recounted a dare from a friend who challenged him to leap into the water below for ten bucks. He claimed he took a leap of faith and jumped. Later on, he clarified that he didn't jump from the highest part of the bridge, or else he probably wouldn't have been there to tell the tale. He described hitting the water feet first, a jarring impact as if he had crashed into concrete, plunging all the way to the muddy riverbed. The water was murky and filthy, and he found himself stuck up to his waist in the sludge. After some wiggling, he managed to free himself and burst back to the surface, gasping for air. Naturally, we were curious if he had collected his ten dollars for the stunt. He laughed and said he had to tackle the guy to get paid.

That was my dad—whether or not it truly happened remains a mystery, but it makes for a fantastic story. Now, whenever I cross that bridge, I'm no longer filled with fear; instead, I simply shake my head and smile at the thought of it.

The 21st Street Lofton Henderson Memorial Bridge

29. My Father, The Robber, And The Can

Here is another one of my father's stories that was hard to believe. He worked in a gas station owned by his own father when he was young. One day, while he was attending the counter, a robber came in with a gun and asked for all the money. My father gave him the money, but when the robber turned to walk out the door, he swiped in one motion with his hand a can of oil and nailed the robber right in the back of the head, knocking him completely out. The police arrived and arrested the robber. His father arrived and gave him a very stern talking. My dad really liked to pretend to throw that can in one swipe, telling that story. It always scares me to think how I will react in certain confrontations: will I do what they say and let it go, or will I fight someone threatening me with a knife or gun? Hmmmm...

30. Fishing, Run, And Laugh

One time, my dad, my uncle, and I went fishing near Lakeview Park in Lorain, just past the beach. We lugged our gear over logs and debris to find our perfect spot. For a while, everything seemed fine as we cast our lines out. Then, I glanced towards the horizon and noticed something eerie—it looked like it was creeping closer. They turned their gaze toward the water, and it didn't take long for us to realize that a line of rain was rapidly approaching. Suddenly, we were hit with a surge of adrenaline, and we hurriedly reeled in our lines and packed up our gear. As we rushed back to the truck, I barely registered the obstacles in our path; it felt as though we were flying. I had never seen my dad and uncle move so quickly. We made it to the truck just as the rain started pouring down; visibility was reduced to nearly nothing. But we got there in time. The relief of finding shelter just before the torrential downpour hit us was a blend of exhilaration and gratitude.

31. My Dad And The Ice Rescue

My father had a knack for sharing stories that left you questioning their validity. One day, he claimed that while ice fishing on Lake Erie, he had to be rescued by a helicopter. To him, it appeared as though it was just an ordinary occurrence as if nothing out of the ordinary had happened. His casual demeanor made it difficult to fully doubt his tale. Perhaps he was simply a master of his own narratives, turning every experience into something bigger than life itself. We exchanged perplexed glances, still unsure what to believe.

32. Sheep Head And The Trip To The Hospital

I've always believed that if someone truly values something you can easily give them, you should share it. There was an elderly couple living just around the corner from my parent's house, and my father was the kind of person who would strike up a conversation with anyone. He discovered that this couple loved to eat fish — all kinds of fish, even those most people would throw back, like carp and sheep heads.

Sheep heads, also known as freshwater drums, have a unique feature: within their heads, there are what we call "lucky stones," small stones marked with an "L." One day, after a successful fishing trip where we caught several sheep heads along with other keepers, I decided to take some over to our neighbors.

When I knocked on their door and announced, "I have fish for you!" the expressions on their faces were priceless; it was as if I had presented them with a treasure. The wife looked delighted and seemed ready to clean and cook the fish right away. I shared the story of the lucky stones, and they listened with genuine interest. However, a gut feeling told me not to overstay my welcome, so after cheerful goodbyes, I left them still beaming.

As I rounded the corner toward my parents' house, lugging the cooler, everything changed in an instant. My brother and father burst out of the house, running toward me, and I initially thought they were about to confront me for some unknown reason. It quickly became clear that my dad was having a heart attack, and they were rushing to the truck.

I tossed the cooler onto the lawn and jumped into the bed of the truck just as my brother accelerated toward the hospital. The ride was chaotic; I clung to the sides, wondering if I would be thrown from the truck with every bump. The blaring horn filled my ears as we sped through intersections, barely avoiding disaster.

When we finally reached the hospital, my father was immediately taken in for urgent care. My heart sank at the realization that this wouldn't be the last health scare we would face with him; it felt like a foreboding sign of more challenges ahead.

I used to carry lucky stones in my wallet as symbols of cherished memories and hope. Now, my wallet contained little more than my license, credit cards, insurance cards, and a mere smattering of cash — reminders of how life changes and how precious every moment with our loved ones truly is.

33. My Dad's Biggest Fish Tail, And I Was There

My father had a deep passion for fishing. For him, it wasn't really about what he caught; he simply relished being out on the water. He had many friends, one of whom, Mr. Willis, generously let him use his boat whenever he wanted. It wasn't a large or particularly remarkable boat, but it got the job done.

On one occasion, my dad, our neighbor Mr. Zalenski, and I went out fishing together. My dad had recently rigged up his level wind reel with a heavy-duty 30-plus pound test line, which felt like a rope. I couldn't quite understand why he preferred it, but then, suddenly, he got a bite. The fish took his rod down towards the water, and I feared it might snap any moment.

Recognizing the small size of the boat — there was barely enough room for the three of us — Mr. Zalenski leaned over to the opposite side to prevent us from capsizing. My role in this excitement was to net the fish. Despite my dad's strong arms, I could see he was getting fatigued, but his excitement was palpable.

As we finally spotted the big walleye, he shouted, "Net it, net it!" I told him not yet, as it wasn't close enough to the boat. He had to carefully work it back towards us so I could net it in a single attempt. When it was finally close enough, I made one swift sweep with the net, just managing to bring it aboard as it barely fit. My dad looked utterly relieved yet exhausted, while Mr. Zalenski wore a satisfied smile. My dad's reel, however, was a tangled mess, but the joy of catching his first Fish Ohio award was worth it.

Another time, we took the same small boat out again, but this time, the engine unexpectedly caught fire. My dad's friend and I almost jumped overboard in panic, but my dad remarkably kept his composure and extinguished the fire with a fire extinguisher. We were then towed back to the dock. Mr. Willis was untroubled by the boat's fate, focusing solely on our safety, never asking for anything in return because they truly valued their friendship.

Eventually, my family acquired a larger boat — not the biggest or the fanciest, but definitely safer and more comfortable. I even learned how to water-ski from it. One day, four of us were out on the water, and my friend Mike and I were catching fish left and right at the back of the boat. Meanwhile, my dad and Herb (Mr. Willis) at the front weren't getting a single bite. Then, Herb suddenly hooked something big. His rod bent precariously as he fought to bring it in, but he couldn't even see the fish yet. It was clear he was getting tired, and just when it seemed he was about to land it, the line snapped, and the fish was gone. Herb set down his pole, disappointment written across his face. Feeling for him, Mike and I decided it was time to wrap up our day as well. My dad and Herb simply loved fishing together.

During my father's time in hospice, when he was somewhat disoriented with his eyes closed, someone asked him what he was doing. He replied that he was fishing. When they inquired where he was fishing, he said he was fishing in Hawaii. I believe that was his way of letting us know he felt ready, calm, and at peace as his time with us was drawing to a close. Fishing, for him, seemed to offer an escape from reality, allowing him to embrace freedom, serenity, and joy, even in his final moments.

34. Cardinals After My Father's Death

You can interpret what I'm about to share however you wish. Is it just a coincidence, or is it a sign from above that everything is alright?

Shortly after my father passed away, we held his funeral. During the wake, my mother sat in her chair beside a planter with a red cardinal on it.

Additionally, my brother placed a red Cardinal brand fishing rod, which was the same color as a cardinal, in the casket.

The next day, while I was sitting quietly in my hot tub, I noticed a red cardinal visiting the bird feeder nearby. The bird stayed for quite a while, singing and often turning its head to look at me.

A few houses down, the neighbors also spotted a red cardinal lingering near their front door. I shared these moments with my mother, hoping they would help her in her grieving process.

A few days later, my father's sister came to visit my mom. While we were sitting in the backyard enjoying some fresh air, she saw a red cardinal fly into a nearby tree and heard it sing.

She remarked that it sounded like it was singing to its loved one.

I glanced at my mother, and we exchanged smiles, keeping the moment to ourselves.

Northern Cardinal at the birdfeeder

35. My Uncle And His Funny Car

My uncle lived with my grandmother, who was my mom's mother. Their house was situated next to a convenience store right on the main street of Oberlin. I never particularly enjoyed visiting my grandmother's house; as a young child, I preferred playing at home, and it often felt dull to me. However, on this particular day, my uncle was working in the garage, that was actually closer to the store than the house. He had transformed a Camaro into a funny car and occasionally raced it down the drag strip.

I was inside when he fired it up and started revving the engine. As the noise intensified, the windows began to vibrate, and I was convinced they might shatter at any moment. Finally, summoning my courage to confront the sound, I peeked outside. I saw the car half in and half out of the garage, surrounded by about four spectators. As he continued to rev the engine, creating both noise and smoke, a crowd of curious shoppers from the store gathered along the fence, drawn to the spectacle.

I'm not sure why he eventually decided to stop pursuing his passion for that car; he simply sold it one day. The show he put on for the store patrons came to an end, as did the shared moment of strangers brought together to witness such an exciting event.

36. The Porch

As a young kid, the world often feels like a swirl of colors, sounds, and fleeting moments that we take for granted. I remember my grandmother's house, particularly the simple screened-in porch that seemed unremarkable at the time yet was a haven of comfort and connection. It opened up to a bustling scene: the Convenience store parking lot and the steady flow of vehicles on Route 58.

Sitting on that porch, preferably in a rocking chair, I found a delightful breeze that brought a sense of ease to the sweltering summer days. Little did I know then that what unfolded before me was a slice of life—a social tapestry woven from the fabric of our small town. The cars that rolled by were not just modes of transportation; they carried people — friends, neighbors, and familiar faces. Each time a vehicle pulled into the parking lot, it was like a miniature reunion. Hands would rise in friendly waves, and conversations would spark.

To me, it was just something that happened — an ordinary backdrop to my childhood. But now, as I reflect on those sunny afternoons, I realize how rare those interactions have become. Life has accelerated; technology has enveloped us in its glow, often at the expense of genuine connection. The simple acts — a nod, a wave, a casual chat — seemed trivial then, yet they held immeasurable value.

In a world racing forward, I find myself longing for those leisurely moments on the porch. They served as reminders of the importance of slowing down, of taking the time to engage with one another, not just through screens but through shared smiles and voices. Those connections, once commonplace, are treasures that deserve to be cherished, much like the memories of a child watching the world go by from a rocking chair on a summer afternoon.

50

37. My Uncle's Dog

Reflecting on my grandmother's house brings back memories of my uncle and his dog. He lived with my grandmother and had a dog named Sandy, whom my uncle affectionately called Bozo (Boz O), not after the clown.

When I was younger, Bozo seemed quite intimidating. I was convinced he would stare at me and attack if no one was around. I even witnessed him push my uncle off the couch while he was sleeping! Bozo would sit in the kitchen like a person, proudly claiming a chair for himself. My grandmother referred to Bozo and another dog named Charlie as her "boys." Charlie was a chubby little Yorkie who was grumpy with almost everyone. He preferred to curl up in his box, eat, and bark at passersby.

As I reached my teenage years, I found the courage to pet Bozo without worrying about being bitten. Slowly, we built a bond that allowed us to go outside and play together. I discovered that I could toss a large plastic ball to him, and he would push it back to me with his front paws. We actually played catch, and I could have sworn I saw him smile! It's amazing how dogs can exhibit such distinct and wonderful personalities.

All it takes is a bit of patience to uncover and enjoy those traits.

38. Sometimes

Sometimes, we crave a **shoulder** to lean on.

Sometimes, we seek an **ear** to be heard.

Sometimes, we need a **voice** to articulate our thoughts and feelings.

Sometimes, we long for **love** to fill our souls.

And, sometimes, we pause and try to **understand** and **see** everything life has to offer.

Live life **strong,** my friends, and do so without regrets.

39. Perplexed

I feel a bit confused at times. I often find myself waiting for my friends to reach out to me, and I wonder if I should initiate contact with those I haven't spoken to in a while. I hold back because I understand that everyone has their own busy lives, and I don't want to disrupt their routines. I've come to realize that I can't change my friends to fit my expectations, and I've accepted the unique ways each of them contributes to our friendship. I just hope they all know that I'm here for them always, ready to share my thoughts and feelings. Do you think this is a healthy perspective?

40. Golfing With A Putter

My friend and I certainly wouldn't be classified as golfers. Looking for a bit of fun, we headed out to a country course, rented some clubs, and jumped into the game with no expectations other than to enjoy ourselves. Larry was always up for whatever I threw his way, cherishing our time together no matter the activity.

I shared with him that on my first visit to this course, I managed to completely miss both the lake and the clubhouse by just a few feet. This course offered a variety of terrain and features, including a bell at the bottom of one hill, used to signal when it was safe for golfers to tee off since the hole was out of sight from above. As we approached the bell, someone hit it while teeing off, causing us to duck instinctively as if avoiding gunfire.

On another hole, Larry had quite the adventure. I happened to be standing a bit farther back by the golf bag. He took a swing, and the ball struck a tree on his left, ricocheting off another tree to the right. He then ducked again as it bounced back, hitting a third tree. It was quite the spectacle.

When we came to another hole, I managed to pitch my ball up onto the green. I turned to watch Larry, expecting him to use his pitching wedge, but to my surprise, he was holding his putter. I shouted, "Hey, you can't use a putter like that!" But he went ahead and hit the ball anyway, and to my astonishment, it plopped right into the hole. I quickly learned to keep my advice to myself; he was having far more fun doing things his way, and watching him enjoy himself was just as rewarding.

This experience reminded me that what works for one person may not necessarily work for another. It showcased the beauty of creativity and the diverse ways people approach challenges.

The emphasis isn't on mastering a sport or strictly adhering to conventional rules; it's about enjoying the adventure with friends. Here's to more whimsical outings filled with laughter and camaraderie.

Thanks, Larry.

41. Its Quiz Show Time

(Game show entrance music begins playing)

Game show announcer: And now, ladies and gentlemen, it's quiz show time with your host...

Rob ... Smiley .... (Applause and music)

Rob Smiley enters, beaming with a microphone in hand, sporting a wild hairstyle and a flashy sports jacket.

"Hello everyone! You all look fantastic, and I'm sure just as lovely at home, too! It's Quiz Showtime, where you in the audience and at home will decide which option is best for you and explain why! Our first question of the day: Would you prefer the sound of a gently flowing brook or the sound of someone mowing the lawn? Bob, in the audience, what is your answer?"

Bob: I would pick the gentle flowing brook, Rob. It's so soothing.

(Ding, ding)

"What? A home viewer wants to weigh in. Ok, caller, what do you have to say?"

Caller: "Well, Rob, I would choose the person mowing a yard."

Rob: "OH, why is that?"

Caller: "Because it reminds me that he works hard and takes pride in his lawn for himself, his family, and his neighbors. While the brook is the same trickling noise time and time again, I enjoy listening to Ray mow his yard at 8 am and occasionally hitting a stone, and then a few choice words come out of his mouth."

Rob: "Well, ok, well, there you have it, folks. A unique perspective! Our next question, would you prefer the tranquility of a living room while reading a book alone or a large family gathering around the dining table? Audience? Jane, in the audience, what is your take on this?"

Jane: "Rob, I'd definitely choose the living room. With four kids, a moment of quiet to read alone is a rare treat!"

(Ding, ding)

Rob: "And it looks like we have another caller. Go ahead! Caller, go ahead."

Caller: Rob, I'd choose the large family gathering any day! As we grow older, people often reflect on the best times spent together with family. Life is too short to miss out on those moments. The memories we create during those times are ones we cherish in our quiet moments.

Rob: "Question number 3, would you rather change your past or receive enough money to clear all your debts? Audience? Rick, in the audience, what is your answer?"

Rick: "Rob, I have to go with enough money to pay off all my debt because if you change your past, there are certain things you would still miss out on, such as your loved ones, family, and friends. We learn from our mistakes, and that makes us all unique, and we all grow from them."

(Ding, ding)

Rob: "Oh great! Another caller. Go ahead, caller."

Caller: "Rob, I would opt to change my past. You see, I'm currently in prison, having made choices I can't overcome. Money isn't everything."

Rob: "Well, there you have it, folks. Until next time on. It's Quiz Show Time."

(Game show music plays as Rob exits)

42. Restaurant Thoughts

I believe that while most people visit restaurants to enjoy good food, I first focus on the atmosphere. I seek an engaging experience and want to be surrounded by something fresh and exciting. The colors, sounds, and overall vibe of a place can significantly enhance the dining experience, making it much more than just a location for a meal. For me, the food is secondary; I can overlook a less-than-perfect dish if the ambiance captivates me.

I understand that many restaurants are struggling to stay afloat during these challenging times, and I've noticed a few that still have decor from the 80s. I wish they would invest in updating their interiors, as I believe it would enhance my meal and enrich my overall experience.

It would also be great if restaurant staff realized that even their off-the-clock conversations are often audible to customers. I want to enjoy my meal without being distracted by gossip from behind the scenes. I truly appreciate it when managers or chefs take the time to check in with diners; it fosters a connection that makes patrons feel valued and more inclined to return.

When it comes to payment, I always try to tip well and leave a kind, thoughtful note for the waiter, waitress, or chef. A small gesture like a friendly message can brighten someone's day and show appreciation for their hard work. Simple acts of kindness can create positive connections, and I hope that a well-written note can go a long way.

43. The Grocery Shopping Pattern

Are you the type of person who can quickly dash in and out of the grocery store? Or do you find yourself going in for one item only to spend hours meandering through the aisles, backtracking repeatedly?

I can swiftly navigate the store with a laser-like focus, which often means I spend less money in the process. I know someone who embodies the other style; this person enjoys leisurely exploring the various food options and items available, finding joy in the experience of discovery.

One of the biggest mistakes you can make is to let this person shop on an empty stomach. It can easily turn a simple trip into a full-fledged adventure, as cravings can lead them to wander even more and fill the cart with impulsive buys.

Patience is key in these situations, as shopping with someone who takes their time can test your limits. It's important to let them thrive in their element and enjoy their shopping experience, as it may serve as their weekly escape or source of joy. So, it's essential to foster a sense of mutual respect and understanding between different shopping styles.

44. Some Of My Funny Short Phrases I Have Used

- An apple a day keeps the doctor away. But an onion a day keeps everyone away.
- A sign near my hot tub: No Skinny Dipping alone.
- Another sign near my hot tub: All Trespassers Will Be offered a shot.
- Is my drink impaired when I speak?
- A knife, a fork, and bottle and cork. That's how you spell New York. (One of my father's favorites)
- A chicken in the car, and the car won't go. That's how you spell Chicago. (Another of his)
- Fishy, fishy in a brook. Papa catch 'em with a hook. Mama cooks them in a pan. Baby, eat 'em like a man. (This was his favorite when fishing.)
- My mom's favorite:
    - Red skies at night – sailor's delight
    - Red skies in the morning – sailors take warning
- Another of her favorites:
    - Don't let the doorknob hit ya where the good lord split ya.
- I was going to get a shirt made of this one:
    - If you litter, FINE
    - Up to $500 in Ohio.
- Down goes Frazier (I use this when someone or I fall down). It is from Howard Cosell during the Ali – Frazier fight.

45. Two Fun Questions

When people ask me what I need, I often reply with "Time and Money." With more time, I could earn more money, and with more money, I could enjoy my time more. I also like to pose a thought-provoking question, "What is the most important thing to you in the world?" Most people respond with something like "family." Then, I challenge them further by asking, "What is more important, family or nothing at all?" They typically stick with their initial answer. I continue the conversation by asking what is more important than family, and they reiterate their response. Eventually, I even throw in the idea of "nothing" to see how long it takes them to grasp the concept. Sometimes, it takes several rounds of questioning for them to catch on, which adds to my enjoyment when I see their confusion. So, do you find this puzzling, too?

46. Get The Knife

When I was a kid, our kitchen table had a distinctive setup. There was an island table with a cupboard that jutted out from the corner, accompanied by some bar stools. One evening during dinner, I was rocking back and forth on one of those bar stools when I lost my balance and hit my head on the sharp corner of the wooden cupboard. I went down quickly, clutching my head as I felt a lump forming rapidly.

Then chaos erupted as my father leaped from his chair and shouted, "Get the knife!" Panic and confusion filled me as I feared he meant to cut me open. They held me down, and it dawned on me that he was actually using a cold steel butter knife to press against the bruise to ease the swelling. I was still terrified that I was going to be hurt. I still wonder why he couldn't have handled it a bit more calmly!

Looking back, it's pretty funny now. Nowadays, whenever someone in the family gets banged up, we all quickly shout, "Get the knife!" and only we understand what that means. It has evolved into a quirky, humorous bonding moment within our family.

47. A Thief Vs. A Liar

I've reached a point in my life where I've realized I can move on from a thief more easily than from a true liar. People steal for various reasons, and that makes it simpler to forgive. In contrast, when someone lies, it feels much more painful. Perhaps it boils down to trust; trust, loyalty, and love are interconnected. We all make mistakes, but it's how we address those mistakes that define us and strengthen our relationships.

Forgiveness is a complex process, and it's often easier to rationalize someone's actions when their motivations are somewhat relatable, even if they are misguided. Lying, however, usually involves a conscious choice to deceive, which feels like a betrayal and deeply undermines our sense of security and trust.

Engaging in open communication and fostering understanding can help us heal from mistakes and betrayals, ultimately building stronger bonds and a deeper connection. Trust and honesty play a critical role in shaping our relationships.

48. Perfectionism Guaranteed

I have always said that if I owned a sleek cigar racing boat or a thoroughbred racehorse, I would name it "Perfectionism Guaranteed." It just has a cool ring to it. However, I have come to realize that striving for perfection can lead to more problems than it is worth, often leading to many potential pitfalls. I have always found it difficult to feel at ease in various aspects of my life, whether it's work, sports, or teaching. Until I feel that I have mastered something, I often find it hard to feel calm about it. There are moments when I come close, and those are enjoyable, but I still tend to feel uncertain in many areas. Once I achieve mastery, I feel confident enough to teach it to others.

Building that confidence is a challenging process that requires practice, patience, and time. While we sometimes feel pressure or become overwhelmed, those elements are essential for developing genuine mastery. Unfortunately, we don't always have the luxury of time, which complicates things even more.

Having strong support is also incredibly beneficial. I still would love to hear just once, 'Coming up on the outside, it's Perfectionism Guaranteed." I can just imagine someone looking at the racing boat and smiling at the lengthy name sprawled across it.

49. Bob And Gladys, The House Wrens

This morning, as I sat outside enjoying the fresh air, I heard two house wrens chirping away. While many might assume they were simply singing to each other, I had the impression they were having a conversation. It went something like this:

"Bob, I'm not sure if this house is the right fit for us."

"Oh, come on, Gladys, it's fine! Here, I'll check it out while you wait up."

"Bob, hurry! I don't want to be left out here alone, especially on this side of town!"

"Look, Gladys, there's plenty of space for the kids. Harold and Ethel have snagged that prime spot on the west side of town for years up on that post. And Bill and Shirley are in that quirky house down the street painted like a hummingbird. I still think that's a bit odd."

"Bob, this side of town makes me nervous. There's so much more going on here!"

"It'll be fine. Trust me, it's a good neighborhood, and the kids will love it. Everyone seems friendly, and there's a seed market just a hop away from the house!"

"Alright, Bob, but let's gather some furniture before we settle in."

50. A Musical Dream

I can't play the guitar, piano, keyboard, or even sing along to written music. I used to play a few instruments in school, like the trombone and a very basic organ. I often wish I had taken singing lessons, as well as guitar and keyboard lessons when I was younger. Our choices shape different outcomes in life.

Once, though, I had a fascinating and fun dream. I found myself sitting on a front porch, playing the guitar. I could effortlessly play any song that popped into my head and even sing along. Friends and neighbors gathered around, enjoying my performance. It felt wonderful to bring them joy and happiness. The carefree feeling of playing and singing was almost surreal, filling me with pride and joy.

Then, my dream shifted. I was in someone's home and was invited to play the piano. I approached the bench smoothly and sat down, placing my fingers on the ivory keys. I began to play a soft, classical piece that I spontaneously created. My audience was intrigued, and I continued, my fingers gliding effortlessly across the keys. As I smiled at their smiling faces, I began to wonder if I could ever perform on a big stage. The thought of playing the piano, keyboard, and guitar and singing from the heart in such an effortless way felt like the ultimate fulfillment. It was something pure and soulful, not tied to a job or career.

Of course, I eventually woke up, realizing I had lost many of my musical skills, and remembered that I usually only sing in the car or when I'm alone.

51. Kids In Restaurants These Days

I enjoy dining out at nice sit-down restaurants, and they don't have to be overly fancy; I just appreciate something a bit different. I believe you truly get what you pay for in this regard. When my son was younger, I never had issues taking him to restaurants because I made an effort to explain the appropriate behavior in such settings from an early age.

However, nowadays, I'm often taken aback by how some parents allow their children to behave. Recently, I observed a young girl who kept leaving her table to look at animals on display, repeatedly going back and forth while her parents seemed completely unconcerned. I've also experienced children sitting behind me in booths, standing up and kicking the back of my seat, or nearly pulling my hair. The loud screaming is the most disturbing part; there's simply no reason for it, yet parents seem to let it happen without intervention. It's as if they're just happy to be out at a restaurant and dismiss any disruptive behavior.

I urge parents to teach their children respect and proper etiquette when dining out. Your actions can influence others, often without your realizing it. It might be beneficial for parents to sit down and have a conversation with their children before heading out to dinner, discussing the behavior they expect, including respect for both fellow diners and the staff. Staying engaged with children through activities like coloring sheets, puzzles, or talking about the menu can help. Additionally, parents should praise their children for demonstrating good behavior, reinforcing the importance of proper manners in public settings.

52. Porches And Decks

As I travel by car, I can't help but gaze at the homes adorned with porches and decks. Are they simple or grand? Do they feature a few chairs? Are any of them rocking? I wonder if these spaces invite friends to gather and share stories. Too often, I spot these beloved areas sitting empty, waiting for moments to come alive.

The time spent relaxing and chatting with loved ones is invaluable, and people should embrace these spaces more frequently. It's a joy to see someone in a rocking chair, smiling as they soak in their surroundings.

I have dreams and plans for my own deck or patio. However, it will take a little while since I have other financial obligations. But even now, while I'm still on that journey, I find happiness in simply sitting on my steps. I savor the sights and sounds of nature around me. Occasionally, a neighbor strolls by, and we exchange friendly greetings with warm smiles. Just imagine how wonderful it would be to have a comfortable rocking chair to enhance that experience, with its gentle sway creating a soothing rhythm.

With age comes reflection. If I spot you sitting on your porch while I drive by, I'll make sure to wave. I hope you'll wave back with a warm smile. Can we truly connect through our porches and decks?

53. First 3 Cars With Names

I knew a guy who named his first three cars: the Rustang, the Gate Mobile, and the Deer Mobile. His first car was an old classic Mustang that he paid way too much for, only to discover that it had a camouflaged and deteriorating frame. It became so dangerously unstable that he could execute a right turn without even touching the steering wheel. It was an accident waiting to happen, so he and his father decided to junk it to prevent anyone from getting hurt.

Next, his father thought it would be a great idea to buy him a canary yellow Chevelle Super Sport equipped with headers, big slick tires, and a powerful engine. However, this car was also a hazard. The dashboard was so loose it could fall apart, and you could start it without a key! His friend would drive it around the parking lot while he showered after football practice, and anyone riding in the back had to keep their feet up because the exhaust pipes made the floorboard too hot.

One day, while driving to a junior varsity football game with two friends, he decided to have a little fun on the straight road to the high school. It was rainy and foggy, and as he gunned it, one of his friends suddenly shouted, "Oh crap, the gate is closed!" In a panic, he nearly swerved to avoid it but ended up crashing into the gate instead. Despite the front end getting wrecked, he went into full panic mode while his friends couldn't stop laughing at his expense. After pulling over, he called his father, and when the police arrived, they ended up just discussing how to fix the gate without charging him. Later, the coach joked, "If you can handle a gate like that, you can handle a nose guard."

Eventually, he sold that car for a simple Chevette, but it began falling apart shortly after. One memorable incident involved a deer; while he was driving home from Christmas shopping, a deer jumped in front of him. As he pointed it out to a friend, a second deer crashed right into the front of the Chevette. They never found that deer and his friend was more rattled than he was. After repairs, another accident occurred when he backed out of a driveway and hit another car, completely unaware of what happened at first. He was confused about why his car was climbing the curb and couldn't understand why the elderly driver hadn't swerved out of the way.

With time, the Chevette started to rust, and the window became stuck, which was a hassle because rolling it down meant it wouldn't come back up easily. The worst part came when it rained, as water would drip from the hood right onto my, oops, I mean, his lap, making it look like he had an unfortunate accident!

We all have some great car stories. I'd love to hear about some of yours!

54. A Quirky Poem I Wrote A While Back

Dazzle and frazzle <u>alakazoo</u>.

Shake and shout what is in <u>you</u>.

Don't let great opportunities go to such a <u>waste</u>.

Grasp them, enhance them, and love them with a flurry of <u>haste</u>.

Twirl and whirl through the whims of <u>time</u>.

Paint every moment with laughter and <u>rhymes</u>.

Leap over doubts like a bright shooting <u>star</u>.

Embrace every day's challenge, no matter how <u>far</u>.

Twist the mundane into a dance of <u>delight</u>.

Let your spirit soar high and take flight through the <u>night</u>.

Savor the sweetness of life's immense <u>spree</u>.

Each fleeting chance is a gift for <u>thee</u>.

Keep your heart wide open and your dreams in full <u>bloom</u>.

Let the passion ignite you in every corner and <u>room</u>.

Dazzle and surprise with your radiant <u>hue</u>.

Shake, rattle, and shout, for the world is waiting for <u>you</u>.

55. Meditate Recipe

Have you ever tried to meditate or just relax and let it all go? Here is a recipe to try. Sit in a calm, relaxing area. Close your eyes. Slowly take all your negative emotions and thoughts at the time and gather them all up in a ball. Throw the ball up into a cloud and let the cloud carry them away. Take all unwanted sounds and blow them up into the cloud as well. Calmly imagine the cloud drifting away. Don't let the cloud ever rain on your happiness. Balance the good with the bad. Find something happy to always offset something negative. Sunshine, laughter, birds singing, smiles, hugs, flowers, flowing water, and animals are instant happiness. Creating a peaceful environment and allowing yourself time to breathe and reflect is essential, too.

56. Opportunity Cost

I once learned in an economics class about the concept of opportunity cost. This refers to the cost of pursuing one option compared to the potential benefits of another option that may yield greater returns. Life is filled with choices, and we strive to make decisions every day without regrets. Each choice we make leads to different outcomes, prompting us to consider, "What if?"

It's important to navigate life with the choices we make, acknowledging that mistakes are inevitable but also serves as valuable teachers. The lessons learned from our missteps can be viewed not as failures but as opportunities for growth and development.

Focus on what you can learn and how you can evolve as a result. Make each decision with the understanding that it might lead to something intriguing. In essence, aim to live without regrets. Continue to move forward, learn, and embrace the adventures that come from your choices. Seek happiness and joy in your decisions, as the lessons they provide can contribute to a fulfilling and enriching life. Even when a poor choice is made, there is often something valuable to be gained.

Every decision we make, whether significant or small, carries its own potential benefits and drawbacks, and the key is to embrace this complexity.

57. The Manipulator Of Conversations

I love to converse with people. When engaging in a passionate conversation, I am full of enthusiasm. When I get on a fun subject, I tend to get overzealous. My voice becomes louder. I get too excited, and sometimes I cut people off before they are done. I hate that I do that. I sometimes have to learn to listen to people more.

Listening gives a sense of respect and understanding. When one feels that they are heard, it creates a more cooperative environment where different perspectives are valued. I have to find a balance between sharing my thoughts and allowing others to contribute to the conversation.

Everyone has different ways of expressing themselves. Some talk faster than others. Others take long pauses. Even a few use their body and facial expressions to help them convey their thoughts. Everyone has their own unique rhythm and manner of expression.

I truly hate a manipulator of conversations. This is a person who seems to be at the center of attention. When I eat at a restaurant, I tend to pick up on this type of person at a table close by. The individual is usually louder and more robust. The other individuals at the table or in conversation usually do not get to talk much. Sometimes, their facial expressions let you know where they stand in the conversation as well.

It is so disheartening, and I have had to walk away from a group where a manipulator would not let anyone start a new subject or put their own thoughts into the subject. I hope I have not gotten to the point where I am talking that someone wants to leave.

Communication is a skill. We all need to improve upon it to make life more pleasant. We need to listen and allow input into each and every conversation. Share your thoughts. Do not preach your views without listening to others respond. You just might learn something and gain more respect.

58. Sparrows In The Morning

I watched two sparrows this morning, their constant chirping drew my attention to them. As I gazed my eyes towards them, my eyes came into focus upon a small plump sparrow. Another sparrow came hopping over to it. I then quickly realized it was a young, fairly newborn sparrow. It was able to fly but still had much nurturing and growing to go. The youngling was saying to the other sparrow, "Feed me now!" It seemed to be having trouble gathering food on its own accord.

The adult bird meticulously gathered bits of birdseed from the hanging feeder and brought it to the young one. As it drew closer, the squawking increased, and small beaks extended outward, waiting for its morsel from the other bird.

The adult bird seemed to know its importance in the relationship as to provide and protect the little one. Then, two raccoons decided to scuffle in a covered tree off in the distance. Their ruckus drifted my attention away. Then, my attention swayed off to a hummingbird that was searching for anything new that I had to offer.

No, it didn't like the jelly-like the orioles do. No, it didn't like the spinning yard decoration thing, either. It then decided to go back to the hummingbird feeder that was almost empty. I think I better get it filled quite soon. Then, I heard the chatter of two wrens as they continued to prepare their nest in a hanging home. Then, I heard a fluttering of sorts.

I turned toward my birdfeeder once again. It was another sparrow. He was alone in his travels. He was very selective in his choice of seed. He spat most of what he did not care for out of the feeder and onto the ground. That is where the lazy birds gather their morsels, as they are not as selective in their choice of food.

A cardinal then flew by, letting me know it was near and dear to me. The morning nature and its sounds can take you away from your daily worries, even if it is only for a moment's time.

59. Life Is Full Of Reciprocals

Life is full of reciprocals. We experience both the good and the bad, the old and the new, the rich and the poor, the weak and the strong.

I aim to find happiness in simply staying in that middle ground and enduring. Life will always have its challenges. By showing kindness, we can make the journey more bearable.

Let's help each other survive. We are not alone in the struggle. We can strive for balance, understanding, and happiness.

60. The Neighborhood Circle Walks

My neighborhood is shaped like a circle. It's neither the best nor the worst place to live. There are both positives and negatives to it. What stands out to me is the warmth of my neighbors. Some residents take great pride in having beautifully maintained lawns and homes, while others seem indifferent. It's not uncommon to find a well-kept yard next to one that hasn't seen a mower in ages. Each home reflects the unique personality of its owners, with every house telling its own story of the lives and challenges faced by its inhabitants.

I might not know all my neighbors by name, but when we pass each other in the circle, we can share a smile or a wave, a simple gesture that fosters feelings of comfort and belonging. The circle is a pleasant route for a leisurely walk, and many residents take multiple strolls throughout the day. Some walk their dogs, some with friends, and some on their own. I've figured out a shortcut that allows me to cover a mile if I make two loops. It's nice to walk in peace without feeling anxious.

While the neighborhood does have a few troublemakers and one individual with mental health issues who sometimes cause disruptions, it remains quiet and calm. I often find myself walking during the early morning hours, where I might catch glimpses of people heading to work or see a deer darting away because I startled it. Dogs bark to announce my presence as I stroll by. I prefer walking in the street because it offers clearer visibility, and the sidewalks often have obstacles.

I enjoy observing the different ways people maintain their homes. While the houses may look similar at first glance, it is evident which neighbors are struggling financially, who seem healthier, and who simply have more on their plates. The trees, flowers, and various sounds all contribute to the comforting charm of my circle, which I truly appreciate.

61. Once Sitting On The Patio To A Surprise

There, I laid relatively quiet and alone underneath my gazebo. It was me and the sounds of blissful nature. A song of a cardinal. A tweet of a finch. The hoot of a morning dove. The tingle of the wind chime. The soft, tranquil, soothing drops of the rain falling soothe one's soul. Then I began to feel reality come jolting back in: A car driving down the street. A truck rumbling in the distance. A crazy person mowing in the rain. My son laughing inside with a friend.

I awoke, turned my head, and opened my eyes. What did I find? A very large raccoon, staring at me not more than two feet away as if I was to be his next meal. I shouted out an explorative or two and watched as he ran to the tree. Gosh, can't a guy get a break on his vacation? Gee, Golly gosh. Can someone please take me away? Well, at least not the raccoon.

62. The Shiny Red Suit Man Dream

I had another strange dream. In this one, I found myself asking an audience a variety of questions, almost like a game show host. Every time a special word was mentioned, a guy in a shiny, sparkly red jumpsuit would dash onto the stage and perform a wild dance for everyone. It felt like someone I knew, and it reminded me of my dad, who would have definitely pulled off something that crazy if he were still alive, younger, and in great shape.

As the dream came to an end, I wondered whether I would be the talk show or game show host in real life or if I'd be the one in the red jumpsuit, dancing around and acting silly. I think most of you can guess the answer to that! Does anyone have a shiny red jumpsuit I can borrow?

63. Can You See The Wind?

I question you now: can you see the wind? In a storm, do you see the trees sway, or is it the wind? Do you see the rain pushing in a different direction, or is it the wind? Do you see the debris being picked up and carried along, or is it the wind? Do clouds move with robust force, or is it the wind pushing them? Is it the trees, objects, and buildings being pounded in a storm that you hear, or is it the wind that you hear? Is it the cool wind hitting against your skin, or is it the particles in the air being thrashed upon you from the wind? Can you see it? Can you hear it? Can you feel it?

64. When You See A Championship

Dear Boss: I wanted to reach out and sincerely apologize for having to call off work today. I do not typically make a habit of doing so, but I feel compelled to explain my situation.

Last night, I watched the final championship game, completely absorbed in the moment. I was waiting for something bad or tragic to occur. Then, the game reached its climax.

When I saw the block, then the shot, then the miss, I could not believe what I was seeing.

When the game concluded, the emotions were overwhelming. I was speechless while my son and his friend erupted in joy. I sat there in awe, with no movement, just my hand over my mouth as everyone around me was screaming and jumping up and down with joy and exuberance.

I was numb as a nova cane shot and shocked.

The experience has a special significance for me. I want to witness the parade first-hand with my son. I want to be a part of it as I hope it will be a part of me. I want to be able to say I was there with my son. It is moments like these that create enduring memories, and I want to share this unique experience with him.

One day, he may not want to engage in these activities with me, so I want to cherish this bond now. I hope that one day, he will be able to say that he was there with me as he tells the tales to his children.

I genuinely regret any inconvenience my absence may cause you today, and I assure you that I will be back tomorrow, ready to give my best, with some parade confetti to share as well.

2016 Cleveland Cavaliers Championship Parade

65. A Simple Flower Has Power

My place of employment is struggling. The parking lot is full of chuck holes. They don't have enough money to fix it. Today, I noticed these small, little pink wildflowers growing amongst the cracks. Even when things are down, look at things differently and see what you may find. This tiny, simple color of pink put a small smile on my face. It took my mind off the woes and worries of work. If only for a brief moment, it still was a small blessing.

Flowers in the parking lot holes

66. Lightning Bugs In The Early Morning Hours

When you were a kid, did you spend any time in the summer trying to catch lightning bugs and put them in a jar? Lightning bugs, or as others call them, fireflies, are a fun spectacle at night.

Recently, I watched the light show in the early morning hours while in the hot tub. The sky was black, with the moon glowing. I began to notice the flashes of light. It was as if nature was putting on a firework show of its own.

I learned that the blinking light is the lightning bugs' way of communicating and courting with each other. I guess some have distinct patterns. Most animals do not eat them as they are usually toxic to them. They do not bite humans. Some actually eat each other. In the daytime, they hide in tall grasses. Their light show usually only lasts a few months because they only stay in the adult stage for about 2 months. It seemed to be only a few days later when the show no longer commenced in the dark. The show was over, and I would have to wait another year.

On your next summer night, stop and see if you are able to witness this fun, simple, free-light show.

67. The Red Solo Cup

I stepped out of front of my house the other day. I was finally finished with most of my errands and yard work for the day. I needed a short break and decided to sit on my cold stone front steps. It was fairly quiet. I heard a faint sound and noticed a discarded red solo cup lying on the street. My mind said I should go pick it up and place it in the trash properly. My body said otherwise and to sit and simply relax. Then the magic started.

As I sat there, the sun began to dip lower in the western sky, casting a warm golden hue across my front yard. The leaves on the fall trees rustled gently, and the shadows grew longer, adding a sense of calm to the moment. My initial impulse to retrieve the solo cup faded further as I surrendered to the soothing embrace of the calming evening.

The cup's whimsical dance had captured my attention, transforming a mundane piece of litter into a grand performance full of life and movement. I found myself smiling, watching it glide with the breeze as if it were a playful spirit just looking for an adventure. Each little movement seemed to tell a short story, a fleeting narrative of its time abandoned on the street, caught in an unexpected ballet of nature. It rolled a bit to the left. It rolled a bit to the right. It spun a little like a dancer doing a pirouette. My mind was still trying to say go pick it up. I had to instead continue to watch.

Suddenly, the breeze picked up again, stronger this time, setting the cup into a wild, spinning motion. It twirled with enthusiasm as if teasing me, bringing forth memories of simpler times when I, too, would dance freely without a care in the world. The world felt alive at that moment, and the cup was a reminder of the magic we often overlook in our busy lives.

As it wobbled precariously towards the car, I instinctively held my breath. Would this be the end of the show? The cup seemed to pause mid-spin, teetering delicately on the edge of its next move. And then, in a final playful flurry, it rolled underneath the parked vehicle, disappearing from my view like a magician's final act.

I stayed seated for a few more moments, allowing the stillness to wash over me. In that instant, I decided that the cup could stay there a little longer to cast a short story and to share a lesson of stillness and presence. I wondered if it might dance once again should the wind call for it once more.

Tomorrow or the day after, I would check back. I would hope to see another magical show or perhaps to just retrieve it or see if it had moved on. But for now, I let my worries go, content to simply watch the fading light and listen to the soft symphony of the evening.

68. Too Many Car-Washes

I don't get it. During these, when consumers are generally more cautious about discretionary spending and filling the workplace with applicable workers is rare, I find it incredible to see an abundant number of carwashes popping up. Brand-new buildings and fancy-free vacuums may seem to be a big draw. But how many do we require in close proximity to each other? I mean, I can count on one stretch, 4 car wash places on one stretch of road with another 3 to 4 not too far from that.

I question the inundation of the car wash market. It must be a convenience factor for the ease of a quick wash rather than spending time and effort doing it yourself, especially with busy schedules. Some may view it as a small luxury or treat, even if they are tightening their budgets elsewhere.

I do not need these places as I tend to wash my own car at my own house when I have the energy and time. I obtain a certain level of satisfaction, and the aftereffect can be quite rewarding. This usually results in rain within the next day or two, or a nice bird tends to relieve itself on my vehicle. I enjoy cleaning my tires myself and making them shine to a brilliant ebony finish. I find that I usually have Mother Nature wash my car most of the time. You can spend your money on those places and help with the economy. I will instead rely on my friend, Mother Nature, a little more. It is a personal preference. Some enjoy the convenience, while others prefer the hands-on approach. Everyone has their own way of managing their car care, and the diversity in the method is interesting. Maybe I should buy a car wash of my own.

69. Cars And People Always In A Hurry

On many days during my commute to work, I notice an overwhelming number of cars and people rushing around. I set my cruise control and take a relaxed approach to my drive. Meanwhile, vehicles zip past me and zoom in and out of traffic as if they're in a race against time. For most, this leads to stress, frustration, and often road rage; I, however, simply smile and shake my head.

I sometimes watch as these hasty drivers fly by, only to hit their brakes in panic when a parked police vehicle suddenly appears, lying in wait for speeders. I've encountered motorists who tailgate me, weave in and out of lanes, and then abruptly stop at a traffic light. In response, I just pull up beside them with a smile. They continue to burn up their gas while I try to maintain decent fuel efficiency.

Why are we always in such a rush? It's important to relax, stay calm, and arrive at our destinations safely. My smile is aimed at those who might otherwise succumb to road rage, and their puzzled expressions, in return, make it all worthwhile. I hope my gesture fosters a sense of calm that counters their frantic behavior. Instead of constantly racing against the clock, we might consider prioritizing safety and tranquility. It's not merely about reaching the destination; it's also about appreciating the experiences we have along the way.

70. Tucker The Scottie Dog Liked Me Today

My neighbor has a small Scottish Terrier named Tucker, who loves to go for walks with his owner around our neighborhood circle. Whenever I pass by his house, Tucker typically barks to assert that it's his territory.

However, today was different. As I was out for my evening walk and approached his yard, Tucker's owner let him outside to take care of business. Instead of barking and running to his owner as he usually does, Tucker bounded over to me, eager for pets and playtime. I clapped my hands, and he joyfully ran in circles before returning for more affection. You could see the happiness on his face.

The owner and I remarked on how unusual this behavior was; he admitted it was one of the rare occasions Tucker acted like this towards someone. Perhaps he sensed that I could use a little pick-me-up, given his enthusiastic leaps of joy. This unexpected display of affection reminded me of life's simple pleasures.

After we waved goodbye and his owner called him back to the house, I continued my walk with a smile, grateful for Tucker's delightful surprise.

Thanks, Tucker.

71. Bobby Blue

Bobby Blue wore a mask each day,

Chasing shadows that led him astray.

He built his castle high in the air,

But inside, it echoed a hollow despair.

He collected accolades, wealth, and fame,

Yet deep down inside, it all felt the same.

In the pursuit of a life wrapped tight in allure,

He lost the true essence of love, pure and sure.

Then, one fateful moment, a light did appear,

A soul that brought warmth and chased off his fear.

With kindness and laughter, they opened his heart,

Showing him that connection was the truest art.

No longer alone, Bobby started to grow,

Discovering joy in giving, not just the show.

As they walked hand in hand toward the setting sun,

He learned that real happiness had just begun.

So, here's to Bobby Blue, no longer in strife,

Finding fulfillment in the richness of life.

With love and respect as the keys to his door,

He finally understood what it meant to be more.

95

72. Swimming Pool Games

Today's children appear to spend much less time outdoors and engage in different types of play than when I was young. Influenced by technology, structured activities, and perhaps even the safety concerns that now permeate modern parenting, they seem to have lost the nostalgia for more physical and imaginative play of the past. They play their activities and games in quite a different way today. They scream more than they laugh. They carry sticks or anything close to it and attack something with it, either a tree, a rock, or another person. It is very violent looking. Maybe it comes from the technology of TV, gaming systems, phones, and social media they watch.

The games I have seen them play outside on a trampoline or pool or a backyard are too simple, it seems. They only last about 20 minutes outside at the most. When I was young, we held the freedom to roam, explore, and engage in creative play outside for hours on end. I wonder how we survived so long without food and water. We played all sorts of games. We played football, baseball, softball. We rode and raced bicycles. We played a game of who could slide the farthest on frozen ice. We walked frozen creeks. We floated cups and cans down creeks. We explored. We played made-up games like Zoo and Spud (a simple game with a ball that was sort of an outdoor dodgeball game) and Red light-green light.

When we played in a pool, we did crazy things. We ran from a distance and jumped and dove over the side. We dove off a deck, and we knew we had to bend immediately or break our neck. We floated dogs on rafts around the pool, sometimes we let them swim. We had contests to see who could stay under the longest. I wonder how we didn't drown. We had chicken fights, and being on the bottom was the hardest. You had to be strong to hold the weight of the other person on top of you, while hoping they never messed around when you went to lift them up. We played made-up games where you could not touch the bottom, or you died. You had to swim or hold on to something. We made it even more interesting when we were creating the ever-popular whirlpools. Around and around we would go, and you would hold on to something and float in a relaxing way with friends. The games and activities we played fostered not only physical skills but also teamwork, resilience, and problem-solving. It built personal growth in ways that structured activities and technology can never replace.

I lived in an era in which children engaged more deeply with their surroundings, often pushing boundaries and taking calculated risks. Our unstructured play allowed us as kids to explore our physical limits, develop problem-solving skills, and learn cooperation and competition in a more natural way. With the greater emphasis on safety, does it come at the cost of outdoor exploration and imaginative play? Has it led to a more confined childhood? Kids should get outside, learn, play, explore, and grow.

73. You Can't Buy Happiness

We wake each day, living our lives in pursuit of happiness. Many of us go to work thinking that by earning money, we can buy our happiness. For some, this elusive quest for joy may lead to an understanding that true happiness isn't a purchasable commodity; rather, it springs from acceptance, understanding, and cherishing what we already possess. The search for happiness often prompts us to look outward — through careers, relationships, and material possessions—yet the essence of happiness truly lies within ourselves and the connections we cultivate with others.

I observe many people in relationships born out of fear of loneliness, clinging to the familiar instead of seeking genuine fulfillment and true companionship. Their facial expressions, eyes, and actions may betray their true feelings. Perhaps they are missing out on authentic happiness. Some may feel obligated to stay in a relationship, while others have yet to discover the acceptance, understanding, and cherishing of their true needs.

In navigating the complexities of life, friends play a critical role in guiding us toward happiness. Real happiness emerges from trustworthy connections, where acceptance and understanding flourish, enabling both individuals to grow and thrive together. True friends serve as mirrors, reflecting our strengths while also revealing areas where we may need improvement.

A genuine friend provides unwavering support and mutual respect, helping us reconnect with our true selves when we falter. While their perspectives may differ and, at times, seem unjust, accepting, understanding, and cherishing our friends in all their actions can unveil a new dimension of happiness.

Ultimately, happiness cannot be found in the acquisition of material goods or the maintenance of superficial relationships. It instead resides in the depth of our connections with others and our appreciation for the richness of what we already have.

In embracing this understanding, we may unlock the door to a fulfilling and enduring sense of happiness.

74. A Fun Birthday Request From Many Years Ago That Was Fun

I wrote once on Facebook that my birthday request was for everyone to respond to this: If you were on an old train, where would you be on it? I would be on an open boxcar, feet hanging over the edge, stuck in the middle, as I look out into the vast openness, pondering life as the sound of rails and engine blows along.

Here are some of the responses I received:

- One said they would have to be in the engine, opening the throttle as far as it would go.
- Another claimed they would be sitting in a chair on the back of the caboose.
- Next was one who would be hiding between boxes with the rest of the transients that snuck on when it was stopped.
- A hungry person asked if they had a dining car? It would be that...always focused on food and giving people what they need to make them happy, which is what they love!
    - An old friend said that he did this as a young teenager. Three of them started out hopping on a moving freight train out of Cincinnati. Then they climbed aboard a coal car just after dinner, ended up in Portsmouth, OH, and then caught the next westbound freight train in an empty boxcar. However, the train did not go back to Cincy, it went to Columbus, OH, where they were stranded in their huge railyard as morning broke! Dirty, hungry, and broke, they hitch-hiked their way back to Cincinnati. Never trust a freight train!
    Where would you be seated?

75. Life Is Like A Speeding Car

Life is like driving a car really fast on a blinding, sharp curve. You don't know what's around the corner. And when you get there, it sometimes goes by way too quick. It is exhilarating and unpredictable, full of many twists and turns. Try to love your drive. Appreciate the sights and sounds of the trip. Experience the thrill of the unknown and the beauty of the moments we capture along the way.

Unplanned detours can turn into the most cherished memories. Life can astonish you with magnificent sights, yet challenges can arise unexpectedly at every corner. However, when you unite with others, you may discover laughter as you navigate through it all.

Treasure the companions you share your journey with. Life is much like a road trip; it's defined by the experience rather than just reaching the finish line.

It's the friendships formed along the way, the joyful moments, and the insights gained from unexpected detours that truly enrich the ride.

Therefore, when we encounter sudden twists and turns, let's take a moment to slow down, enjoy the view, and value every laugh and memory created in the driver's seat of life.

76. Do You?

Do you hear the blissful music in the quietness?

Do you see the twinkling of light in the darkness?

Do you feel the wind caressing your face?

Do you smell the fragrance of a new day?

Do you see the happiness in sadness?

When someone speaks do you listen?

When you care do you love?

When you awake do you live?

77. The Smell Of Outdoor Cooking

How can you not enjoy the smell of outdoor cooking? The aromatic fragrance may radiant to wherever you might be and provide a sensory experience that goes beyond just the act of preparing the food.

As you walk through neighborhoods or drive with the windows down, the smells wafting through the air become a part of the fabric of the environment, creating a vivid tapestry of memories for those who catch a glimpse or take a deep breath. The warmth of grilled meats, the smokiness of charred veggies, and the sweet notes of desserts mingling with nature form a language of their own, inviting interaction and camaraderie among strangers.

The aroma dancing through the air has a unique ability to invoke nostalgia, bringing back memories of summer barbecues, family gatherings, and carefree moments spent with friends and family. It draws people in, creating a common spirit and strangers might even bond over the tantalizing scents as they stop to chat, sharing recipes or tips.

The artistry involved in outdoor cooking is something to be admired, too. I can picture in my mind the happy soul that sits and inspects their masterpiece. Each chef brings their personal flair, from the choice of spices to the preferred method of cooking, whether it's grilling, smoking, or roasting. Their passion becomes evident as they tend to their creations with the fire crackling and smoke curling up into the sky, capturing the attention of all who are nearby. The smile on their face as they dissect their labor of love.

I enjoy passing by someone preparing for a gathering of friends or family. Sometimes even some smoke will signal that the artist is in charge of the succulence. And let's not forget the joy of anticipation. Those mouthwatering smells can stir excitement, whetting the appetite long before the food is ready to be served. The sizzle of meats on the grill, the smell of charred vegetables, or the sweetness of a fruit dessert roasting under the open sky. It is all part of the culinary theater and I am truly happy just to even have the opportunity to smell these wonders. I love to imagine the individuals embracing the food with energetic vigor as the chef smiles at his accomplishment.

Moreover, outdoor cooking brings us together. It's not just about the food, but also about gathering loved ones together, sharing stories, laughter, and love around a fire or a Barbeque. The shared experience of enjoying a meal prepared in the open air strengthens bonds and creates lasting memories.

In essence, the smell of outdoor cooking is a celebration of life, flavor, creativity, and togetherness. It invites everyone to partake in the joy of good food and good company, reminding us all to savor not just the meal, but the moments spent creating and sharing them.

78. I Am Always Hoping I Raised My Son To Be A Good Person

Every day, I struggle with the hope that I raised my son to be a respectable individual. I was once married, and we had one son together, dreaming of a life where we could support and nurture him as a family. However, our divorce shattered that vision. I worked hard to provide him with a life full of happiness and opportunities, wanting him to experience things I couldn't as a child. I offered guidance and encouragement, even when I didn't agree with all of his choices.

I could sense his emotions—his joy, curiosity, and frustration—even without him expressing them aloud. Often, a shared glance between us would speak volumes, highlighting the deep bond we had forged over the years. It felt as if we had developed our own language, sculpted by moments of understanding, laughter, and silent support. In our playful smirks during lighthearted moments or solemn nods during tough times, those quiet exchanges became the fabric of our relationship. Each look, each pause, held significance, underscoring a connection that transcended words.

Now that my son has graduated high school and college and moved far away, I find comfort in our conversations, believing that I've guided him enough to help him make sound decisions. I appreciate the person he has become and notice small traces of my influence in how he interacts with friends and the world around him. His growing appreciation for music, love for the outdoors, and caring nature toward loved ones are just a few examples of this influence. I'm hopeful that his interests in games, sports, and outdoor activities were inspired by me. Even in our discussions today, I feel we're mentally connected in a deeper way. He is making a positive impact in his career, while I remain focused on navigating my work life, finding solace in the belief that I set him on the right course.

However, there is one interest he clearly lacks. I used to ride road bikes for exercise and got him a bike when he was quite young. One day, I took him for a reluctant ride on a bike path. Still new to riding, he struggled with stopping. During one turn, he was going too fast and ended up colliding with a telephone pole. Though his pride was more hurt than anything else, that incident seemed to mark the end of our biking adventures together. To this day, I don't see any interest in biking from him, and I can't help but think I played a role in that.

Now, even with the miles between us, our conversations foster a bond that brings a sense of warmth and closeness. His calls instantly lift my spirits.

79. Spencer Atomic Bomb Hot Sauce

There is a YouTube channel out there in which a host asks the guest questions as they progress through a series of hot wings with increasingly hotter hot sauces. One particular sauce was intriguing to my son. He purchased a bottle of it. It is called Da Bomb Beyond Insanity hot sauce.

He was working for a time at a pizza shop. He went on a break to get something to eat. He decided it would be a good idea to dab some of the hot sauce on some wings he was going to have for lunch. The chaos then ensued. The sauce was so strong that the vapors traveled up into the duct work and into the kitchen area. All of a sudden, all of the workers in the kitchen started complaining that their eyes were burning. All work was stopped until the crying burning tears and noses stopped running intensely.

I have never tried that hot sauce, nor will I ever. The bottle does not even reside in my home anymore. It is amazing what some hot sauce can do to you and others. It is not for me.

80. The Journey

I wrote this about a year after I started running. I had it posted on Facebook and did receive some positive input. I then added some writing to the end of it.

My One Year Journey: Please read only if you have the time. I am posting just to put it out there. It helps me see how far I have come. It is long and jumbled. But I got it out there.

My one Year Journey:

Today I will complete my one-year journey. It was a journey to try to lose some weight and get in better shape. Along the way I learned a lot more than I expected. I lost close to 25 pounds. I dropped a waist size or two. I learned that I could actually run and compete. I started out a year ago looking at the scale at work and I did not like what I saw. The number was not pleasant. I was not feeling great. I was depressed, down, lethargic, no energy, and needed a boost.

I wanted to check out the Margaritaville restaurant in Cleveland. A friend said that I should do a 5k that they were putting on. I didn't think I could run a 5k. But I knew I needed to do something to get me out of this funk and this would be a good inspiration.

I began by running 1 mile from my house and back. Going out and stepping out the door was the hardest part. The next day I went a bit farther. Then I mapped it out, and went all the way to downtown and back. I did it I ran 3.2 miles a bit farther than a 5K of 3.1. I then knew that I could do it. I then asked my son if he would like to run our first 5K for my birthday and he said sure. I kept running uptown and back and tried to run the best I could.

We completed the Parrot Head 5K run. We both were happy we just completed and finished. At the time we did not know that my son was running with a health condition. It's nice to know that we can run together now at the same pace if we want to. My first 5K time was 34:38:6. I was just under 35 minutes with a pace of 11:10 per mile. It is hard to believe that I improved to a point where I kept placing a bit better in my age group to the point where I finally placed third and set my personal best pace at 8:27 and was 16 seconds off of 26 minutes. Then I got my first 2nd place finish. Then I ran one race and got my first, 1st place in my age group win. I have run in 24 races now. I have done 5Ks, 5 miles, 10ks, and back-to-back races in 2 days. I ran in the morning. I ran at night. I ran in the rain. I ran in the snow. I ran in the heat. I have learned many things on this journey. I learned how to run. I learned that you can improve. I learned that it is more mental than physical. I learned that my surgically repaired knee from 20 plus years ago can still hold up well. When I was young, I hated running. I was slow, it hurt, I was made fun of. Now I am not doing too bad for my age group. I learned it doesn't matter what anyone thinks because it's all about what you think and feel yourself. I started out running with basketball shorts, heavy shirts, and very bad worn-out shoes. I learned what chaffing is again. I learned how a nice pair or two or three, etc. ... of running shorts helps you. I learned cool shirts are great in the heat. It was hard to learn how to run in the cold. Long thermal pants and hoodies are great in the winter. Gloves, socks and head gear of all sorts are important too. Lights and bright colors are for visibility. Shoes: I bought the most expensive pair I have ever bought and the extra insoles are the normal price I pay for shoes. I am wearing the soles out. I have bought other shoes for training. I also bought shoes because they look cool. I get some interesting comments on my shoes. I learned that when I run by myself, I can burn stress and get away from all the bad stuff of the day for a while. I learned that small pieces of encouragements are huge. I love spectators with signs and ones that make noise. I love officers that slap high five. Races are like mini vacations for me. They are exciting and are the icing on the cake of working hard to try to get better. Running with 100 to 3000 of your closest friends for 30 minutes is exhilarating. I have run in big races. I have run in little races. I have met many people. I have witnessed all kinds of runners and walkers. I have been passed by faster guys. I have been passed by faster women. I have been passed by old men. I have been passed by young kids. I have been passed by dogs. I have been passed by strollers. But now I am beginning to be the one to do some of that passing. I learned that some of those people that tend to win in and around your age group have their own story to tell and are helpful and encourage you on your journey. I learned that winning is in many forms. It is first at the finish. It is your personal best. It is competing. It is finishing. It is watching others overcome their obstacles.

I learned that hill is a four-letter word, just like wind. I learned that a slow incline is even worse. I learned that you have to be careful running downhill. I learned what all these people at the beginning and end of these races were pushing. They were pushing their watches. These watches tell you the time and much more. Yes, I own one, and a heart rate strap. I started with just my phone and phone aps. I ran in beginning just holding my phone, using an app. It is hard to run with it in your pocket. On one ran it fell out at the finish. I learned how to run with arthritis, a bone spur. I learned that you can get runners toes. I didn't lose my toe nails but, some were definitely ugly. I figured out different ways to carry my phone. I ran with and without headphones, and of many types as well. I learned what vo2 rate is and hit excellent for my age a few times. I learned how important heart rate zones are. I learned when to say when during training. I learned to run different types of runs for training, slow, fast, interval, fartlek, long, and short. I have run by myself for 10 miles. I did it without water. I consider doing a half marathon or a marathon. I consider it, but not yet. I love my family and friends, that don't laugh at me but support and encourage me instead.

Today, I will have my fiancé' and mother watching me with the spectators on the end of this one-year journey. I probably won't win. Well, I mean I won't finish first. But winning would be blowing my personal best time away in tough heat. I want to enjoy the crowd and climb the big hill with ease. I want to celebrate afterwards. Hey I learned how to drink beer after these races. I learned how to have fun. And I will have fun today once again.

If you actually read this to the end, then you are a winner in my book too. Thumbs up, and run hard in whatever you are running.

Then I continued to run when I could and ran in several events. I decided I could do the Cleveland Marathon Challenge. It was a 5k the first day and the 10K the second day. The event was filled with tons of people and spectators. When I ran the 10k, I ran alongside some of the ½ marathon and marathon runners at different points. I was amazed and intrigued. I was wondering if I could train enough to do a ½ marathon. I was doing good. My training was getting farther. I was doing more events of longer distances like 10ks. I registered to run in the Cleveland ½ marathon. Then Covid hit and shut everything down. Then Covid began to affect my work and the stress level at work began to grow. Then the race was back on the following year. I began to try to get in even more longer distances in. I completed a 10-miler event. My time was not too bad I felt. It was not easy and my body hurt afterwards. The Marathon weekend got moved to later in the year, which made training a strain. Work became more stressful and training time became harder to get runs in. Then I got hit with a stye in my eye. In ended up with 2 surgeries. The race day was getting close. I had to realize that I did something a little over zealous. I had scheduled not to just do my first ½ marathon but to do one of the challenge series again. This time I would be doing a 10k the first day and my first half marathon the second day. I was not fully confident in my training. Race day had approached and I drove to Cleveland on a wet Saturday dark morning. The 10k had a bridge. Hills are always a challenge, but with wet shoes it added to it a bit more. I survived. My legs told me that I may have pushed a little too much and didn't save for the next day. Adrenalin and all the people tend to do that. I was hoping my legs would recover enough that I could run the next day. Surprisingly, I was feeling pretty good. I met a friend at the starting line and it was reassuring to start with him to relieve some of the apprehensiveness I was feeling. We had to go over the same bridge and back again. I remember a couple running behind me. She noted to her husband that she needed to go to the restroom. He spotted a porta potty. He told her to run to it and then to catch back up with him. She did and they later passed me. That started to take a little wind out of my sail. I was hanging in there. Then we made the turn by the Rock and Roll Hall of Fame Museum. I looked and saw a very long steady uphill grade for miles. It crushed me. My mind and my body started messing with me. I needed anything positive to keep me going. It was spectators on the side of the road cheering their loved ones along the way. It was a friend running as a pace setter at a pace I couldn't keep that said hi and smiled at me. It was the next water station for a sip of water. It was a group of dancers doing a dance routine. It was dogs barking and cheering. It was all the different levels of people, mostly passing me as I went along. I hit a section of the run that I had run in parts of different events. The homes felt comforting to run alongside as it also seemed that the runners tightened up also. On the way back after a turnaround section I was heading back to the city. You could see the buildings in the distance. I could also see hills. Hills and wind will always do more to me mentally than they do physically. I was starting to really get hit mentally and physically as I was counting down how many more miles to go. I was by myself. No one running with me. No one cheering me on. I then said to myself that after all the trials and tribulations that I had gone through that I was going to finish this. I was not going to stop even once to walk. I was going to have a decent time. When I made the last turn the announcer said that the lead runner of the full marathon was nearing the finish line. I was determined to finish my ½ marathon before he finished his full marathon. My mind was almost shot. My knees and quads were really hurting. I need one more push. I saw another runner and I wanted to pass someone instead of getting passed. I sprinted past that person and finished. I rang the bell of accomplishment. I got my stuff and left. That race hit me mentally and physically and I shut down for a time. Work got even crazier. I ran less and less. I was able to do a turkey trot, slow and fun. I then did a Santa run, dressed crazy, slow and fun.

I then got hit with Covid. Christmas with my fiancé' in quarantine and through the window with my visiting son from Seattle. I ran one more event. It was a January Resolution run. It hit me. I had to stop 3 times. I did not realize that Covid had messed me up. I tried to get a run in here and there but stress messes with you. I could walk each day, but running was difficult. My vo2 which is how much oxygen you can take in dropped really bad and so did my pace. I then got transferred at my workplace adding more stress. I then got hit with a bad case of poison ivy. The medicine made my heartrate go funny. I managed to get through all the stress and recovered from the poison ivy and started out to see if I could get a run in. I was in a quarter of a mile and my good knee popped. I continued somehow, thinking it would warm up and get better, and finished a normal run. I paid the price. I was limping bad while walking. We went on vacation and every resting stop on our drive it took some time to get out of the car as the leg was stiff and sore. I walked in a pool. I walked on a trail. I walked at home. I could not run. I used ice. I used elevation. I bought different knee supports.

As of this writing I ran again, but with knee supports. This journey has been tough. Recovering from something is hard. I can't get my speed and endurance up. My vo2 and pace are so far down. I changed some habits a bit. I have dropped a few pounds. If I run again, during my next event, I may have to stop and walk, but I will get one in. My running and racing will be different from now on. My running changed to walking each day for an entire year. I have had the knee pop again. I went to therapy. To run now is physical pain and a danger to me blowing the knee out. I was able to do one more turkey trot. Cold weather has hit my body and mind and running has become an afterthought at this time. Change comes with age and obstacles. The journey of anything you attack is different each time. The journey for each of us is different in our own unique ways. Find support to get you through it. If it is not from others, find it within yourself. Keep running after something in your life. Do not stop. You will have ups and downs. There will be changes. Chasing the goal is just as important as achieving it.

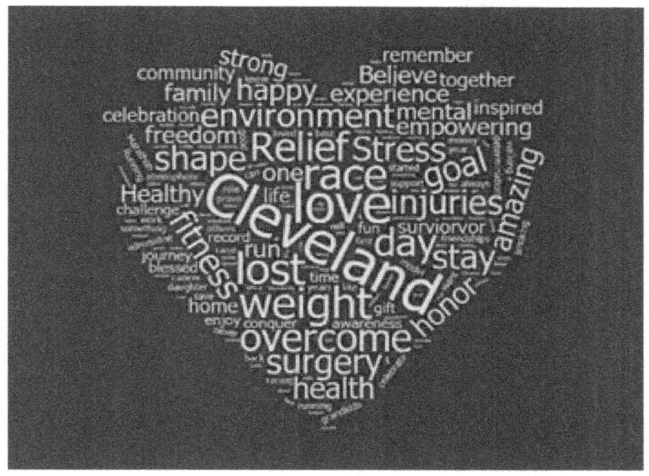

This was an inspiration on the journey

81. The Hidden Box

A young man had quickly rose to become a successful vice-president in a large marketing company. His position was challenging as he was tasked with meeting the company's expectations but also to be the driving force for the company's success. He was having trouble sleeping and dealing with the stress. He received weekly phone calls from his parents as they "checked in" on him. During these calls, the conversation often felt stiff, with obligatory inquiries about his health and work. "I'm fine, nothing new," he would reply, his voice lacking any warmth or enthusiasm. His parents, well-meaning, yet persistent, would prod him gently, reminiscing about family gatherings and milestones they had celebrated together. But for him, those moments felt like echoes from a distant past, stories he preferred to keep locked away. He often glanced out the window, watching the world pass by as he engaged in the call, wishing he could hang up and retreat into the comfort of his solitude and become engrossed in his work. Each call ended with the same familiar words of love, which felt more like a duty than a sentiment he could reciprocate.

As the days between calls stretched on, he found himself wrestling with a mixture of guilt and relief. The guilt of not sharing more, of denying his parents the connection they craved, clashed with the relief of preserving the distance he'd carefully constructed. It was a fragile balance, one that often left him feeling hollow, with only the echoes of unspoken memories to keep him company. Work was the most important aspect to anything in his life. He was constantly taking notes and writing ideas and putting them in his briefcase. He stopped going out to dinner with his friends as he felt it was more important to work on his ideas and notes for the company. He wasn't watching much tv or listening to any music at all. He was out of touch with the outside world. He would take lunch breaks outside, only to be seen sitting at a park bench with his eyes glued to his work.

One day he received a phone call from his mother telling him that his father was gravely ill. She begged of him to come home. He became irate and yelled back at her that the company needed him to finish his project. He ended the phone call and quickly went back to his office. As he sat at his desk, the weight of his decision began to settle heavily on his chest. The clatter of keyboards and the low murmur of conversations around him felt distant and unreal. He poured himself deeply into his work, but every keystroke was reverberated with guilt. Images of his father, once vibrant and full of life, flickered in the back of his mind, battling against the glowing spreadsheets on his laptop.

Hours passed, and the frantic ticking of the clock became a drumbeat of his anxiety. He glanced at his phone, half-expecting it to ring again, a reminder of the call he'd cut short. But the screen remained dark. Each moment stretched on, tainted by his earlier harshness and the fear that time was slipping away, time he could have spent with his father. The drive home was a blur, the city lights streaking by as he wrestled with his emotions. Regret gnawed at him, but his work responsibilities remained intact.

A few short days later he received another phone call from his mother. His father had passed away. She pleaded for him to come home for his father's funeral. She knew that he would not talk much more on the phone and quickly said, "Your father loved you, he wanted so much to tell you, but could never find the right way. He said he left something for you, but he would not tell me what it was or where it is." The young man quickly said he had to go back to work and abruptly hung up.

Several days turned into a few weeks. Time passed as he worked tirelessly at work on his next business project. Each day more boxes would pile into his office along with paperwork. One night the young man went to bed as usual. This particular night he had a dream of a simple cardboard box sitting on a wooden shelf. He shook it off and went right back to burying himself into his work the very next day. As he walked to his old familiar office door, he noticed various cardboard boxes lying on or near many of the office cubicles. None of the containers looked like the carboard box in his dream so he again shrugged it off. While in his office he was working so hard that he put his head down and said to himself that he would close his eyes, only for a brief moment. Quickly he found himself inside a daydream. It started, by seeing himself reaching his hand out to the handle of an old wooden door. He grabbed the handle and slowly opened the door. Inside the door were old pots, gardening tools, broken parts, old cleaning supplies, rusty tools, and a small double-pane window. He moved the cobwebs away to obtain a better view of what he was seeing. Suddenly the sunlight cast a beam of light into the small room to a shelf. Upon the shelf, behind some old rags, sat a simple cardboard box.

Suddenly the young man was bolted back to reality as an intern from accounting entered with another stack of paperwork. "Hey, I thought you could use these,' the intern said, his enthusiasm profound. "You're always buried in your work!" "Yeah, thanks," he replied without eye contact or a smile. His mind was still swirling with dreams of the mysterious cardboard box of his dream. It became increasingly difficult for him to shake the sensation that it was quite significant, pulsating with a meaning that eluded him. As the intern left, he found it to be difficult to focus on all of his spreadsheets, reports and data that loomed before him. Instead, he felt an inexplainable urge to explore the contents of that dream box. He wondered what lay beneath the dust and the rags on that shelf. He sat there, staring at his computer screen, as his thoughts drifted back to the fading image of the old room filled with the unexplainable items. The allure of the unknown began to strangle his productivity. He shook his head, forcing himself back to the task at hand. Yet, in the back of his mind, the simple box loomed large, a silent call to his mind.

After leaving the office he decided to take a longer than normal walk back to his car. He began to think about the dream from the night before and also the daydream. He made his way to a local park. He was going to go sit on a bench when he instead stopped by a swing set and watched a father and son. The little boy giggled, his laughter ringing through the crisp air. It reminded him of simpler times, of moments spent playing without a care in the world. He envied the carefree innocence of childhood, a stark contrast to the burdens he had been carrying.

Turning his gaze, he noticed a young mother with a newborn in a stroller. She smiled down at her baby, her eyes filled with love and wonder. The fleeting time felt almost tangible, as he too longed for connection, for tenderness, and the warmth of a loved one beside him.

He heard laughter for the first time in a long time as he watched kids play on a playground. It reminded him of a time when laughter was not a distant echo but a constant companion and uncomplicated happiness.

He approached an older woman on a bench, who was gently scattering crumbs for the birds. She glanced up, her wise eyes sparkling with kindness. "Beautiful day, isn't it?" she said, her voice soft yet clear amidst the rustle of leaves. "Yes," he replied, his heart swelling slightly. "It really is." He then thought of his own mother's face and realized he could not see it clearly in his mind. He reached into his pocket and drew out his phone. "I am sorry, I will be out of the office for a few days. Please cancel all my appointments. I will contact you when I get back." He then prepared to set off for his journey back home.

The young man parked his car and then opened the latch on the white picket fence. As he touched the white tip something hit him deep within his soul. He felt like he was 10 years old again, if only for a brief moment. He then slowly began to walk up the sidewalk and approached the front door. It was a red door with a brass door knocker that struck his emotions hard and he had a very difficult time touching it. He forced himself to knock. He heard nothing for what seemed like an eternity. Just when he thought of returning to the car and leave, the door slowly opened. In front of him stood a short silver haired woman. She was dressed in clothes that were not over the top and yet they were not inexpensive as well. They were comfortable and practical looking. She wore upon her a red and white checkered apron that was full of flour. Despite its wear, there was a certain charm to it. She was not frail, nor was she looking strong and fit. Her face was sullen with years of struggle, worry, and fear. Love was filled into each and every wrinkle. Then the young man noticed her eyes. They were full of sadness. They were filled with a depth of wisdom that seemed to tell untold stories. Shadows lingered beneath them, fragments of sleepless nights and burdens carried alone, yet there was a glimmer, a flicker of resilience that hinted at a spirit not easily extinguished. He felt he saw the faint traces of laughter alongside a bit of sorrow upon her face. He was not even sure it was his own mother, but out the words came. He simply said, "mom." Her eyes changed like magic from sadness to tears of jubilation as she finally recognized her son. She instantly threw her arms around him, flour and all. He at first was hesitant until he felt her love enter him. He grabbed her tighter. Her tears were dripping upon his chest and he said the simplest of things, "Mom, I'm home." She pulled him away and towards the kitchen. Along the way he touched the rough textured walls of the hallway of his youth. He felt something, but could not place what it was. As they entered the quaint kitchen, the aroma of his favorite homemade pasta dinner hit his senses and all of his thoughts of work were gone. The warmth of the room began to fill him with memories. The rich scent of garlic and basil drifting in the air began to dissolve a bit of guilt and to be replaced by the comforting embrace of familiarity. He looked at the kitchen table and saw two place settings. He thought to himself that she might still be placing a setting for her late husband. It did not seem quite right. He looked at her and said, "Where you expecting someone?" She replied, "yes." He then asked where they were. She said, "They are right here." He then realized the place setting set forth was for himself. He asked, "How did you know I would be here?" She replied, "Hope, love, and faith." The young man simply walked over to his mother once again and kissed her on the forehead. He quietly said,

"I'm sorry." She said, "I know, he knew, we both knew. You are here now and that is all that matters."

For the first time that day, he felt a warmth that transcended the fear and sorrow. In that moment, he found clarity amid the chaos of his busy life. The relentless deadlines, meetings that stretched into the night, and the pressure to excel suddenly felt insignificant to the love he felt for his family. That realization promised to change him forever.

They ate together and spoke little. With each bite she took, she gazed at him and smiled brighter. With each bite he took as he gazed back, he felt his youth and comfortable relaxed-self come back to form. He prepared a fire in the fireplace after dinner as she cleaned up the kitchen. She quietly brought in some warm cider and said to sit in his father's old wooden rocking chair alongside her by the warm fire. He placed a blanket upon her legs and she smiled and held his hand in a thankful gesture. He gazed into the fire. The flickering flames danced and twisted, morphing into the distinct silhouette of the cardboard box. He then had to ask his mother the question. "Did Dad have an old workshop or tool barn?" She said the only thing she could think of would be the old decrepit wood shed behind the garage. He gazed into the fire and the hair on his arms became stiff. A small drip of nervous perspiration began to form upon his brow. His mother drew a long yawn and then proceeded to her bedroom for some tranquil sleep. He sat still by the fire and did not hear the fire crackling. He instead heard the old grandfather clock meticulously clock its time. He then realized it was telling him that time was ticking away. He became tired. He was so tired from work and the drive to his childhood home that he laid upon the couch near the fire. The fire slowly died but he did not sleep well as he was very restless throughout the night. Just when he was finally asleep a bright ray of sunlight came through the window like a prism and struck upon his weary face.

He knew it was time to face it. He slowly gathered himself and proceeded through the musty old garage to the small shabby doorway at the back end of it. He entered through it and made his way around to behind the garage. He found upon his eyes a small old wooden structure. His dream came back to him as he reached out his hand to the door handle. He hesitated for a brief moment, the weight of anticipation setting heavy upon his chest. The dream had come so vividly, whispering with it the importance and igniting a curiosity inside him. As he slowly turned the handle, he felt a small sense of energy rise in him. He entered into the room that was in his dream. He brushed away the cobwebs and saw the items from the dream. As his eyes found the double-pane window the sun began to shine through casting a bright straight beam of light straight to a small shelf. His hand automatically moved some old rags that were in the way. In front of him on the shelf sat, what seemed to be glowing in a yellow hue, a small cardboard box. He grabbed the dusty old box off the shelf and placed it upon a small bench with an area that had more wear than any other area of the bench. He pulled up a small wooden stool that had its own share of wear showing and sat down. He was extremely nervous as he thought he would have to blow dust off the lid before lifting it. To his surprise it was quite clean. With both hands he slowly pulled the lid away and placed it upon the bench. He was totally at a loss at what he might find inside. He then reached inside. His hands first came upon an old faded folded sheet of notebook paper. His eyes slowly began to read the faded words and he realized it was his father's writing. It became clear that it was lyrics and music to an unfinished song. He quickly read it in astonishment, but did not think too deeply into it. Something inside him told him to turn the paper over to the back side. To his amazement he found circled the words Hemlock Tree Records, a phone number, an address, and a date from a long time ago. He folded the paper and set it aside. He then reached back into the box and pulled out a simple Hot Wheels car. It was bright blue. He somehow recognized it as a 1967 Ford Shelby Mustang. He rolled it a bit on the bench then set it alongside the paper. The young man's eyes full of inquisition, searched more. His eyes came upon a small 4 x 6 photograph. The corners were worn from repeated touch but the subject was still clear and bright. It was a picture of 2 young men at the summit of a mountain. The man's father was not in the picture. Once again, he was propelled to look at the back of the photo. Written with a black sharpy pen was written, "One day man, One day. Peanut and Doof." He thought that was all there was until he looked once again and found a seed package inside the box. It was titled "Columbine – Rocky Mountain Blue Variety. He shook the package and placed it also on the bench. Last but not least, his eyes peered inside one final time. Propped up against the side corner of the box stood one more photograph. The edges were worn from being touched many times. It then came into focus for him. It was himself next to a car packed fully with college stickers on the side. He was shaking a hand. It was the hand of his own father. Suddenly he felt a cold presence behind him and then what felt like a hand on his left shoulder. As he stood, still with the picture in hand, he turned and the cold presence was gone. What he found next was his mother's glowing face shining through the double-pane window. He smiled back and lifted the photo to show her. She simply nodded a yes. Then she stepped inside, grabbed his hand, and told him to come back inside the house and bring the box. She went straight to her phone. All he heard her say was, "Hi, it's time." She then abruptly hung up. She then told him to gather all his things, including the box, and to be ready. The young man, with some internal force, did not question her but went straight to gather all of his items.

After he had gathered all of his possessions, the young man sat in a chair with his beloved mother in the quaint and comfortable kitchen. Time past slowly as he waited patiently wondering what was to come of his mother's phone call. His fingers were hovering slightly over the edges of the cardboard box. A noise startled him and his heart quickened. It was a jarring sound of a loud car. It wasn't just any car, it sounded like a vintage muscle car, the kind that commanded attention and turned heads. The rumble and roar of the care came to a stop as the breaks squealed in a protesting screeching halt. He then heard a car door open and close and then what he thought might be a stumble. A knock came upon the door. Surprising him even more was that his mother was already at the door and she began to open it. As she opened the door a tall thin man with grey hair appeared in the doorway. She said to the man, "Did you trip on the sidewalk again?" The man replied, "as I do every time." The tall thin man turned to the young man and said, "Are you ready? Let's go", not even allowing the young man to respond. The young man grabbed his items, including the cardboard box, and looked at his mother. She was simply glowing with glee. She held the door open and said, "Go on son, it's time." The young man stepped through the doorway and put his eyes upon the sharpest looking car he had ever seen. It was a 1967 Ford Shelby Mustang, just like the one in the cardboard box. The tall thin man helped him put his stuff in the car. His mother walked out and handed the tall thin man a bag. He looked inside, smiled, and laughed. He said to her, "You never forget, do you?" She simply smiled back.

The ride began slowly and quietly as the young man was examining the interior of the car. The polished dashboard, the classic steering wheel, and the faint scent of gasoline mixed with leather filled his senses. Silence enveloped them, as the young man let the purr of the engine sooth him in a tranquil way. The young man was simply marveling at the sound of the car, the feel of the cool wind outside the window, and the excitement into the unknown of this journey. He finally asked the tall thin man next to him what his name was. The man replied, "What do you think it is?" The young man quickly realized he was one of the young men in the picture from the cardboard box. He asked him if he was Peanut. The man replied with a laugh, "I wish." He then said that he could call him" Doof".

Without giving the young man any chance to ask, he began to tell him that ever since he was young that he always seemed taller for what his body was supposed to be. He would trip over everything. When he was in school with the young man's father and Peanut, he tripped right in the hall way in front of everyone. They called him a doofus and everyone laughed. He was pulled up by his two best friends for life. He said, "I might still be a doof but without Peanut and especially your father I would not be the person I am today." He continued, "Without your father, we would not be in this special car." The young man asked, "This sure is a special car. It has really been kept up nice. It must be worth a little." Doof smiled a cynical smile and said, "This particular car is worth $200,000." He continued, "Your father always said that this car could talk to you through her exhaust pipes. She talks to me though, through her steering wheel." The young man was taken aback. The mystery and questions in his mind continued. He was about to ask more, but Doof merely said, "I know you have a lot of questions. Have patience, relax, and enjoy this ride and what will come next. All your questions will soon be answered."

The ride continued for many hours, then began to meander through an immense forest. The fragrant smell of the crisp pines flowed through the car taking the young man's soul deeper into an unknown realm. As they continued to drive with more twists and turns the traffic seemed to get less. Doof slowed as he came to an intersection and made an abrupt turn. They drove through what appeared as a tunnel of trees. Then it appeared in the distance. It was a beautiful wood log home. As they grew closer a sign appeared that told the young man that it was not a home but rather a large wood lodge. Brightly written upon the sign was "Welcome to Alliance Lodge".

They pulled up to the entrance and parked right there. Out came running a short man with round wire rim glasses. He yelled out, "Doof!" Doof replied," Peanut!". He asked if they had everything. Doof then handed him the bag from the young man's mother. Peanut smiled and jumped up and down a bit. He pulled out a container of peanuts of what seemed to be a special kind. Peanut couldn't resist and with a huge smile on his face he opened it and popped a few in his mouth. Peanut said that it was time to come inside and that they must be exhausted. The young man said that he was too excited to be exhausted.

As they entered the door the young man's face gazed at the intricately carved woodwork on the beams above to the richly woven rugs that adorned the floor, each one telling a story through its vibrant colors and patterns. The subtle fragrance of polished wood and the faint sound of a piano filled the air, enveloping a warm embrace. Massive comfy couches, glorious chandeliers, and intriguing displays were found all around. On each side of the massive front desk check-in table were two grand staircases that led to an upper floor of rooms. A small can of peanuts were quickly found on the check-in table near the computers. Peanut told the young man that he became addicted to them at a very early age, and hence they called him Peanut. Behind the desk on the shelf sat many keys, papers, brochures, maps, and one simple mahogany box. The young man could not contain himself as his continued to take in the splendor of the mass space. Peanut told them to rest for a bit as he would gather their items inside. Doof then said to the young man, "This place would not be here if it were not for your father."

The three ate together in the adjoining dining hall a wonderous meal. They told the young man to eat well, sleep well, and prepare for tomorrow as many answers would be answered. Peanut said, "Tomorrow is an important day. You must embrace it with an open mind and a courageous heart." Doof then said, "The answers you seek may not come in the form you expect." The young man was then taken to a comfortable bedroom to rest, sleep, and prepare for the next day. Sleep came quickly and it was some of the best sleep the young man had in years.

The fresh aroma of breakfast drifting up to his room led him to arise fresh and invigorated. He quickly dressed and freshened up and went to the lobby first to take in all the energy of all the patrons as well as the pleasant staff that assisted them. He proceeded to the breakfast area and found Peanut and Doof sipping away coffee at a quaint table in the corner. They nodded for him to join. They filled him up with the most delicious eggs benedict he had ever had. The excitement, anxiety, and reassurance from the two built inside him. After their meal, they led the young man to an entrance to the backside of the lodge which contained a wraparound porch. As the young man stepped out onto the porch, with his hands instantly leaning on the railing, he saw before him a majestic looking mountain. It contained rock formations with vast amount of pine foliage. He was then approached with a hand from each of the men on each shoulder. They told him that it was for them to climb today. As the young man turned to say that he was not ready, not in shape, and had not the proper attire, they handed him with all the clothing, shoes, and equipment he would need. They then prepared for their climb.

They embarked on a small trail that meandered and weaved its way around clusters of trees and over patches of wildflowers, their colors vibrant against the backdrop of earthy greens and browns. After a short time, the path began to rise gently, and the soft earth began to give away to more rugged terrain. The rocks, initially small and scattered, gradually formed into larger boulders and outcroppings. The young man could not see the top but was encouraged each step of the way to forge on. They continued for what seemed a long time as they twisted back and forth up the trail. Each step felt heavier, the air thick with the scent of damp earth and pine.

Suddenly as the young man was coming around a turn he saw before him a bright blue sky with soft white clouds and emerging from the rocks was the most unique hemlock tree he had ever seen. The tree stood resolute against the rugged landscape with its roots fixed into the crevices of the weathered stones. He stopped dead in his tracks and instantly thought back to his father's unfinished song. He told the two men that after they finished the journey of the day that he had something to finish for his father at another time and place. The two men smiled and continued on.

The young man began to hear in the distance the soft tranquil falling of water. Around the next bend they came across a simple but beautiful waterfall. The young man said that he thought they reminded him of falling tears. The men explained that they were instead, tears of happiness because he was now on the mountain. They continued and with each step it became steeper and more difficult to climb. The young man was growing tired. He paused for a brief moment to catch his breath, glancing at the nimble figure of Peanut just ahead. Despite his shorter legs, Peanut moved with a grace and energy that seemed almost effortless. Doof occasionally would trip over roots or even his own feet as he was the embodiment of enthusiasm mixed with a touch of clumsiness. Suddenly the summit was seen up in the distance. With renewed vigor the young man's energy bolted. He passed Doof and soon passed Peanut as well. He reached the summit, and before him unfolded a breathtaking panorama of a grand ridge stretching endlessly into the horizon. A view like no other, it was a tapestry of rolling hills and jagged peaks, bathed in the golden light of the setting sun. The vibrant colors of the sky transitioned from deep blue to warm oranges and purples, casting a magical glow over the landscape. In that moment, all the struggles of the climb faded away, leaving only the sheer beauty and tranquility of nature, a gift that filled his heart with awe and gratitude.

The other two soon joined him. They said to him, "you did it!" The young man replied with a single tear falling from his eye, "I wish my father was with me." Peanut quickly said, "He is with us." He then proceeded to pull the mahogany box from the shelf of the lodge. The young man was told to sit down. He noticed an area that reminded him of the picture from the cardboard box. He noticed around him an array of blue columbine flowers as he sat upon a sturdy boulder. He pointed to the flowers and Doof told him to pull the seeds package from his backpack. They must have placed his carboard box items in his backpack as he saw the package in the first pocket he came to. Doof explained that they had planted these flowers for his mother up there every year. This time would be his opportunity to plant them for his mother. He thought back to her and her apron. Peanut spoke first, "We all have our mountains to climb, both literal and figuratively. Today, you faced yours. Your father wanted to summit this mountain and to feel the vastness and wonder. Now he has." Doof continued, "Today you will release him onto the mountain as he so wished." The young man asked for the mahogany box. He solemnly opened it and took the contents and lifted it high above his head and the wind carried it away. They sat down once again and they proceeded to tell their story of the two of them and the young man's father.

They explained that they had, and always will be lifelong friends. They would do anything for each other. They laughed and shared their dreams with each other. The young man's father dreamed of one day climbing the mountain. He dreamed of owning the Blue Shelby. He fell in love with the love of his life. A son was born. The young man's father was smart, but he loved his family more than chasing his dreams. Peanut and Doof decided to climb the mountain one day. The young man's father refused to go as he would miss his son's championship ball game. They tried again exclaiming the jubilation they found in climbing it. Once again, the young man's father refused as he wanted to see his son graduate. Peanut and Doof then spent almost all of their money in obtaining land on the mountain. The last of their money was given to the young man's father. He being smart and wise invested it properly for them. One day, they approached the young man's father with an idea for a lodge. He took the money he had invested and gave it to them. They soon built it. They began to grow a strong and striving business at the lodge. Then the young man's father became ill. The young man never even knew of it. It was kept a secret from him somehow. The young man's father was running out of money. The two other men paid for the young man's college expenses. They paid his parent's home off. They were at his bedside as death came knocking. They paid for the funeral. He sacrificed his dreams for the love of his family and friends. Doof then pulled the keys from his pocket and handed them to the young man. He said, "The car is yours now, your father will be with you in spirit as you drive it the rest of your life." The young man did not shed tears but instead hugged each man tightly. He asked if they would help plant the columbine flowers. They would be to him, his mother's flowers of life, and they did so. The young man pulled the picture of him and his father out. As he looked closely, he saw what appeared to be a bandage on his father's arm. He told them that he understood now.

They enjoyed their time on the mountain. The young man spoke again, "I wish I could have said goodbye". His voice steady but filled with considerable emotion. Peanut placed a reassuring hand on his shoulder. "He knows, and he will always be with you. His spirit lives on in the man you are."

The young man had embarked on a journey of self-discovery after his time at the lodge. He felt a sense of clarity wash over him. The mountains had not only inspired him to finish his father's song, but they had also ignited a passion within him that he had never fully embraced before. The melody and lyrics resonated with memories of laughter, warmth, and the bonds that tied him to his family and friends. He packed his belongings and jumped in the blue Shelby and let the engine purr to his father's lifelong friends as in a thank you. He slowly drove away.

One day the young man's mother received a special delivery. She brought it inside and opened it. It was from Hemlock Tree Records. It was a recording. The recording. The title was Sacrifices for love and friendship. She felt a rush of pride and nostalgia as she listened to the recording for the first time. The heartfelt vocals and the symphonic background struck a chord within her, reminding her of the late nights spent singing with her husband and watching their son grow. It was as if her husband's spirit was woven into each note. His sacrifices, his love and his devotion to family was evident in every line. The young man had brought this to life.

The recording quickly became a testament to their shared memories, a bridge connecting the past and the present. Friends and family who received a copy were equally moved, finding their own stories within the lyrics. The echoes of his father's song served as a constant reminder that while life might take different paths, what truly mattered remained rooted in the heart. And that understanding, that beautiful clarity about love and friendship, became the melodic refrain of his new life. The young man never went back to his place of work, instead he found new employment. It was no longer work, but instead it became a rewarding and fulfilling experience. He was happy in life and found what he needed in life. The lodge was visited each and every year, as was the summit reached. He communicated regularly with his mother as well as Doof and Peanut. A career might be great, but love and friendship out way it all.

82. Lightning

The awe-inspiring nature of a lightning strike is indeed a blend of fear and fascination. As children, we often react instinctively to such sudden bursts of energy. I would be in an instant state of fear. As we age, our relationship with nature's phenomena can shift. Instead of fear, the rumble that resonates within us during a close strike can become a reminder of the raw power of the natural world. It is a vivid manifestation of energy that connects us to something greater than ourselves. That power is like a melodic bass song of nature to me.

That sharp white brightness is striking. It luminates in a way that rewires our senses momentarily. It grabs our attention, making us acutely aware of our surroundings and our own existence. The ground shakes, the air crackles, the walls shake, and for a fleeting instant, time seems to pause. It's in these moments of intensity that we can appreciate the beauty and chaos of nature, and perhaps even find a sense of grounding amidst the tumult.

Lightning to me is both furious and a beauty. It reminds me how moments of stark clarity can awaken a deeper appreciation of everything around us. The blinking, perhaps, is a response not just to the brightness but to the sheer wonder of being alive in the presence of such immense power regardless to when others are trembling near me in deep fear.

83. Cemetery Misconduct

Many people never go to a cemetery. Some people go occasionally to pay respect or to remember someone or reminisce on past experiences. Other people may even go regularly talking to the deceased and enjoying the peaceful surroundings. Then there are those that use it as a place to walk their dogs. It is upsetting to many when the owners allow their dogs to urinate and defecate on headstones. They sometimes do not even clean any messes up. Some do not even care where they park, where they walk, how loud they may become, and have no decency or compassion to others nearby. I wish people be would have more respect to others. What is fine for you might be quite irrespective to others. Cemeteries act as resting places for the deceased and are a remembrance for those who visit, but there are those individuals that show no empathy to the grieving visitors. They are public spaces that for some carry the weight of loss and remembrance. It deserves a level of respect that acknowledges their significance to many. A simple awareness of what is appropriate in these settings can go a long way in ensuring they remain peaceful and respectful spaces for all.

84. Sam's Pretzel And The Drink

While shopping at Sam's Club, I took a moment to enjoy a quick, budget-friendly lunch at the cozy café. I was eager, having missed the chance on my last visit due to a long line that sent me to the drive-thru at Steak and Shake, where I ended up paying three times as much for just a drink. But today, the line was short, and I couldn't wait to indulge in a hot dog and soda for only $1.50, boy what a steal.

As I settled at my chosen picnic table, I observed fellow shoppers checking their lists and moving to the register. Some hurried past, while others looked intrigued or put off by the café's offerings. Amidst this scene, I noticed an older gentleman in a motorized wheelchair patiently going through the checkout. His eyes lit up as he spotted the café menu, and a broad smile spread across his face—he couldn't wait for his meal.

Then, something remarkable happened like a spark of inspiration: he rose from his wheelchair and walked, filled with excitement, to the line for food! It reminded me of how small joys can ignite immense happiness in our lives. Just as I was soaking in this heartwarming moment, I received a call to pick up my fiancé. I quickly refilled my drink, leaving with a smile on my face, inspired by the little things that can brighten our day. Always remember, sometimes it's the simple moments that can touch our hearts the most.

85. The Island

This is a story of an enchanted island. Why was it enchanted? Sometimes things are just magical.

There once was a small village of people that lived on a small island. The townspeople would interact occasionally with the mainland for supplies and items they could not obtain on the island. Usually, these boat trips were from the mainland merchants trying to trade with the island merchants. Once a month, small boats would be used to travel back and forth between the mainland and the island. They took pride in the fact that their island was untouched by the turmoil and noise of the outside world. But hidden beneath the idyllic surface was a strange, powerful magic that occasionally revealed itself.

The island had a secret. The townspeople at first never had any problems or any issues. Then small incidents began to occur. Small items would occasionally become missing from their homes. The items were anything from sewing needles, buttons, watch parts, small spools, and much more. The pets of the townsfolk occasionally would run from their owners into the dense tree line areas. At times, dogs would come meagerly back with what looked like a nose full of yellow pollen. Some suggested mischievous children, others blamed wild animals, while others believed it was the work of an evil spirit.

One day the owner of the local island baker was walking behind his bakery shop, cleaning up the area when he thought he saw something move in the brush. He pushed his broom through the low-hanging brush and he thought he heard some sort of movement further in. It was a strange ruffle of a sound. He found himself scurrying through more dense foliage he had never seen. He continued on until he came across so much foliage that he thought he would need help lifting and moving it out of the way.

He returned to town to gather someone familiar with the woods who could assist him. The first person he came across was the seamstress of the island. He explained what he encountered to her. They traveled back through the dense brush area to once again find the dense thick area he could not move. "See? I wasn't exaggerating," he said, motioning toward the seemingly impenetrable wall of vines and branches. The seamstress looked at in wonder and said they should go back to town to gather a few more people to help. A few townspeople along with a few dogs, were then gathered with some tools to help cut through the blockage. They made their way through and they began to chop and move the massive green grasses, vines, and branches. Suddenly to the baker's eyes, he saw what seemed like a small dirt path no wider than a potato. It was too small for a human and much larger than an insect trail. He thought it might be from a small animal, but then thought otherwise as the path led to something amazing. He quickly pointed it out to the seamstress. The small quaint dirt path led to a tiny picket fence. Beyond the fence were small sewing spools set up as what looked like a miniature table with thimbles for seats. Then in the corner was a small mound of stones and sticks made into a small house. It had an entry door and even windows. The baker got down on his stomach and peered inside. He found many of the small items that had been taken from the islanders. A gold watch face glistened from the sun shining into the small house. The seamstress let out a squeal as something poked her ankle abruptly. She saw the grass near her ruffle and she looked down toward her ankle. She found lying on the ground next to her shoe a small pin. The rest of the townspeople quickly gathered around. They could not see what was living in this house but they knew it was not normal. "Something dark is lurking amongst us," said the seamstress. The baker said, "It's a threat we cannot ignore and must be stopped as more may be found." One of the men came running saying his dog came out of an area with yellow pollen on his noise and the dog ran from him back towards the town. They then looked at where the dog had run from and found another small house similar but different than the first. More of the people began to find more hidden homes. Suddenly they realized that these tiny homes were all around a large oak tree. The baker ran back to his store and came back with some torches. He exclaimed, "If we can't see this evil, then we must burn it." And then it commenced. They began to light the tree and all the tiny houses they found. They contained the fire to just that area. Many believed they heard small screeches and screams. Many believed they saw the grasses scamper and ruffle against the wind. The fires were put out and they returned back to the village. They all felt relieved and thought the evil was gone for good and they would be able to rest peacefully and quietly.

The islanders all were in their beds when the air began to take quite a turn. The wind began to pick up and turn the leaves on the trees. A strange darkness began to set in. Shudders on houses were suddenly being shut close. Loose items began to roll down the street with dirt and other debris. The wind grew even stronger and the light became quite dark. Lightning was forming off shore now. Then in the distance a very dark dense fog began to roll in. It came in like a thick blanket and covered the entire island. A bleak silence set in and everything became completely quiet. It was an eerie stillness. Then as quickly as it disappeared the fog and darkness left the island. The townsfolk, once lively and spirited, had seemingly vanished without a trace. Only a rocking chair squeaked as the wind swept by. No dog could be heard barking. No laughter was heard from any children. The swings they played on hung motionless, swaying slightly only when touched by a stiff breeze. No music was being played from any home. No fire was burning for any meal. It was complete silence on that island. Soon a month passed and not a stir was made anywhere. Only the trees swayed with the wind. The grass whipped back and forth as well. A few insects could be heard and very rarely was a bird seen. A windmill still spun when the wind breezed by. The grist mill's wheel still turned as well as water still trickled through it. The silence echoed on to the distant murmur of the sea.

This silence lasted for many days until a peddler from the mainland came on a row boat and pulled his boat and goods ashore. He instantly knew something was quite different. He usually was greeted from an islander or two assisting him pulling his boat ashore. There was no one. His favorite dog would come wagging his tail and barking a happy tune to him. There was no dog to be found. He continued towards the village and began to notice the odd silence that was abound. The wind whispered to him with a repressive weight, waiting for something or someone. As his feet traveled across the cobblestone road it had a sense that the stones were grabbing at him, but he thought how could that be. As he crossed a small bridge the large grasses seemed to reach out to him. On the other side of the bridge a large willow tree seemed to stretched its limbs towards him. He continued on. He began to enter each of the empty buildings. No person or animal were to be found. Everything was still in its place as if someone left abruptly. As he continued to search the island he came to the area of the burned tree. He did not get too close because an unnerving feeling grew inside him. He saw a ruffle in the grass. That was enough for him and it startled him so badly that he quickly headed back to his boat with a sense of evil around him and vowed never to return.

Weeks, month, maybe even years passed as the rumors spread that the island was now haunted and full of evil. Boats would slow as they traveled nearby, but none would venture ashore to investigate. Then one day a new elder traveler and his young granddaughter were exploring the area as they had traveled long and far to explore many new places. They had no reason to believe any stories of the island and they felt it proper to explore the island. Their boat came ashore and the young granddaughter was smiling with excitement. Her grandfather stroked his white beard as his eyes scanned the shoreline. They slowly made their way to town. As their feet hit the cobblestone road the elder traveler felt a sensation rise up his legs but thought little of it. His young granddaughter instead just gazed with excited eyes at all the empty buildings. As they searched the buildings the elder traveler spoke not a word but simply stroked his beard once again. The young granddaughter asked to roam by herself and the elder traveler simply nodded yes.

She began to explore not in the building as her grandfather but instead behind and into the grasses and tree areas as any kid would do. She came upon tall grasses that seemed to be swaying back and forth as if playing with her, even though there was little wind. She walked over a bridge and came across a large willow tree. It too began to sway, but with no wind. She simply smiled and giggled. As she continued on, she saw small movements in a grass area and proceeded towards it. She made her way through the grasses and came upon a small line that led to the smallest and frailest looking of piled stones that somewhat resembled a home. She recalled her grandfather telling her of the importance of looking closely at the world around them, and of finding beauty in the small things. As she focused and gazed at it in more detail, she noticed an overturned spool. She reached down and straightened it back up. She did not gaze into the structure. She did not even try to straighten the stones. She thought it simply amusing. She reached into her pocket and pulled out a small mushroom and placed it next to the spool. She thought to herself that it would make a nice tiny table and chair. She then pulled out a tiny piece of bread from her pocket. She placed it ever so gently upon the tiny table spool. She thought she saw two tiny eyes peeking out of the grasses. She smiled and giggled a small laugh. She quietly said, "Have no fear, we mean no harm." She then reached once again into her pockets and pulled out a small polished stone. The stone was something that had washed to shore that she had found in her travels with her grandfather. It held a brilliant blue color that made it look as if it were a priceless gem that shimmered in the sunlight. She bent down and placed it next to the bread and said, "Here this is for you." She rose and turned back to the village.

She found her grandfather in one of the homes. Place settings for food were still out on the table as if a meal was being prepared. She grabbed her grandfather's big strong hands and said, "Grandfather, please come with me. I want to show you something special." She proceeded to walk him to the small area she had just found. When he saw the small stone shelter before him, he asked his granddaughter,

"TaTonga, do you see it?" She stated that she thought she had a glimpse of it through the grasses. He then pulled from his coat a small bottle of honey mead. He placed a drop of it on the underside of an acorn top. He gave it to TaTonga and told her to place it near the edge of the grass. He stepped back a few steps. Suddenly to TaTonga's eyes out of the grasses appeared a small frail beautiful creature. It was green with hints of blue upon it. It had large inquisitive looking eyes. It had upon its back a pair of wings that looked to be damaged. The little creature slowly took a drink of the honey mead. TaTonga smiled. Her grandfather asked, "Do you see it now?" She replied, "I do." He said to her, "It is a special gift for a fairy to show herself to you. May her magic warm your heart as I hope your heart warms her." He said he would go back to the village so she could better acquaint herself with the fairy.

Once he left, she sat down in the grass and began to ask the fairy questions about what had happened. The fairy would nod her head yes or no. At times she had to try to act out some of the events. The fairy ate the bread and seemed to gain a bit of energy. The two were so engaged with each other. They had a unique way of telling each other their stories to each other. Sometimes they communicated stronger than two humans can ever do in words. At one point the fairy put her small hand upon TaTonga and began to cry. The small girl was sad for her new friend. She told the fairy that they would travel the world to find more like her. She told her that they would do whatever they could to make her place more comfortable.

Soon her grandfather returned with some small items. He fixed the stone roof and placed a small metal pipe that would now be a chimney for a fire place. He placed a soft red pin cushion with a portion of his handkerchief to be used as a warm bed and blanket.

TaTonga laid out her hand on the ground. The fairy stepped upon it. She lifted the fairy ever so gently to eye level with her grandfather. He could not see the fairy but smiled knowing its presence was upon him. He felt the fairy brush across his thick beard. The fairy was placed backed down and she quickly examined her new gifts. A small smile rose across her face to TaTonga.

She motioned for TaTonga to follow her upon a small path. It led to the tall grasses swaying towards them. The fairy reached out her hand and touched the grasses. She closed her eyes and the magic began. Before TaTonga's eyes the grasses were slowly making noise. At first, she could not make out what it was, but then she realized it was the sound of children's laughter. Then the grasses slowly began to turn into children. They began to jump around in joy and laughter. The fairy and TaTonga smiled at one another. The children ran to her grandfather and hugged him. The fairy continued on. She reached out to large stones, boulders, frail looking trees, and weathered looking bushes. They suddenly turned into the townsfolk and their pets. They ran to the children. TaTonga and her grandfather noticed the weeping willow tree swaying and leaning towards them near the bridge they had once walked over. The willow tree was abruptly losing all its leaves as if it were crying tears. The fairy looked upon TaTonga and TaTonga picked her up and carried her to the base of the tree. She turned and looked at TaTonga's grandfather with a uncertain look. He said unto her with a touch of light glinting wisdom in his eyes, "While magic is a special, sacred, and a beautiful gift, many unjustly misinterpret it into evil ways. The blindness of one's ways can sometimes be opened up with the forgiveness from others." The fairy turned and reached out once again to the willow tree. This time a sparkle of light flashed and out of the center of the tree the seamstress fell upon the ground. With deeply sadden eyes she arose and simply said, "I am so sorry." The townspeople gathered around the seamstress in silence in a comforting way. TaTonga was on her knees at this point in front of the fairy. Only she could see the fairy. The fairy was tired from the magic she had used and was also upon her knees. TaTonga lowered her head in a thankful way. The fairy rose and slowly began to walk across the bridge. She reached the edge of the bridge and got down on her knees once again. She closed her eyes and placed both hands upon the cobblestone road. Suddenly the stones began to rumble. Each stone began to rise and shape into the form of a stone man. The stone man had eyes and looked upon the townspeople, TaTonga, and her grandfather. Tears came flowing down like a river flowing over rocks. The fairy looked up at the stone man. He said unto her, "Please, do not change me back into the man I once was. I have done unto you something that I could never repay. I have destroyed your home, your kin, and your way of life. Leave me to be ever in this state as my punishment for the wrong I have committed." The fairy turned and looking back at TaTonga and her grandfather. She remembered what he had said. She rose her hands and clapped them together. The stone man seemed to shatter like glass exploding. From the ground arose the baker with red eyes full of tears as he looked out to the townspeople. The seamstress ran to him and embraced him with a warm hug.

The stories were shared with TaTonga and her grandfather of their wrongdoings with the fairy and her kin. The seamstress explained how she tried to reach out to anyone on the trail as she was a willow tree. Other townspeople felt that they would decay away as foliage.

The children said their cries when they were the grasses could never be heard. The baker said he felt the pain of weather and everything that stepped upon him as he was the cobblestone road. TaTonga explained that the yellow pollen on the dogs' noses was fairy dust magic that kept them away from barking and showing the fairy homes. She had to explain to them that in their recklessness they had also damaged the fairy's wings to the point of no repair. She would no longer be able to fly. TaTonga explained that they would never ever be able to see the fairy because that magic was damaged forever. In the ensuing days, the townspeople quickly built a new home for the fairy with the finest materials they could gather. It included twinkling twigs, soft moss, petals of the brightest flowers, and a great assortment of food. They really tried to provide her with everything she needed,

The day came soon that TaTonga and her grandfather were to leave. Everyone had gathered around the town center. They prepared rations and items for their journey. TaTonga held the fairy upon her hand as her grandfather began to speak. "We will travel the ends of the world and journey across the lands and shall seek out any of her kind. We will not stop until thus found." Suddenly the fairy pulled out of her satchel the blue stone. She placed both hands upon it. A bright light appeared around the stone. It began to glow and then with all the magic the fairy could put forth it changed into the most brilliant of blue sapphires one had ever seen. The magic in that stone would help the two find other fairies on their travel. With a final wave and shared promises of remembrance, the town sent them off with a chorus of well-wishes and hopes. As TaTonga and her grandfather set forth, the sapphire pulsed softly, leading the way like a star shinning in the night sky.

Time had passed on by, and visits had begun from the mainland people. The magical island kept their secret from the mainland people. They protected the fairy until the day TaTonga arrived back by herself, now tall, strong, old, yet wise beyond compare. And yes, she had with her two fairies of innate beauty and magic. With their magic they repaired the fairy's wings and she joyfully flew in the air all over the island with them. The entire island was celebrating the beautiful reunion. TaTonga's heart was full of joy as she saw that the children had grown into adults and had taken good care of their elders. She smiled as she saw an old married couple and realized they were the baker and seamstress still with a look of a tint of guilt and sorrow upon their face. It was time to go and TaTonga and the fairies were saying their goodbyes. The fairy, now flying with new wings stopped in front of TaTonga. Their eyes gazed at each other and words not spoken. TaTonga said, "She stays!" The townspeople yelled out in exuberating delight. The old couple smiled and hugged one another with newfound hope in their eyes. Their guilt began to dissolve as well. The magic stayed, as did lessons learned that love and understanding can mend what fear and anger have broken. If you ever are granted the gift to see magic, may you keep it deep within your soul.

86. Hummingbird Haikus By My Son And I

Hummingbirds fight on

All fight for something else

As Steve watched on

The nectar is at hand

Hummingbirds struggle to obtain it

The fight continues

87. The Special Animals At The Hospice

Loving Hospice Center, a haven for terminally ill patients, offered compassionate care during their final stages of life. Featuring ten quiet rooms, a welcoming front desk, a cozy common room, a small library, a quaint chapel, a modest kitchen, and a tranquil outdoor patio, the facility ensured a serene environment. The dedicated staff consisted of six nurses, two cleaning personnel, and a doctor available as needed.

Among the caregivers was Joan, a seasoned nurse with three decades of hospital experience. The passing of her mother had prompted her to transition into hospice care, where she flourished in providing support to her patients. Hellen, a younger nurse, found her calling in hospice care through her religious upbringing, believing deeply in the spiritual dimensions of her work.

Their bond with the patients deepened when a dying man requested that his beloved dog, Sandy, be allowed by his side. Joan and Hellen worked tirelessly to fulfill his wish, witnessing the profound connection between the man and his dog. A smile and glow were seen on the man's face. The sandy brown medium sized dog wagged his tail happily. Then on the final day Sandy sat in a chair upon the man's side with the dog's head lying quietly upon the man's chest. There were no wagging tails to be seen and no barks to be heard. Sandy simply offered a comforting presence at the time of his final moments.

When the man passed away, the nurses learned that Sandy had no one to care for him, as the man had no living family. Determined to keep him safe, they arranged for Sandy to stay at the hospice center.

Sandy quickly became a cherished part of the atmosphere, wandering the cream-colored hallways and bringing joy to patients and families alike. The dog mainly stayed in the common room, and of course, found his way towards the kitchen for morsels of food. Sandy would slowly stroll the cream-colored hallways and would peek inside to wag his tail and smile at the patients. His gentle demeanor provided solace amidst the sadness, and his playful interactions with visiting children warmed hearts. Staff members enjoyed the company of the quiet dog, who rarely barked and seemed to understand the emotional needs of those around him.

One sunny afternoon, while Sandy napped in the sunlight of the common room, he awoke to find a small black cat sitting at the sliding glass door, gazing intently at him. Sandy left the common room to find Hellen going through some patient's paperwork. Hellen looked up and found Sandy standing at attention. He wasn't sitting. He wasn't wagging his tail. He was simply frozen in place, gazing intently at Hellen. She recognized the change as well. She called out to Joan who was also nearby emptying a trash can. They exchanged glances at Sandy, who then turned around as if encouraging them to follow him. They followed Sandy into the common room where he went straight to the glass patio door. There they spotted the small black cat sitting at the door. Joan sighed and suggested that they should feed the little one. Hellen opened the door and the cat quickly walked in and touched noses with Sandy ever so softly. Hellen and Joan looked at each other in bewilderment. Joan said to the cat, "Hey, Little One, would you like some milk?" The cat turned towards Joan with no change of expression and proceeded to walk towards the kitchen. After introducing the cat, whom Hellen suggested they name "Coal," the nurses quickly decided to take in the new arrival. In the days that followed, Coal and Sandy developed an unlikely companionship, often seen together as they wandered the halls.

Their bond became even more mysterious when Joan observed Coal seeming to fixate on Sandy. One day, as Sandy entered a male patient's room, Coal stayed behind at the threshold. Joan peeked inside, only to find Sandy resting his head on the patient's bed. When she confirmed the patient had passed, she turned to go back to the front desk to make the call to the doctor and other details. She noticed the cat stared directly into her eyes and got up and walked out before she even left the room. Hellen met up with Joan at the front desk. They discussed the situation and were baffled. The patient had been talking about how he wished to see his son one more time before dying. Later on, after many phone calls were made, Hellen and Joan found out that the son had tragically died in a car crash on his way to the hospice. Joan asked Hellen whether she thought the man had some sense that his son would never return to see him again.

Days later, Hellen was putting some magazines away in the common room. She was about to go back to the front desk when she noticed Coal get up and head towards Sandy. The dog stood up and proceeded to the hallway. The cat followed. Hellen slowly followed as well. She observed Sandy enter the room of a lady who was so frail that she could no longer speak. She could nod with her head, but her illness restricted her ability to communicate and move. Hellen watched as the cat stayed at the doorway. She then noticed Sandy moving towards the bed and gently resting his head on the lady's left hand. The woman smiled at the dog before turning her gaze to the doorway, where she saw Coal the cat. Her expression shifted to a frown as she nodded in response. She glanced at Hellen with a faint smile before closing her eyes. Hellen approached her and noticed she wasn't breathing, so she checked for a pulse. There was none. Hellen left and went back to the front desk, where Joan was waiting. Upon seeing Hellen's expression, Joan asked, "Again?" The phone calls had been placed, and the doctor had arrived as well. Shortly after the woman was taken out, a member of the cleaning staff entered the room. He stripped the bedding, but when he reached the other side of the bed, he paused. There, he spotted a trail of rose petals leading to a small dresser tucked away in the corner of the room, far from the bed. The dresser was locked, so he reported his findings to Hellen and Joan, who had keys to all the dressers. They unlocked the dresser and discovered the woman's clothing and personal belongings. In the last drawer, they found an envelope addressed to Hellen and Joan. They took the letter back to the front desk and opened it. It was a note from the woman expressing her heartfelt gratitude for the extra care they had provided. She mentioned that she had found peace within herself. The letter concluded with a comment about Sandy, the special dog who offered love when it was needed most. Joan asked Hellen how the woman managed to write the letter, and Hellen simply shook her head in confusion.

Another brief week had come and gone. A family had come together as their beloved matriarch approached the end of her life. The children gathered in the common room, engrossed in board games, their quiet demeanor reflecting their awareness of the gravity of the situation with their cherished grandmother. Meanwhile, most of the adults were engaged in fervent prayer in the chapel. Sandy sat patiently near the children, enjoying their gentle affection as they took turns petting him, while Coal rested quietly in a corner.

Suddenly, Coal stood and made his way toward Sandy, prompting Sandy to rise and slowly head for the door. Feeling a magnetic pull, the children instinctively followed the dog. As they all walked down the hallway together, Hellen and Joan glanced up and noticed Coal trailing behind. Without exchanging words, the two women made their way to the chapel to inform the family they should go to the grandmother's room. Upon reaching her room, the adults and nurses found the young children sitting in a circle, with Sandy's nose resting against the woman's hip. The grandmother was gently petting Sandy's head, a look of contentment gracing her face. As the rest of the family and nurses entered, Coal reappeared in the doorway. The elderly woman, surrounded by her grandchildren and children, noticed the cat's presence. Turning to her family, she spoke, "I love each and every one of you. May my love for you grow within each of you. Stay strong as a family, and share your life's journey together." With that, she looked up at the ceiling, closed her eyes, and peacefully passed away. Sandy then turned and made his way back to the common room. No tears were shed; instead, smiles and hugs filled the air. The nurses carried out their duties, while the family left not in sorrow, but in a warm, uplifting glow. Hellen and Joan beamed, eager to go and pet Sandy after this poignant moment.

As time passed, small incidents continued to unfold. One day, an elderly patient named Lowe was in the company of his twin brother, Lloyd. During this visit, Lowe revealed to Hellen that he had once dated her mother many years ago. He mentioned that their relationship ended due to his own shortcomings and mistakes. Each time Hellen entered the room, an unmistakable tension and hostility seemed to emanate toward her, making her feel uncomfortable. Despite this, she diligently carried out her duties and left the room as quickly as possible. Meanwhile, Joan was checking the chapel to see if any candles were lit in prayer for loved ones. Hellen was finishing up a phone call at the front desk when she stepped out of the serene chapel into the common room. As she closed the chapel door behind her, her gaze locked onto Coal, who was staring intently back at her. Coal then walked over to Sandy, who was lounging near a couch. Sandy rose to all fours, and Hellen observed as the two animals ventured out of the common room and into the hallway. She decided to follow them. The two animals briefly turned to glance at Joan, who stood in the common room. Hellen stepped into the hallway and caught Joan's eye. "Here we go," Joan remarked. Sandy entered Lowe's room and settled next to his bed without actually making contact with it, instead moving his gaze back and forth between Lloyd and Lowe. The nurses gradually made their way in as Coal allowed them to pass. Just as they were preparing to conduct a routine wellness check, Coal suddenly appeared at the doorway. Lowe fixed his gaze on the doorway, although his eyes seemed to look right over Coal. Suddenly, he shouted, "Get her out of here!" Joan thought she saw a vision of her mother standing in the doorway. In response, Lloyd turned and headed towards it, but in his rush, he tripped over a monitor cord, fell, and struck his head, losing consciousness. Hellen hurried to help Lloyd, who was lying in a pool of blood. Meanwhile, Joan continued to stare at the doorway, hoping for one last glimpse of her mother. At that moment, Coal entered the room for the first time ever, heading straight for the bed and jumping onto Lowe. Though he said nothing, Lowe's face registered sheer terror as his eyes widened and sweat poured down his face. The tension in the room was palpable as Coal slowly turned to look back at Joan. In a panic, Lowe cried out an apology before he died. Coal then walked towards the door and seemed to fade away into the hallway. As Hellen focused on Lloyd, Joan dashed through the doorway. Hellen remained by Lloyd's side while Joan burst through the door, searching for her mother and Coal, only to come up empty-handed. Frustrated, she headed to the front desk to call for assistance. Lloyd sustained a significant concussion, which ultimately impaired his ability to communicate effectively, leaving him forever changed.

A few weeks passed, the serene yet somber atmosphere of the Loving Hospice Center began to feel a bit more like home again. The nurses worked diligently, tending to their patients with a renewed sense of purpose, yet the shadow of Coal's absence lingered in the back of their minds, a gentle ache that they could not let go. It was a shift change and the other nurses approached Hellen and Joan. They asked how they were fairing. Hellen said that they were doing better and Sandy helped with their stress and sadness. Joan then said how she even missed Coal the cat as they never found where the cat went to. The other nurses exchanged puzzled glances, their brows furrowing. "What cat?" one finally asked, incredulity evident in her tone Hellen and Joan exchanged a quick, knowing look, the kind that speaks volumes of shared experiences. "You never saw a black cat here?" Hellen asked, tilting her head slightly, as if willing the memory of Coal to spring to life within their minds. "Nope, never! Just Sandy," came the unified reply, laughter and disbelief mingling in the air. A warm smile blossomed between Hellen and Joan; a shared acknowledgment of a unique little secret that seemed to bind them closer. It was as if Coal's presence was a gentle reminder that love transcended the physical realm, manifesting in the hearts of those who believed. They kept their musings about the mystery of Sandy and Coal to themselves, as it fueled their efforts into the care of their patients even more.

88. Halloween Music Changes

As a young child, I would eagerly pull out a 33 RPM record of Halloween music produced by Disney. The eerie yet exciting sounds from the Haunted House, Disneyland 1964, along with its album cover showcasing a spooky haunted house, would captivate me. It depicted elements like light, grass, trees, and lightning. I'd place the needle on the record and settle down on the floor, taking a moment to gaze at the cover before closing my eyes. My imagination would run wild with vivid scenes inspired by the enchanting sounds emanating from the humble record player. I replayed it countless times, letting all sorts of visions unfold behind my eyelids.

As I grew up, my collection transitioned from records to CDs. On Halloween night, I would blast my Halloween music CDs, sharing the spooky sounds with the entire neighborhood. I had speakers arranged in the front yard, and while I worried that the volume was too high, some of the neighbors signaled for me to turn it back up when I lowered it. I also set up microphones so we could give the trick-or-treaters a good scare as they walked by. I developed a deep appreciation for the work of Midnight Syndicate, who elevated the genre to new heights. Eventually, I embraced the digital era with Spotify, allowing me to effortlessly discover exciting new Halloween music. I enjoy researching the tracks and uncovering intriguing facts. One piece that fascinated me is "Tubular Bells," the theme from The Exorcist. I learned that it's actually a 26-minute composition and had already become a major hit in Europe before the film was released. I still love listening to "Danse Macabre," imagining death playing his fiddle while ghosts and skeletons dance around. I can almost picture the rooster crowing as dawn breaks, signaling the return of the phantoms to their graves.

89. The Cloud Show

The brisk breeze caressed my skin like a gentle reminder of the changing seasons, the temperature sitting at a cool 51 degrees. I settled onto my garden swing-glider, a cozy retreat amidst nature's embrace. The warm sun streamed down, banishing any lingering chill and bathing my face in its comforting glow.

As I sat there, the clouds began their dance—an ever-changing tapestry of white and grey, weaving stories against the canvas of the sky. The wind whispered through the trees, and the distant songs of birds became my soundtrack, creating a serene symphony around me.

From right to left, the clouds glided gracefully, each one distinct yet part of a larger performance. One audacious cloud seemed intent on overtaking its counterpart, while a grander formation stood its ground, majestic and unyielding. Others drifted lazily, like wanderers lost in a vast ocean, savoring the journey above me. The trees, still adorned with hints of autumn, swayed gently as if swaying to the rhythm of the heavens.

A sudden break in the cloud cover unleashed a brilliant flood of sunlight, illuminating everything around me in a golden hue. But as quickly as it appeared, the clouds regrouped, casting shadows and transforming the landscape into a soft, muted palette. Shapes shifted, morphing into fleeting figures that sparked my imagination.

Though my escape to this cloud performance was fleeting, the beauty of nature engulfed me profoundly, leaving me refreshed. I couldn't help but smile—how easy it is to step outside and allow the wonders of the world to draw us in. Friends, take a moment today;

step outside and witness one of nature's most spectacular shows. Your own imagination awaits among the clouds.

Clouds in the backyard

90. My Frankenstein Discovery

I occasionally find myself reading a book that's quite challenging. One particular book presented a significant difficulty due to the author's philosophical insights. The vocabulary was complex, and I quickly recognized that many classics are hard to navigate because they use language that's not commonly found in our everyday conversations. Nonetheless, I persevered. While reading these works, I sometimes have to pause to look up unfamiliar words. This process helps me understand the author's choice of vocabulary, making it easier to grasp their thoughts, messages, and imagery. In my own writing, I strive to avoid overcomplicating my language with unnecessary words. Using sophisticated vocabulary doesn't necessarily make me appear more intelligent; instead, I believe it's more important to communicate my message clearly and effectively. I've never been fond of reading digital books; there's something so warm and comforting about holding a physical book and turning its pages. As Halloween approached, I began searching for "The Legend of Sleepy Hollow." My initial quest led me to various videos about the story, including the classic animated version featuring Bing Crosby. I also stumbled upon other film adaptations and clips showcasing people visiting the locations tied to the story, as well as gravesites of the characters and the author. Realizing I wouldn't have time to read the book, I turned to Spotify, my go-to music app, in hopes of finding an audiobook. To my delight, I found a version where someone narrated the story. I listened to the tale during my commutes, allowing the imagery to unfold in my mind. It was truly a pleasure to revisit Ichabod Crane and his adventures.

Next, I decided to check if I could listen to "Frankenstein" on Spotify. To my delight, I found it available. While "The Legend of Sleepy Hollow" took me about a week to get through, "Frankenstein" offered around 9 hours of listening time. Within the first 5 minutes, I realized that this novel would be challenging to read. Fortunately, I was listening to the audio version. Once again, the vocabulary reflected the 1800s and was quite different from our modern speech.

Interestingly, the original novel differs significantly from its cinematic adaptations. Frankenstein's creature is not the iconic green figure with bolts in his neck. Instead, he is described as having yellow skin that barely conceals the muscles and arteries underneath. His hair is glossy black and flowing, and his teeth are pearly white. He possesses watery eyes, a shriveled appearance, and straight black lips. There are no characters like Igor or Fritz, and Victor Frankenstein is not a doctor, as he never completed his education. Contrary to popular portrayal, he never exclaims, "It's alive!" In fact, when the creature first comes to life, he is so horrified that he flees. The narrative reveals that all of Victor Frankenstein's friends and family meet tragic fates. The story explores the inner thoughts of both the creature and Victor, prompting the question of who the true monster is. Themes of life, loss, and monstrosity are consistently examined, challenging our understanding of humanity. Readers often feel sympathy for both the creature and its imperfect creator, highlighting the need to take responsibility for our creations and their consequences.

Mary Shelley, the author, and her friends embarked on a challenge to write the most frightening tale. The inspiration for her story came to her in a nightmare. Mary's mother passed away due to complications during childbirth, and her first child also died shortly after being born. She later married Percy Shelley following the suicide of his first wife. Tragically, two of her subsequent children died as well, and eventually, the body of her husband Percy was found washed ashore after drowning. The novel's full title is "Frankenstein; or, The Modern Prometheus." It would be wonderful to see a film adaptation that more accurately reflects the essence of the original novel, as it would provoke meaningful discussions about morality, the ethics of creation, and the importance of looking beyond initial impressions, among other themes.

91. The Dead Mall

I once took my son and his friend on a college tour, visiting two schools. We stayed at a hotel in Fairfield, just north of Cincinnati. With some free time on our hands, we decided to check out the nearby Kohls department store and explore the mall adjacent to it. The Kohls was quite typical, and we were eager to see what the mall had in store for us. Soon, we discovered an entrance that connected Kohls directly to the mall.

As we stepped inside, we immediately noticed how dim the lighting was, and at first, it puzzled us. We spotted a small Chuck E. Cheese-like area with a food section and a space for young children to play. Observing the mall, I realized it spanned two levels. Yet, an unsettling feeling began to wash over me. The dimness was unnerving—where were all the people? Was the mall already closed on a weeknight?

It dawned on me that the stores weren't simply locked up for the evening; they were permanently shut down. Suddenly, the mall transformed in my mind, taking on an apocalyptic aura. I felt as though I had stepped into a video game—something akin to Silent Hill or a survival horror scenario. I braced myself for the possibility of creatures, people, or zombies creeping out from the shadows at any moment.

My son and his friend chose to embark on their own adventure. They ascended the non-functioning escalators and delved into their imaginative exploration of what this place might hold.

I continued my solitary walk, noticing the sparsely populated corridors. This quietness compelled me to venture deeper, curious about what lay ahead. My perception shifted from the aftermath of a disaster to ghostly echoes of what once was and what might have been. In the center, I came across a simple kiosk, which I imagined as the hub of information for the mall—a place where joyful visitors would come to rent strollers or wheelchairs. Nearby, a lifeless water fountain caught my eye. I could almost hear the splashing of water as children laughed and tossed coins into the basin, making wishes with each plink.

To my right, a stage area brought to mind the celestial voices of young performers that once filled the air with music, resonating in the hearts of patrons. I couldn't help but notice the soft lighting that highlighted the mall's color palette. Once vibrant and joyful with playful cartoonish hues, it now appeared dark and dreary, casting a somber shadow on the walls—a poignant reminder of the sadness that led to the decline of this once-thriving place.

The ghosts of passersby lingered in my mind. I saw them, heard them, felt their presence. Where had they gone? Why did they leave, and why had they never returned? Was it a reflection of the changing times in an area struggling with economic hardship? Was it a consequence of poor management and steep rents? Or was it simply an unfavorable location, uninviting for potential visitors? The true reasons behind the mall's decline were unclear to me, but I couldn't help but envision what this place could become—a vibrant hub that offered employment opportunities, revitalized the community, and breathed life back into its dimly lit walls. I imagined a mother with her children shopping for clothes. I envisioned an elderly couple walking hand in hand as they took in the sights and sounds. I could hear the joyful teenage laughter as they giggled looking for their next boyfriend.

I continued on my journey as my son and his friend explored the second level dark and dreary. I stumbled upon a food court where only one business was open, but it had no customers. There was also a video arcade that seemed to be barely hanging on. At the far end, there was a cinema, likely struggling for customers as all the movies were priced at just $3.

My son and his friend discovered an area that used to be designated for police or security purposes. They couldn't resist diving into their imaginations and created a fake video where they were being chased by zombies and racing to find help. They even visited one of the closed food establishments and pretended to sell food to each other. Additionally, they found another store that was connected to the wall.

What was amusing was that the security guard was riding a Segway. The sight of a rundown, abandoned mall combined with a guy cruising around on such a fancy device reminded me of Paul Blart from "Mall Cop."

Why do wealthy individuals create impressive structures only to undermine their potential with poor management decisions? As time passes and life progresses, I will still recall the ghosts of this mall.

92. Required Community Service

What would happen if we were all required to participate at least once a year some sort of community service or some sort of way to pay it back to others. I think our lives would be much better. Some people are too stuck on taking care of their selves to even think of something like this. A piece of humble pie will make you more thankful for what you have. Many people can smile on the outside but are being crushed on the inside. A little help to each other will makes us all grow in so many more ways. Spread happiness and help to each other.

93. Mr. Hobbs And Mr. Brenner

I recently found myself reflecting on two neighbors from my childhood. One was Mr. Hobbs, a quiet, slender man. I remember wandering around my neighborhood on my bike, playing hide and seek, searching for a lost dog, or simply exploring the backyards. Back then, that kind of freedom was completely normal. Mr. Hobbs had a garage that functioned as his workshop, where I learned he crafted spring stretchers—what we now call picture frames. His frames were of exceptional quality and craftsmanship, and I discovered that some of them adorned priceless artworks in the Oberlin Art Museum. I wish I had recognized then the true craftsman living so close by; it would have been wonderful to observe him at work with the perspective I have now as an adult. I also learned that he contributed to the restoration of a Frank Lloyd Wright home in Oberlin and was involved in the committee responsible for building the police station. I had no idea he served in the army during World War II, fighting in the 5th Armored Division during Normandy, the Battle of the Bulge, and the Rhineland. It pains me to think of the fascinating stories I missed out on hearing from him. You never know what incredible people are right in your neighborhood.

Another neighbor who comes to mind is Mr. Brenner, whom I remember mostly for one of his Christmas traditions. He would set up a beautiful train set for the holidays and invite us over to see it. While I can't recall much about the train itself, I distinctly remember him taking wax paper and cutting it into tiny shreds to create a snow-like effect around the train. As I've grown older, I've come to appreciate the care he took in those small details. It would have been nice to express my gratitude back then. Nowadays, I find myself paying more attention to the little details in my own decorations, perhaps inspired by that wax snow from my childhood.

Though I may not remember the faces of these two men clearly, I still cherish the small memories of the joy they shared with me. I strive to learn from these experiences and to build my character as I continue to grow.

94. Christmas Snow Globes

When I was a kid, getting my picture taken with Santa Claus was an essential part of Christmas. I remember the annual trip, bundled up in my winter clothes, with my boots likely looking bulky and silly. My jeans might have been those sturdy Sears Huskies, and my coat was probably a bit worn and not particularly stylish. My hat was likely oversized and adorned with a large pom-pom. I may have even worn a scarf, and my gloves, at least hole-free, didn't seem to handle snow or water well—I distinctly recalled my hands freezing when I tried to make snowballs.

We would journey to the Ben Franklin store, and I always felt a thrill of excitement as we made our way to the back, where the big empty chair awaited Santa. A small line would form, and the anticipation of seeing the jolly man in the red suit with his big boots and fluffy beard filled the air. When it was finally my turn, I would sit on his lap and share a few of the gifts I hoped to receive. I honestly can't remember if I smiled for the camera, but I might have received a little coloring book and crayons. My mom always chuckled at the silly black-and-white Polaroid picture, though that wasn't the highlight for me.

What I enjoyed most came next. It was picking out a snow globe. I loved shaking them and watching the snow swirl around the images inside. Unfortunately, these snow globes were often of such poor quality that by the time Christmas arrived, the plastic would have cracked, or the water would have evaporated or leaked out. I wish they had been made better because I would have treasured them forever.

I I always looked forward to visiting Pandy's Garden Center during the holidays. It didn't matter if I bought anything; the place just put me in the Christmas spirit. Walking among the beautifully lit trees felt like strolling through a Christmas Forest. I knew they were trying to entice you to buy a tree or some unique lights, but the atmosphere was magical. I remember the quirky animatronic decorations, like the alley cat popping out of a trash can. I still am not sure what it had to do with Christmas, but it still sticks in my mind. Then there was the clown that did flips, his wood worn down from countless performances. And of course, the large Santa Claus that moved up and down—what a sight that was! I often gazed at the train displays, dreaming of having a grand train set running in my yard, complete with presents in the cars for neighbors to enjoy.

Nowadays I collect musical or animated Christmas ornaments and music box decorations. I spend a few hours installing all the batteries but I enjoy playing each one. I enjoy it most when someone stops by and enjoys them as well. Take the little things in life that you enjoy and expand upon them.

95. The Snowman Wishes

In the heart of winter, when the world is cloaked in a glistening layer of snow, whispers of the snowman wish flutter through the chilly air like delicate snowflakes. For those who take the time to craft a snowman with joy and affection, there lies a hidden magic waiting to be discovered.

As the snowman takes shape—his rounded form getting more defined with every loving snowball—you may notice a sparkle in his coal-like eyes, and perhaps his smile growing broader as warmth from your heart breathes life into him. It's his way of showing appreciation for the care you've taken in creating him.

But to unlock the enchanting secret of the snowman wish, one must embark upon a little ritual. Before the sun tucks the day into a cozy slumber, gently form a small divot where his ear would be. Lean in closely and with the softest of whispers, share your heart's desire. Whether it's a wish for kindness, friendship, or even for happiness to blanket the world, make it sincere and unique.

Once your wish has danced from your lips into his snowy ear, lovingly pack the snow back into place to keep your dream safe. The final touch is a gentle breath—blow softly, watching as a few tiny flakes drift away, carrying your wish to a hidden, magical realm where snowmen come to life.

Here, your snowman finds fellowship among others just like him, frolicking in the ethereal snowflakes, sharing your wish with all who will listen. The kindness and uniqueness of your wish echo through their enchanted realm, strengthening the bond they share as they play.

May your wishes be a gentle nudge towards kindness and joy. Let each wish be a reminder of hope and the power of love—because in the world of snowmen, every wish has the potential to blossom into something beautiful. So, cherish those snowy days, build your snowman with love, and let the magic unfold!

96. Finally A Nice Gesture

I have a nice red leather theater seating couch, but one of the remotes for the recliner I usually sit on had stopped working. I checked the cord to see if it was snagged on anything and discovered that the wires were exposed, indicating something had come loose. I tried wiggling it, but it still didn't function properly. I decided to take a few screwdrivers to see if there was an issue inside the remote. Upon inspection, I noticed that the wires were on the verge of breaking apart. After some effort, I managed to reassemble the remote, but I realized that the plastic casing had separated and the wires were damaged. Thankfully, the recliner was in the down position since I couldn't raise it anymore. Unfortunately, the remote was beyond repair, and I needed to figure out my next steps.

I contacted the furniture store where I purchased the seating system and learned that it was no longer under warranty. I was still hoping to obtain a new remote. They provided a few options. One option was to have a technician come to my home to diagnose whether the issue was with the remote, the motor, or something else. However, this would involve a trip fee, a service fee, and an hourly charge, plus I would have to cover any replacement parts and shipping costs. The other option would be for me to disconnect the remote and take it to the store for a replacement. Unfortunately, I could not inspect anything in the dim light of the early evening, and with the holiday season approaching, I had preferred not to incur any repair expenses at the time.

After getting home from work one day, I decided to turn on some lights and see if I could remove the broken remote. I quickly discovered that the remote had slipped through a hole in the back of the seat, which meant I needed to take the top of the seat off. I appreciated the design of the seating, as it was engineered to allow for this.

Despite my efforts to wiggle it free, it didn't budge. Then I noticed that the bottom was secured with Velcro. Once I removed that, the top of the seat back came off easily, revealing the path where the remote had slipped through. However, I was still at a standstill since I couldn't see where the remote connected.

To solve this, I had to maneuver behind the couch, reaching into a tight spot to locate the connection. I reached down in this tight spot to see where it connected. I found it and was able to disconnect it, but there were still cable ties holding the wires in place. Climbing back over, I grabbed a small pocket knife to cut the ties. Getting back behind the couch was tricky because I couldn't see what I was actually cutting. I then had to actually had to lift this very large couch up and almost over on its side; while ensuring I didn't break anything in the process. I moved all obstacles out of the way and then climbed back over again. I managed to balance the hefty couch on my knee while attempting to cut the cable tie. Unfortunately, I realized I had cut the wrong one. I had to try again, and it almost bent the blade of my pocket knife. Finally, the right cable tie was cut and finally the remote was free. I slowly took the couch off my knee and lowered it back to the ground. I called my mother and asked if she wanted to go with me for a ride to the furniture store. She may have ended up being my lucky charm for the day.

As I stepped into the furniture store, I was greeted by a diverse collection of furniture — some pieces were elegant, others extravagant, and a few even bordered on the bizarre. The absence of sales personnel in the front area left the space feeling somewhat quiet and inviting. Intrigued, I ventured toward the back of the store, where I found a small sales desk staffed by two employees. Holding up my broken remote, I approached the sales lady, handing it to her. She quickly assessed the situation and offered me two options: I could order a new remote, which would take time, or I could take one from a floor model and have it immediately. Opting for the faster solution, we walked together to a recliner that was on display. As I explained how I had managed to remove the original remote, I noticed the sales team working diligently to prepare a replacement. After a bit of teamwork and some initial struggles with cutting a stubborn cable tie, they finally secured a remote from a recliner on the sales floor. Handing it to me with a warm smile, the sales lady said, "You are all set." Surprised, I expressed my disbelief. "Really?" I asked, still feeling a bit cautious about the generosity of the gesture. "Yes," she replied, reassuring me that they would replace the remote on the recliner in due time. My appreciation bubbled over — I was more than ready to pay for the part and cover any shipping costs, but they had already put my needs first. "You just gave me a wonderful Christmas present!" I exclaimed, shaking both of their hands and beaming with gratitude.

Their kindness made a significant impact on my day, and I could only hope that others would experience the same thoughtful service. As I left the store, I felt a renewed sense of goodwill, both for the people who assisted me and for the holiday spirit they had just ignited within me.

I took my mother to Bob Evans for a casual dinner to celebrate. Sometimes, a thoughtful gesture can mean so much. It really brightened my day!

97. His Christmas Gift Beyond Measure

There once was a man who cherished the ideals of family life. He worked long hours at a demanding job, striving to provide for his wife and children. Each Christmas, he would exhaust his savings on gifts he thought would bring them joy. They always tore open the gifts he presented them with the speed of a gazelle. He believed that fulfilling every wish on their lists would show his love, but deep down, he wrestled with anxiety about money and wondered if his efforts truly made his family happy.

Tragedy struck one fateful evening while he labored late in the office. His family was involved in a horrific car accident, and he rushed to the hospital, heart racing. He found his kids lying side by side, connected to machines buzzing with sterile urgency. In another room, his beloved wife lay unconscious. She opened her beautiful blue eyes and turned her head towards him. She could not speak. He felt as though she was speaking to him within her eyes. He knew he could not understand what she was telling him but, he that one day he may. Moments later, she slipped away, taking his heart with her. Within minutes of her passing he heard the monitors and a sea of activity in his children's' room. They too soon passed away within minutes of each other.

In the weeks that followed, the man's life drifted into a solemn routine. He found solace in solitude, observing the world around him from a distance. While his social interactions dwindled, he began to notice the vibrant tapestry of everyday life. As he walked to his car and his way to the grocery store, he found himself more observant of the actions of others around him. He socialized very little as all his family were gone or lived far away. The few friends he had left were afraid to talk to him as they were afraid to talk about his wife and family.

He smiled and was cordial with his neighbors and in his quietness, he began to watch their interactions with each other and their subtle nuances of their daily lives. This took his mind off of his grief and through his observations he grew an idea. He watched the old lady next door struggle to make a very small path to her mailbox in the deep white snow. She shrugged her head and with each movement of the shovel she looked like her pain in her back was intensifying. The couple across the street seemed to exit their car and argue on their way into their house with their groceries. Another neighbor had a white picket fence. And every day he squawked at the squeaky gate. Some of the fence boards were falling and coming loose. Another single mother had two small girls that played on the front steps of their home with nothing more than pretend wings made with their hands. One last young woman took her energetic dog for a quick walk on a daily basis. She was constantly being pulled by the dog and seemed very annoyed.

Inspired by his observations, he devised a plan while sitting alone at his kitchen table. He gathered items from within his home, scouring the internet for ideas, fueled by a renewed sense of excitement. It was as if Christmas again was beckoning him to be part of something larger than himself.

It was Christmas eve and a huge freshly fallen snow had blanketed the area. He observed the old lady open her door to go to retrieve her mail and then shake her head and return back to the confines of her home. He heard the couple arguing as they too were stuck in their driveway and returned back to their house as well. The man with the picket fence threw a snowball at it. The kids flew their hand/wing birds around two small evergreens and then were told to return back to the house. Finally, the lady walking her dog got pulled so hard she slipped and fell right into a snow bank.

Night had fallen and the lights of his neighbor's homes had gone out. He began his final tasks. He quietly went into action. First, he cleared a path to the mailbox for the elderly neighbor, making sure to salt it well. He placed a little wrapped gift at her doorstep. He then moved on to the couple's home, leaving behind a surprise package meant to brighten their day. The man with the picket fence found his gate repaired and his fence mended, with a can of oil waiting for him to smooth his creaking gate. The children's play area sprouted little surprises amidst the evergreens. Finally, to the dog walker, he left a simple dog bone on her step.

The man returned home buzzing with excitement, feeling vibrant for the first time in a long while. It was time for him to go to bed. He was so excited that he could not sleep. He went to his living room and sat in his recliner. He looked beside himself and looked at the picture of his beloved wife and kids. He thought if ever for a brief moment, that his wife's smile widened ever so little. In a cozy warm blanket, he fell asleep.

On Christmas morning, soft sunlight streamed into his room, mingling with sounds of laughter and joy drifting from outside. He peeked through the window to find no signs of arguing, no squeaking of a fence. Instead, he heard the song of children's laughter instead and the dog bounding around joyfully barking. A warm feeling enveloped him, stirring the first glimmer of hope in his heart. He smiled and drifted off to another nap.

He was awoken by the sound of what was increasing in volume, the singing of a Christmas Carol, We Wish You a Merry Christmas. The sound seemed to be coming right out his front door. He walked to the front door and opened it. He was taken aback to the sight of all his neighbors full of the largest smiles he had seen in years. They were swaying back and forth as their song filled their hearts as much as his.

First the young couple approached him and they pointed to a simple red painted heart in the snow with the words, thank you, underneath it. They approached the man with a picture frame of them kissing each other. They said to him that they did not know how he found it but that the picture was the greatest gift the two of them could ever have. It reminded them of what happiness is and how to forgive and live a better life. Next came the old lady, bringing a tray laden with warm, fragrant cookies, filling the air with sweetness. She gave him one of the warmest hugs he had received in quite some time. The man then went to the picket fence. He repaired the gate and mended the fence. He left a can of oil waiting for the owner to smooth his creaking grate. He then walked to the children's play area and sprouted little surprises amidst the evergreens. Finally, he left the dog walker a simple dog bone and a dog walking harness on her step.

The two small girls came forth with the simplest but most thoughtful handmade picture of birds flying around a group of people and evergreen trees. He smiled and said that he would frame them and place them on his wall for all to see. For as he looked over their shoulder, he saw his work of origami cranes hanging all over the evergreen trees. Their innocent creativity evoked a warmth in his heart.

At last, the dog leaped up and showered the man's face with excited licks, while the young lady shared how her companion could now stroll with ease, all thanks to the well-designed harness he had left behind. With a grin, she expressed that their walks would be so much more enjoyable from now on.

He expressed his heartfelt gratitude to everyone present. He emphasized the importance of caring for one another and the positive impact that a simple smile can have in brightening someone's day.

As Christmas day came to an end, he found himself reflecting on the time spent with his friendly neighbors. Sitting in his chair, a warm smile spread across his face as he glanced once more at the picture of his wife and children. In that moment, he recalled the message his wife had tried to convey to him in her final moments; she had wanted him to know that love isn't measured by the quantity or grandeur of the gifts we give. Rather, it's about the joy we bring to others through thoughtful gestures that require little expense. Acts of care and generosity will always hold more significance than even the most lavish presents. Thus, he began a new chapter in his life, discovering hope within his community and honoring his family's love by spreading kindness through each meaningful action, one kind deed at a time.

98. Christmas Wrapping

The art of wrapping Christmas gifts encompasses a delightful array of techniques, each reflecting the personality and intentions of the giver. Some individuals invest a significant amount of time and energy into their gift-wrapping process, selecting wrapping paper that sparkles with a festive allure or displays intricate patterns bursting with color and joy. These meticulous wrappers often take pride in their craftsmanship, ensuring that each fold is precise and that each name tag is placed just so, creating an aesthetically pleasing presentation that heightens the anticipation of the recipient.

In contrast, there are those who prioritize speed and efficiency over appearance. Their wrapping jobs might appear haphazard, with paper that is unevenly cut and corners that are less than perfect. Yet, there is a certain charm in their approach; these givers are simply eager to share their gifts, and the thrill of completion brings them joy. The spirit of giving, after all, transcends the need for perfection.

Some opt for the convenience of gift bags, which can be adorned with or without tissue paper, adding layers of surprise and simplicity. This method, while less traditional, allows recipients to dive right into the moment without the need to unroll and tear the wrapping paper.

Then there are the bold few who skip wrapping altogether, choosing instead to present their gifts with a casual flair, handing them directly to the recipient. This straightforward approach speaks to the warmth and sincerity of the gesture, emphasizing that the true value of a gift lies not in its presentation but in the thought behind it.

Ultimately, the diverse ways people wrap gifts reveal our unique perspectives on giving, with each method carrying its own significance. Whether meticulously wrapped, hastily prepared, or simply handed over, every gift is a token of generosity and love. As we celebrate the season, what truly matters is the spirit of giving, which is appreciated in all its beautiful forms.

99. No New Year's Resolution

This year, let's move away from typical New Year's resolutions. Instead, I invite you to engage with your friends during the good times. Take a moment to reach out, check in, and lend your support. You might be surprised at how much your message can uplift someone's spirits. If you're facing challenges, don't hesitate to seek help from your friends. We have the power to uplift one another. Always keep in mind that there are friends who are willing to offer support, even during difficult moments. Stay modest during your successes, and remember that brighter days often follow the tough ones. Together, we can cultivate a more positive environment for everyone.

100. Hector The Cricket And Freddie The Frog

Hector the Cricket and Freddie the Frog lived near a neighborhood pond.

They frolicked and played and grew to have such a common bond.

At night when the fireflies flew and the moon cast beams,

Hector played his banjo while Freddie tapped his foot upon his pant seams.

The fish joined in and danced to his tune.

Then came Bob the old racoon.

Bob pulled out his fiddle and joined in the fun.

Oh, how the party kept going before they saw the sun.

When the orange glow began to rise,

They knew it was time to cut their ties.

The fish swam away as the fireflies put out their lights.

The moon frowned as he soared away to great heights.

Bob climbed a nearby tree.

Freddie tapped Hector upon his knee.

They smiled at each other and gave a high five.

Away they went as Hector jumped away and Freddie took a big dive.

101. Picnic On A Hill

If you picnic on a hill, do you mind a few ants?

If you go on hike and a snake crosses your path, do you get upset?

If the sidewalk you take is full of cracks, do you jump or head back?

When the water drains to a trickle do you dry up as well?

Do small things bother you or do you relish in the tiniest of things?

102. When Tears Fall May You Look Upon The Moon

When tears stream down, may you find comfort in gazing at the moon. It might send down a moonbeam as a whisper from a cherished one. In your quest for love and hope, seek the moon in quiet reflection. The old man in the moon may just offer a wink, showering you with hope. And if you're enveloped in love and filled with hope, share that magic by scattering and blowing moondust into the air for someone in need.

103. Redundant Control Surprise

Sometimes, the smallest and most unexpected discoveries can bring the greatest joy. I had owned my car for over a year, and although I felt I might be paying too much for it, I truly enjoyed its features. Whenever I get a new vehicle, I make it a point to read through the entire owner's manual in the glove box. I always thought one feature I wished it had was redundant controls for the stereo on the steering wheel.

It was during one of my son's Christmas visit from Seattle that I stumbled upon a delightful surprise. As I shared with him how much I liked my car, its features, and even its decent gas mileage, he mentioned how much he enjoyed driving it while he was here. I then expressed my wish for the redundant controls. To my amazement, he reached over from the passenger seat and touched the back of the steering wheel, revealing small buttons! I was shocked; my hand typically doesn't position itself to reach those buttons.

A huge smile spread across my face as I felt a rush of happiness from this little discovery. My son couldn't help but laugh at the realization that I'd driven the car all this time without knowing about these controls. Reflecting on my experience with the salesperson when I got the car, I recalled that he never pointed out these buttons. Perhaps he assumed I already knew about them, or maybe he wasn't aware himself since car designs can change. It's funny how sometimes the simplest things in life can bring the most unexpected joy and surprises.

104. Drip Candles

When I was a young kid, my father, brother, and I used to make dripping candles together. Now that I think back on it, it seems quite risky. We would use an old glass bottle, whether it was a wine bottle, a soda bottle, or something else; the type of bottle didn't matter. I remember we'd lay down some old newspapers on the living room carpet. I'm not certain that it was really a clever idea back then!

At the time, I never considered the fire hazard. Next, we'd position the bottle right in the center of the newspapers and place a candle on top.

Once lit, the candle would start to drip wax down the sides of the bottle. We even had other lit candles that we hand-dripped onto the bottle, creating intricate and beautiful designs with the wax. We felt a rush of excitement as we completely coated the bottle, enjoying the mix of colors. I hope we never left it unattended during our sessions!

Recently, I've had the wild idea of trying it again. A quick search online revealed that there are now pre-made kits available with candles and bottles in various colors. The times have certainly changed. I was shocked by how expensive candles are now! I often wonder how we managed to have so many candles back then.

If I do decide to drip candles again, I will make sure to take every precaution and never leave the hot wax and flames unattended.

Is it really worth it to see what designs emerge from the dripping wax? Will the scent of the melting wax transport me back to my childhood? Or are those memories cherished enough just as they are?

Drip Candle

105. I Attempted To Make A Snowman At The Age Of 55

At the age of 55, I set out to create a snowman. When you're young, the goal is to roll the biggest snowball you can, usually with the help of a few friends. But as I got older, I found myself questioning whether the snowball was big enough, especially with my back aching from bending over. I quickly decided it was sufficient, understanding that I still had two more snowballs to stack on top of the first. I glanced around, hoping for assistance, but the person inside my house just waved and chuckled. The kid down the street watched but didn't venture out of his yard, and the neighbors walked by with their dogs, unable to leave them unattended.

Determined, I gathered the next two snowballs and added them to my artistic creation. I packed the snow tightly, feeling for a moment like a pottery artist. Next came the fun part of adding details. I found some sticks from the fire pit to use as arms and headed indoors to gather more supplies. I managed to find a knit hat, a colorful scarf, a tape measure, and some gloves. But I still needed eyes, a nose, and a mouth. In a flash of creativity, I used two stress balls for eyes, a compact mirror for the nose, a tape measure as a tie, and a ruler for the mouth and tongue. I even found three small trays to use as buttons. With a bit of effort, my goofy snowman took shape, and it felt like a fitting reflection of my own silliness.

I was pleased with my creation until the next morning when I looked out the window. Note to self: always consider the impact of building on a sloped front yard. When I checked outside, I discovered my snowman leaning forward, as if he, too, was suffering from back pain. His lean was quite dramatic. After work, I knew repairs were necessary. I reached out to my neighbors and friends, asking for their help to rescue my snowman and expressing my gratitude for their support. One neighbor kindly offered to paint him yellow, enlisting her dog's help in the process. I made some adjustments, moved him around, and gave him a little makeover. Then I had hoped that he would stick around long enough to bring a smile or two to those who pass by.

A goofy snowman just like me

106. Humans Are Creatures Of Habit

It's fascinating how humans are indeed creatures of habit. When we examine how we engage in the same repetitive actions each day, it becomes quite evident. From the moment you wake up, your routine often follows a familiar pattern. You might stretch before heading to the bathroom, put on your right sock before the left, or enjoy a cup of coffee or orange juice before starting your day. Do you find yourself taking the same route to work every day? Do you open doors with the same hand? Do you prepare meals in the exact same way each time?

What occurs when we introduce a change? Sometimes, breaking our routines can lead to moments of clarity and renewed energy. One of my favorite ways to mix things up is by changing the music I listen to during my commutes. I'm not suggesting we completely overhaul everything, like trying to write with the opposite hand, which would surely result in some messy signatures! However, tweaking your routine can help you discover what you truly enjoy even more.

It's also important to recognize that many people resist change, clinging to their established habits no matter what. So, what small change could you make to your routine that might bring you some added benefit?

107. Scary Unaware Trust In Each Other

I'm not trying to alarm you, but it's worth considering the trust we place in one another in our everyday lives. Have you ever thought about what might happen if a driver coming towards you sneezed and lost control of their vehicle, crashing into you? Every day, we travel at high speeds on highways, relying on the assumption that every driver will stay in their lane and avoid collisions. What about crossing a bridge? Do we not have faith in the strength and stability of its supports? We have faith that the buildings and structures we encounter are designed to keep us safe, not harm us. The items we use daily are built to be safe, allowing us to interact with them without fear. What would prevent someone from sabotaging your water supply? What if someone managed to send electrical surges through your connections and caused damage? Could our food be tampered with? Even as we wait in long lines, we generally exercise patience. But what if someone loses their cool? I trust you, and I hope you can extend that same trust to me.

108. The Debate Of Roadside Memorials

In writing this piece, I conducted research that deepened my internal debate about roadside memorials. While driving on highways of various sizes, you might encounter numerous memorials such as crosses, flower arrangements, markers, photographs, signs, balloons, stuffed toys, candles, lights, liquor bottles, cans, handwritten notes, T-shirts, white bicycles, and many other tokens, all often bearing names of the deceased. These are commonly referred to as roadside memorials, which has sparked a contentious discussion about their appropriateness.

For many, these memorials provide a means for families to honor the memory of loved ones who have died in tragic circumstances. By marking the site of an accident, survivors create a living tribute to the deceased's life. As the number of cremations rises and cemetery spaces become less common, the roadside memorials often become a long-lasting remembrance maintained by family and friends. For some, these displays represent the hidden, yet palpable, grief of a community or family. A white-painted bike, for instance, symbolizes a cyclist lost at that location, embodying a part of the grieving process for some individuals. Many see these memorials as a fitting tribute in an era that struggles to confront death, marking the place where a spirit has departed. They act as sobering reminders that safety should always be a priority while driving, serving as symbols of grief and remembrance. In New Mexico, for example, roadside memorials, known as "descansos," are protected as "traditional cultural properties" by the state's Historic Preservation Division, a custom that has been observed for over 200 years.

However, there is a counterargument to the existence of these memorials. Critics argue that they distract drivers and pose safety hazards, creating unnecessary risks for road maintenance workers who have to deal with them. Some believe these memorials represent an imposition of private grief into public spaces, suggesting that individual sorrow should remain private rather than being displayed publicly for all to see. They contend that such displays not only draw attention to one person's loss but may also overshadow the grief of others. Opponents worry that if memorials continue to proliferate, roads will resemble graveyards, with markers every few feet, leading to questions about why individuals don't erect tributes at every hospital bedside, as well. Some object on religious grounds, arguing that religious symbols on public property violate the constitutional principle of separation of church and state, with instances of individuals replacing memorials with offensive alternatives as acts of protest.

Despite their presence across the nation, roadside memorials may not always be legal, as state and local laws vary widely. Some states impose fines on individuals who create memorials, while others penalize those who remove them. Local governments often take a hands-off approach, recognizing the sentimental value of these memorials for grieving families and their potential to serve as warnings for motorists. For instance, in Ohio, roadside memorials can be placed along public sidewalks or roadways without a permit, and local governments are responsible for removing materials that pose safety hazards.

Alternatives to roadside memorials do exist. Families might choose to decorate headstones in cemeteries, create memory boards for social media, or make charitable donations in the victim's name.

There are also local spaces that allow for engraved bricks as a tribute, and some states offer permanent signs that can be purchased. Ohio even has an "Adopt a Highway" program to honor victims through designated stretches of land.

The debate continues: Who should be responsible for the upkeep of these memorials? Should it fall to the families and friends who create them, or to local and state agencies? What may provide comfort for some can be seen as offensive to others. It might be worthwhile to consider allowing these memorials to stand for a specified period unless a compelling hazard arises, after which they could be removed. As we seek to become more sensitive to each other's feelings and beliefs, reaching a compromise on this issue could foster understanding across the country.

109. Is It Better To Be In Love Than It Is To Love And To Be Loved?

Is it better to be in love with someone or to love that person and receive their love in return? Being in love is about desiring someone, while loving them means wanting what's best for them. It involves a deep understanding of who they are, accepting their flaws, and embracing all aspects of their personality. Being in love tends to focus on how your partner makes you feel, whereas loving someone requires you to actively seek their happiness.

When you're in love, you might experience infatuation, joy, excitement, and even nervousness, often characterized by feelings of pleasure and euphoria. Conversely, loving someone is a conscious choice you make, and to be loved is a true gift from that individual. While you can't dictate how someone else feels, it's essential to invest your energy into genuinely loving them.

To truly love someone means to care for them deeply, accepting both their strengths and weaknesses. While being in love emphasizes your personal feelings, loving someone involves proactive efforts to ensure their happiness. Loving someone can be challenging and demands dedication. Ultimately, it is more meaningful to love than merely to be in love. This can lead to vulnerability, but it also makes us more human. The richness of loving someone may not always lead to the rush of infatuation or reciprocal love, yet it defines you as a compassionate individual.

110. Love Is Slow Dancing With The One You Love

Love is slow dancing with the one you love, where it does not matter if you are in sync, stepping perfectly, or even hearing the music at all. It is about the connection in your eyes and the warmth of your smiles that touches your hearts. She might still be peacefully asleep, but I continue to dance with her in my thoughts and feelings. Hold onto the beautiful memories of your loved ones in the recesses of your heart, and remember to bring them out when you need a little extra warmth.

111. Murrrder Against The Maytes

Let me provide some background for this story. I once produced a murder mystery event with my fiancé for some of our friends, which had a wine theme, and it turned out well. Inspired by that, I decided to produce a pirate-themed version, which also went over successfully. Afterward, I thought it would be entertaining to adapt it into a written story. Converting my notes and materials from the murder mystery into a readable format proved to be quite a challenge. While it may not be perfect, my goal is for it to be enjoyable. Naturally, there are elements of confusion, as is typical in murder mysteries. I've aimed to infuse it with humor and surprises, particularly at the conclusion.

The full moon hung low over the horizon of Port Royal, casting its light on the town below. A local resident strolled along the boardwalk when he suddenly heard a commotion emanating from the grand ship docked nearby. This vessel was the Queen Anne's Revenge, renowned for its storied past on the high seas. As he approached, a large woman staggered out from the ship and fell into his arms. She appeared disoriented and possibly intoxicated. With a frantic cry, she exclaimed, "He's dead! Someone killed him! Help me, help him!" Before he could react, she collapsed against him.

Quickly regaining his composure, he contacted the local authorities, who promptly boarded the ship. Agent S. Wash Bucket, alongside Lord Oliver Cromwell, stepped into the captain's cabin only to be met with the grim sight of the captain lying lifeless.

"Well, it's clear he's dead," Agent Wash Bucket remarked.

"Indeed," replied Lord Oliver Cromwell, pausing to examine the sword nearby. Close to the captain's body lay a striking red gem, gleaming in the dim light. A pouch of gold coins spilled from the captain's pocket, while a white handkerchief embroidered with a Jolly Roger lay crumpled on the floor by his side.

"There's a lot happening on this ship," Cromwell noted.

"Absolutely," the agent replied. "I think we need to consult Captain Morgan on this matter. Hopefully, he can unravel this mystery."

Captain Morgan was summoned aboard the vessel, where he quickly recognized both the ship and its captain. Determined to get to the bottom of the situation, he agreed to assemble a group of individuals from the ship for questioning. He was confident that he would uncover the truth behind this shocking incident.

The following day, the diverse group of individuals began to board the ship as summoned. Captain Morgan stood patiently, watching each one step onto the grand vessel. Among them was a strikingly robust lady, a force to be reckoned with. Her bright, large eyes sparkled with enthusiasm, and a voluminous bun of hair sat atop her head. She carried a commanding presence, accentuated by her ample figure. She greeted Captain Morgan with a warm smile, and he directed her to a spacious table.

Next came a frail, elderly man whose weathered body bore the marks of countless sea voyages. Clad in a well-worn sailor's outfit and a faded cap, he squinted at Captain Morgan, saying nothing as he took a seat next to the large lady.

A couple strolled in arm in arm afterward. The woman appeared proud and stern, her nose held high, adorned in elegant clothing with a sparkling necklace and earrings. In contrast, the man seemed quiet and sullen, embodying the role of a supportive partner. They exchanged greetings with Captain Morgan before settling into their seats.

Before anyone noticed, another figure slipped into the room—a woman dressed in a fusion of gypsy and clairvoyant attire, radiating an aura of peace and freedom. Her dark dreadlocks framed her inquisitive eyes, which seemed to peer right into the soul. Captain Morgan was momentarily taken aback by her captivating presence and gestured for her to take a seat.

A heavy-set man entered next, walking with a noticeable limp that produced a disconcerting sound with each step. His attire suggested aspirations of higher status, yet it bore frayed edges—a hat with a small hole, and his coat and pant leg were similarly tattered. He placed a friendly hand on Captain Morgan's shoulder, offered a smile, and seated himself beside the fragrant woman.

Suddenly, a young lady in a flowing cream-colored dress appeared, rushing to the ship. Her hair whipped wildly in the wind as she lifted her dress to avoid tripping. Barefoot and without shoes, she careened into the nearest chair, collapsing into it with a sigh of relief.

Finally, trailing the scent of rum, a stumbling man entered, careening into the first empty chair he encountered. A few observers speculated that he might already be dozing off, seated and snoring softly in his newfound resting place.

Captain Morgan gathered his small crew ready to set sail. Captain Morgan began, "Ahoy there mateys! Me be Captain Morgan. We are in a time when pirates scour de sea like sharks, attacking even de most prominent of ships. Ye have all been asked here to board this here mighty ship: The Queen Anne's Revenge, ye most well-known vessel to sail these here waters. Its Captain was none other than ye famous Captain Grisly Meed, the longest serving captain at her helm. De ship was set ta sail to Parrot Island, a land said to behold a massive, buried treasure. Last night, Captain Meed's reign has been stolen from him with a slash of a blade, his own blade, his prized treasure, the Sword of Galgano. Captain Meed has been found murdered. Well, shiver me timbers and sharpen me sword! A night of seamen, secrets and scallywags await you as we leave next to the Salty Sea Dog Inn here in Port Royal, and set sail to Parrot Island. We shall discover that ye murderer is amongst us. Everyone aboard is a suspect in his murder, and ye person shall walk the plank and face his judgment with Davy Jones himself.'

"I think it be best if we introduce ourselves. Let's start with you me lady." "My name is Jamaica Parrotless mawn. I telz ya your future mawn. That's if yeez really wants to know. Meed gave me my first set of Tarrot cards from a merchant sailing into Port Royal. Twas one item of many I obtained to help me see into da future. Me was working with a new and exciting crystal ball mawn and was to tell the future to all the Caribbean. But my tools have been stolen. Ol' Grisly always challenging my futures I told. I shall miss his interpretations."

"I go next. Ayee. Me name is Bad Leg Pete. Me be a humble rum runner from Bermuda. Me travels around the Caribbean for my employer, Bacardi Rum, shopping for de best tasting rum a landlubber could find. Then me purchases large amounts for distribution throughout the whole Caribbean. Me been comin to Port Royal for quite some time. Me have many Hearties in the island areas and me has been quite impressed with the quality of rum found. The Queen Anne's Revenge has been a great help in me purchases and distribution. Tis such a tragedy that Captain Meed is gone."

"I'll be next, Hidey Ho, I am Christy Crabcakes. I once lived in Port Royal and made quite a name for myself. I left Port Royal to help grow my handkerchief business across the Caribbean. I recently came back to Port Royal to see how my business was doing here. I will miss Captain Meed. He gave me the idea of putting the Jolly Roger on all my handkerchiefs. I don't know what my business will do without the help of Captain Meed and The Queen Anne's Revenge. She then wiped her eyes with a handkerchief."

"Wait a minute now. I am Henrietta Fluffbucket and I don't think I am a suspect. I am a bar maid in the Salty Sea Dog Inn. I had been drinking a bit of rum with Captain Meed late into the evening. I thought at one point I saw him go upstairs with someone, but I cannot remember. I guess I had a bit too much rum and when I awoke, I found myself here in the captain's quarters of The Quenn Anne's Revenge. It is so sad that Captain Meed was killed. He was one of the Salty Sea Dog's best clients in more ways than one."

"Now wait a minute, Henrietta. Me be Long John Popper. Me be de first mate. Captain Grisly Meed was my long-lost cousin. Me believes now that I am the rightful captain of this here Queen Anne's Revenge. Me wife, Penny Periwinkle and me have great plans for de big ship. We have plans to extend our boundaries as soon as we can set sail ourselves. Me mother was a Meed, but de family disowned her after she had a terrible public incident in which she was runnin' from a drunken sailor and she tripped and ripped her clothing on a broken barrel of rum, and everything "popped' out. Me mother and me moved to Neverland. Henrietta and me found each other in Neverland. We fell in love, and we started a new life there. The only person that kept in touch with me was Captain Meed. Me received correspondence from him occasionally. That be why me came back. When me did comes back, Captain Meed gave me a job as a swabby and me swabbed the deck well. Me worked my way to be his first mate."

"Oh, John how I love you. Hi, I am Penny Periwinkle. I am married to Long John Popper, but I kept my maiden's name. I just hate John's last name. Can you imagine hearing, Penny Popper? I have supported John as first mate for a while now. He kept an eye on the captain and I kept an eye on him. We keep a tight ship together."

"Me be Samuel H. Teach, but everyone calls me Squint Eyed Sam. Me left my wife and child in Neverland to get a better job on The Queen Anne's Revenge as a simple deck hand. Me never saw them again. Me worked hard and learned de tools of the trades on the high seas. Me men's call me an old salt. Me've been under Captain Meed as the Master Gunner for his entire reign. Long John Popper is a good young lad to be his first mate. Me would like to retire and go back to Neverland or maybe even Parrot Island and rest me tired hands."

"Ahh, but me be last. Me be Jack Sharkbait. I be a loyal patron at the Salty Sea Dog Inn. Me don't believe me be a suspect. I knows all the happenings of Port Royal. Me went with the investigators to help identify the body of Captain Meed. Boy, I'll miss that guy. He was my favorite captain. Hic up."

Penny Periwinkle exclaimed, "Oh, my poor Captain Meed, I hope he is sailing to lands never seen." Squint Eyed Sam then said, "Well, blow me down! Captain Meed be gone and killed with his own sword." Long John Popper then cut in, "Aaaarrrrgghhh. Well, it be a damn nuisance if you ask me. Now they be a going over this here ship with a fine-tooth comb looking for clues. Me yikes to keep a ship shape ship. O' me hate those bilge sucking landlubbers. Penny Periwinkle then questioned Long John Popper, "Long John Popper you show little compassion for your dear cousin. He cared enough about you to give you a job. You were able to start a new life." Long John Popper replied, "Yeah, right! As a lousy deck hand, while he played lord of the ship. Cousin or Captain ye did me no favors. Bad Leg Pete added, "Tis sounds like you be happy he's gone to Davy Jones Locker deep in de bottom of the de sea. Mr. Popper, maybe ye not so surprised his body was killed with his own sword aye?" Jamaica Parrotless addressed Bad Leg Pete, "Bad Leg Pete, you are just as much a suspect as Long John Popper. You are all over Port Royal and on The Queen Anne's Revenge with your rum. Bad Leg Pete replied, Aye, Me was here, but me be no killer. Me business would dry up if me murdered one of my best suppliers. You, on the other hand, Jamaica Parrotless, you and Captain Meed seemed to always be in an argument over your predictions it seemed. Me wonders why ye were so angry with him?" Christy Crabcakes cut in, "I guess the price I have to pay for all the popularity I have with my handkerchiefs is that everybody wants to see me fail. In case you hadn't noticed Jamaica Parrotless, my success happened only after I came back to Port Royal and Ol' Captain Grisly Meed helped me with the Jolly Roger idea. I worked hard and earned every bit of it." Henrietta Fluffbucket laughed, "I bet you did," and then laughs again. "I need a drink or something for my aching head. Oh, that Captain Grisly Meed. That rum and him, Oh, what a scallywag." Jack Sharkbait asks Henrietta Fluffbucket, "Arnt ya three sheets to the wind? Another rum please." She replied, "Not! now, but I might have been last night, hey there Jack, I think I have never seen you without rum in your hand." Jack, "RRRRRRRRRR!" Squint Eyed Sam concludes, "Yo, Ho, Ho. De truth will call out to us all. Captain Meed is gone and we be his family and hearties. Together we discover who it be. Now me have a few questions." Captain Morgan looked out a port hole and saw a seagull flying in the brisk wind. He told them to continue.

Penny Periwinkle approached Squint Eyed Sam, "You have grown increasingly resentful that you have not been treated properly by Captain Meed. Did your resentment grow enough for you to kill Captain Meed in an act of vengeance?' Squint Eyed Sam replied, "I put in many years of hard work ta make the Queen Anne's Revenge a success. Every single captain of de Queen Anne's Revenge has promised me I would receive a piece of land in recognition of me service, but Captain Meed refused to honor his predecessor's promises. There was no respect." Squint Eyed Sam then turned his attention to Long John Popper. "Long John Popper ye have always been the black dog of the family. Before ye came to the Queen Anne's Revenge, ye spent years in a dungeon for filling a town well with rum. Wherever ye goes, trouble follows. Ye is cursed". Long John Popper responded, "Yeah, it be true me served time in a dungeon but me paid for me crime and that's all behind me now. Me've not been in trouble once since me release from that stinky ol dungeon." John turned his head towards Christy Crabcakes, "Ye was seen with Captain Meed last night. He walked with ye on the boardwalk near Lucky Bluffs. Captain Meed was never seen alive again. What did ye do to him?" She jumped right back at him, "Yes, Last night, Captain Meed and I took a nice walk on the boardwalk near Lucky Bluffs. It was a nice night so the two of us simply took a stroll and had a pleasant talk. He dropped me off at the Salty Sea Dog Inn late in the evening and I went to home to bed alone." Jack Sharkbait slid in his seat making a scratching sound on the floor and everyone turned towards him. He said, "Tells us more about your "talk" with Captain Meed when ye walked at Lucky Bluffs. What were ye talking about? Why would ye be in an area for lovers?" Christy with a fake smile on her face, "Oh, Jack, It was just a nice chat and it had a nice view of the sea." She waved her hand in the air as if to say no. She looked next at Bad Leg Pete, "You seem to be a man who lives well beyond your means. You only own one very small longboat, yet your pouch is filled with gold coins. You dine extravagantly at the Salty Sea Dog Inn. It is said that you own a small island off the coast of Bermuda. When Captain Meed was still alive, he was suspicious about Bad Leg Pete's source of income.

You did something here did you not?" Pete sitting upright and proud, "I be a very resourceful man. Over de years I have invested my income wisely and have reaped the benefits . . . a nice little boat, a small piece of land on an island off of Bermuda, and a few Parrots. Ye don't throw your money around foolishly like a scallywag. Rrrrrrrrr!" Henrietta then added, "Pete why don't you open that pouch of coins you have there and reveal how much doubloons you are carrying on you. Isn't that quite a large amount? Where did you get it?" He slowly pulled out the pouch but the vast amount falls all across the table. Pete, "Me manages me money wisely." Bad Leg Pete quickly change the subject to Long John Popper, "Long John Popper gains the most from Captain Meed's death. Ye now becomes captain of the Queen Anne's Revenge. Ye receives control of the Queen Anne's Revenge and everything attached to it. He also is married to Captain Meed's close friend and now be a wealthy man. These were all powerful motives for Long John Popper to kill his cousin Captain Grisly Meed. Long John Popper quickly replied, "All the motives Ye claim me had for killing Captain Meed were things that would have happened even if he was alive. Captain Meed was a sniveling weakling. In this world, only the strong survive and take what rightfully belongs to them."

Long John Popper then produces a memo:

March 1654, Oliver Cromwell, Lord Protector of England,

Port Royal, Jamaica

From: Lord Oliver Cromwell

Date: March 18th, 1654

File: Murder Investigation Case #555023 Meed, Captain Grisly

Comments: Let it be known that said body was found face up in the captain's quarters of the Queen Anne's Revenge while docked at bay in Port Royal. Body was found to have a large 3- foot silver sword protruding from the chest of the victim. A torn white handkerchief, a money pouch with a small amount of coin, and a red ruby were found near the pool of blood surrounding the said victim. The sword was clean and sharp, with an engraving with the word Galgano on it.

It should be noted that a Penny Periwinkle was interviewed shortly after the body being found. She claimed not to be missing any red ruby. She was extremely nervous and angry over something. Official noted Periwinkle to have stated something about prize jewelry missing under her breath while investigators were leaving.

Sincerely

Agent S. Wash Buckle

Long John Popper looked at Penny Periwinkle and continued, "This here be a murder investigation case memo that was filed by Lord Oliver Cromwell. Lord Cromwell reported how the body was found and what items were found near the victim. Lord Cromwell speculated that Captain Meed had met with foul play and Penny Periwinkle was questioned as a leading suspect. Why did they question you right away?" Penny Periwinkle, "The Lord Cromwell is a scallywag and his memo is a pile of seagull guts. That agent S. Buckle has no leads to explain Captain Meed's death so he made me appear suspicious just to hide his incompetence. I have lots of jewelry, so even if I did lose a really nice looking ruby, it wouldn't be a big loss." Penny looking a bit nervous turned to Jamaica, "Jamaica Parrotless you grew a nasty little grudge against Captain Meed. You say your clairvoyant items were stolen. I think that Captain Meed may have stolen the items to get back at you for something they disagreed on? You seemed so certain the thief was Captain Meed." Jamaica snapped back, "I be certain it be Captain Meed who stole me clairvoyant items mawn. He be trying to get back at me for telling him a bad fortune I gave him. He was trying to get me a new crystal ball to start a new approach and move on. The theft was a blessing in disguise as me fortunes have "grown" new power. I tell yam awn, it's just too "high"." A slight laugh was heard from a few. She was sensing some people were looking at her and seemed not to believe her. She then spoke to Christy Crabcakes, "Now Christy, ya was found to be frequenting many rooms at the Salty Sea Dog Inn last night. One room may have been Captain Meed's. It be strange that this murder only happened when ya came back after leaving Port Royal for so long. Why did ya come back, tells us now?" Christy quickly responded, "I left Port Royal to help grow my handkerchief business all across the Carribean. I came back to see how sales were doing in the city. I met with Captain Meed to discuss some of the Handkerchief business as well. I am just so busy meeting people over this handkerchief business." Sam, squinted even more and let out a, "rrrrr." He then turned to Jamaic Parotless, "Jamaica you knew there was a secret passage into Captain Meed's Quarters on the Queen Anne's Revenge. I showed it to her one time when she was visiting the ship. Jamaica could have used the passage to sneak inside to kill Captain Meed quite easily." Jamaica looking somewhat dumbfounded, "I had forgotten about the secret passage into the Captain's Quarters. It has been a long time since you showed it to me mawn. I doubt I even remember how to get through it." Jack then cut in, "Jamaica, can you describe the secret passage as best ya can remember? What does it look like? How long is it? How does someone get in it?" He cringed his eyes judging how fresh her memory was of the passage. Jamaica, "I remember seeing a dark passage or a hidden door, but I tells yam awn, I can't remember much of it at all." A creek in the wood of ship paused everyone's attention for a moment, then Christy spoke to Squint Eyed Sam, "Sam you were living below deck on the Queen Anne's Revenge while the murder happened. It seems strange that you did not hear or see anything that night. Can you explain that?" Sam replied, "Me had way too much rum last night. It was a jolly o'l time and me had celebrated with me mateys. Me passed out sometime around midnight. A large ship could have run aground and me would not have heard it." Everyone looked at all the rum in abundance at the table. Jamaica pulled a piece of paper out. "I have here a flyer from a exotic parrot sales place. It was found in Captain Meed's quarters. There is a threatening note to Pete from Meed on the flyer. Pete, Me hears you're not happy with the deal. Maybe you don't understand the consequences! What does this mean mawn?" Pete proudly answered, "Me have never seen the note Captain Meed wrote to me on the Exotic Parrot sales flyer until this very moment. Captain Meed must have intended to give it to me but was killed first. I have no idea what it means." Out of the blue Pete attacks Penny, "Me knows for a fact that Penny Periwinkle and Captain Meed were once very close to each other. It seemed as though Penny Periwinkle wanted marriage. They had a huge fight about it. Could Penny Periwinkle have killed Captain Meed because he decided to dump her? Penny, "Yes, my dear Captain Meed and I were once an item. I loved him but he had a reason why we could never be together. You see Meed was going to gain a mass fortune then give himself to religious faith. Can you believe that? He would then give all his treasures of gold, jewels, and coin to the poor. By naming the sword Galgano it reminded him of his religious faith. Captain Morgan will tell you the story of the sword of Galgano."

The Story of the Sword of Galgano

Saint San Galgano was born in 1148 and lived a wild life as a fierce knight, driven by lust and untamed passions. At the age of 20, he encountered Archangel Michael, who guided him toward salvation and instructed him to seek solitude on a nearby mountain. This encounter led him to become a hermit, settling in a cave. While riding his horse, he experienced a fall, but a spirit lifted him to the summit of Monte Siepi. There, he found a circular temple housing Jesus, Mary, and the Apostles, where he was called to renounce his worldly pleasures. Galgano expressed skepticism, asserting that while giving up such pleasures sounded appealing, it would be as challenging as using his sword to split stone. To demonstrate, he drew his sword and aimed it at a rock, expecting the blade to break. The stone instead, yielded effortlessly, sinking to the hilt.

From that moment on, Galgano chose to remain on the hill, embracing a life of poverty. He formed bonds with wild animals, and local farmers came to seek his wisdom and blessings. One day, the devil sent a disguised assassin who posed as a monk; however, the wolves that dwelled with Galgano defended him, attacking the would-be killer and feasting on his remains. A year later, at the age of 33, Galgano passed away, and his funeral turned into a significant event. A chapel was erected over the sword, which became a site of reported miracles visited by many. It was said that his head continued to grow golden curls for years after his death, one of which was displayed on one side of the chapel, while the gnawed bones of the assassin were placed on the other side. The sword has been verified to date back to that era and remains embedded in the stone to this day. Notably, there may be a cavity beneath the sword that could contain Galgano's body.

Additionally, it is suggested that legends of King Arthur may have been inspired by Galgano's remarkable story.

Penny simply answered, "I tried to convince him to think twice about it. But we will never know if he would have changed. Thank goodness I have Long John Popper to help me through this ordeal." Henrietta added, "Can you repeat the words that were exchanged with Captain Meed and you when he broke off the relationship?" She answered, "It was just as simple as this must end now. This can no longer go on. I was sad and I yelled and begged him to keep our relationship. I may have even slapped him I was so upset." Captain Morgan then stirred a bit and asked Jack Sharkbait if he thought he was brought on board to help solve the murder. "Why do you think you are here? Does any of this have to do with any of your drinking?" Jack answered, "I just don't understand why help is needed in solving this murder. I just have a little memory problem after drinking some rum. I'll be fine. I'll remember everything soon. Maybe if I could have some more rum it may help my memory." Then Captain Morgan asked Henrietta about her drinking as well, "How much did you really drink with Captain Meed? Henrietta laughed a good chuckle, "I really can't remember how much we drank. It is quite funny how I have no idea how I ended up in the captain's quarters. I wonder if it was something else besides rum that someone gave me to drink. I tell you; I see everyone that comes into the Salty Sea Dog Inn and I wish to get back after this all over."

Captain Morgan stood up and slowly walked around the entire table. With his left hand upon his chin and finger upon his nose his eyes gazed at each of the suspects at the table. He began to speak, "As me watched and listend to all ye, me couldn't help but think of de old song, yo ho ho and a bottle of rum. It seems ya scallywags are full of secrets. Let's review what been revealed so fer. Pete, you certainly know how to do so much with so little; selling rum to merchants with such a small boat. Maybe the note Captain Meed sent ye were to get yeeze to meet him at the Salty Sea Dog Inn fer some advice." Pete simply shook his head. He then stood right next to Penny Periwinkle, "Penny, how ironic it is yer good friend broke off your relationship due to his fear of everyone finding out his religious faith, yet geets killed by the sword that reminded him of his faith. Ye were so quick to jump ship and hook up with Long John Popper. Tis curious that they found a red gem near the body. And when you were questioned about your jewelry you became nervous and angry." Penny shrugged her shoulders and turned her head away. He turned to Long John Popper, "John, well, blow me down. Ye have been doin an outstandin job as first mate, supportin Captain Meed in all of his toughest times, especially with such a limited sailing experience. It is an incredible feat how ye went from being chained in the dungeon to swabbin the deck to first mate of the most revered vessel sailing these here waters. Ye could be an inspiration to anyone chained to bars." John smiled thinking he was being appreciated, then turned a frown upon his face as he wondered if Captain Morgan was simply mocking him. Captain Morgan then put his hand upon Christy Crabcakes shoulder, "Christy, Please don't leave today without giving ye one of yer famous handkerchiefs. We love how ye put a special Jolly Roger on each one. Tis amazing that ol' Grizzly gave ya the idea. Interesting how they found one of those special handkerchiefs on his possession when they found his body." She blushed and was about to give him one when she realized that it linked her to the murder as a suspect. He then pointed at Squint Eyed

Sam. "It's a shame you don't own your own sailing ship. Ye are so knowledgeable of guns, ammunition, and weapons. Captain Meed must have been very lucky to have ye take care of the ship after all these years; and ya seem to be enjoying sampling the rum near the powderkegs as much as ya tend to the supplies." Sam squinted even more, if it was even possible. Captain Morgan raised his hands in the air and looked at Jamaica Parrotless. "Your new crystal ball is amazing, especially after all your clairvoyant items suddenly disappeared. Meeze wonder who took em all. Ye must have been quite angry. By the way, meeze didn't see ya come down the steps of the ship. Did yeeze use the secret door?" She smiled and shrugged her shoulders in a way as if to say maybe or maybe not. Captain Morgan wanted to sit down with Henrietta Fluffbucket but there was no room. "Ye keep a good bar there matey, can't wait to go back to a seat at the Salty Sea Dog Inn with ya." She winks her eye back at him. Then he pointed at something on Jack Sharkbait's shirt. "Is that a spill from rum on ye shirt or some tis else dere?" Jack raised his glass. Captain Morgan continued. "This is all so interesting. Usually, me be the one tellin de stories, but now me content ta just sit and listen. Let's continue with ye conversations and let's see if we can plunder some more answers to de mystery."

Penny turned to Long John Popper, "John, did you kill Captain Meed to keep me closer? I am madly in love with you. Were you afraid that Captain Meed was going to steal me away from you?" John responded, "Me not have to kill Captain Meed to keep you close to meeze. You seemed to be getting angrier with Captain Meed each day. So why would me haves to kill Meed to keep ya away from him? Me had the best of both worlds; your love and being second in command, so why would me ruin it by killing Captain Meed?" He chuckled and shook his head. Jack added, "Have ye done this sort of thing before? What did the real Long John Popper look like?" John slouched and said, "I have never been an imposter before this time. It was a chance of a lifetime to start a new life and get out of the mess me was in. Me would describes him as a crazy looking guy with big eyes and long black hair. He was very scary looking." Captain Morgan then produced a sketch and asked if it looked like him. John gave no reply.

John then turned to Jamaica, "Your new fortunes seem to be "growing" in strength. What happened to your clairvoyant items? Who did this to ya? Did someone give ya a new crystal ball?" She turned towards him with a large smile and piercing eyes, "I was starting to move around the area with many new fortunes and they were "growing" rapidly. Just when I thought that I was going to do more, all of my items were stolen mawn. I believe Captain Meed stole the items because he did not like the fortunes, I gave him. He gave me a new

221

crystal ball to start me on a new path. I tinks he did it to cover up all his theft of my items mawn." Henrietta then asked, "Did you bring your crystal ball so you could do a fortune or two for us all?" Jamaica reached down and pulled out a small orange cloth bag. She pulled out another cloth and then a crystal-clear glass ball. She then began to ask each of the individuals at the table to come closer to her as she called them one by one. She first asked Long John Popper to come close. He was skeptical but did sit next to her. She wrapped the ball onto of the cloth and moved her hands around the ball as she gazed at John. Her eyes brightened up and she read, "It seems that the people who know the least about you, always seem to have the most to say about you." John said not a word, but turned his lips and turned his head a bit in contemplation. She then called Penny to sit next to her. Penny was somewhat reluctant but made her way to her seat. Jamaica cast into the glass ball again and then said, "A beautiful face in youth is the result of fortune, a beautiful face in old age is earned by kindness and wisdom." Penny smiled and fluffed her hair and went back to sit next to Long John Popper. As she was sitting down Jamaica added, "I see a second fortune for you madam. A good time to keep your mouth shut is when you are in deep water." Penny's smile instantly turned to a frown. To Jack she turned to next. She was having a difficult time getting close to him as he reeked of rum and it was a bit overwhelming at times. She did gaze into the ball and came up with one for him. She said, "An apple a day keeps the doctor away, but an onion a day keeps everyone away." Jack smiled. He somehow had the whitest smile one could imagine. Jamaica then asked if Christy could come by her next. Christy pulled up her dress and made her way next to her. She gazed into the ball once again. With a gasp she said,

"If you look for happiness in the darkness, do not be surprised that you cannot see it." Christy was puzzled and could not figure it out. She simply went back to her seat. She then said she would move close to Pete so he would not have to move. He was glaring at the ball intensely. He waited patiently as she read the fortune, "You have a secret admirer you will never meet." He took his hat off and scratched his head, unsure of what he thought of the fortune. She then asked Sam to sit next to the crystal ball as she was already waving her hands above it. She said, "He that waits upon a fortune is never sure of a dinner." Sam may have even squinted his other eye after this as he was puzzled to the telling. She then said that she saw an extra fortune for Jack. He might have been snoring, but he awoke alert and attentive to his extra fortune. She said smiling at him, "Doesn't expecting the unexpected make the unexpected become the expected?" He said, "huh?" and then looked for some more rum. She then spoke to Captain Morgan, "I see a special one for you as well." "Friendship is like a garden. It needs a lot tending. Truly good friends are hard to find, tend to them well. Captain Morgan simply looked upwards and said, "Oh my dear friend." Everyone was deep in thoughts of their own of Captain Meed when Jamaica said she had one more for everyone. "All good things must come to an end, but all bad things can continue forever." They then thought if it was Jamaica just coming up with some sayings, or if she did use the crystal ball to obtain these fortunes.

Jamaica then stood up and then pointed at Pete, "Let it be known that Pete was to meet up with me at the Salty Sea Dog Inn for a possible romantic rendezvous and for a new fortune telling. He was extremely late and his clothes were covered in dirt when he arrived. I tinks back that night and tink his actions that night seemed highly suspicious." He frowned and spoke, "Yes, me was on me way to meet ya at the Salty Sea Dog In. Me thought we might get it to turn romantic and me really wanted that fortune telling Me bad leg buckled on the boardwalk and me fell onto the ground. Me had no time to change clothes. Me be so embarrassed. Me didn't stumble from drinking too much rum, it was that darn bad leg." Everyone at the table held back their chuckling laughter the best they could. Pete then pulled out a picture he was given. It was a picture of a fisty fiery woman.

Anne Bonny

It was a picture of the famous female pirate Anne Bonny and her trial document. Captain Morgan then began to tell story of Anne Bonny.

The Story Of Anne Bonny

Anne Bonny was born in Cork, Ireland, as the illegitimate daughter of Mary Brennan, a servant, and William McCormac, a lawyer who was also her employer. To escape from his wife's family, McCormac moved to London, where he began dressing Anne as a boy and calling her "Andy." When this was discovered, he relocated to the

Carolinas, bringing along Anne's mother. To conform into the citizenry of Charles Town (now Charleston, South Carolina), McCormac dropped the "Mc" from their Irish surname. Although the family faced difficulties initially, McCormac's legal expertise and trade skills soon enabled them to acquire a townhouse and eventually a plantation outside the city.

Anne's mother passed away when Anne was just 12 years old. Attempting to establish himself as an attorney, McCormac struggled and eventually switched to a more lucrative career in merchant trade, amassing a significant fortune. Anne was noted for her striking red hair and was seen as a desirable match, though she was also rumored to possess a volatile temper; at the age of 13, she allegedly stabbed a servant girl with a table knife and hospitalized a young man who tried to assault her.

Anne married James Bonny, a poor sailor and small-time pirate, hoping to secure a portion of her father's estate. However, her father disowned her. There are accounts suggesting she retaliated by setting fire to his plantation, though there is no evidence to support this claim. Still, she did move with James to Nassau on New Providence Island, a known refuge for English pirates in what was called the Republic of Pirates. Many residents had received a King's Pardon or were evading the law. After the arrival of Governor Woodes Rogers, James Bonny became an informant for the governor.

While in the Bahamas, Anne began socializing with pirates at local taverns, where she met John "Calico Jack" Rackham, the captain of the pirate sloop Revenge. They became romantically involved and had a son in Cuba, though various theories suggest different fates for the child, including abandonment. Bonny ultimately rejoined Rackham, abandoning her husband and marrying him at sea.

Alongside Rackham and fellow pirate Mary Read—who some sailors claimed was also in a romantic relationship with Bonny, they seized the ship William while it was anchored in Nassau harbor and set out to sea. The trio recruited a new crew, targeting smaller vessels and accumulating treasure over the months. Bonny fought alongside the men and earned a reputation as a capable and respected pirate.

Governor Rogers listed her in a "Wanted Pirates" notice published in The Boston News-Letter. Although Bonny gained historical fame as a Caribbean pirate, she never commanded her own ship. Rackham and his crew faced an attack by a King's ship captained by Jonathan Barnet under a commission from the Governor of Jamaica, Nicholas Lawes. Most of Rackham's crew offered little resistance due to intoxication, but Read and Bonny fought bravely and briefly held off Barnet's troops.

After their capture, Rackham, Read, and Bonny were brought to Jamaica, where they were convicted and sentenced to hang. According to reports, Bonny's last words to the imprisoned Rackham were: "Had you fought like a man, you need not have been hang'd like a dog." After the sentencing, both women claimed they were pregnant, requesting mercy. Under English common law, they received a temporary reprieve until they gave birth. However, Read ultimately died in prison, likely from a fever after childbirth.

There are no historical records confirming Bonny's release or execution, leading to various speculations about her fate. Some suggest her father may have ransomed her, while others think she might have returned to her husband or resumed piracy under a new identity. Some evidence implies that her father purchased her freedom from Governor Lawes and married her to a wealthy Jamaican political figure, where she supposedly took on the name Annabele, bore eight children, and lived until the age of 88, outliving her husband. The ambiguity surrounding Bonny's final years continues to fuel intrigue about the life of this legendary pirate.

Captain Morgan continued, "Captain Meed figured out that she was the renowned female pirate. Captain Meed had threatened to reveal Christy Crabcake's secret to the world. Christy/Anne knew if she was found, she would not survive another trial. What did ya do to stop Captain Meed from "exposing" ya to all?" Christy, "I was young and foolish when I ran around as the famous female pirate Anne Bonny. I escaped death in prison and miraculously disappeared. I then began a new "service" to others. Captain Meed recently found out about my hidden past, but instead of reporting it to the authorities he pressured me to grant him special favors. He was killed before I decided what to do." Christy was upset and she began to cover herself with her dress. She then pulled from inside her dress a piece of paper. She told them all that it was a death certificate for Long John Popper, signed by the dungeon master. The real Long John Popper died in a dungeon just before being released. "If the real Long John Popper died in dungeon, then who are you? What is your real name? What the heck happened in that dungeon." John was taken aback and fell back in his chair. "RRRR, Me was Long John Popper's cell mate in a Neverland dungeon. Me learned all about the Queen Anne's Revenge and Captain Meed. When Long John Popper died shortly before my release, I stole his identity and came to Port Royal to try my hand in

the ship business. Me real name is Peter Teach. I paid my dues. I
want to move on." John then turned everyone's attention to Sam, "Ye
have spent an unusual amount of time below deck. It seems ye never
goes ashore much. Ye is constantly down der tinkering and doing
repairs. Could ye have been secretly "carving out" a place to kill
Captain Meed?" John sat up in his chair, "The Queen's Anne's
Revenge be a massive ship that is in constant need of repair and the
weapons must be kept in tip top shape. That is the reason me spends
so much time below deck, fixing things down there. Me had no idea
poor Captain Meed's body was found in his own captain 's quarters.
May god rest his soul." Henrietta then added, "Could you please
elaborate on some of the repair work you have done on the ship's
arsenal and supplies over the years." She crossed her arms in wonder
if he will tell the truth or not. Sam replied, "As me be the Master gunner
me be responsible for de ship's guns and ammunition. This includes
sifting the powder to keep it dry, prevent it from separating; ensuring
the cannons and ordnance, which are the mounted guns and artillery,
keep em free of rust and that all weapons be in good repair. A
knowledgeable gunner be essential to the crew's safety and effective
use of their weapons." Sam then addressed Pete, "It be said that ye
came to the Salty Sea Dog Inn and gave Captain Meed gold
doubloons from a pouch. It was filled with lots and lots of gold. It was
said that ye seemed very unhappy about giving the gold to Captain
Meed and left in such a hurry ya forgot your pouch. What was with this
pouch and gold and Captain Meed?" Pete replied, "Captain Meed and
Me had conducted a business deal. The money me gave him was his
share of the profit. The payoff was in gold doubloons and the deal was
not totally legitimate. That's all me can say about it." Pete turned it

back onto Sam, "The investigation of Captain Meed's body concluded that whoever used the sword to fatally slash Captain Meed was very skillful in its use. No one has more access to all the weapons than ye, Squint Eyed Sam." "It is true me be skilled with weapons like swords. The sword is a tool that must be respected. It is for cutting rope as well as defense of others." Sam quickly pointed to Penny, "All this time, ye has shown an absolute fear of being in the confines of Captain Meed's quarters. Is it because ye knew where Captain Meed was killed and was afraid of his ghost?" Penny with a scared nervous look said, "Your theory that I knew Captain Meed was going to be killed in his captain's quarters is ridiculous. In truth, I have a phobia about confined spaces." Jack then added, "Why ya be so nervous to be comin into de confines of de captain's quarters? Penny nervously answered while looking to be shaking a bit, "I have been nervous ever since I came inside here. I was accidentally locked in an empty treasure chest one night as a child and it has had a traumatic effect on me." Penny in her nervous state noticed Christy staring at her and then said to her, "Your explosive temper is legendary. There are constant reports of your outrageous tantrums. It is reported that you went ballistic when you found out you're your handkerchiefs were once made wrong. It is said you chased each worker with a sharp knife. You might have been alone with Captain Meed last night. If you lost your temper, you could have killed him in an uncontrollable rage." Christy looking shocked, "People will do anything they can when they are jealous of someone else being successful. There is no truth to the rumors that I have an explosive temper. I had a couple of mild tantrums and everyone has blown it out of proportion. I never lost my temper when my handkerchiefs were made wrong." Christy looked at Jamaica who was smiling back at her with a silly grin. She said to her, "All the time you have conducted fortunes, yet, you only produced a small amount of money. There always seems to be one misfortune after another. Yet, you appear financially sound. How are you able to keep her business afloat." Her smile stopped and she replied," I be providen fortunes for years to various individuals. Some have remained silent in how they pay me for my "services". Even in the bad times they have remained true to me and wish to remain anonymous in helping me with my expenses mawn." Captain Morgan then asked Henrietta, "Can ye recall who was in the Salty Sea Dog Inn Last night and how much rum dey drank?" She said, "I can only remember seeing lots and lots of rum flowing in and out of the Salty Sea Dog Inn last night, although Jack Sharkbait always drinks the most of anyone. I can't remember who had what and of how much. I thought I saw someone go upstairs with Captain Meed. I did lose my memory at some point in the night and somehow found myself in the captain's quarters." Captain Morgan then asked Jack how many years he had been going to the Salty Sea Dog Inn. Jack stated, "Me can't remember how many years but me been coming for quite some time. Me can tell that everyone had a lot of rum. Can me have another?"

Captain Morgan rose and declared, "Ahh yes Mateys: Me must say, me be somewhat overwhelmed by what me have heard ye sa far. Tis hard to keep track of ti all. Let me get this straight." "Squint Eyed Sam: Let me commend ya on keepin da ship in tip top shape for such a long time. Tis a shrine to yer dedication. Me always wanted ta learn proper swordsmanship. Maybe ya could teach us all Sam, as you seem to know how to use one so well." "Christy Crabcakes: You are really sailing off with that handkerchief venture of yers. We must say we are bit envious of ya. Also, me should tell ya that they say when you found them making them there handkerchiefs with the Jolly Roger not in the right spot you chased em all over and almost pushed em overboard. Me not like to get in ye in such a frenzy." "Bad Leg Pete: Me curious, just how much coin was in ye pouch you left with Captain Meed? Just seems odd that you dealt a deal in such a way. But, then again ye are a man of many secrets. Me loved the one about you and Jamaica Parrotless having a midnight rendezvous in the Salty Sea Dog Inn, Intriguing indeed." "Jamaica Parrotless: You've had the worst 'fortune' haven't ya? Ya barely got back telling fortunes after your items disappeared. Is the new crystal ball as good as the ol one? "Long John Popper: John or do we call ya Peter Teach now? Whoever ye are, ya certainly like to live dangerously. Under the circumstances me take back my compliments about the success of your rise through the ranks. Cheating with Captain Meed's close friend and using the identity of his long-lost cousin to get a job on the ship, tsk, tsk, tsk." "Penny Periwinkle: You and Long John Popper seem to have a lot in common. Dishonesty. Playing around with Captain Meed and Long John Popper, gives me de impression that ye aren't sincere with your relationships with men. But me understands ye fear of confined spaces. Me have ordontophobia. Ye fear of teeth, or more specifically in me case, the fear of missing teeth." "Ye certainly rrrr an entertaining group of seafaring foes. And me things we are getting close to solving this mystery. Shall we sail along?"

Long John Popper said to Christy in a raised voice, "Christy Crabcakes, - ahh, Anne Bonny. Why don't ya 'bare your soul with de truth about Captain Meed's murder." She replied, "You're pathetic, Long John Popper, or is it, Peter? Who are you really?" Penny

Periwinkle began to cry, "I can't believe I'm married to an imposter. Or am I married to a man who died in a dungeon years ago? I'm so confused." Bad Leg Pete then cut in, "What else be new, Penny? But, don't despair, your men seem to be interchangeable as long as dey be rich, rrrrr?" Penny responded back, "My dear Bad Leg Pete, maybe I'll leave Long John Popper and marry you. I could help you run your 'not-so-legitimate' business deals." Pete said, "Me think not, Penny Periwinkle, me think me would like Jamaica Parrotless for me partner. She must have a good "sense" of "smell" for business. All these years producing very little fortunes, yet living a good rich life. Meeze would like to know her secret." Jamaica rose up in her seat and shot back at Pete, "It shouldn't be hard for you ta find out Bad Leg Pete. From what I've heard you're pretty good at secretly flying around situations mawn." Squint Eyed Sam then spoke to divert the conversation, "Me don't know if it's important but whoever killed Captain Meed right here did a good job. In all me years me not found one out of place board or weapon. De killer must be handy with ye hands." John added, "Right, and someone who be happy with a blade. That be narrowing the list down. I'd say ya be at the top of it, Squint Eyed Sam." Christy then added, "Your name would be next on the list Long John Popper. Don't you have a lot of experience of "cutting" like your "slice" of a deal, back in the dungeon?" Sam cut back, "Thank ye Christy Crabcakes. Ye always be such a nice wench. But ye temper . . . Shiver me timbers!" Henrietta sitting back listening to it all then asked if anyone needed anymore rum. She said the chatter made her just want to poor more rum drinks. Jack raised his glass with a hiccup and said, "rum rrrrrr! Jamaica then asked if they could get back to business as her fortunes were waiting and growing.

Penny began again, "Captain Meed told me he had discovered that Bad Leg Pete was using his rum distribution job as a cover to run his exotic Parrot sales theft ring. He mingled with the rich and famous at parties, taverns, and inns all across the Carribean, then planned the theft of their exotic Parrots. Did Captain Meed blackmail you for a piece of the action?" Pete replied, "If me steals a few birdies from wealthy people, it is not such a serious crime. They simply can get another one. But, murder – that is not something me would do, even if Captain Meed was "cutting" into me hidden profits. I be a chivalrous, courteous, and honorable man." Pete then turned to Christy, "Christy Crabcakes, ye used to be Anne Bonny. One of your lovers was Calico Jack. He was captured and hanged for his crimes. Anne Bonny vowed to get revenge for Calico Jack's needless death. Did Captain Meed play a part in his hanging?" Christy raised her voice and her hand, "It is true that I believed Captain Meed helped to capture and hang one of my lovers: Captain Jack Calico Rackham. I was grief-stricken when I vowed revenge, but I've long since gotten over my anger." Christy then approached Penny. She began, "You have a history of marrying men for their money. Before you came to Port Royal, you were married twice to elderly gentlemen who conveniently passed on shortly after their weddings from supposedly stab wounds, leaving everything they owned to you, Penny Periwinkle." Penny stood face to face to her and said, "My two previous husbands died of natural causes. That comment about them dying from stab wounds is hog wash. Captain Meed was never in danger of me. Besides, Long John Popper is living proof that I am not a 'husband-killer'. I have been married to him for quite a while now and he's still alive." Long John Popper then quickly added, "Ahh, but me saw Penny Periwinkle stumble out of the Salty

Sea Dog Inn. Before me said good night to her she began to stumble with her words. While being very intoxicated from of course rum, Penny started talking about a confession of killing Captain Meed. Me have kept her secret until now." Penny staring right back at his face, "I could not possibly have confessed to Captain Meed's murder while being drunk on rum because I never killed Captain Meed. In fact, I really don't remember too much from last night at all." Penny was now red to the face and very angry. She rose and then pulled out a flyer.

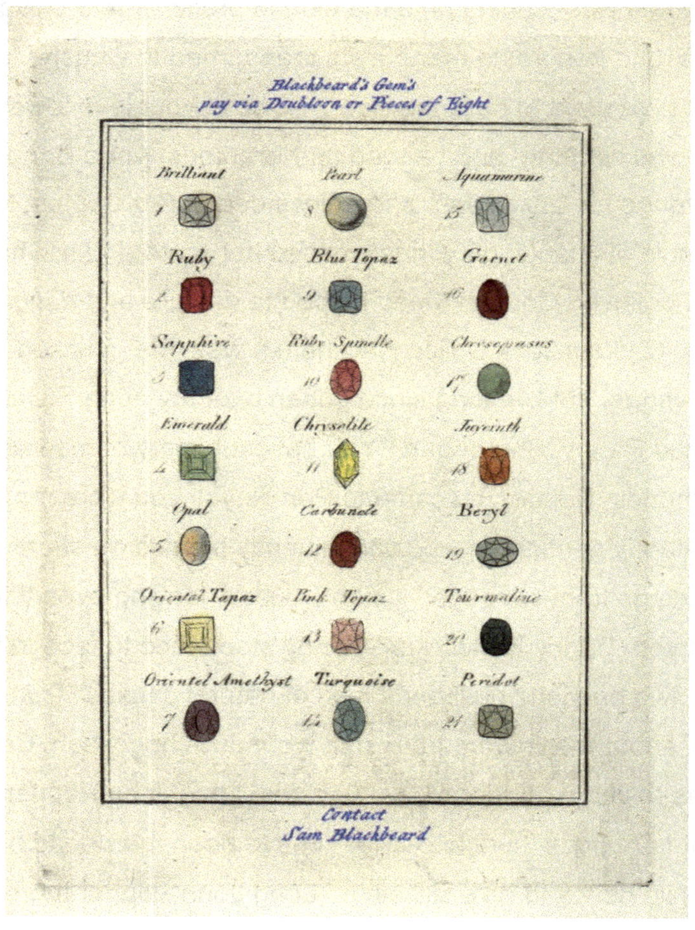

It was a flyer for ordering exotic gems. It appeared that Squint Eyed Sam may have been stealing some gems from the Queen Anne's Revenge's treasure chest. He may have passed the flyers out wherever the ship was docked at port. Captain Meed may have discovered Squint Eyed Sam's theft ring. Sam quickly responded, "It be true me made a little extra Pieces of Eight and Doubloons selling the gems across the Caribbean. Me simply took just a few from the ship's treasure chest once in a while. What did it hurt? Nobody would miss it. There was so much treasure and me was paid so little for me service on the ship for so many years." Jamaica then added in, "Tis be true that Captain Meed discovered that Squint Eyed Sam had been stealing his rare gems from the ship's treasure chest. Captain Meed was going to Court Martial Squint Eyed Sam and then have Sam leave the ship for good. Squint Eyed Sam swore that only Captain Meed's death would satisfy his vengeance for such an unforgivable insult mawn." Sam looking sorrowful replied, "Me have worked a very long time on the Queen Anne's Revenge to build it from the bottom to a mighty fine ship. This be me home. How could Captain Meed think me could make you leave me home? Me was so angry me drank a gallon of rum and when me woke up the next morning Captain Meed was gone - murdered." Jack added, "Just how angry was Captain Meed? What did he say to ya?" Sam replied, "Captain Meed was extremely angry. He threatened to make me walk the plank, but instead he changed his mind and said he was going to court martial me instead. Court martial, can ya believe it." Sam began to cry with his eyes covering his face. Sam quickly tried to change attention to someone else and asked Christy, "Did ye gain any special skills when ye was Anne Bonny?" Reluctantly, Christy replied, "When I was Anne Bonny I had to learn to survive in many ways. One way was to become a master swordsman. It may be unusual for a woman, but I am very good at it. It doesn't make me the killer though." Christy then pointed to John. "Long John Popper, or is it Peter Teach now, you have murdered twice. It is doubtful the real Long John Popper's death was accidental. It wasn't an accident, was it? If you murdered once, it would be easy for you to murder twice." John looking strong and proud said, "Me had nothing to do with da real Long John Popper's death in de dungeon. As far as me knows, he died from an accident. It was suggested to me to assume Long John Popper's identity and move to Port Royal to start me a new life rrrrr." John noticed Pete's money pouch. "Your money pouch looks quite interesting. Did ya get it back from Captain Meed after he blackmailed ya? How did ya get it back? Did ya kill him to get it back? Pete scoured pack, "Ahhh, me pouch is the same type as Captain Meed's personal pouch. It be easy for someone ta say I took his pouch from him. Me pouch can only carry a few doubloons and pieces of eight. Whereas a treasure chest can carry much much more." His eyes lit up with the thought of a full treasure chest. Pete then hobbled over next to Jamaica, "Rrrrr, me remember last night walking near the boardwalk and overhearing Jamaica talking to some men. She was saying something about "roll him up", "light it", and "smoke em". It didn't make any sense at the time. What was this all about? Was it something to hide your murder?". Jamaica looking a bit nervous said, "The sea lads on the shore and you were conducting some business. I can't remember the conversations we had mawn. I tells you that me clientele last night really "grew" by leaps and bounds. My best guess is that they were setting up private meetings with me. That be all." Sam then pulled out a picture of an herb that he was told that Jamaica was selling.

He continued, "Is it true that ye have been using your fortune telling/clairvoyant activities as a cover to ye "herbal" distribution "gig". Captain Meed discovered this and blackmailed ya for a share of the "green" profits. Did ya kill Captain Meed to silence him?" She reluctantly replied, "It be true mawn, that I do sell this. Captain Meed foolishly tried to blackmail me over my "herb" selling operation but he backed down after he realized that my silent partners really are very powerful with that funky weed. He knew better than to take on the Cartel. That was the end of the matter." Jamaica turned her attention to John. "I was told the murder weapon was found to have traces of blood dripping down the blade to the body. It was not from Captain Meed. I see that you have a small bandage on your hand. Did you get cut when you were attacking Captain Meed?" John trembling a bit, "De blood dripping down de sword be not mine. Me was cleaning me own sword because me didn't trust Sam ta clean me sword. Me slipped and cut me self and placed a bandage upon it." Henrietta then grabbed the murder weapon right off the middle of the table and tossed it to John. John grabbed it firmly with one hand. She asked Sam if John looked like he knew how to really use it. Henrietta was not done. She grabbed the sword right from John's hand and put in right in Christy's own hand. She said to her, "You have an interesting past. You must have been good with a sword in your secret past. Raise the sword to show us your strength." Christy reluctant to show her past frowned but stood up and raised the sword high in the air. Her eyes twinkled and her face lit up for a brief moment, then she came back to reality and sat down. Captain Morgan stood up and walked towards Jack. "Is there anything ye drink besides rum?" Jack in his slumbered state sat up. "Yo, ho, ho, and a bottle of rum, me only drinks me rum." Captain Morgan continued questioning him. "What be a pirate's favorite letter of the alphabet?" Jack answered smartly, "Some say it might be the RRRRR, but me say it be the CCCCC." Captain Morgan then turned to Henrietta, "What be the name of your next rum concoction and what will it contain?" Henrietta peeked right up. "It shall be called the Captain Meed Grog. It will contain:

5 oz of Captain Morgan Cannon Blast

25 oz of Bulleit Bourbon

6 oz of Red Stripe Lager

1. Combine canon blast and bourbon into a shot glass
2. Pour red strip lager into a pint glass.
3. Balance shot on 2 chopsticks over beer.
4. Slam table to make the shot glass blast into the beer."

Captain Morgan then became serious. "Tell me now, each of ya one final time, why ye are not the murderer." Bad Leg Pete rose proudly. "Me be guilty of stealing a few exotic birds but that be all, and so what. Me only took these things from rich people who could afford to buy new ones. Me be telling you the truth when me say, me never met with Captain Meed last night. Me bad leg buckled when walking on the boardwalk on my way to meet Jamaica Parrotless and got my clothes dirty, nothing more than that. Me was not happy about Captain Meed blackmailing me but he had me over a barrel so me paid him a lot of money to keep his mouth shut. Me accepted it as a cost of business. Me be glad me got my pouch back. Me swear it be the truth." He sat down and rubbed his leg. Captain Morgan gave a look at Christy. She looked back at him and stood up. "I thought I had left all this trouble behind me when I left my life as Anne Bonny. I still think Captain Meed helped with Calico Jack's death. I'll admit I wanted revenge for that, but I never got the chance. Someone else beat me to it. As far as my handkerchief and other services I provide, it really doesn't change anything. I would still have gone on to sell things, one more than the other. Who knows, the notoriety I gained may have even helped me. At least people will have something nice to say about me instead of my 'non-existent' temper." She wiped her eyes with her handkerchief. Jamaica raised both her hands in the air. "Captain Meed was sticking his nose in my business. He didn't like my fortune telling and he didn't like my new "herbal" business as well. If he was snooping around and checking on my business, it's a safe bet he was doing it to others as well. Obviously, someone didn't like what Captain Meed was doing and killed him. It wasn't me. When I explained who my "supporters" were, he was smart enough to back off. As far as the stealing of all my clairvoyant items, I had first accused Meed to cover up the fact that I had actually sold them to purchase some of my new "green weed". Since Captain Meed was not responsible there is no motive there." Slowly, Henrietta took her stance. "I did not kill my close friend Captain Meed, and I certainly did not confess to the murder while I was drunk. I am not a 'husband killer' – I've just had bad luck with men. I was upset with Captain Meed when he called off any chance of a relationship because of his religion. But I had hoped that he would have come around to his senses if someone hadn't killed him first. That Lord Oliver Cromwell investigation report was a pile of rubbish. And just because I have a fear of being in a confined space is no proof either that I knew Captain Meed's body was down in his captain's quarters. What a lot of ridiculous accusations I've had to put up with today." John rose and asked Henrietta to sit. "You be no murderer, me love, and either be me. Me may be an impostor, but me no murderer. Me didn't kill either Captain Meed or the real Long John Popper. The blood on the sword was not mine. Me cut my hand on my own blade. Me worked hard to keep the ship and its crew in order. You'll find everyone knows Meeze knows the ship well. Me know I've gained a lot since arriving at Port Royal, the Salty Sea Dog Inn, and the Queen Anne's Revenge, but me believe it was my destiny to come here and take control of the ship. What does it matter now that me not be related ta Captain Meed?" Sam then put his hand on John's shoulder and he began to speak. "Captain Meed be like a grandson to me. Yes, he could have treate me with more respect, but ye was still a good captain. In time ye would have realized that Long John Popper, Meed, and I were family, and family takes care of family. They forgive each other's sins such as stealing a few gems and selling them across the Caribbean. Me wonders what was going on in poor Captain Meed's head all these years. Me guess we shall never know. May he rest in peace. Sam began to sweat profusely. Jack who by now had several bottles in front of him simply raised his bottle in the air and said, "Rum! Rrrrrrrrr!" Henrietta rose up and raised a glass and exhaled, "I shall miss that old scallywag Captain Meed and his business at the Salty Sea Dog Inn. I would like to thank all you crazy people. You see, now I will be able to concoct so many new rum recipes from your exploits and in his honor as well. Three cheers to Captain Meed - hip hip hooray hip hip hooray hip hip hooray."

Captain Morgan began to quietly walk around the entire table. They were all looking upon him. His quietness was quite unnerving. They were all getting more nervous. He began to speak. "Tis been quite an enlightening sail. In the end tis safe ta say that ye all had motif and opportunity to kill Captain Meed." He continued and walked around each of them until he came upon Sam. He went on, "The evidence shows that there only be murderer and he is none other than **Squint Eyed Sam**. Ye did it to get the ship for his grandson named Peter Teach who was once living in Neverland. Of course, ye know Peter Teach better as Long John Popper. Sam received a fortune telling/reading explaining he had a grandson named Peter Teach living in Neverland. Squint Eyed Sam contacted de dungeon master to have his grandson convicted of stealing food and sentenced to de same dungeon as the real Long John Popper was in. Ye dungeon master was bribed to put Peter Teach and Long John Popper in de same dungeon cell so that Peter Teach could learn about Long John Popper's past. The, just before Long John Popper was ta be released, Squint Eyed Sam had Long John Popper murdered by de dungeon master at de price of a pretty gem. Squint Eyed Sam then convinced Peter Teach to take Long John Popper's identity and move to Port Royal near the Salty Sea Dog Inn and start a new life. Peter Teach had no idea he was Squint Eyed Sam's grandson when he arrived at the Salty Sea Dog Inn. Ye helped him obtain a job on the ship and helped him to work his way to the next in command of the ship as first mate. As he worked his way up the ship's ranks, Peter Teach acting as Long John Popper was accepted as the next in command of the ship. After Peter (acting as Long John Popper) was accepted as cousin of the Meed family, you murdered Captain Grisly Meed leaving your grandson as the new Captain of the Queen Anne's Revenge. Squint Eyed Sam had planned to keep Peter Teach in the dark about his relationship with him until after Captain Meed's body was laid to rest. Then, Squint Eyed Sam could retire back to Neverland or relax on Parrot Island, knowing that his life's work could benefit his grandson and future generations with a smile on ye face."

Sam was sunken to a small hump of a man. The entire table looked upon him. Then Captain Morgan continued. "I will end this by speaking in the proper dialect that my great friend Captain Grisly Meed taught me. I will honor him and continue to talk with respect to him. Now at this point I must confess that I have gained knowledge of many untold and surprising facts. I have given you enough information for you to cast your own judgement upon Sam as well as everyone else. I must add that each of you had Captain Meed all wrong. He was a mighty captain, a mighty good man, and a man full of surprises. He was always looking out for his fellow person in the sea of life. He had something specially planned for each and every one of you. Although his death may prevent us ever truly seeing it and the potential of a good man and his dreams." To Jack, he grabbed him in a big hug and picked him upright in his chair. "Very few people know, except Henrietta, I, and a few others that Squint Eyed Sam is the actual owner of the Salty Sea Dog Inn. You are in a financial ruin as you have drunk most of the profits away. Captain Meed knew you had a severe drinking problem with the rum and vowed to help save your life. He planned on paying you handsomely to be his private guard and assistant if you vowed to leave the rum alone for good. Captain Morgan went to Henrietta next. He leaned forward and kissed her wrist. "Captain Meed loved to converse with you. It is said that when he spoke with you, that he always had a smile to his face and a twinkle in his eye. He thought you were a hard worker with good spirit and a creative mind. He planned to build you your own inn so you could mix any o'drink with any o'friend that would sit down with ya. His only request was that the inn would have a signature drink named Meed's Mead, and that it would not contain any rum." Henrietta began to cry uncontrollably. Sam hugged her. Captain Morgan went to Bad Leg Pete next and put his hand on his shoulder. "Yes, Captain Meed knew of your exotic Parrot theft ring, your rum running, and your extravagant lifestyle. He had a better plan for you. He was going to offer you a substantial deal if you gave up the rum running and stealing of birds. He knew your true passion was your love of birds. The captain was about to build a store on Parrot Island and have you legitimately sell exotic birds all across the Caribbean." Pete put his hand to his mouth in shock. To Jamaica Captain Morgan turned to. "Captain Meed actually thought someone did steal your items, even though you sold them yourself to get the green herbs. He actually acquired the new crystal ball even though he never thought you gave a true or honest fortune ever. He still believed in you to be a good kind person and wished to assist you. Many people thought the two of you met up for sexual encounters. I know that not be the case. He may have listened to your fortunes, but he enjoyed your secret talent you seemed to only shared with him, that of singing. He was intrigued by your vocals. He was about to introduce you to a new group of musicians that played a new type of music, something called, "reggae". Captain Meed once said that with her voice she could really get "high". Her eyes began to fill with tears. Captain Morgan looked right into Penny's eyes next. "Captain Meed really liked you, but once he found his religion he enjoyed that even more. He continued to converse with you because he wanted to teach his religion to you. He could never think of doing anything more with you than being just friends while you were married. He was going to try to convert you to his religion in order to help you with all of your anger issues. He was set to also support your marriage and relationship problems." Penny simply looked at John in awe. To Christy he turned next to. "Captain Meed was very uncomfortable with you being a lady of the evening. He tried to promote your handkerchief business to have you leave the life as a strumpet. He found out that you were actually Anne Bonny. He did not like that side of you as well, but always found a special place in his heart for you. He could not find it in himself to have you walk the plank but, instead had you put on probation with Lord Oliver Cromwell." She covered herself up into a ball. To John he shook his head towards. "Captain Meed somehow knew of your entire past. He knew your mother as well. He always wanted to help you grow. He was on the brink of handing to you a new captain's hat and the control of the Queen Anne's Revenge as captain. May you run it as close as you can to the greatness he accomplished." John nodded back. To Sam he asked to rise. Sam slowly rose and placed his hands upon the table ready to be tied. "Captain Meed had planned to buy Parrot Island and offer most of it to you so you could retire in comfort after your years of service to him. He may have known your master plan? It could be that he knew that Samuel and Peter Teach were related to the great Edward Teach, better known as

Blackbeard. He may have made a deal with Blackbeard as well. It is strange to think that the Queen Anne's Revenge is the same name as Blackbeard's ship. Is it possible that they are one and the same? Sam it is up to this gathering to determine if you shall walk the plank or not."

It's up to you to determine whether Squint Eyed Sam truly faced his fate and walked the plank. Perhaps each of the suspects felt a sense of guilt for their own actions, leading them to keep the events and discoveries aboard the ship a secret. Would they choose to spend the rest of their lives striving to be better individuals and to improve the lives of those around them? The ship was manned by men and women, all pirates in a different era. Yet, the world still holds its pirates; they simply appear and dress differently today.

112. An Interesting Restaurant Experience

After our weekend of refueling the car and shopping, we decided to seek out a small quaint breakfast spot. Debbie was quite hungry, while I was in the mood for something light and simple, and I had a strong craving for morning juice. We considered a few nearby options.First, we pulled into a popular diner, but the parking lot was packed. We then moved on to another place, only to find it equally busy, with cars circling in search of parking. Undeterred, we continued on our journey and ended up at a restaurant we had never tried before. The area wasn't the most appealing, and the exterior didn't exactly invite us in, but we parked after maneuvering around some potholes and made our way to the front.As we walked to the entrance, we noticed several things that gave us pause. The narrow pathway felt perilously close to the street, and nearby, an outdoor table seemed rather pointless. I spotted someone lighting up their cigarette as they exited their car, which added to the uncomfortable atmosphere.

Upon entering, we were greeted by a "seat yourself" sign—perhaps a sign of the disarray that awaited us. I approached the cashier to ask where we should sit, and she simply pointed us to the bar or the back. Opting for the latter, we navigated through a crowd of diners, skirting around tables before reaching the rear, where we settled in.

As we sat down, I noticed the Christmas decorations still on display, despite the holiday being over for more than two months. To my right, broken window blinds sat on a shelf, abandoned rather than discarded. The hostess brought us menus that featured reasonable prices, though I noted the limited choices and the conspicuous absence of orange juice, which was substituted with Sunny Delight instead. I guess it was their way of passing on the savings to the customer or to just try to keep the prices more affordable.

As Debbie examined her surroundings, glancing at the decorations and the blinds, I observed the hectic scene unfolding around us. A waitress was not having her best day. I witness four tables that she had problems with. The waitress seemed overwhelmed and was repeatedly apologizing to each table for various issues. She devoted significant time to a table behind us, neglecting to notice us at all. The hostess promised to fetch someone from the back to take our order, but I could see the waitress struggling with other tables, one of which had a visibly frustrated diner who was cursing about her order. Another table, with a mother trying to feed her baby, found that the eggs the waitress brought were cold and unappetizing.

Just as we contemplated leaving due to the lack of service, a friendly girl approached us claiming she could take our order. She wasn't a waitress, but she was warm and polite, bringing us water before taking our drink orders of apple juice and Sunny Delight. As we waited, I noticed the busser, dressed in a winter hat, old jeans, and a motorcycle shirt, cheerful but I questioned the cleanliness of his rag and the spray he was using on the tables. He even shared a rather odd joke about a broken toaster being old with a patron. It was just a bit off.

To our surprise, our food arrived quickly, well before meals at the other tables. I enjoyed a pleasant Belgian waffle, while Debbie had eggs, bacon, hash browns, and rye toast, which she found satisfying. As we finished, our fill-in waitress offered each of us a cup of soup to take home, which struck me as a peculiar after-breakfast offering. She also suggested we take home drinks of Sunny Delight and apple juice.

When we were ready to pay, we were instructed to bring our bill to the cashier, and as we made our way through the restaurant once more, I noticed a small Christmas tree leaning against an unlit fireplace. I couldn't help but wonder why it was still on display.

At the cashier's desk, a collection of mismatched ceramic figurines caught my eye. They did not match with the restaurant. When I went to sign my bill, the cashier asked if I wanted to add a tip, which was unusual since I typically write it on the bill myself.

As we exited and headed back to our car, we reflected on our experience. This restaurant seemed well-suited to its clientele. The meal was perfectly fine, and it offered an affordable option for those who might not have the means to dine at pricier places but still wished to enjoy a decent breakfast.

113. Change Is Inevitable

Change is a certainty. In fact, change is always happening. Perhaps change is a constant presence in our lives. I will shift my perspective to consider different approaches. My thoughts are not static; they are continually evolving. Maybe I should just rewrite this entirely and embrace that transformation.

114. A Man Once Drove His Car To A Lake

A man once drove his car to a serene lake.

He perched on the hood of his car and considered what was at stake.

He listened to the silence,

yet heard much in essence.

The flutter of a bird,

Was quite heard.

Then he threw a rock into the lake,

Wondering if his life was a big mistake.

To his surprise a fish jumped out.

It made him realize what life was all about.

To live, to see, hear, and feel,

Life is full of experiences that are truly real.

115. The Glance, The Eye Contact, And The Smile

In that bustling café', amidst the clinking of cutlery and the gentle hum of laughter, he found himself lost in a moment that felt both fleeting and eternal. He was seated quietly alone at a table eating a small meal. While aware of the noise of people conversing with one another, he looked upon his food. Something made him look up. At a table not too far away but far away that it was not in speaking distance, sat a table of four women. Back to the meal at hand and another bite was taken. As he glanced in her direction, their eyes met. She looked directly back deep into his eyes as the others continued to converse at her table. In a blink of a second, he saw and read into her mind as he imagined many thoughts. Their eyes talked to each other stronger than any words of a lifetime could. Their shared gaze held unlimited stories of dreams and fears, of joys and sorrows. A vision of an instant bond was seen.

With each heartbeat, the intensity of their connection swelled, a silent conversation blooming in the space between them. Where they meant for each other and could they live a happy life for eternity? Would their journey be filled with laughter, adventure, and a mutual understanding?

In that same moment, a trace of sadness lingered in her eyes. He envisioned a woman with a devoted husband and three children, standing at the crossroads of meeting the needs of her family and seeking her own happiness—a struggle reflected in the intensity of her gaze. This made him appreciate his own marriage, recognizing the delicate balance required to ensure both his wife's contentment and his own.

Then she smiled at him. He returned the smile warmly. In that exchange lay unspoken words of encouragement and joy shared between them. Their gaze was a fleeting moment, brief yet significant, as life would carry on. They discovered happiness in the simple act of sharing a knowing glance.

As she rose to leave, she turned back one last time, offering him another smile. He smiled in return before redirecting his attention to his meal. Thoughts of his wife filled his mind, and with each passing moment, his smile deepened as he finished his food.

116. Second Chances

Does everyone merit a second chance? I am uncertain. I believe it largely depends on the situation. It is true that severe crimes are particularly challenging to justify in terms of offering a second opportunity. Personally, I strive to learn from my own mistakes. In my life, I have granted many people second chances, and sometimes I question whether that was the right choice. While some individuals genuinely learn from their errors, others may take advantage of those chances without appreciating their significance. Can we support one another in today's society by offering opportunities while also providing guidance? I think we can grow together by helping each other navigate life's journey.

117. Reach Out Your Hand

Step outside and extend your hand. Are you offering it to a friend in greeting? Is it a welcoming gesture for a business associate? Are you reaching out to lend a hand to someone in need? Or perhaps you're simply inviting the breeze and natural elements to touch your skin, reminding you that you are alive and in tune with nature. What or who will respond to your outstretched hand?

118. A Merry Heart

A merry heart is like good medicine.

It can cure one out and in.

When you see someone rundown,

Open your heart to turn their frown around.

Kind hearts can cure much sadness.

Smile at each other to share happiness.

A smile goes a long way.

To make someone's day extend a warm friendly handshake.

And, when you send a kiss give it from your heart for goodness' sake.

119. A Nice Diner

During our travels, Debbie and I often gauge the popularity of restaurants by the number of cars in their parking lots. One particular diner consistently had a large influx of vehicles whenever we passed by. Curious, I looked it up online and discovered it primarily served breakfast for limited hours on specific days, along with dinner and brunch options. We decided to check it out.

As we pulled into the parking lot, we were fortunate to find a spot right in front, despite the lot being nearly full. Upon entering, we encountered several groups waiting to be seated in an entirely packed restaurant. The hostess informed us we would have to wait about 20 minutes. Inside was bustling with noise, as diners chatted and the staff navigated between tables to serve their guests.

The hostess took note of how many were in each waiting party, looking for opportunities to seat them as tables became available. Spotting a few stools at the bar, she kindly asked the patrons if they would shuffle down a seat to accommodate us. Once we settled onto the barstools, we were warmly welcomed by both the people seated there and the waitress behind the bar.

The bar featured a shiny, sparkling counter, with the kitchen visible behind it. My eyes darted around, taking in the scene: a TV broadcasting the news, waitstaff bustling about, taking orders, finishing dishes, and serving customers. The kitchen staff, consisting of two dedicated female cooks, was busy fulfilling orders for the entire diner, while another person washed dishes and stocked supplies. The cashier at the front was occupied folding silverware. The dynamic energy of the staff was impressive.

The waitress approached us, and we mentioned we were from out of town. She and the locals beside us offered a warm welcome. I had my heart set on the unique French toast crunch meal, but sadly, the waitress informed me they had just run out of the crunch ingredients. A nearby patron had one, and it looked delicious. In the end, I opted for a simple blueberry pancake, adding a French toast to my order as well.

As we enjoyed our meal and chatted, the waitress apologized for the delay, explaining they were short-staffed in the kitchen. We reassured her that we were patient and perfectly fine waiting. When our food arrived, it was excellent. While paying the bill, I noticed the waitress had removed the charge for our beverages, likely due to our wait.

The diner sold interesting t-shirts, and when I asked the price, a staff member hurried to find out for me. Although I didn't purchase one, the generosity, reasonable prices, and delicious food promised that we would return.

On subsequent visits, the staff began treating us more like friends than mere customers, engaging in brief conversations with us. It was always a busy place. I recall one instance where a pair of patrons expressed their frustration over the wait time for their food. The waitress overheard and informed the owner, who then approached the customers to explain, "We are not a fast-food place. We serve quality food and make it worth the wait." She was absolutely right; our experiences there were consistently wonderful, thanks to the food, the people, and the lively atmosphere. Oh, and I did end up getting that French toast crunch meal and the t-shirt!

120. You May Whisper In My Ear To Give Me A Thrill

You may whisper in my ear to give me a thrill.

I will take your thoughts and treat it like a pill.

A wink and a curl of your lips,

and you might see me do a few flips.

My lady says oh my god,

I just give her a simple nod.

Do a simple jig,

and watch my heart grow really big.

121. Smile, Heart, Adventure

Embrace each day with a warm smile, a peaceful heart, and a zest for adventure. Always be on the lookout for something fresh and thrilling.

When you infuse your journey with music and laughter, it becomes a joyous experience. Life is too brief to dwell in sadness. Support one another on this journey. Let positivity triumph over negativity. Explore the vibrant colors, enticing scents, and delightful flavors that surround you.

The world is brimming with magic and wonder, and while discovering it may require some effort, it is absolutely worthwhile.

122. The Wagner Statue

I participated in a 5k event at Edgewater Park in Cleveland, and before the race, I took several photos of the Cleveland sign with the downtown skyline behind it.

On my way back to my car, I stumbled upon a large statue in a small section of the park. A sign revealed it was a statue of Richard Wagner, prompting me to snap a picture of it, along with a plaque inscribed in a different language on the back. I found myself wondering why this statue was located there and planned to look into it when I got home.

After the event, I shared a photo of the statue along with images from the 5k and the Cleveland sign on my Facebook page. However, I later decided to remove the pictures of the statue after doing a bit of research, as I didn't want to unintentionally offend anyone. I discovered that the statue honored the renowned German composer and writer. It was commissioned in 1911 by the Goethe-Schiller Society, comprised of German immigrants and German-Americans, and sculpted by Herman N. Matzen. Notably, in 1924, Wagner's son, Siegfried, visited the statue with his wife.

However, as I delved deeper, I came across an article detailing Wagner's staunch anti-Semitism and his influence on Adolf Hitler, who was known to have visited Siegfried Wagner's home frequently. Wagner's music, characterized as the musical embodiment of 19th-century European nationalism, overshadowed his hateful views that later fueled the atrocities of the Nazis. While many Clevelanders appreciated his music and supported the statue's presence, opinions began to shift, with some advocating for its removal as of 2016.

A friend of mine raised a valid point about the dilemma of removing the statue, comparing it to people who drive Ford vehicles despite Henry Ford's well-documented anti-Semitic beliefs. Intrigued, I started researching Ford's views. I discovered that he leveraged his position as an employer to socially engineer his workers, aiming to make immigrants more "Americanized." He opposed labor unions, perceiving them as a Jewish conspiracy, and even purchased a newspaper to spread his anti-Jewish sentiments. His views became so notorious that Hitler mentioned him by name in Mein Kampf.

Whether or not you drive a Ford or have mixed feelings about the statue, this experience underscores a vital truth: sometimes, what appears before us carries multiple interpretations and meanings. It's essential to approach life with an open mind and recognize both the positive and negative aspects of everything around us.

123. Bourbon And Whiskey Insights

I was introduced to the world of Bourbon one day, and what started as a casual interest quickly turned into a fascination. The history, the proper ways to savor it, and much more captivated me.

Throughout my journey, I stumbled upon many unexpected insights. I have managed to build a small collection that I share with friends and family, creating lasting memories as we experience the tastes.

Bourbon And Whiskey Insights

This structured guide can provide a solid foundation for tasting and appreciating spirits. Enjoy your tasting experiences!

What defines bourbon? While all bourbon is whiskey, not all whiskey qualifies as bourbon. According to regulations, bourbon whiskey must be:

- Produced in the **United States**

- Distilled at no more than **160 proof** (80% alcohol)

- From fermented mash of not less than **51% corn**

- Entered and stored in a barrel at not more than **125 proof** (62.5%)

- Bottled at no less than **80** proof.

- Contain no additives except **water**.

- Aged in **new charred oak** barrels.

Types of Bourbon

Straight Bourbon Whiskey:

- Aged in **new charred oak** for a minimum of at least **two** years.
- It can comprise multiple straight bourbons as long as they are produced in the **same state.**

Blended Bourbon Whiskey:

- Produced in the U.S. and must comprise at least **51% straight bourbon** whiskey base on proof gallons
- The 51% figure does not include alcohol from any added **harmless coloring, flavoring, or blending agents.**

Blended Straight Bourbon Whiskey:

- A mixture of **straight whiskies** crafted in the **U.S.**
- Must consist of straight bourbon whiskies.

Bottled-In-Bond Bourbon Whiskey:

- Produced during **one** single distillation season by **one** distiller at **one** specific distillery.
- Required to be aged in a federally bonded warehouse for at least **four** years.
- Must be bottled at 100 proof (50% alcohol by volume).
- The label must indicate where it was distilled and bottled.
- Product of **one distillation season** by **one distiller** at **one distillery**. It must have been stored in a **federally**

bonded warehouse for at least **four years** and bottled at **100 proof**. The label of the bottled product **must identify the distillery where it was distilled and bottled**.

- The Bottle-In-Bond Act of 1897 was introduced to ensure quality for consumers.
- Colonel Edmund Haynes Taylor (founder of Old Taylor Bourbon) was instrumental in promoting this legislation.

Whiskey vs Whisky

- Whiskey – (adds the "e") Generally refers to spirits made in the United States (e.g., American whiskeys like bourbon, rye, and Tennessee whiskey) and in Ireland (Irish whiskey).
- Whiskey (drops the "e") typically refers to spirits produced in Scotland, Canada, and Japan.
- Notable exceptions:

While American whiskeys typically include an "e" (e.g., Jack Daniel's, Buffalo Trace), some brands like Old Forester and Maker's Mark opt to omit the "e."

Fireball Whisky - Although it is produced by Sazerac in Louisiana, the base alcohol originates from Canada, following the "whisky" spelling.

Tennessee Whiskey, Tennessee Whisky, Tennessee Sour Mash Whiskey, or Tennessee Sour Mash Whisky:

- Manufactured in **Tennessee.**
- At least **51% corn**.

- Distilled to no more than **160 proof** or 80% alcohol.
- Aged in **new, charred oak American barrels** in Tennessee.
- Filtered through **maple charcoal prior to aging** (the Lincoln County Process)
- Placed in the barrel at no more than **125 proof** or 62.5% alcohol.
- Bottled at not less than **80%** proof or 40% alcohol.

Tennessee whiskey is still essentially bourbon that's aged in Tennessee and filtered through maple charcoal prior to aging. Although Tennessee whiskey shares similarities with bourbon (it can be classified as bourbon when it meets specific requirements), local pride prevents many Tennessee residents from labeling it as such. Notably, brands like Jack Daniel's often face criticism from bourbon enthusiasts who may consider them less authentic to the bourbon tradition.

Tasting guide for Bourbon:

Appearance

- **Color** - Observe the hue of the spirit. Is it clear, amber, dark brown, or another shade? This can indicate age and potential flavor.
- **Swirl** - Gently swirl the spirit in the glass to observe how it moves.
- **Legs/Tears** - Watch how the liquid clings to the glass after swirling. Thick legs can suggest higher viscosity and potentially more sweetness or higher alcohol content.
- **Stems** - Inspect any remnants left on the glass after the swirl. This can indicate the spirit's texture and body.

<u>**Nose**</u>

- **Closed Mouth** - Inhale deeply to catch the initial aromas without tasting. This helps to identify volatile compounds.
- **Open Mouth** - Inhale again while slightly opening your mouth. This can change the perception of aromas, allowing you to pick up different notes.

<u>**Taste**</u>

- **Small Sip** - Take a modest sip to acclimate your palate to the spirit.
- **Swirl in Mouth** - Roll the liquid around your mouth to engage all taste bud areas—sweet, salty, sour, bitter, and umami.
- **Chew** - Mimic chewing to further release flavors and aromas.
- **Water/Ice Cube Addition** - Add a drop of water or an ice cube to open up flavors and aromas, especially in cask-strength spirits.
- **Burn vs. Spice** - Understand the difference between a burn (high alcohol heat) and spice (warmth from peppery notes). This distinction can help identify balance in the spirit.

<u>**Finish**</u>

- **Duration** - Observe how long the flavors linger after swallowing.
- **Taste Notes** - Identify which flavors persist. Are they sweet, spicy, herbal, fruity, etc.?

Flavor Notes to smell and taste:

Fruits - Apples, Apricots, Blueberries, Cherries, Oranges

Spices - Black pepper, Cardamom, Cinnamon, Nutmeg

Sweetness - Caramel, Butterscotch, Honey, Maple syrup

Nut and Herb - Almond, Basil, Rosemary, Walnut

Unique Notes - Leather, Cigar box, Campfire, Fresh-baked bread

Allspice, Anise, Anise seed, Apples, Apricot, Baked and fried pie crust, Bananas, Basil, Bay leaf, Bell pepper, Black pepper, Blackberry, Bleach, Blueberry, Brown sugar, Butterscotch, Campfire, Caramel, Caraway, Cardamom, Cedar, Celery, Cherry, Chocolate, Cigar box, Cilantro, Cinnamon, Citrus-general, Citrus-lemon, Citrus-lime, Citrus-orange, Clove, Cocoa, Coconut, Coffee, Coriander, Corn, Cornbread, Cornmeal, Crème Brulé', Crushed grapes, Cumin, Dill, Eucalyptus, Fennel, Fenugreek, Floral, Fresh-baked biscuits, Fresh-baked bread, Heated caramel syrup, Herbs, Honey, Lavender, Leather, Lemon zest, Licorice, Lilac, Mace, Malt-O-Meal, Maple syrup, Marjoram, Marijuana, Marzipan, Mint, Mustard, Nutmeg, Oak, Oatmeal, Orange, Orange Juice, Oregano, Pan-melted caramel, Parsley, Pear, Pecans, Pepper, Peppermint, Petrol, Pine, Pineapple, Pink pepper, Plum, Poppy, Praline, Pumpkin pie, Raisins, Raspberry, Rose petals, Rosemary, Rye, Rye meal, Saffron, Sage, Sassafras, Savory, Sesame, Sweaty gym socks, Tarragon, Tea, Thyme, Toasted nuts, Tobacco, Toffee, Turmeric, Turpentine, Vanilla, Varnish, Walnut, Wheat, White pepper.

Neat vs on the rocks:

Neat - Two ounces right out of the bottle, usually served in an old-fashioned glass intended to be sipped, no chilling, no ice or any other mixers.

On the Rocks - Served over ice in a straight-walled, flat-bottomed glass, which can help open up flavors and aromas through chilling and dilution.

Up - A cocktail shaken or stirred with ice and then strained into a stemmed glass.

Straight Up - Often used to mean "neat," but verify to avoid confusion.

Twist - A thin strip of citrus peel, typically lemon, which can enhance the aroma and flavor of the drink.

The Glencairn Whisky Glass is a groundbreaking vessel that allows enthusiasts to truly appreciate the taste and intricacies of fine whisky. It is perfect for enjoying single malt whiskies, Irish whiskeys, and single barrel bourbons. The glass's tapered mouth enhances the ability to detect the rich aromas and nuances each whisky presents. While spirits like champagne, brandy, and wine each have their designated glass, whisky—the most complex spirit—has often been served in a variety of vessels, from highball tumblers to Paris goblets. In 2001, Glencairn Crystal addressed the quest for the perfect whisky glass. Originally conceived by Raymond Davidson nearly 25 years earlier, the design was refined through collaboration with master blenders from the five largest whisky companies. This innovative glass received the Queen's Award for Innovation in 2006.

<u>**3 main cocktails**</u>:

Manhattan –

- Ingredients -

  - 1 oz Rye Bourbon (or Bourbon for a sweeter flavor)

- 0.5 oz Sweet Vermouth

- 3 dashes Aromatic Bitters

- 1 Cherry (for garnish)

- Instructions –

    1. Use a jigger to measure and pour the rye bourbon, sweet vermouth, and bitters into a mixing glass.

    2. Stir the mixture and strain it into a cocktail glass.

    3. Garnish with a cherry.

For an added twist, you can rub the cut edge of an orange peel around the rim of the glass and twist it over the drink to release the oils (but don't drop it in). Traditionally, rye is the whiskey of choice for this cocktail, which is one of five drinks named after New York City boroughs, alongside Brooklyn, Queens, The Bronx, and Staten Island.

Old Fashion –

- Ingredients -

    - 1.25 oz Bourbon

    - 2 bar spoons Simple Syrup

    - 3 dashes Bitters

    - 1 Orange Peel (for garnish)

- Instructions -

    1. In a large rocks glass, combine the simple syrup, bitters, and bourbon.

2. Add ice and stir gently until the ice and liquid are level.

3. Zest the orange peel over the glass and add it to the drink as a garnish.

Alternatively, you can prepare it by dissolving a sugar lump in a bit of water in a whiskey glass, adding two dashes of bitters, a small piece of ice, a slice of lemon peel, and one jigger of whiskey. Mix it with a small bar spoon and serve, leaving the spoon in the glass.

Sazerac –

- Ingredients: -

  - 1.3 oz Bourbon

  - 0.25 oz Absinthe (for rinsing the glass)

  - 1 Sugar Cube

  - 3 dashes Bitters

- Instructions

  1. Muddle the sugar cube and bitters in an old-fashioned glass.

  2. Add the bourbon and stir with ice.

  3. Strain into a chilled glass that has been rinsed with absinthe.

Another approach is to coat the inside of the glass with absinthe, stir the rye whiskey, bitters, and syrup with ice in a mixing glass, and then strain it into the absinthe-coated glass. Garnish with lemon peel.

The Sazerac became New Orleans' official cocktail on June 23, 2008. It was initially made with Sazerac cognac, but due to the phylloxera epidemic that devastated French vineyards, the main ingredient transitioned to rye whiskey.

A Shot:

The term "shot," as it relates to a small serving of liquor, is rich with various theories regarding its origin. One popular idea suggests that it derives from the act of consuming a small amount of whiskey in one go. Upon finishing, the drinker would emphatically slam the glass down on the bar, producing a distinct sound referred to as a "shot."

Another narrative connects "shot" to the Western saloons, where patrons might trade a bullet or cartridge (a "shot") for a glass of whiskey, hence the phrase "a shot for a shot." This highlights a bartering practice that underscores the rugged culture of the Old West.

A different perspective attributes the term to Friedrich Otto Schott, who established a glass factory in Germany around 1884. The glassware produced there became known colloquially as "shot glasses," further embedding the term in drinking culture.

In the 1940s, the word "shot" was formally documented in relation to regulating liquor servings, likely as a way for bar owners to ensure that bartenders poured accurate amounts and to prevent excessive pouring. This practical application helped solidify the role of the shot in modern drinking customs.

Together, these origins showcase how "shot" has evolved and adapted over time, reflecting various cultural practices and the way alcohol consumption is perceived and standardized in social settings.

Through various acts and cultural shifts, bourbon has evolved not only as a drink but also as a cultural icon, deeply embedded in American history. Its recognition as "America's Native Spirit" highlights the pride associated with bourbon and its diverse production techniques.

Key Historical Events in Bourbon Production:

1783 –

- The Samuels family claims the title of the oldest bourbon family still active today. The family did not produce bourbon commercially until T.W. Samuels (grandson of Robert Samuels, who created the "secret" family recipe) constructed a distillery at Samuels Depot, Kentucky. In 1943, after a break during Prohibition, Bill Samuels Sr. burned that famous family recipe. Bill Sr. wanted to create a bourbon without the bitterness and smoother, and so he did: **Maker's Mark.** The company is now in the hands of his son, Bill Samuels Jr.
- **Evan Williams** opens his distillery on the banks of the Ohio River in Louisville, which was the first commercial distillery in Kentucky. It still bears his name.

1785 –

- Bourbon County, Kentucky, is established, although production centers primarily around Louisville, Frankfort, and Bardstown. Some say it's from Bourbon Street in New Orleans, where Sazerac was.

1789 –

- Elijah Craig opens a distillery in Georgetown, Kentucky. He is often credited with inventing bourbon by aging the already popular corn whiskey. This claim remains disputed.

- Some say those who emigrated from Pennsylvania because of the Whiskey Excise Tax also had a part.
- It is a fact that in 1789, Elijah Craig, a Baptist minister, opened a distillery in Georgetown, Kentucky.
- Heaven Hill Distillery produces a bourbon named after the "inventor" of bourbon.

1794 –

- The Whiskey Rebellion occurs as farmers in western Pennsylvania protest the 1791 Whiskey Excise Tax, testing the federal government's authority.
- President Washington called up 13,000 militia to deal with the rebels, but the band dispersed before any conflicts.
- These events encouraged Kentucky and Tennessee distillers, who were not subject to the federal law at the time. The Whiskey Rebellion was the first real test of the federal government's ability to enforce laws.

1795 –

- Jacob Beam sells his first barrel of "Old Jake Beam Sour," marking the beginning of the Beam family legacy in bourbon production.
- Since that time, David Beam, David M. Beam, Col. James Beam (the Jim Beam), T. Jeremiah Beam, Booker Noe (Booker's Small Batch), and now, Fred Noe have carried the family craft into what it has become today.
- Jack Beam (Jim's uncle) founded Early Times.

- Parker Beam was renowned for his great whiskeys, which receive a tribute every year with the annual release of Parker's Heritage Collection.

1792 –

- Kentucky becomes the 15th state in the U.S.

1821 –

- The first advertisement for bourbon is printed in the "Western Citizen" newspaper in Paris, Kentucky.

1823 –

- Dr. James C. Crow developed the sour mash process at the Pepper Distillery (now the Woodford Reserve Distillery), which is crucial for bourbon production.
- This method of recycling some yeast for the next fermentation revolutionized the way most bourbons and Tennessee whiskeys have been produced since.

1840 –

- Bourbon whiskey officially gains its name.
- Prior to this, it was known as "Bourbon County Whiskey, or Old Bourbon County Whiskey."

1856 –

- The Lincoln County Process, involving charcoal filtering, is perfected by Jack Daniels.

1861-1865 –

- The Civil War led to a whiskey shortage, disrupting production.

- Not only were many men drawn from their day jobs to fight in the war, but many battles were fought in the major America whiskey distilling regions. Major Benjamin Blanton, who before the war hit it big in the California Gold Rush and owned a large portion of downtown Denver, Colorado, sold everything to buy Confederate War Bonds. Those bonds were worthless after the fall of the South, leaving Blanton broke. Shortly after, he opened a distillery in Kentucky (later the Stagg Distillery), producing Blanton's Bourbon Whiskey.

1869 –

- The Ripy Family Distillery is established in Lawrenceburg, Kentucky.
- The Ripy family began a long tradition of bourbon production on the site, and their whiskey was chosen from a list of 400 bourbons to represent Kentucky at the 1893 World's Fair.
- The distillery is now the home of Wild Turkey Bourbon.

1870 –

- Jugs of bourbon are first shipped from Ohio River ports, allowing for easier transportation.
- The decision to bottle bourbon was a matter of convenience for the consumer, as jugs were a more attractive and portable vessel than barrels.

1872 –

- The A. Ph. Stitzel Distillery is founded.
- It was not until the early 1900s that the distillery became significant in bourbon whiskey's history. Julian P. Van Winkle,

Sr., or "Pappy," and a partner acquired the distillery, which was known for its excellent sour mash whiskey.

- Just before Prohibition, Pappy began producing Old Rip Van Winkle Bourbon, and he later became the oldest active distiller at age 89.

- During the country's dry period, the Stitzel-Weller Distillery held one of the few licenses to produce medicinal whiskey, and when the country was once again wet, they produced brands like Old Fitzgerald, Cabin Still, and Rebel Yell.

- It was not until 1972 that Pappy's son, J.P. Van Winkle, Jr., resurrected the original Old Rip Van Winkle brand, which lives on today as one of the most sought-after rare bourbons.

1897 –

- The Bottled in Bond Act is enacted, establishing standards for bourbon.

1920-1933 – U.S. Prohibition

- Prohibition enforces a nationwide ban on alcohol, which devastates many distilleries. Some, like those of the Samuels and Beam families, persevere.

- The Temperance Movement finally got what it wanted when the U.S. Congress passed the 18th Amendment, prohibiting the manufacture and sale of alcohol. The entire adult beverage industry was shattered, hundreds of businesses were shut down, and many went underground. The majority of bourbon distilleries were closed, many to never reopen, but a few, like the Samuels and Beam families, came back after the repeal of Prohibition and resurrected the craft of bourbon distilling.

- The government issued 10 licenses to produce whiskey for medicine at the time, only six of which were ever activated. One of those companies was Brown-Forman, which now produces Woodford Reserve Bourbon on the site of the Prohibition-era distillery.

1940 –

- **Wild Turkey** gets its name after a distillery executive shares his bourbon with friends on an annual hunting trip for wild turkeys.

1964 –

- An act of Congress designates bourbon as **"America's Native Spirit"** and the country's official distilled spirit.
- At this time, the current regulations defining what can be called bourbon whiskey were established.

1973 –

- Vodka outsells whiskey for the first time in the U.S., reflecting changing consumer preferences.
- Many factors played a role, including James Bond and an increase in younger, female drinkers looking for a lighter drink.

2004 –

- The American Whiskey Trail launches, promoting the historical significance of whiskey distilling.
- The American Whiskey Trail is an educational trip to many of the distilleries and other historical sites in Kentucky, New York,

Pennsylvania, Tennessee, and Virginia, along with two rum distilleries in Puerto Rico and the Virgin Islands.

- The focus of the continental section of the trail is on the history of the whiskey distilling business, which has long dominated the area.
- The trail includes distillery tours of Jim Beam, Jack Daniels, and Maker's Mark, along with George Washington's Distillery at Mount Vernon and Fraunces Tavern, where he gave his farewell speech.

2007 –

- In August, the U.S. Senate declares September as National Bourbon Heritage Month, honoring the bourbon industry's contributions to American culture.
- While this may not have much impact on the average consumer, it is an honor for the craftsmen in the bourbon industry. The designation is designed to celebrate "America's Native Spirit" and the significant historical, economic, and industrial role the bourbon industry has player in the country's history.
- Gave his farewell speech.

2011 –

- **Wild Turkey** and **Old Crow** engage in litigation over the slogan "Give 'Em the Bird," highlighting the competitive nature of the bourbon market.

Other Legal and Cultural Impacts

- The interplay between legislation, familial legacy, and innovative practices shapes the dynamic and ever-evolving landscape of bourbon, reinforcing its place as a central element in American drinking culture.

- The **Kentucky Distillers' Association** sued **Buffalo Trace** for using its trademarks, specifically "**Kentucky Bourbon Trail**", as well as logos. **Buffalo Trace** is not part of the Kentucky Bourbon Trail.

- When a company comes out with a **wax seal** on its liquor bottle top, **Maker's Mark's** lawyers send letters to make sure the wax doesn't drip down like it does on that brand's bottles, which federal courts upheld.

- **Sazerac**, which owns **Buffalo Trace**, sued **Bison Ridge Distillery** in Minnesota for adopting a similar name and packaging.

- **James E. Pepper** sued his **mother, Nanna**, for control of the Pepper Distillery when Oscar passed away in 1865. After many changes in hand, it now produces Woodford Reserve. Was even run by E.H. Taylor. Look for old bottles of Old Oscar Pepper.

- Bourbon icons **E.H. Taylor** and **George T. Stagg** sued each other's companies in the 1800s. **Buffalo Trace** makes brands named after both men.

- **Brown-Forman**, parent company of **Jack Daniel's,** sued the brand **Ezra Brooks** over label confusion in the 1960s and lost. Nearly fifty years later, **Brown-Forman** sued **Barton Brands** to protect another brand, **Woodford Reserve**, and won.

Other notes of interest

- The history of distilled spirits, particularly whiskey, is intertwined with various cultural and economic dynamics, especially during the time of early settlers and traders in North America. Unfortunately, many traders took advantage of Native American communities by exploiting their desire for alcohol, often resulting in unfair trades for valuable goods like pelts.

- Yeast plays a critical role in the fermentation process of whiskey, converting sugars into alcohol. Distillers may keep yeast in a controlled environment, like a refrigerator, to maintain its viability for future fermentation batches.

- Kentucky is renowned for its limestone-rich water, which is considered ideal for whiskey production. The natural filtration properties of limestone help remove impurities and provide a balanced mineral content that enhances the flavor of the spirit.

- The term "Angel's Share" refers to the portion of whiskey that evaporates during the aging process in barrels. This evaporation is a natural part of maturation, and it contributes to the overall character and flavor of the whiskey, though it means that the distiller ultimately loses some of the product to the atmosphere. The nuance of whiskey-making is both an art and a science, with each step of the process carefully influencing the final product.

- **Angel's** Envy is finished in Ruby Port barrels for its finishing process.

- **Buffalo Trace** derives its name from the buffalo migration trail that crossed the Kentucky River on its way to the Great Plains, a route later utilized by settlers. It holds the title of the oldest distillery still in operation. During Prohibition, it was able to remain open by producing whiskey for medicinal purposes. The distillery is recognized as a National Historic Landmark. Originally known as the **George T. Stagg Distillery**, it also included parts of the O.F.C. (Old Fashioned Copper) Distillery. A fire in 1882 devastated the facility, which was promptly rebuilt at a cost of $44,000. Additionally, the distillery faced significant flooding in 1937. Currently, **Harlen Wheatley** serves as the Master Distiller, while Freddie Johnson, a third-generation tour guide, has even inspired a root beer named in his honor. The remains of the **O.F.C. distiller** were discovered and are referred to as "Bourbon Pompeii." Other notable Master Distillers at Buffalo Trace include **Colonel Edmund Taylor Jr.**, **Elmer T. Lee**, **Albert B. Blanton**, and **Orville Schupp.**

- **Jim Beam** was established in 1795 and was acquired by **Suntory Holdings** from Osaka, Japan, in 2014. The list of Master Distillers includes **Freddie Noe** (1988-Present), **Fred Noe** (1957-Present), **Fred Booker Noe II** (1929-2004), **T. Jeremiah Beam** (1899-1977), **James B. Beam** (1864-1947), **David M. Beam** (1833-1913), **David Beam** (1802-1854), and **Jacob** Beam (1760-1834).

- **Knob Creek** is named for the small creek that flows just south of the distillery, which is located near **Abraham Lincoln's** childhood home.

- **Longbranch** is a bourbon brand created by **Wild Turkey**, recognized for its distinct mesquite charcoal filtration process, which reflects **Matthew McConaughey's** Texan roots. The brand embodies a philosophy that likens a good handshake with a friend to a "long branch." The bottle showcases the signatures of **McConaughey**, **Eddie Russell**, and **Jimmy Russell**, distinguished for being the longest-serving master distillers in the industry. Together, they are the only three individuals whose signatures appear on a **Wild Turkey** bottle, highlighting the brand's collaborative and personal essence.

- **Maker's Mark**, located in Loretto, Kentucky, is renowned not only for its distinctive red hand-dipped wax bottle top but also for its strong commitment to craftsmanship and heritage. To celebrate the distillery's 60th anniversary, founder **Rob Samuels** sought out famed Seattle glass sculptor **Dale Chihuly** to create a unique piece of art that would reflect the distillery's handmade ethos.

  Samuel's, an eighth-generation whisky maker, faced challenges initially in reaching Chihuly for collaboration. After several unreturned calls and emails, he resorted to a handwritten two-page letter, passionately detailing his family's history in whisky making and the beauty of the Maker's Mark brand. This heartfelt approach got Chihuly's attention, leading to a collaborative project that would beautifully embody the essence of Maker's Mark.

Initially, the plan was to position the artwork above the bottle-dipping area in the gift shop. However, after being inspired by a documentary showcasing Chihuly's pieces displayed in Venice's narrow alleys, Samuels envisaged a more fitting location: the aisle of an aging warehouse. This space became the perfect backdrop for what would be known as "**The Spirit of the Maker**."Chihuly's sculpture incorporates over 1,000 unique, multicolored glass pieces that reflect the brand's iconic red wax as well as blue tones reminiscent of the nearby lake. The artwork also features cherubs, symbolizing the "angel's share" — the whiskey that evaporates from barrels during aging. It took Chihuly's team five days to meticulously place every piece, resulting in a stunning installation that hangs above guests as they exit the tasting room.

During the reveal of the piece, Chihuly remarked that he believed this was one of the most interesting environments he had ever displayed his work. The combination of colors—rich reds, blues, and caramel hues echoing the bourbon—creates a mesmerizing spectacle, celebrating both the artistry of Chihuly and the craftsmanship that defines Maker's Mark.

- **Jimmy Russel** is the longest tenure Master Distillery, as of 2023, at age 83 Wild Turkey.
- **Elijah Craig**, a Baptist minister, is often credited with either inventing bourbon or at least discovering the technique of charring barrels.
- **George Washington's Mount Vernon Distillery** was a significant operation in 1799, featuring five copper-pot stills and producing nearly eleven thousand gallons of whiskey. The distillery was managed by a Scottish distiller named James Anderson and was one of the largest of its kind during that period.

Interestingly, Washington had previously procured whiskey from Pennsylvania distillers. However, tension arose when the U.S. government enacted an alcohol tax to help pay off war debts, which led to widespread discontent among whiskey makers. This culminated in the Whiskey Rebellion, where more than 400 distillers and farmers revolted against the federal government's taxation policy, refusing to pay the tax. In response to the escalating unrest, Washington took the unprecedented step of federalizing 12,950 troops to quell the rebellion and restore order. This event underscored the challenges faced by the young government as it sought to establish its authority and navigate issues related to taxation and rebellion.

- **President Ulysses S. Grant** became embroiled in the infamous **Whiskey Ring scandal**. He faced allegations of being an alcoholic with a particular fondness for whiskey, especially Old Crow. A number of distilleries collaborated to defraud the government of tax revenue, using the illicit funds to support the Republican Party's national campaign for Grant's reelection. In 1875, investigations led to the arrest and indictment of the distillery owners, as well as Grant's close friend and **General Orville E. Babcock**. At the time, $3 million in taxes was owed, with $1.2 million remaining unaccounted for, prompting the public to question what Grant knew about the situation. Grant ultimately testified on behalf of Babcock, who was acquitted. However, 240 distillers, government officials, and others were indicted, with 110 ultimately found guilty, though many served little jail time. Notably, Grant's testimony marked, at the time, the only occasion in U.S. history where a sitting president had testified in a criminal case.
- **Jefferson's Bourbon** is intriguingly tied to historical figures and events, notably **Thomas Jefferson**, despite his personal aversion to bourbon. The brand, founded in 1997 by **Chet** and Trey Zoeller, showcases a commitment to innovation in the

bourbon-making process, utilizing unique wood and cask finishes to enhance flavor profiles. A fascinating tidbit about the family's history includes the arrest of their grandmother in 1799 for "Production and sales of spirituous liquors," which underscores the family's long-standing connection to the spirit industry.

One of their standout offerings is **Jefferson's Ocean Aged at Sea**, which began with a small batch of 3 to 5 barrels placed on the **M/V OCEARCH research vessel**. This journey involves a three-year trek across global oceans, allowing the bourbon to mature uniquely as it travels to 30 ports, crosses five continents, and makes three equator crossings. Currently, the brand has expanded to 180 barrels at sea, further enhancing the distinctive aging process that characterizes Jefferson's Ocean Aged bourbon.

- **Woodford Reserve**, introduced in 1996, boasts a rich history that traces back to the **Old Oscar Pepper Distillery**, later known as the **Labrot** and **Graham Distillery**. Today, it holds the title of **the official Bourbon of the Kentucky Derby**, celebrated with special commemorative bottles featuring unique artwork inspired by the event. The watercolor artwork adorning these bottles is crafted by Louisville resident **Richard Sullivan**, an artist who has a background in minor league baseball and honed his artistic skills at the Savannah College, where he studied Art and Design. This collaboration perfectly blends the worlds of bourbon craftsmanship and artistic expression, enhancing the heritage and prestige of both Woodford Reserve and the Kentucky Derby.

- **Four Roses Bourbon** has a charming origin story rooted in romance, starting with its founder, **Paul Jones, Jr.** Legend has it that Jones fell in love with a Southern belle and, after proposing, awaited her response with bated breath. She informed him that if her answer was affirmative, she would wear a corsage of roses to the grand ball. When she arrived, adorned in a beautiful gown featuring a corsage of four red roses, Jones was overjoyed. He named his bourbon "Four Roses" to symbolize his enduring passion for her, a love that he channeled into crafting the bourbon.

Today, Four Roses Bourbon is produced by the **Kirin Brewery Company** of Japan and boasts a distillery in Lawrenceburg, Kentucky, established in 1910. The distillery features exquisite Spanish Mission-style architecture and has earned a place on the National Register of Historic Places, reflecting both its historical significance and the legacy of the brand.

- **Suntory Holdings** Limited from Japan owns several notable companies, including **Beam Suntory** (famous for **Jim Beam**), **Pepsi Bottling Ventures LLC**, and **Subway Japan**, among others.
- **Rabbit Hole Distillery** was founded in 2012 by **Kaveh Zamanian**, who holds a PhD in psychology and has a deep passion for wine and spirits. The name "Rabbit Hole" was inspired by his wife, Heather, who is from Kentucky. Upon hearing Kaveh express his ambition to start a distillery, she remarked, "You're taking the family down the rabbit hole," which perfectly encapsulated the adventurous spirit of their venture into the world of distillation. Rabbit Hole Distillery is

known for its innovative approach to crafting high-quality bourbon and whiskey, blending tradition with modern techniques.

- **Nathan "Nearest" Green's** legacy as a master distiller and his influence on the whiskey industry, particularly through the **Jack Daniel's** brand, is a significant story of friendship, mentorship, and racial history in America. Green, a skilled craftsman and an enslaved man, played a crucial role in developing the Lincoln County Process, which is a charcoal filtering technique that defines Tennessee whiskey.

Jasper Newton, better known as **Jack Daniels**, came from a challenging background, losing his mother at a young age and becoming essentially an orphan. His early employment on the Dan Call Farm presented him with the opportunity to learn about whiskey-making from Green, who was not only his mentor but also a friend. Their collaboration and the relationship they built may not have been well-documented at the time, but it reflects a profound bond that transcended the era's social and racial divisions.

The continuance of Green's legacy through his descendants working for Jack Daniel's adds another layer of depth to the story, showcasing how familial connections can persist across generations. While there is a lack of visual documentation of Nearest Green himself, historical records and photographs of his family, including his son with Jack Daniels, help preserve the narrative.

In modern times, **Fawn Weaver's** initiative to create her own distillery further honors this legacy. As the first woman and person of color to own a distillery, Weaver not only taps into a rich tradition but also revitalizes the story of **Nearest Green** by hiring his descendant, **Victoria Butler**, as the distiller. Through their work, they have established scholarships for Green's descendants, ensuring that the impact of **Nearest Green** is recognized and celebrated as part of American whiskey history.

This narrative not only highlights the contributions of African Americans to the whiskey industry but also encourages a broader reflection on historical injustices and the celebration of diverse voices in this space.

- **Jack Daniel** passed away in 1911 due to blood poisoning. A popular story suggests that the infection originated from an injury to one of his toes, which he reportedly hurt one early morning while attempting to open his safe in frustration, as he often struggled to recall the combination. However, Daniel's contemporary biographer claims that this narrative is inaccurate. Still, it's an intriguing tale nonetheless.

- According to Daniel's biographer, the origin of the "**Old No. 7**" brand name was the number assigned to Daniel's distillery for government registration. He was forced to change the registration number when the federal government redrew the district, and he became Number 16 in district 5 instead of No. 7 in district 4. However, he continued to use his original number as a brand name, since his brand reputation had already been established. An entirely different explanation is given in the 1967 book 'Jack Daniel's Legacy', which states that the name was chosen in 1887 after a visit to a merchant friend in Tullahoma, who had built a chain of seven stores.

- **Heaven's Door Whiskey** derives its name from **Bob Dylan's "Bootleg Series"** of albums. The brand was established by Bob Dylan in collaboration with **Marc Bushala**, the founder of **Angels Envy**. The bottles feature designs showcasing Bob Dylan's artwork from Black Buffalo Ironworks, which reflects his distinctive wrought iron style.

- **High West American Prairie Whiskey** takes its name from the American Prairie Reserve, which aims to establish the largest wildlife reserve in the contiguous United States, located in Montana. The bottle features the pronghorn antelope, known for its remarkable speed, capable of reaching up to 55 mph, making it the fastest land mammal.

- **Fireball Whisky** (notice no "e")

Fireball was originally part of a line of flavored schnapps developed by Seagram in the mid-1980s. The manufacturer's storyline is, in part, that it was the product of a Canadian bartender's efforts to warm up from an Arctic Blast. The Sazerac Company purchased the brand rights and formula from Seagram in 1989. It was marketed as **"Dr. McGillicuddy's Fireball Whisky"**. Ostensibly, the named doctor was **Dr. Aloysius Percival McGillicuddy**, allegedly more commonly referred to as "the shot doctor," who was "born" in the year 1808. Later, in 2007, the product was rebranded as "Fireball Cinnamon Whisky." An April 2014 article in Bloomberg Business Week said, "It's also one of the most successful liquor brands in decades. In 2011, Fireball accounted for a mere $1.9 million in sales in U.S. gas stations, convenience stores, and supermarkets, according to IRI, a Chicago-based market research firm. In 2013, sales leapt to $61 million, passing Jameson Irish whiskey and Patron tequila. In 2012 and 2013, the product had a surge in popularity, which the company achieved by using social media, cultivating bartenders, word of mouth, and a relatively small advertising budget. It is said that the sharp increase in sales early in its resurgence (late 2011/early 2012) can be attributed to a grassroots effort by **Beer Can Alley**, a Des Moines, Iowa, Country bar. Several national country music acts would perform at the establishment during this time, and inspired multiple references in many popular songs. In 2013, it became one of the top ten most popular liquors, displacing Jose Cuervo tequila. In 2016, Bloomberg reported that with estimated sales of at least $150 million in 2015, the brand had overtaken **Jagermeiste**r in popularity to become the top-selling liqueur in the United States. In 2014, Finland and Sweden reported that Fireball contained amounts of **propylene glycol** that surpassed the EU limitations of 1g/kg. Although not part of the EU, Norway also decided to recall the product. The company responded by saying the product was "perfectly safe to drink and called it a "small recipe-related compliance issue" related to the difference in regulations between the North American and European markets. The recalled batches were replaced with a compliant product, and sales could resume for the EU-compliant formulation. As of 2018, Fireball does not use **propylene glycol** in any of its products.

- **Tin Cup Whiskey's** bottle top is a tin shot glass in honor of Colorado's first whiskey drinkers and the tin cups they drank from.

- **Freedom Whiskey Bourbon**

On a summer day in Helman Province, Afghanistan (2011), Have A Shot of Freedom Whiskey Co. was born. The Marines of Alpha Batter, 1st Battalion, 10th Marines engaged enemy forces with a barrage of artillery shells. Marines moved tirelessly to reload cannons as steel rain poured down over the mountain tops. Through the booming of the howitzers, the units' Senior Staff NCO shouted, "Marines, enjoy this day! For those who fight to protect it, Freedom has a flavor the protected will never know!" Freedom Whiskey Co. exists to harness that flavor into each bottle of bourbon, paying homage to those who served, while honoring the individuals who have toiled to make American great. Freedom Whiskey Co. strives to provide the highest quality bourbon in America while building a family of passionate whiskey drinkers. The company is dedicated to creating whiskey that honors the heritage of our country while providing employment opportunities to veterans who have served or are currently serving, their family members, and those who seek to make a difference in general. The company's mission was always bigger than making great whiskey for Zach. Despite its success, he never took anything out of the business for himself. All profits were either reinvested back into the company or given away to help veteran causes. Freedom Whiskey was created to pay homage to those who served, while honoring the individuals. In all military branches that have toiled to make America great. Zach Hollingsworth died at the age of 35. He was born in Wilmington, Ohio.

- **Bib and Tucker Bourbon**

It gets its name from what was often referred to in pioneer days as "bib" and tucker" clothing, usually reserved for special occasions.

124. The Goldfinch Chirp

The Goldfinch chirps a cheerful tune.

I really hope it lingers until the afternoon.

The Cardinals sing and chat off in the distance.

Enjoy nature today, even if it is only for an instance.

125. The Rag Doll

A new family had just settled into their home, brimming with excitement. As they unpacked their boxes, they began to realize they were running out of places to put their belongings. The mother turned to the father and recalled seeing a door that might lead to an attic. "Here, take this box and put it in the attic," she said, handing it to him. He studied the box, marked with a bold black marker simply labeled "attic," and securely taped shut.

Glancing over at his son, who was engrossed in a handheld video game in the corner, he decided to leave him be. Turning to his daughter, he asked if she wanted to join him. She hesitated, her long brown hair framing her face as uncertainty flickered in her eyes. Sensing her hesitation, he spoke gently, "We can go explore and turn it into an adventure."

They made their way up the steps to the old wooden door. He asked her to open it since he was carrying the box. With a sense of unease about what lay behind it, she slowly turned the handle. It was stiff and resisted her efforts as she began to pull it open. The door creaked ominously, its sound echoing the weight of age and neglect.

Unable to step inside first, she quickly moved aside, wary of the darkness within. Her father reassured her, saying, "Don't worry, I'll find a light once we're inside." He stepped into the gloom and discovered a light cord hanging from the center of the dusty room. Chuckling, he realized there was a light switch right by the door. He called to her, "Hannah, come on in!"

Hannah cautiously poked her head through the doorway. As she took her first step into the attic, her father's reassuring smile greeted her. He set the box down in the center of the room and moved to the side to explore what was stored away. Hannah scanned the attic, her eyes adjusting to the dim light, revealing piles of assorted boxes, old lamps, chairs, clothing, blankets, sheets, various pieces of furniture, and much more.

Then her gaze landed on what appeared to be a small pony. Upon closer inspection, she realized it was an antique rocking horse. A thought crossed her mind: she was far too old for such a toy. Yet, she couldn't resist the temptation and immediately climbed onto the rocking horse, beginning to rock back and forth.

The father was rummaging through a pile of old clothes and rags, pushing them aside to form a small heaping pile. Suddenly, he tossed what appeared to be a small rag toward the center of the attic, where the light streamed in. Hannah's gaze shot to the object, and she halted her rocking. To her, it wasn't just a rag; it was two somber, cold black eyes gazing back at her from atop a small bundle of fabric. Curiosity piqued, she stepped over and gently picked it up.

As she unfolded the cloth, she revealed two legs and two arms. The doll was quite worn, with its limbs seemingly crafted from various scraps of clothing and fabric. Hannah gazed deeply into its eyes. The doll's face showed clear signs of age, with no nose or mouth left painted on. The hair appeared to be made from the end of an old mop, and the limbs were so patched up that it resembled a small, mismatched quilt.

Suddenly, she experienced a sensation, whether it was a wave washing over her or a stirring from within, she couldn't tell. A rapid sequence of images flashed before her eyes. The first depicted an elderly man with grey hair, leaning down to a tiny child. He reached out, offering her a small rag adorned with an even smaller rag tied in a ball on top.

The stream of images continued. Next, she saw an elderly woman in an apron, who took a small piece from the bottom of a mop and placed it atop the rag, transforming it into something resembling a doll. She then handed it to a petite girl. The following image featured a muscular man sporting a thick mustache, holding a paintbrush in his hand. He painted a face onto the doll, then passed it to a curly-haired girl.

Soon after, the scene shifted to a slender man sitting with a little girl in pigtails on his lap. An apron-clad woman approached them, carrying scraps of fabric. The man started sewing what looked like arms and legs onto the doll, while the woman ripped a small piece from her apron and handed it to him for incorporation. The subsequent images revealed various small girls joyfully playing on a lawn, near a fireplace, on a bed, and on a porch of a house. In every scene, the children's wide smiles were mirrored by even broader grins from the adults surrounding them.

At last, the father turned to Hannah and asked, "What do we have here?"

She replied, "It's a doll that many girls once cherished and played with." He raised an eyebrow, glancing between her and the doll. Then, reaching out, he requested to take a closer look. Hannah carefully passed it to him.

As he examined the doll's solemn eyes, he said to his daughter, "Follow me."

They made their way downstairs and then stepped outside to a small shed. The father quickly discovered some paint and a tiny brush. He carefully decorated the doll's eyes with cheerful details, added a small nose, and gave it rosy cheeks. Finally, he painted a delightful smile on its face. The doll seemed to radiate joy, looking back at him with a playful gleam. He returned it to Hannah, who excitedly dashed back to the house to show her mother.

In the kitchen, the mother was busy preparing a meal while her brother sat at the table munching on a cookie, accompanied by a glass of milk. As Hannah entered, her mother turned, wiping her hands on her apron. Hannah eagerly extended the doll toward her loving mother. With tenderness, the mother picked it up, examining it as her son chuckled, "What an ugly doll!"

"Jimmy, be nice to your sister," their mother reprimanded, though she quickly glanced down at her own apron and the patch on the doll. It struck her that her apron was missing a small section.

Just then, the father walked into the kitchen, and the mother showed him both the apron and the doll. They exchanged a meaningful look of curiosity and then embraced each other, sharing a silent understanding.

Hannah spent countless hours playing with her cherished rag doll. Meanwhile, the parents decided to get Jimmy a dog to encourage him to step away from the video games. The two of them enjoyed endless frolicking and playtime together. As the family settled into their new home, the father discovered a variety of crafting tools in the shed.

Inspired, he began making dolls of his own. The mother often came in, smiling as she watched him immersed in his work. She would wrap her arms around him and say, "These are wonderful, John."

He would smile back and reply, "Thank you, Hellen. Their smiles remind me of your love."

Their life was going smoothly until one day, when John returned home with devastating news. He informed Hellen that he had lost his job due to downsizing. They were both deeply upset but made an effort to maintain love and support for one another and their children.

Hellen found herself pacing the kitchen restlessly, while John, frail and visibly weighed down by anxiety, sat rocking in a chair on the porch. As their financial situation grew more precarious, both of them became increasingly anxious about what the future held.

One day, Jimmy was playing in the yard with his dog while Hellen busily tended to her garden, pulling out weeds. Nearby, Hannah sat near a tree, engrossed in play with her rag doll.

On the porch, John nervously rubbed his chin and mouth, rocking back and forth as he pondered how to best support his family through their struggles.

Suddenly, as Jimmy chased after his dog, Hannah became startled and accidentally tossed her rag doll into a thicket. When she reached in to free it, it got caught on some sharp thorns, splitting the doll open.

John, witnessing the whole scene unfold before him, saw a brilliant blue object fly out of the rag doll in slow motion. He immediately sprang to his feet, calling for Hellen as he stepped off the porch. Hannah, having successfully freed her rag doll, was saddened to find it torn and began to cry.

Seeing this, Jimmy rushed to help her up. As he did, he noticed the bright blue object lying on the ground and picked it up. At that moment, John and Hellen approached them. "Look, Dad! What is this?" Jimmy asked, handing the object to his father.

With sheer optimism in his voice, John replied, "This is our solution to our troubles." He quickly took Hellen in his arms and kissed her as he realized the blue object was, in fact, a rare blue diamond.

They quickly realized they could use the money to invest in transforming the shed into a rag doll shop. He took the money from the gem and purchased a variety of supplies, converting the shed into a space that served as both a workshop and a storefront. He crafted numerous charming rag dolls while Hellen managed the shop, selling them all. The venture proved to be quite lucrative, enriching their lives as they shared the joy of rag dolls with others.

Time had moved on, and John lay on his deathbed with Hellen, Jimmy, and Hannah by his side. In silence, he reached out and handed Hannah, now a grown woman, a small, vibrant blue diamond. She smiled warmly as Jimmy assisted their elderly mother to her feet. One by one, they each kissed John gently on the forehead to say goodbye.

Hannah had outlived her parents and brother, continuing the rag doll-making business on her own. One day, as her weary hands ached with age, she sewed a blue diamond into the final doll she would create. After completing the last stitch, she flipped the doll over and thought she caught a glimpse of it winking at her.

In her final years, she found a sense of peace. The business, the dolls, the shed, and the home had become overwhelming for an elderly person to manage. She gently rested her hand on the realty sign that read "for sale," with a "sold" tag dangling beneath it. Stepping back for one last look at the shed that had transformed into a beloved shop, she glanced at the sign in her hand that proclaimed "Hannah's Special Rag Dolls."

With a smile and a playful wink toward the attic, she turned away for good.

126. Have A Vision

I came across this concept in one of Arnold Schwarzenegger's books. It emphasizes the importance of setting personal goals. To help you reach those goals, you should take the time to visualize yourself successfully achieving them.

For instance, if your objective is to run a 5K, don't merely declare it; instead, visualize yourself crossing the finish line. The key is to combine that vivid visualization with dedicated effort to make your goal a reality.

127. The Sludge

His eyes began to flutter open, but his vision remained hazy. He felt as if he were standing waist-deep in what appeared to be a small river or stream, with the banks rising steeply around him, made entirely of dirt.

As he took another step forward, he realized it wasn't water he was wading through but rather a dark, muddy sludge. Each step made him feel heavier, pulling him down deeper. His sight was still clouded, and he couldn't see far ahead. He knew he needed to escape. But 'how' he wondered. He felt the need for assistance.

Then, he noticed what seemed to be hands reaching out from the banks and a bridge ahead. A sudden thought, or perhaps a feeling, overwhelmed him. Could he really trust these hands to pull him to safety? What if they only dragged him further in? He couldn't make out any faces clearly, though he thought he might have caught a glimpse of someone he recognized.

Ultimately, he realized that to escape the sludge, he had to take action himself. As fewer hands reached out to him, his vision grew even murkier.

Taking a deep breath, he closed his eyes and cautiously took another step. He felt as if someone might have helped him from behind, but he couldn't be certain. Gathering his strength, he reached up with his eyes still shut and felt the cool stone of what he believed to be the bridge. Voices began to float to him, but their words were indistinct. With one final push, he pulled himself up.

Was this all a dream? Was it a metaphor for the personal struggles we face as we navigate life's challenges? We often seek help and support, but ultimately, we must first help ourselves. Is there unseen guidance aiding us along the way? What do you think? What struggles do you face? Who lends you a hand? Do you prioritize your own efforts first? Feel free to reach out; you can count on me to offer support in whatever way I can.

128. He Knew

He held her soft hand as the twilight sky cast an array of stars dancing upon the water ripples surrounding their small boat in the middle of the still water. Her effervescent smile was all that he needed to know that all was right in the world.

129. The Big 6 Club

When I was younger, there was a type of social media known as CB radios, primarily used by truck drivers to share traffic updates with each other. They exchanged information about speed traps and other road conditions. There were even movies and songs that revolved around CB radios. Specific channels were set aside for law enforcement, safety, and emergency communications. Even today, boats continue to rely on CB radios for communication and safety purposes.

While I refer to it as a form of social media, back then it wasn't labeled that way. It functioned as a means for people to converse back and forth, similar to using telephones. This communication method had its own unique language, featuring call signs and handles instead of real names. Certain words stood in for phrases, and numbers conveyed specific messages.

Occasionally, I could use a walkie-talkie to connect with CB radio users. During my early teenage years, I adopted the handle "Little Spanky," which suited me since I was often said to resemble Spanky from The Little Rascals. It was enjoyable to connect with complete strangers, and the intention was never to meet in person; instead, the joy came from having simple yet engaging conversations.

At times, this mode of communication became so popular that communities began to form around it. My aunt and uncle were once part of The Big 6 Club, where my uncle went by the handle "Grave Digger" and my aunt was known as "Little Red." They used Channel 6 to connect, chatting while at home or in their cars. It's interesting to reflect that a telephone could have provided a similar experience, but for those involved with CB radios, it was all about the fun of it. Meeting someone face-to-face would have made it even better.

Nowadays, we primarily communicate through cell phones, and often we don't talk at all; we just text. I find it somewhat frustrating that at work, I communicate so frequently through chats, emails, or texts that I miss the opportunity to share the same physical space and have genuine eye contact with my colleagues. As the world evolves, it feels like we're becoming more disconnected from one another.

It was frustrating for some people when certain CB operators had large antennas set up at their homes. They had such powerful setups that I recall some memorable evenings when I was watching my favorite TV show, only to have the CB conversations interrupt the broadcast. The Big 6 Club did a lot of things that I wish we could see more of today. The members wore jackets that represented their group, and they participated in local parades, beaming with smiles and pride. They also raised funds for various charities.

Time has a way of changing things. While CB radio had a limited range, now with cell phones, we can connect with nearly anyone, anywhere in the world. We often adapt to the technology available to us, but I truly hope we can prioritize more face-to-face interactions and meaningful physical connections moving forward.

130. The Merchant Of Venice

A close friend recently gifted me an old book: "The Merchant of Venice" by Shakespeare. I was instantly thrilled to recognize it as the very book I had to study as a freshman in high school, and a wave of memories washed over me. I remembered that we were assigned to read it, memorize a passage, and then recite it in front of the class.

At that time, my self-confidence was quite low, and I could have really benefited from more encouragement and guidance. I did read the book, though I only grasped some aspects of it back then. When it came time to select a passage to memorize, I picked one that I thought I could manage. However, when I stood in front of the class to recite it, I realize now that I delivered it just as if I were reading it, without any true emotion or feeling.

My only goal was to get through it. Meanwhile, a renowned Shakespearean actor was visiting the school to assist some English classes with their studies on Shakespeare's works, but unfortunately, my class was not among those chosen for his guidance.

As soon as I had the opportunity, I eagerly searched for the passage I had memorized all those years ago. Upon finding it, I shared the significance of the book from my youth and my connection to it with a few others.

To my astonishment, as I read the opening line, I recognized how much I had grown both as a person and a reader. I was able to articulate the entire passage fluidly, grasping its meaning more clearly than ever.

As I began to read it aloud, I embraced my adulthood, skillfully embodying the character and conveying his emotions through my voice and physical presence. I couldn't help but wonder how different my journey might have been if I had possessed this confidence and understanding during my uncertain freshman years.

With age comes wisdom and insight, and I only wish I had experienced some of this earlier in life. Sometimes, we find ourselves on paths that neither we nor those around us anticipated. Embrace life with the energy of an exciting character in a story, and cultivate growth through compassion and understanding.

131. Work, Family, And Friends

You can choose your friends, but you can't choose your family or your coworkers. Treat your colleagues like family. We are all in this together, both with our loved ones and our teammates. By supporting each other through life's challenges and triumphs, we can make the journey a bit smoother for everyone.

132. Total Solar Eclipse

We recently experienced a rare total solar eclipse, and the excitement surrounding it was intense. Accommodations were quickly booked up, businesses rushed to sell various items, particularly eclipse glasses, and we were warned about potential traffic jams, cell service outages, gas shortages, and empty grocery shelves. It felt as though everyone was preparing for an impending apocalypse. Some businesses even closed for the day, and many employees at my workplace called in sick, while others only worked part of the day. I was at work the entire time, but when I drove home, I encountered traffic that was surprisingly light, even for a normal day.

Once I got home, I changed into my swim trunks, eager to unwind after a tough few days at work. I grabbed a special beer from the fridge, slipped into my robe, and gathered my phone and flip-flops before heading outside to the hot tub. As I cracked open the can and sank into the warm water, I put on my eclipse glasses and leaned back, watching the celestial display overhead. I took my time observing the moon gradually crossing in front of the sun, trying to set aside my work worries and simply enjoy the moment in a peaceful state of mind.

It was certainly a strange experience to see an eerie darkness descend during a bright day. I noticed that many people were treating the occasion as if it were a picnic or cookout, almost like a holiday. Schools had even closed for the day. Meanwhile, I could hear children in the neighborhood playing, seemingly unaware of the eclipse unfolding above them. Sure, they might have looked up during the moment of totality, but most seemed to view it merely as a day off from school, while adults enjoyed their own break from work.

For those who did watch, they described it as amazing, but to me, it felt unique rather than awe-inspiring. I began to wonder if missing it would truly have been a significant loss, probably not.

This led me to reflect on what I truly value more: a rare total eclipse or witnessing a sunrise over the ocean from the beach. It's easy for me to say that I prefer an ocean sunrise over an eclipse.

Despite the rarity of the total eclipse, the sunrise holds far more meaning for me. To me, it signifies the start of a new day and all the possibilities and opportunities that come with it. It is a chance to temporarily set aside all struggles and worries. We never know what each day will bring, but we can always strive to make the best of whatever life presents us.

133. The Troll And The Bridge (A Children's Story)

Once upon a time, a grumpy old troll once lived under a bridge. The bridge was the path to the land of sweet treats. The grumpy old troll guarded the entrance. He would not let anyone pass unless they could answer a riddle. If you got the answer right, you could have all the sweet treats you wanted. If you got it wrong, the grumpy old troll would eat you all up. Quack the Duck, Skippie the Fox, and Henrietta the Chicken were on their way home from school.

Quack the Duck yelled out, "I want some sweet treats."

Skippie the Fox said, "So do I."

Henrietta the Chicken said, "I don't think it is a good Idea. I don't want to be eaten all up by the mean old troll."

Quack the Duck said, "I will run as fast as I can, and the grumpy old troll will not catch me."

Skippie the Fox said, "I will sneak right by the grumpy old troll. He will not see me."

Henrietta the Chicken said, "I will not run. I will not sneak. I'm not sure what I shall do."

Quack the Duck began to run. He ran as fast as he could. He made it halfway across the bridge. Then he was almost at the end of the bridge. That is when the grumpy old troll jumped out and ate him all up.

Next, Skippie the Fox began to quietly sneak across the bridge. He made it halfway across the bridge. Then, he was almost at the end of the bridge. That is when the grumpy old troll jumped out and ate him all up. Henrietta the chicken did not run across the bridge. She did not sneak her way across. She slowly walked right down the middle of the bridge. She made it halfway across the bridge. Then, she was almost at the end of the bridge.

She stopped and called out to the grumpy old troll, "Hey, Mr. Troll."

The grumpy old troll jumped onto the bridge. The grumpy old troll then asked, "Do you want some sweet treats?"

"Yes," said Henrietta the Chicken.

"Then you must answer my riddle to cross the bridge. If you guess right, then you can cross the bridge. If you guess wrong, then I will eat you all up."

Henrietta the Chicken thought long and hard and came up with a plan. "Mr. Troll, I will answer your riddle, but if I guess right, then you shall let anyone cross the bridge at any time except for me. If I guess wrong, then you can eat me all up."

The grumpy old troll laughed and said, "Even if you guess right, you will never have any sweet treats. I will make this deal with you then."

Henrietta the Chicken said, "What is the riddle?"

The grumpy old troll then said, "What can run but never walks, has a mouth but never talks, has a head but never weeps, has a bed but never sleeps?"

The grumpy old troll laughed full of delight. "I will soon eat you all up!"

Henrietta the Chicken said, "Wait, I have not answered yet." She thought for a moment and then stared straight up at the grumpy old troll and said, "A river."

The grumpy old troll began to jump up and down in anger. He then said, "You may have guessed right, but you may never go across to get sweet treats." He laughed with a big smile on his face.

Henrietta the Chicken then said, "That's ok, because now anyone can cross the bridge and bring back all the sweet treats I want to me." The grumpy old troll began to cry and created such a fuss.

Henrietta the Chicken said, "Don't cry, Mr. Troll. It will be all right. I will give you some of my treats." And it was all right. The grumpy old troll continued to guard the bridge and became friends with all who wanted sweet treats.

The end.

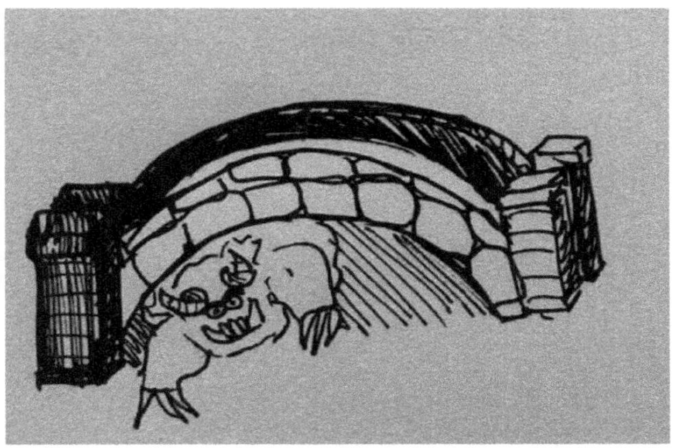

134. The Stillness Of The Night

In the stillness of the night and the glow of early dawn,

I wander through shadows, where dreams are drawn.

Just past 4 a.m., I take a solitary stroll,

As a few neighbors head to work, rushing towards their goal.

I hear the spring peepers singing their song,

While in the distance, the highway hums along.

The robins have yet to awake and begin their chirping.

No rooster either, stretching and crowing.

My mind races with a flurry of thoughts and feelings,

But the calm of the night helps my passions find their meanings.

135. Music Can Fill Your Soul

There are numerous occasions when I find myself driving alone in my car, celebrating in the discovery of music with deep bass and captivating rhythms. I crank up the volume, allowing the vibrations to resonate through me.

Occasionally, I roll down the windows and select a distinctive classical piece that plays a vibrant, immersive melody, often catching the attention of individuals at traffic lights and in downtown spots. I enjoy the sensation of truly "feeling" the music, and I appreciate how it can elevate my mood.

136. Classic Video Game

Many years ago, I had two knee surgeries. Part of my rehab was to elevate and prop my leg up high while I sat in a chair or couch. An outlet was to play a computer game I picked up. This is way before the technology of video games and graphics of today. The game was called "Phantsamagoria". It was a graphic horror game. It was like watching a horror movie. I would have my young nephews come over and visit. I was at one point in the game when my nephew stepped into the room while I was right at a point in the game where a death scene happened. He was traumatized for life.

The game was hard to get after the evolutions of various platforms and systems. But recently, there has been a streaming service in which you can play classic games on your laptop. I recently picked the old "Phantasamgoria" up and texted my nephews and son. They said, "Awesome."

Great old memories came back, even of one when my son begged to play an "adult" Grand Theft Auto game of theirs. When they gave him the chance, he played a part in which he stepped out of a building with a big sword and, in one swipe, chopped 3 heads off. He was also traumatized, and my nephews tried repeatedly to re-create it, but never were able to.

137. Jewelry And Relationships

I believe, at times, we treat jewelry like our relationships with one another. When we first acquire a piece of jewelry, we can't help but smile and admire it. We eagerly show it off to everyone as they express their admiration.

The same can be said for new relationships; they dominate our thoughts and conversations, and we become completely infatuated. However, over time, the shine of the jewelry may diminish, just as relationships can become stale or stagnant. Just as we can clean and polish our jewelry to restore its brilliance, investing effort into our relationships can reinforce our bonds with deep love.

Sometimes, when we take older jewelry to be appraised, we often discover its hidden value. In the same way, long-term relationships can prove to be incredibly priceless.

138. A Walk In The Rain

When was the last time you walked in the rain with someone you love? Some may never have that experience, and many may never get the chance. Don't let this opportunity pass you by.

Walking in the rain with someone you love can strengthen your bond. Just as the umbrella offers protection and shelter, rain jackets and parkas provide warmth as well. The rain creates a soothing melody as it bounces on the umbrella and rain jackets.

As the couple draws closer together, it radiates warmth inside. The "Splish" and the Splash" of the puddles are mere distractions on a clear path. Together, in an embrace under the umbrella, the warmth shall carry the couple steadily forward.

Though the rain may obscure their view ahead, their shared closeness offers a fresh perspective on love.

139. What Color Looks Good On You?

I once came across a quote, surprisingly, above a urinal in a bathroom. It was by Coco Chanel and read, "The best color in the whole world is the one that looks good on you." This phrase has lingered in my mind, and I find myself interpreting it differently each time I reflect on it. To me, it suggests that the colors we wear can influence how others perceive us. However, it's also about the individual wearing the clothes—their ability to convey an image through their attire, which in turn enhances that image.

Even if someone chooses to wear dull colors, their vibrant personality can shine through, making those drab hues more impactful.

Conversely, those who opt for bold colors might be seeking out a way to stand out in a crowd. Ultimately, what looks good on you should reflect your inner self and make you feel good, each in your own distinctive way.

140. Spread Kindness Like Wildflowers

This message is inscribed on a small collectible jar I own: "Spread Kindness like Wildflowers." A single act of kindness can spark a chain reaction of happiness, smiles, and laughter. Just like planting wildflower seeds, which is easy to do, the blooms that emerge bring joy to those who notice them.

If we focus on being kinder to one another, rather than allowing hate to prevail, the world could be as vibrant and beautiful as a field of wildflowers.

141. Identity Theft

I was going about my usual tasks at work when I received a phone call. Unfortunately, I was in an area where it was difficult to hear or see clearly. All I could determine was something regarding my credit card. I pulled my card from my wallet, flipped it over, and attempted to call the credit card company, or so I thought. I mistakenly dialed 1-800 instead of 1-888.

While on the line in a poorly lit corner with background noise, I spoke with someone who asked for my name, credit card number, and address. Despite my efforts to clarify the situation, the person kept trying to sell me things, and I repeatedly said no until I finally hung up. I decided I would call back when I was off work and could hear and see better.

When I got home, I flipped my card over and discovered that I had called the wrong number. After being transferred multiple times, I finally reached someone who understood the situation. We quickly canceled my credit card and arranged for a new one to be sent. In the days that followed, I noticed someone attempting to use my old card, so I called my credit card company back to have them review and dispute each unauthorized transaction.

As time passed, I experienced no issues with my new credit card. One day, while I was at work carrying out my usual tasks, my phone began to ring. I glanced at the screen and was taken aback to see that it displayed my local police department's name. As my curiosity quickly grew, I answered the call.

A man on the other end introduced himself as a police officer of my local department, providing his badge number and mentioning that he worked directly with the police chief and cited his name. He asked for my name and then inquired if I had recently purchased certain chemicals.

He went on to explain that it was a matter of homeland security and that my name was linked to these types of purchases. He claimed that homeland security had contacted him about the situation and emphasized the importance of my cooperation, providing me with a case number.

During the conversation, he recited the first four digits of my credit card and then gave me the last four digits of my old credit card that I'd closed after the previous identity theft incident. He asked if I wanted to have an attorney represent me or if I preferred to have the government do so. Although I had some reservations and questioned a few things, I decided to continue the conversation.

With the need to return to work, I asked him to call me back around 4 PM when I would be home. He agreed to contact the government to discuss what I had said, and I resumed my workday.

During my next break, I called my local police department to verify whether the officer I encountered actually worked there. The dispatcher confirmed that he did. I still felt very uneasy and unsure of everything.

I left work earlier than normal and called my local police department again to speak with the officer. I was asked about the nature of my call, and I explained that I was supposed to discuss something with the officer at 4 PM and wanted to know if we could talk now or if I needed to come to the station in person.

When the officer got on the phone, his voice sounded different from the first person I spoke with. I explained the situation, and he revealed that I was dealing with a scam.

It involves a scammer impersonating a police officer who collects information about the officer and details about their workplace, such as the police chief's name. The scammer provides a fake badge identification number and a fabricated case number. Individuals like the one I encountered often obtain stolen credit cards to gather as much information as possible for malicious purposes. This scammer already knew part of my credit card number, my name, and my address, and he was beginning to threaten me.

The real officer assured me that he would look into the matter and keep me updated. He also confirmed that I had handled the situation correctly.

Later, the scammer called me once again, attempting to pressure me further. When he claimed there was a warrant out for my arrest, I told him to serve it in person, and then I abruptly hung up. I called the officer back to inform him about the call, and he reassured me that I had done the right thing. We discussed the fact that many people, particularly the elderly, can easily become victims of these predatory scammers. He mentioned that there had been similar incidents reported in the county by other departments, with some individuals even sending money to these fraudulent people.

The officer then took to social media to share this incident in hopes of preventing others from being deceived. Please stay vigilant; if something doesn't sound right, it likely isn't. Don't hesitate to reach out to your local authorities.

Let's band together to protect one another.

142. Solo Hiking Walks In The Parks

My arthritis and a pesky meniscus injury in my knee had sidelined me from running, leaving walking as my only option. I even went to therapy for it, and my running was limited to just one 5k Turkey Trot. I had to wear two knee supports that gave me protection from injury. As I write this, I had been walking one mile each morning between 4 and 4:30 AM for five months. I then discovered that Lorain County Metroparks offers a hiking stick program.

Once you complete ten hikes in at least six different area parks, you earn both a hiking stick and a pin. I thought this would be a perfect opportunity to increase my walking and explore some parks I hadn't visited before. I was thrilled to complete the challenge, as I walked each walk with knee supports, and submitted my form. I did receive my hiking stick and pin. I was impressed that all the hiking sticks were made by volunteers of the park service.

As I hiked these trails alone, I became more attuned to my surroundings. I often heard the trees communicating with each other as the wind rustled against their branches. The soothing sounds of flowing water from creeks, rivers, and waterfalls were always calming, while the gentle trickle over rocks created small rapids that fascinated me.

The tranquility of the environment, combined with the rustling leaves, blooming flowers, and the songs of birds amidst the diverse terrain, provided a soothing experience. Quiet solo walks sometimes reveal insights about oneself.

I managed to walk daily for an entire year, but then I hit a wall. The cold weather took a toll on both my body and mind. Knee pain and mental fatigue pushed me to prioritize rest and recovery.

Sleep has been a struggle for me lately. I recently started taking medication for blood pressure and cholesterol, something I never imagined I would have to do. I suppose such challenges come with aging.

Writing has been a wonderful stress reliever for me, and with warmer weather just around the corner, I look forward to resuming more outdoor activities.

143. College Visits

During my senior year of high school which I spent at a vocational school for the last two years, I had the opportunity to visit a few college campuses instead of participating in regular classes. I went on three visits in total, and one of them was with my friend Brad.

Unfortunately, I don't recall much about that particular visit because it was quite disappointing. Upon our arrival, we were simply handed two meal tickets and given no guidance or tour. We found ourselves wandering aimlessly, feeling completely lost. As a result, I quickly lost interest in considering that school within just a few minutes.

My second college visit was with a different friend, John, and it was an improvement over the first. We were ushered into a room filled with other prospective students, where we received some information about the college. Although I tried to pay attention, I know I missed a lot and would have easily lost a trivia contest on the school's mascot; I could not remember it to save my life.

Unfortunately, the tour left much to be desired. I do not think we even spent the night on campus, which would have given us a better feel for the place. The highlight of that day was the banquet for all prospective football players. That was where I experienced two standout moments.

The first was Bob Golic, who played for the Cleveland Browns and was the guest speaker for the event. The other was an image that I could not shake of a massive incoming freshman who looked like he was twice my height and weight, which made me realize instantly that playing football at this level was far beyond my reach. The thought of competing against someone like him was both awe-inspiring and intimidating, and it crushed any lingering ambitions of joining that team.

During my third college visit, John accompanied me once again. This time, we stayed in a fraternity house where two students generously offered us their beds for the night. Unfortunately, I can't recall much about the tour or even the meals. I do remember that it was a party night, and we were presented with alcohol and marijuana, but we chose to pass on that and went to the gym instead. I still find it hard to believe that we were still in high school and they did not even think twice about what they were offering us.

The gym had a unique hard-padded floor, quite different from a traditional hardwood court. While we were there, we participated in a pick-up basketball game, and to my surprise, I managed to hit a three-pointer, which earned me some congratulations.

Given that I wasn't particularly good at basketball back then, it felt amazing to be accepted in that moment. We also visited the baseball team, where the coach encouraged us to consider joining. I distinctly remember watching a "Tears for Fears" music video in the fraternity house as well. The college offered strong academic and scholastic programs. The football team ended up winning several national championships.

I was not able to attend the colleges where I had hoped to play football or baseball. A lack of guidance, support, and financial aid prevented me from reaching those institutions.

Ultimately, I found myself enrolling in a community college, which wasn't what I had originally envisioned. I often feel I could have done more and should have pushed harder. Instead, I earned my Associate's Degree and started working at a grocery store, eventually moving on to my current job, where I've been for over 34 years. I sometimes feel like I've underachieved, but I focus on making those around me happy while trying to find my own happiness as well.

I never found out where Brad ended up after high school, but John went on to join the Air Force and played quarterback. He later shared with me that his body paid a price for it, enduring multiple concussions and injuries. Each day, he wakes up dealing with the aftermath.

Despite this, he was able to channel his education into a successful career and has since achieved semi-retirement. He eventually moved to Florida and Tennessee in his later years.

When I helped organize a reunion for my JVS class, I was truly touched that John made the effort to fly in for the event. I can't express enough how grateful I am for that gesture.

My son requested to move in with me during his freshman year of high school, having lived with his mother in another city since our divorce. I agreed to go to court to facilitate this transition, and his mother consented as well.

While I may not have been perfect, my intention was to provide him with support and direction during his final years of high school as he prepared for college. I encouraged him to enroll in a Baccalaureate program offered by the high school, which ultimately aided him during the college application process. He also took advantage of a program designed for first-generation college students at the community college, recognizing that it wasn't a full-fledged four-year institution.

We discussed his aspirations for after high school, and I accompanied him on three college visits. My goal was to empower him to make his own decisions while ensuring he avoided the path I took.

At each visit, we received tours and were presented with enthusiastic pitches from representatives trying to convince us that their college was the best fit. Financial aid packages were significant in the decision-making process, alongside his gut feeling about where he belonged.

He chose an excellent college and swiftly changed his major after the first few months, gaining valuable education along the way. He discovered a lot about himself, formed friendships, and built a network with professors and professionals.

Now, he has moved to Seattle and successfully established himself as an online journalist. I sincerely hope that I provided him with enough guidance to grow into a successful individual.

144. Trick Or Treat Mirror

Over the years, things have certainly evolved. Each Halloween, I usually like to mix in some fun and occasionally spooky activities for the trick-or-treaters. I have set up haunted houses, donned various costumes, and had help from others with special effects and music.

However, it seems like both the neighborhood and the weather have worsened a bit each year. The kids themselves are different, too, and fewer people appear to be out walking. I have also been struggling to endure the cold and rain on those nights, and I just do not have the energy to create the elaborate setups like I used to.

One setup I did once was quite simple, though. As the kids and their parents came up for the candy, I asked them a simple question, "Do you want to see the scariest thing in the whole neighborhood?"

The kids would look at me with fear as I said it. Was it the way I said it? Was it my eyes glaring at them? Or was it simply the fear of not knowing what I had behind the wood doors? I then enticed the parents to see it. They reluctantly moved up and slowly peered around the doors. The children would still look quite scared as to what their parents may find.

The parents would then look at what they saw behind the doors and would either simply smile or start laughing. They then would encourage their kids to look behind the door. Some would do it, while others would wholeheartedly refuse.

To their unexpected delight, they found themselves looking at a mirror. I may do this again soon on one of the next Halloween nights.

I once watched a video of a school teacher who did something quite similar. She informed her students that she had placed a picture of her favorite student inside a box on her desk.

As each student took their turn to approach and peek inside, they were surprised to find a mirror staring back at them, leading to smiles and laughter filled with joy and realization.

Perhaps I should consider modifying my mirror concept to something like this. However, upon reflection, I think I'd prefer to keep the sense of mystery and fear associated with the frightening unknown behind the door much more daunting.

145. Mr. And Mrs. Champney And Mr. And Mrs. Bechtel

When I was younger, I'm not sure I fully appreciated my neighbors next door. Mrs. Champney, a former school teacher, would generously give me books to enjoy during the summer, always greeting me with a warm smile.

Mr. Champney was a quiet yet talented man, known for his exceptional gardening skills. He could grow cabbages with four heads on a single plant and cultivated a variety of vegetables. Neither of them ever reprimanded me for sneaking a few cherry tomatoes or picking daffodils to make a bouquet for my mother.

The range of plants they had was remarkable. Mr. Champney would even shape his yard into forms resembling fish; a tree would serve as the eye, and you could clearly make out the tail, all bordered by walking pavers. You would often find him tending to his garden, and sometimes he would simply sit and take in the beauty around him.

To this day, I've never witnessed a hummingbird landing on someone's shoulder as I did with him.

Mr. and Mrs. Bechtel had a nice boat, and one day they went out of their way to take four neighborhood kids for a ride on Lake Erie. For a kid and three of my friends to receive such a generous offer was quite meaningful. They must have believed we were decent kids who didn't create much trouble.

Unfortunately, we never properly expressed our gratitude, especially after I accidentally broke the garage window while playing basketball in their driveway when I shouldn't have been.

May we open up our eyes to the kind-hearted souls around us. Let us express our appreciation and gratitude to them often, before it is too late.

146. Some Observations At Some Vegas Pools

I've been to Las Vegas on vacation a few times, and I often spent my mornings by the pool. I could never quite adjust to the time difference, so I was usually wide awake. It was warm; actually, it was quite hot for that early in the day. The first hotel I stayed at featured several pools and an intriguing lazy river. True to my thrifty nature, I refused to pay to rent an inner tube for the steep price which was the same as buying two or three at a store. Instead, I brought my own, which I had packed in my suitcase. Yes, I stubbornly opted to inflate it by hand instead of paying for the hotel to do it for me. It took a while, and no, it wasn't a full-sized tube, but I was determined. I also avoided spending on overpriced food and drinks, which were five times the normal cost.

I enjoyed lounging in a chair and soaking up the sun while the upbeat music played in the background. As I relaxed, I began to observe the people around me and their little idiosyncrasies. I noticed that men often went off to buy drinks for their partners, usually gathering near one corner of the pool.

When groups of friends got together, their conversations tended to get louder. Meanwhile, kids were energetically playing, with the usual boisterous sounds of laughter, splashes, and excited shouts of, "Look what I can do!" The guys who seemed to be flaunting their wealth always had a drink in hand as they waded through the water.

When I grew weary of lounging by the pool, I made my way to the lazy river with my rather small inner tube. It was quite a feat to find any semblance of comfort on that tiny ring without falling off, especially with my large butt barely fitting in it. I also had to bring my phone with me, as I was not comfortable leaving it by my towel, flip-flops, and hotel key. Remarkably, I managed to keep it dry, even when I decided to take a dip under the powerful waterfall. I sat it down within sight for just a brief moment. Some onlookers might have laughed at how snug I looked in my inner tube, but I took solace in the fact that I hadn't paid the exorbitant fees that others had.

The lazy river offered a glimpse into others' adventures as well. There were groups of folks who seemed to have battled for what they believed was the prime spot, complete with buckets of drinks, piles of snacks, and numerous towels. These gatherings tended to be on the larger side, both in numbers and the size of the individuals as well. Meanwhile, the kids zipped around like tiny tornadoes, always racing through the water. Occasionally, I'd get bumped by someone, and they would apologize. This area was truly a melting pot of strangers, all united in their quest for relaxation or a bit of fun.

Another amusing observation was the picture-taking happening all around. Some folks were snapping casual selfies, while others were busy capturing moments of their kids. But there was one couple that really cracked me up. The guy was overly eager to show off his girlfriend, or whoever she was, while she seemed to think she was the star of the show. In reality, however, she wasn't all that impressive. He had her posing in various stances against different backdrops, determined to ensure everyone noticed their antics. You would have thought he was photographing a celebrity, but it was anything but that. Meanwhile, I just floated along the lazy river, enjoying the scene. The hotel boasted a separate invite-only pool that featured a DJ and an array of fancy drinks, but I didn't even bother to try and get in. Sometimes, the simplest pleasures are all you need.

On another Las Vegas trip, I stayed at a different hotel, and its pool area was quite different than the last one. I quickly discovered a lovely pool area featuring three pools, one of which was adults only. On my first visit to the pool, I longed for nothing more than to lounge in a chair and unwind. The gentle strains of soft jazz filled the air in the morning, creating a soothing atmosphere.

Unfortunately, the tranquility was quickly disrupted by an individual eager to showcase her vibrant personality. I chose a lounge chair positioned a row behind the pool's edge, hoping to maintain a bit of distance from a woman who was trying to read her book. Just as I settled in, a woman, likely the mother of a nearby family, grabbed my attention, if not my ears. She was not petite and was perched on the edge of the pool, a cup of some drink in hand. I was unsure of her husband's whereabouts, but her teenage and young adult children were happily swimming nearby.

This woman felt compelled to engage anyone within earshot in a loud conversation about her children and their vacation adventures. It was certainly not a subdued discussion. I couldn't help but feel for the lady attempting to enjoy her book, her concentration shattered by this boisterous exchange.

I could not stand it any longer and decided to switch to a different pool. This one was bathed in sunlight, so I opted for a lounger with an umbrella for shade. I convinced the concession guy to give me a collector cup filled with ice and water, and then I poured in my own little bottle of Fireball, keeping it my little secret. This pool had a few loungers partially submerged, allowing for the perfect combination of relaxation and cooling off. Just when I thought things couldn't get better, the show began.

A couple accompanied their elderly mother to the pool. While they weren't as boisterous as some of the other guests, they certainly engaged in plenty of conversation. The older woman wasn't particularly small, but she carried herself with dignity in her bathing suit, clearly enjoying the chance to walk into the water and cool off.

One day, she even expressed to the staff that the water felt too warm and wondered if the heater was on. In reality, it was just the sun blazing down in the sweltering 100-degree heat. The couple attentively cared for her, ensuring she was comfortable and had everything she needed. I thought that was truly heartwarming.

The beverage girls would return to inquire if I needed anything. Naturally, I replied, "No, thank you," as I could not justify spending such inflated prices. These servers likely walked several miles each day, shuttling food and drinks to the guests. They were dressed in similar swimsuits with cover-ups, though I honestly thought shorts would have been a more practical choice; then again, it was Vegas.

The next intriguing moment was when four or five women gathered in the water, each holding an alcoholic drink. One woman seemed to dominate the entire conversation, rarely allowing the others to speak. It seemed they had just returned from a trade fair event, but they appeared to be more interested in enjoying the free trip to Vegas than in their work, which they didn't seem to be happy with at all. This woman was more focused on complaining, drinking, partying, and steering the group in her direction. I even noticed one girl subtly veer off on her own, trying to distance herself from the dominant presence.

It's fascinating how some individuals are completely unaware of how they come across to others.

My attention was then drawn to an older lady with her daughter on a soft bed that required a significant extra cost to rent. I was trying to figure out why this older mother and this girl, who looked to be in her late 20s to early 30s, needed this bed. It all came into play when the daughter proceeded to ask her mother to start taking pictures of her.

With playful elegance, she struck various poses, twisting and turning, and at one point, cheekily revealing a thong. I could not help but chuckle, shaking my head in disbelief. I found it to be rather unusual.

As I shifted in my lounger, my gaze then fell upon a lone woman sitting under an umbrella, her dark sunglasses shielding her eyes from the sun. At first, she seemed unremarkable until she reached for her lipstick. Not just any lip balm, but a bold shade of lipstick that demanded attention. Instantly, I wondered, "Who is she trying to impress? It certainly isn't me.

Next, my gaze landed on a simple mother with all of her energetic kids. She was balancing an impressive array of goggles, masks, inner tubes, floaties, towels, and whatnot, all in her hand. She appeared overwhelmed, and my heart ached at the thought of mentioning that her brand-new bathing suit still had the price tag attached. In that bright moment, she radiated happiness, fully embracing her vacation. The new bathing suit felt like a little gift to herself, and I didn't want to disrupt her joy.

Suddenly, my attention was drawn to an older gentleman standing at the pool's edge, wearing simple dark swim trunks and sunglasses.

The sun shone brightly on his face, and a broad smile rested easily on his lips. He shuffled his feet gently, clearly enjoying the warmth as he soaked in the sun's rays, already tanned yet seeking more. He rarely dipped into the water, exchanging just a word or two with his wife, who checked on him. His smile spoke volumes: a life of accomplishments, financial freedom, and a carefree attitude. He radiated a sense of contentment, reminding us all to embrace who we are and enjoy the little things in life without worrying about the opinions of others. He stood quietly by the pool's edge, never disturbing a soul.

My last bit of entertainment came from an older couple who seemed to have wandered in from another world. With their striking white hair, no trace of gray in sight, they displayed a youthful spirit. The lady sported a shiny green bikini that, while eye-catching, was a bit hard on the eyes, and her partner wore a bright yellow Speedo that was equally bold.

She eagerly asked him to snap her picture, and he obliged, capturing moments of joy as they splashed in the water, lounged about, and strolled hand in hand. Their happiness was infectious. They swam close to my lounge chair when a young guy with a nipple piercing glided by. The lady immediately complimented him on it, to which he responded, "Thanks, my boyfriend got it for me."

Her reaction was unfazed, and I caught myself shaking my head in amusement as I adjusted my lounge chair. It's a reminder that joy knows no age and love takes many forms. So, let's all embrace our uniqueness and celebrate those unexpected moments that bring laughter and connection.

I had an amazing time enjoying this free entertainment! It's incredible how the simplest joys in life can bring such a smile to my day. Keep watching for those little moments, they are often the most delightful!

147. Swimming At Findley State Park As A Kid

As a child, Findley State Park was a cherished escape from the sweltering summer heat. This park was brimming with life and adventure, still draws families eager to camp, boat, hike, mountain bike, and fish. I strongly remember my parents taking us there, ready for a fun-filled day. The parking lot was often crowded, and finding a spot sometimes felt like a small adventure of its own.

Once at the beach, you would find a sprawling patch of grass and a narrow strip of sand leading to the cool water. That grass, unforgiving and sharp, never cut your ankle, but I always thought it would. Maybe it was because it seemed never to be mowed, just worn down by the beachgoers. Despite its sting, we raced to the water, splashing joyfully. Sometimes, I would be carried out to the deep end that was marked with a line and buoys. The lifeguards would often yell at anyone going past that line. The lifeguards would receive breaks and ordered everyone out of the water.

At this time, it was a feeding frenzy in the grass areas. You did not dare shy away from the blanket and towels you had marked as your territory, or the blades of the grass would cut your legs. I look back now and I think how within a few feet from your area, another group of people could be smoking, eating, drinking beverages, and playing music loudly from transistor radios.

As I grew into my early teens, a friend, Sue, would take me and her niece and nephew for camping. If we wanted to go swimming, we had to ride our beat-up, shabby bikes miles away from the campsite to the beach. We pedaled those seemingly endless miles, savoring every moment, all to bask in the refreshing embrace of the beach for just a little while. Findley's beach area could get so busy at times that the parking lot could become completely full. Parking would extend off the roadway entrances. This was the place to be for summer cool-offs if you did not want to travel to Lake Erie.

During my high school days, my friend Joe and I would drive to Findley's beach with his old station wagon and a massive black inner tube. We would drop the inner tube in the sand, claiming our spot. You would think we would just use that inner tube just to lounge in the water, but the reality was far different.

The murky water hid all kinds of mysteries, and we had no idea how we escaped unscathed all those years; back then, we simply didn't think about it.

Once we floated that tube out, the real fun began. The unsanitary waters drew in huge horse flies, turning our day into a wild game of swatting. With each landing insect, we would swipe our hands, counting our "kills," and hoping not to become their next target. It was chaotic, ridiculous, and undeniably fun! Those carefree summer days taught us to embrace the adventures, no matter how messy they seemed.

Times change, and with the rise of public swimming pools, Findley's swimming hole has faded into the background. Once a lively spot filled with laughter and carefree days, it now stands quiet, empty of lifeguards and bustling crowds. Kids today find solace in the glow of screens, and the vibrant world outside often feels forgotten.

Yet, there's magic in those untouched places. The beach may be empty, but it invites imagination and adventure. Remember those horsefly battles with Joe? They were more than just a game; they were moments of joy, laughter, and camaraderie. It's essential to cherish those memories and inspire the next generation to step outside, explore, and create their own unforgettable stories.

So, let's encourage kids to unplug, embrace nature, and rediscover the beauty in simple pleasures. There's a whole world waiting, just beyond the screen—full of hidden treasures and adventures, ready to be explored!

Joe may believe he's the reigning champ, but I've snagged a win or two in our horsefly games.

148. Skiing In Lake Erie

My family once owned a 21-foot boat, modest in size but rich with meaning. It made my father's fishing trips on Lake Erie a little easier, stored comfortably in a spacious garage at Beaver Park Storage, and launched into the water with the help of a hefty forklift. My brother and dad often took it out, returning with tales of adventure that often left the boat a bit messy.

As my father grew older, though, the upkeep became a challenge. I, too, loved to fish, but I also relished the long rides and the thrill of learning to ski in those shimmering waters.

My brother somehow managed to borrow a pair of skis, a ski vest, and a tow rope from a friend, and I still wonder if he ever returned them. While most people start skiing on calm, serene lakes, we jumped right into the thrilling, unpredictable waves of Lake Erie. The currents and chilly water added their own challenge to the experience.

My brother and I learned how to get up on those skis, teaching each other along the way, and we took joy in encouraging our friends to join us.

When it was your turn, you donned the life jacket, not sure if it was a fishing life jacket or a skit vest, and jumped into the water. Sometimes, it was quite cold and would take your breath away for a bit. The next step was for the lookout person to toss the skis your way. This was the tricky part, as you had to fit your feet into the bindings of the skis while trying to keep your head above the water. With a hopeful catch, you grabbed the tow rope on the first try, trying not to tangle your legs in the skis. Then, facing the back of the boat, you positioned your skis upward, with the rope between your legs. The lookout person ensured everything stayed clear of the boat's propellers, and the engine was always turned off as a person would near the rear of the boat by the props. When the line became taught, the skier would signal the lookout person a thumbs-up. The lookout person would signal the driver to speed up.

Several thoughts raced through one's mind: Would I be able to get up with no problem? Would I wipe out and do several somersaults underwater and smack my lower section as I had done a few times in the past? Would the driver stay away from other boats, rocks, tree limbs, and debris?

I remember one time that I frantically waved to the lookout person to, "go, go, go!" There was a large dead fish heading right in my direction as the line was getting tight. Just as the boat picked up speed, I managed to rise just in time, and that dead fish zipped right between my spread legs.

My brother and I eventually got bold enough to cross the boat's wake, which felt like jumping a railroad track. As the driver turned, we would whip ourselves across both wakes, doubling our speed. If the driver turned the boat, you, as the skier, would try to whip yourself across both wakes, and you would double your speed. It was exhilarating as you were leaning hard to the side at a sharp angle, as the skis pounded the water hard. It was intense, it was scary, but it was so rewarding.

I recall briefing my friends on all the safety measures before I ever dipped a toe in the water. When I climbed back into the boat one afternoon, I was curious about their speed. A cheeky grin spread across their faces as they confessed, they had the throttle wide open.

My heart raced, and I exclaimed, "You could've blown the engine!"

There was a moment when the boat soared above the water, and I suddenly knew I was about to be slammed by a massive wave. Fear had no chance to take hold as the wave crashed down, and I found myself unable to grip the rope, and into the water I went.

Another time, I was pulled through an illegal break wall area, my heart racing at the thought of what would happen if I wiped out. I focused on staying upright for miles, my thighs burning with effort. In the end, I tossed the rope and surrendered to the water, a mix of relief and exhilaration washing over me.

Some friends never made it up. Johnny got tired just putting the skis on. Larry had feet too big and could not fit the skis comfortably. As for Joe, well, he had a history. He once tried fishing with us and ended up getting so seasick that he actually hurled on the Walleye I was reeling in. The poor guy actually turned a shade of green. We got him home, but he spent three days recovering and never set foot on a boat again. Lake Erie can be a real bad demon for some people. We still feel bad for him. His brother, Steve, tried so hard to ski. He would start out, and instead of rising up out of the water, it pulled him face forward, and it was pulling him outstretched in the water. This is what we saw from the rear of the boat: the rope, his hands still holding the rope handle with a death grip, and his eyes wide open under the water with his mouth wide open. We felt so bad for him, but it sure was a bunch of laughs.

I'm not sure if my old body can handle skiing anymore, but I truly cherish all the incredible moments we shared on and in the water.

149. Time Portals

I often wonder if a future awaits us where time portals redefine travel. Imagine stepping through a shimmering gateway, bypassing the need for cars, planes, trains, or even the simple act of walking or biking. What if, by the end of our lives, the streets were filled with people gliding and hovering effortlessly to their destinations?

At present, it seems unlikely that time portals could be a reality. The costs would likely be astronomical, accessible only to the elite, leading to significant social divides. Moreover, the potential for misuse, such as criminals escaping through portals, raises serious concerns.

Yet, we can also envision the remarkable benefits they could offer. Imagine being whisked away to a hospital in seconds in an emergency or traveling effortlessly, cutting expenses, and improving comfort. While technology does present challenges, it also holds immense promise.

By embracing its potential and advocating for equitable access, we can work towards a future where these advancements uplift everyone. Together, we can navigate both the challenges and opportunities that lie ahead.

Let us hold onto hope as we strive to enhance the lives of everyone, from the homeless to those facing mental health challenges, medical conditions, addiction issues, and domestic abuse. It's vital that we work together to uplift every individual, regardless of their background. Instead of merely addressing symptoms, let's dig deeper and tackle the root causes.

Together, we can create meaningful change and build a brighter future for all.

150. Bob Evans Message

While dining at a Bob Evans, I noticed a phrase on the wall: "We treat strangers like friends and friends like family."

What a great concept that could enrich our everyday lives. Imagine applying this mindset while at work, strolling down the street, or engaging in casual conversations.

When we extend kindness, it often comes back to us, creating a ripple effect of positivity. The bonds we form with friends can feel just as vital as those with family. Consider the impact of a warm demeanor of a waiter or waitress. Could their kindness lead to a more enjoyable dining experience and perhaps even better tips?

I love sparking friendly chats with strangers, as these moments can brighten our days. So, let's embrace this idea. Each interaction is an opportunity to make someone's day just a bit better. Together, we can spread warmth and joy in our world, one small act at a time.

151. You Can't Change Your Friends

You can't change your friends. You can only offer guidance and support. Keep dreaming, hoping, and wishing because it is what keeps your spirit alive.

Sometimes life brings you many pitfalls. When you are at the bottom of the hole, know that you are not alone. Someone is always there for you. We just need to find each other.

When things are going great, stay humble and look out for your friends.

152. Hocking Hills

I absolutely love the great outdoors, filled with adventure and the thrill of discovering new places. When I first heard about Hocking Hills in southern Ohio, I dove deep into research and uncovered a world brimming with captivating waterfalls, scenic hiking trails, thrilling ziplines, cozy cabins, and so much more. I've made the 3-hour journey to Hocking Hills in Logan, Ohio, multiple times, and every visit reveals something fresh and exciting.

Recently, several friends expressed interest in exploring this incredible destination, so I decided to create a little guide to help them on their adventure. I encourage everyone to experience the magic of Hocking Hills.

The first thing I ever did in Hocking Hills was an exhilarating zipline experience. You glide through the air, suspended on a cable system between two trees. It is a joyful thrill as the zip of the cable resonates in your ears.

Sometimes, you walk on canopy bridges from tree to tree as they sway a bit. Guided by experts, you usually are guided to rappel down at the end. The views are great, and they usually explain some of the interesting traits of the area and trees, and such.

Experiencing the charm of Hocking Hills by staying in a cozy cabin promises comfort and tranquility. These inviting retreats are always clean, plush, and equipped with all the amenities one would need for a relaxing getaway. I have had the pleasure of staying in a few different cabins of various sizes with different amounts of people, ranging from 4 people to 8. The more people in the group, the lower the cost per person. It has been as low as $40 a person per night.

The journey to your cabin is half the adventure, filled with winding roads and beautiful hills, all surrounded by a canopy of trees. Embrace each twist and turn as part of the charm. I suggest stopping at the Walmart in Logan for all your cooking essentials. This eliminates filling up heavy coolers, and you can pick up fresh burgers and veggies.

If you need a breakfast stop on the way down, Waffle House in Sunbury is a place to try. I know someone who swears by their grits, and I usually am ok with their waffles, as the quality varies. And for a quick pit stop, a McDonald's on the way up Route 33 has your back.

Your first hiking adventure at Hocking Hills is truly special, and starting at Old Man's Cave is an absolute must! This place, often thought of as a cave, is actually a fascinating recess with intriguing stories to tell—legend has it, the remains of the old man who once called this spot home are buried nearby.

Begin your journey at Upper Falls, conveniently located near the parking lot. Here, you'll find stunning waterfalls that change with the seasons. They shimmer in the summer sun or glisten with winter's snow. As you stroll along the river, keep an eye out for two small caves, but they are a tight squeeze.

Next, discover the curious Devil's Bathtub, a small rush of water that is said to be very hard to get out of if you fall in. If you are visiting in the winter, make a stop at Eagle's Rock near the visitor center.

Along your path, enjoy crossing unique bridges, including an A-frame one that leads to the upper rim trail. As you approach Old Man's

Cave, a fun little tunnel will guide you to its heart. Be sure to look for Sphinx Rock before you arrive.

If you're feeling adventurous, skip the stairs and venture towards Lower Falls. This path is lined with picturesque views, a beautiful bridge, and a challenging yet rewarding uphill tunnel that offers incredible perspectives from above the cave.

Wrap up your Old Man's Cave visit at the nature center, where you can pick up lovely souvenirs to remember your adventure. The center has been beautifully upgraded, providing both education and enjoyment. Nearby is the newly rebuilt lodge that was burned down in a fire, and it has other offerings.

The annual winter hike is on the Grandma Gatewood Trail. It takes you from Old Man's Cave to Cedar Falls and onto Ash Cave. The ice formations, hearty bean soup, cornbread, and steaming hot chocolate are worth the 6-mile hike.

Once you reach Cedar Falls, do not miss the stunning sight of the largest flowing waterfall in Hocking Hills. It is unique how it splits and then joins back together. Take the wooden steps down and keep an eye out for the hidden cascades along the way.

The path back has you following the river with unique bridges and views. Look for iron in the water, giving the water a brownish-red color. This is the halfway point during the winter hike. They feed you homemade bean soup from very large kettles, cornbread from the Millstone BBQ, and hot chocolate at the stop.

After refueling, you then embark on Ash Cave. It is easy to walk back to when not on this hike and you travel by car instead. It is more of a large recess, but it is quite interesting. The area around the cave and waterfall is sandy. Look for old 1800s or early inscriptions on the walls.

During the winter, sometimes the ice forms a cone from the bottom to the top. The upper rim is walked down into Ash Cave during the winter hike.

Ash Cave is the easiest hike. I have done the winter hike a handful of times until Covid hit. I did it with different people each time, with different levels of walking. I did it with my son and his friends. I have done it with just Jake. I have done it with my brother. He unfortunately almost broke his ankle when he slipped and fell. Debbie did it with me in the worst, rainy, yucky, cold mix weather. She completed it, but hates talking about it to this day.

Patches can be purchased commemorating your winter hike. I have seen some people wear clothing or scarves with patches from just about every year. I have seen people from Canada do the winter hike. The winter hike is done in all weather conditions and can have over 5,000 people attend on the scheduled day.

Just a short drive away is the John Glenn Observatory, a place I haven't visited yet. However, my friend told me that on certain nights, more than 300 visitors come to experience the wonders of the night sky.

The latest hiking adventures in the area beckon with the Whispering Cave and Hemlock Bridge Trail. Though the steps can be steep, they lead to delightful discoveries. There is a quaint cave, a picturesque waterfall, and a charming little bridge.

Conkle's Hollow is another gem, where I explored both the upper and lower rim trails. The upper rim offers a thrilling challenge, rewarding you with breathtaking views that plunge 200 feet into the chasm below. The lower rim trail ends at a waterfall set into the corner.

Rock House may take some effort to reach, but its unique allure makes it worthwhile. Legend has it that treasure lies buried nearby, adding an air of mystery. Just remember to bring a flashlight for safety in its shadowy depths.

Cantwell Cliffs posed a challenge for my son and me, and though we didn't complete the entire trail, we were eager to return and conquer it next time.

Rockbridge remains on my list, and while access seems tricky and the views modest, every trail is a new adventure waiting to unfold.

I've also yet to discover hidden gems like Balance Rock and Airplane Rock, tucked away from the usual paths.

Before you set off, take a scenic drive down Clear Creek Road in Rockbridge, just off Route 33. Keep an eye out for the intriguing Leaning Lena. Look into the legend of her haunting.

Further along the road is Written Rock. It is a section of very colorful rocks and some very old inscriptions as well. You will spot them easily along your route. It's a lovely drive, with a serene stream accompanying you, perfect for those who enjoy a peaceful atmosphere. They say it is a great place for trout fishing.

A fun little stop that most people miss is the pencil sharpener museum at the visitor's center just off of 33. It is a little shed with thousands of pencil sharpeners. You don't see that every day.

You won't want to miss the Moonville Tunnel Rail Trail, rumored to be haunted, adding a thrill to your adventure! Nearby, Lake Hope offers a unique delight. I think you can even hand-feed hummingbirds. There is also Jack Pine Glass Art Studio, where I've picked up some charming glass pumpkins. It's a wonderful spot that even offers glass-blowing classes for those feeling creative.

If you're planning a trip to Hocking Hills, you're in for a treat! Start your culinary journey at Millstone BBQ, where the cornbread muffins and tender ribs are simply irresistible. If you prefer a buffet experience, check out Old Dutch Restaurant near Walmart. It even includes a charming goat petting zoo nearby.

Just a short drive away, you'll find Grandma Faye's General Store and delightful shops like a windchime shop and a magical Christmas store. While in town, be sure to visit Hocking Hills Moonshine for fun, informative tours. The Hocking Hills Winery has a great atmosphere, even if the wine isn't your favorite.

One of the hidden gems is the washboard factory and museum, the oldest of its kind, where you can learn more about this unique craft and pick up a miniature washboard as a souvenir.

If you're visiting in winter, don't miss the stunning ice sculpture festival in Logan! Whether you're staying in a cozy cabin or planning a day trip filled with adventure, make your escape! Nature beckons, so lace up your hiking boots and get ready to explore the beauty that awaits you.

Embrace the adventure, my friend.

Hocking Hills – Leaning Leana – Cedar Falls

153. I Am A List Man

As the years go by, the weight of bills, relationships, work, and life can sometimes feel like a heavy anchor. However, I have discovered a simple yet powerful tool to navigate the chaos. I make lists.

Yes, I am a list man.

Imagine lying in bed, with a whirlwind of thoughts racing through your mind like a strobe light. In those moments, I grab a pen and paper or open a note app on my phone, pouring out all my responsibilities onto the page. Organizing those thoughts into priorities becomes my lifeline. I focus on what needs immediate attention, while also including my dreams and goals.

It is so easy to overwhelm myself with too much on the list, but with age comes wisdom. I've learned it's perfectly fine to tackle just a few items at a time.

Each task I complete feels like a small victory, a little boost that fuels my motivation. These little endorphins keep me going. Embrace the power of the list. Celebrate each crossed-off item as a step forward.

154. Feeding The Birds

Debbie and I are getting old. We find ourselves buying bird food when we should be buying other items. It seems to be more important. We are at the point that we can identify the various birds that come to our feeders by their appearance and songs. We get excited when one of the rarer birds lands and feeds upon the feeders.

In our backyard sanctuary, hummingbirds often find themselves in a playful chase, vying for space at the feeder instead of sharing. The male, with his brilliant plumage, seems to have a small harem of three or four lady friends. Meanwhile, flocks of sparrows gather in joyful chaos, feeding their young with tender mouth-to-mouth care, showcasing the beauty of nurturing.

The cardinals, ever a dynamic duo, flaunt their striking colors as they dart about together. You might catch a glimpse of a solitary robin, rummaging for worms on the ground, though they rarely visit feeders. Wrens and house finches bring unique shapes and songs to the mix, while nuthatches and tufted titmice delight in their acrobatic antics, often hanging upside down.

Goldfinches swoon over thistle, their vibrant yellow feathers attracting admiration. Sweet chickadees serenade the garden with their lovely melodies, while mourning doves coo softly in their inseparable pairs. Downy and red-bellied woodpeckers eagerly feast on suet, and Baltimore orioles, alongside catbirds, indulge in their favorite jelly treats.

Yet, amidst the harmony, a bold blue jay swoops in, scattering the others with its assertive presence. Though he may seem unfriendly, he adds a touch of excitement to the vibrant dance of life in our garden.

The rare guests in our backyard include the charming rose-breasted grosbeak, the vibrant bluebird, the striking red-headed woodpecker, and the impressive pileated woodpecker. We truly stop what we are doing if they stop by for a rare visit. While we are still hoping for an indigo bunting to drop by, the birdwatching is nothing short of magical.

However, this delightful feeding frenzy attracts some lively folks as well. Squirrels and chipmunks seem to multiply overnight, bounding joyfully around the feeders. At night, the playful opossums and raccoons join the fray, turning our space into a nighttime carnival.

Though they may dig up our hostas and tulips, their presence adds a layer of excitement to our garden. Embrace the delightful chaos! Every little hole tells a story, and every visitor, be it feathered or furry, enhances the beauty of our backyard.

It is still quite contentious to simply sit and watch the birds. It is usually better than any negative thing on television and your phone.

Now, we have even reached the point where I created a backyard bingo sheet. We get excited when we can cross one off the list before the other person playing the game can.

155. Skeeter Speeder

Skeeter Speeder was a speeder.

As Skeeter Speeder sped past Patty Petunia, Skeeter Speeder saw Patty Petunia in a perplexing situation.

Patty Petunia's shiny pearl-colored stiletto was stuck in a small precipice in the sidewalk.

Skeeter Speeder simply pulled Patty Petunia's stiletto off of Patty Petunia's pink sock.

Patty Patunia shoved off her other stiletto and simply smiled at Skeeter Speeder.

So too did Skeeter Speeder smirk a smile back as he sped off.

156. My Uncle And My Dad's Truck

I vividly recall the days when my dad owned a mid-sized Ford pickup truck. As a kid, climbing into that vehicle felt like an adventure itself. The way it sat high above the ground gave me a bigger view of the world around me. I can still picture those orange lights glowing around the cab and the unique sound echoing from the wheel well that my dad never bothered to fix. I loved being able to hear him approaching from a distance.

Eventually, I was relieved when he sold the truck. As he got older, I worried it might become too cumbersome for him. While many friends sought his help with that big truck, my uncle was the most daring.

One Christmas, without my mother's knowledge, he asked to borrow it, knowing Dad would never refuse anyone. Off went my uncle on a wild escapade down the old railroad tracks, which is now a bike path.

With a saw in hand, he sprinted onto a golf course and hacked off a pine tree, tossing it into the bed of the truck before speeding back down the tracks. It's astounding to think he got away with it, and even more so that my father allowed him to borrow the truck for that wild venture.

It's unbelievable my mother didn't unleash her wrath on either of them. This experience reminds us that sometimes, outrageous moments lead to the most cherished stories.

Life is full of surprises, and every crazy memory adds a unique chapter to our journey.

157. The Kids That Could Fly At Night

Picture a time, whether in the past, present, or distant future, when children aged 10 to 16 received a remarkable gift. This magical ability, fleeting and precious, would last only until they turned 16, and sometimes even less.

One night, as they slept, a gentle nudge woke them, drawing them to the window. Rising on their toes, they felt an urge to float effortlessly into the night sky. Initially, filled with trepidation, fear soon transformed into exhilaration as they glided above trees and rooftops, performing loops and playful dives.

As they soared through the starry air, curiosity sparked. They gazed into homes, watching families tucked in slumber, and felt drawn to the few who wandered the night. Yet, they soon discovered an enchanting truth: they were unseen, living out their midnight adventures invisible to the waking world.

Night after night, they embraced this gift, delighting in the freedom and wonder it brought. With no fatigue to hold them back, they awoke refreshed, though the memories of their flights remained hazy.

In time, they began to encounter other dreamers in the sky, sharing silent gestures that connected them with an encouraging wink or a gentle wave to join in their dance.

On one occasion, two boys observed an old man in a recliner, staring at the TV with a haunted expression. The older boy shot a glance at the younger one, silently saying, "Watch this." He approached a nearby table, cluttered with an empty glass, a half-eaten bowl of cereal, and a framed photo of the old man with a woman and child. With a gentle nudge, he knocked the picture off the table.

The old man, startled, reached for the photo, and as he looked at it, tears began to cascade down his cheeks. Inspired by the older boy's cue, the younger one then intentionally let the old man's phone slip from the edge of the recliner. The old man retrieved it, his hands trembling, as he dialed a number.

In that moment, two simple actions sparked a connection, reminding us all of the power of reaching out and the hope that can be reignited from even the smallest gestures.

One time, two girls were flying together when they spotted two men attempting to break into a car. With quick thinking, one of the girls toppled a hefty metal trash can, creating a thunderous crash that echoed through the street. The men exchanged glances but continued their attempt to break into the car.

Undeterred, the second girl sprang into action, bouncing from car to car until one of them set off a loud alarm. The sudden noise roused nearby neighbors, who began flicking on their lights. Seeing the commotion, the two men bolted in fear.

As a man was on the side of the bridge, consumed by despair and ready to leap, a determined older boy saw this and flew as hard as he could and tackled the man just as he began to jump. The older boy had a sense this was his last time flying and stared long and hard at the man before he flew away.

Inspired by the unexpected intervention, the man looked upwards into the night sky. With renewed resolve, he turned and made his way toward the welcoming glow of a hospital entrance.

In another instance, an old woman living in an assisted living apartment was sitting in her rocking chair in her quaint room. She was gazing at a picture of her late husband and herself.

A young girl observing this flew behind her and gently rubbed and caressed her shoulders in a tender embrace. The old woman instinctively reached up with her hand as if to grab a hand on her shoulder, and a sense of peace enveloped her. With a gentle sigh, she surrendered to the warmth of the moment, drifting off into a comforting sleep.

The children would reach an age when they would no longer wake up at night and fly. Their memories would turn into only dreams and fade.

For some, their helpful ways led to a life in which they served society in many different capacities. Some rose to become compassionate leaders, advocating for the voiceless, while others dedicated themselves to healing, protecting, and uplifting their communities. Each choice they made echoed the kindness they once were given as a gift.

When you feel an unexpected surge of comfort or guidance, know that it just might be a guardian angel at your side, maybe it is one of these gifted children.

158. Reverand Jones

I had a dream that wove together people from my past with the present. Dreams often come with their own unique quirks that seem nonsensical at the time. It never ceases to amaze me how I can recall fragments of these dreams upon waking. Inspired by this experience, I transformed my dream into a short story, playfully altering some facts and names along the way.

As I strolled into Walmart on that particular day, I found myself pondering the passage of time. Many of my family and friends had either moved on or left this world, leaving me in a quiet solitude that carried no weight of loneliness. I felt settled and at ease, focused on gathering a few essentials for the week: milk, orange juice, bread, cereal, and perhaps some ground beef for a burger or two.

With my shopping cart in tow, I turned a corner and nearly bumped into Tony, an old classmate from high school. We had shared a close bond during our sports days, but life had nudged us apart since graduation. He had aged, yet his eyes still sparkled with that familiar, attentive glimmer, as if he had always been tuned into our shared moments.

"Hi Tony! What brings you back to town?" I asked, pleased to see a familiar face.

He smiled warmly and replied, "I'm here with Reverend Jones."

Reverend Jones was more than just a childhood friend. He was a kind soul who lived just a few houses away. Our summers were filled with laughter and adventure, as we played for hours in the backyards and fields nearby. Now, he has blossomed into a well-respected religious leader, amassing a devoted following and becoming something of a celebrity in the faith community.

As the doors of the modest Walmart swung open, a tall, elderly man stepped inside, his distinguished gray hair and lined face telling a story of wisdom and experience. He wore a well-tailored suit that showed dignity without being flamboyant, topped off with a cherished brown fedora that hinted at his baldness. Accompanying him were three individuals, each playing their part as escorts and a subtle line of protection.

Leading the group was a man in a simple black suit, his urgency setting a purposeful tone. Behind him lingered another man, solemn and slightly disheveled, his unbuttoned coat reflecting a deeper contemplation. Beside the reverend stood a poised woman, elegantly dressed in a black skirt and blouse, dark sunglasses shielding her gaze, radiating both strength and grace as she carried a black notebook portfolio.

I turned back my gaze to Reverend Jones, and in that instant, our eyes locked. His gaze was a silent testament to his sorrows, reflecting deep pain and the burden of the world he carried. He furrowed his brow, squinting slightly as he spoke, "I feel as if I should know you."

Before Tony or his companions could interject, I stepped closer and leaned in to whisper in his ear. "Transport yourself back to your childhood," I began softly. "To a time when you had no worries." He looked surprised but intrigued, urging me to go on.

"Remember the endless afternoons spent playing in our backyards and fields, throwing a baseball, kicking a football, and exploring all kinds of games?" A flicker of recognition crossed his face, and a smile began to form. "Think about climbing trees, swimming, and splashing in the creek. We would go sledding down snowy hills, lost in laughter for hours. We were just friends enjoying life."

As he stared into my eyes, he suddenly asked, "Georgie, is that really you?"

I nodded, "Yes, Bobbie, it's me."

In that moment, his once-cloudy gaze cleared, and a single tear rolled down his cheek.

"I've been so focused on work that I forgot what it felt like to be carefree," he confessed. "Oh, to be young again."

I replied earnestly, "Though we may be older, and the world's pressures weigh on us, we can always choose to feel young at heart when we cherish our friendships." He wrapped his arms around me tightly, and I smiled back at Tony, whose eyes glistened with emotion and a large, warm smile upon his face. The spark of our shared joy was not lost, instead, it was ready to ignite once more.

Reverend Jones turned to his team with a spark in his eyes. "Forget the food. We're here to bring joy to the kids with toys." He paused to shake my hand warmly, gratitude radiating from him. "Thank you, my dear friend."

With that, he grabbed a cart and charged into the store.

"Let's get to work, everyone." His enthusiasm was contagious, and as they rushed forward, I watched with a warm smile, filled with hope for the magic they were about to create.

159. The Fly And His Buddy

Fly number one darted into the house, his tiny wings buzzing with urgency. He was on a mission: find food! After flitting from room to room, he met fly number two in the living room.

"Hey, how long have you been here?" fly number one asked.

"Not long," replied fly number two. "Just searching for food. I think the kitchen is that way, but I'm a bit scared to go in there."

"Don't worry! I'll check it out and come back," fly number one reassured him, his excitement palpable.

With a determined buzz, he zipped into the kitchen and spotted a tantalizing plate of food. The aroma was irresistible! He turned and entered back into the living room to guide his friend.

"Hey, buddy, I found it, right this way!" he said and then motioned toward the kitchen.

Without hesitation, fly number two bolted into the kitchen, enthusiasm lighting his tiny eyes. But then, *'Smack!'* echoed through the air.

Heart racing but driven by hunger, fly number one braced himself and entered the kitchen. Yet, just as quickly, he too met the same fate. *'Smack!'*

Though their adventure ended abruptly, their brief journey was a testament to their courage and camaraderie. The thrill of the chase is what made it all worthwhile! Remember, sometimes taking risks for what we desire leads to unexpected lessons. Keep buzzing and exploring, as every experience helps you grow.

160. It Started Off As A Friendly Gesture

It started off as a friendly gesture. A gesture, too, which would change Walter's world. Walter was widowed, retired, and calm and content in his modest home. Walter truly found solace tending his modest yard. Each trim, each weed pulled was a reflection of his pride, and his neighbors often offered cheerful compliments as they passed by.

Neighbors would commonly yell out while on a walk, "Looks nice, Walter, keep up the good work." Walter would instantly boast a strong smile and wave quietly back, not saying a word, and then contently go back to his work.

Janet, the next-door neighbor's little girl, would often watch Walter from her backyard and see Walter in his yard diligently working. She would run into her house and come back with a crayon drawing of Walter working in his yard surrounded by whimsical flowers, bushes, and trees. Each piece captured the joy of his work, complete with his trademark smile and wave.

As time went on, her art evolved from crayons to colored pencils and even watercolor, yet the theme remained the same. At just 15, Janet carried an air of maturity beyond her years.

One sunny afternoon, while Walter was busy tending to his yard, he caught snippets of a conversation from the neighboring yard.

"I'm so sorry, Janet. I can't help it that they called me into work. You know I must go in as they need me, and we sure could use the extra cash." Walter stopped what he was doing and coughed lightly to make his presence known.

"Walter, we are in such a jam." Walter leaned over the fence. "Janet has won two extraordinary tickets to see her favorite performers, Zeek and the Soft Tones." Walter continued to listen. "The problem is that I got called in to go to work." His voice wavered, nearly breaking, he continued, "All I want to do is to let her experience something special. Times have been so tough lately, ever since. . ." He paused as he could not get the words out.

Walter spoke simply and calmly, "I understand, Jeff, Nancy was a wonderful mother. If it helps, I can take Janet to the concert."

"Oh, Walter, I can't thank you enough," Jeff exclaimed, relief washing over him. In an instant, Janet dashed to the fence, her tall frame glowing with appreciation. She threw her arms around Walter, planting a gentle kiss on his cheek. Walter felt his cheeks warm as a smile spread across his face, feeling proud to uplift Janet's spirits.

Walter hesitated for a moment, unsure of what to wear to the concert. After some thought, he settled on a comfortable pair of khakis, loafers, a soft orange polo shirt, and his beloved light tan jacket that was the last birthday gift from his late wife. He considered wearing a hat but decided against it, fearing it might get knocked off in the excitement of the crowd.

As he pulled into the driveway, Janet burst through the door before he could even beep the horn. She looked radiant, sporting distressed blue jeans with a trendy hole at the thigh and a vibrant mosaic shirt that seemed to spring from an art gallery. Her long, dark hair flowed gracefully, and Walter couldn't help but think how much she resembled her mother.

"You look more and more like your mother each day," he said, and she beamed at the compliment.

"I hope you don't mind, but the tickets I won are for front row seats, and we won't have actual seats!" Janet said, her eyes sparkling with excitement.

For a moment, uncertainty flickered in Walter's mind, but he pushed it aside. "We'll be just fine," he encouraged, ready to embrace the adventure ahead.

As they stepped into the concert venue, Walter couldn't help but feel the buzz of excitement from the crowd. Many attendees sported vibrant, artsy shirts, which made him rethink his choice of jacket over something more colorful. They settled in just off-center to the left of the stage.

Janet eagerly turned to him, her eyes beaming, "This is a great spot. It's going to be amazing!"

Walter returned her smile, taking in the spectacle—the colorful lights, the eager faces. Leaning closer, Janet whispered, "Pay attention to the lyrics; they might resonate with you like they did with me." He absorbed her words as the crowd's energy swelled, slowly transforming into a rhythmic chant of "Zeek, Zeek, Zeek."

A man stepped to the mic announcing, "Ladies and gentlemen, I present to you Zeek and the Soft Tones!" The crowd erupted in cheers as each band member took the stage, instruments in hand, greeting everyone warmly before easing into a gentle melody. Then, with a flurry of beats, the drummer set the stage for Zeek, who entered dressed in black jeans and a vibrant mosaic shirt, decked in unique handmade jewelry.

Walter watched as Zeek worked his way around each area of the stage, waving at the crowd, then Zeek began to sing. He glanced at Janet and noticed a tear glistening in her eye, and it clicked; this moment was profoundly meaningful for her. As the performance unfolded, Walter leaned in to listen closely. The lyrics were light and kind, yet they carried a powerful connection to nature that struck a chord within him.

Turning to Janet, he said, "I get it now." Her smile radiated joy. The atmosphere grew electric as the crowd chimed in, singing, swaying, and jumping along, fully immersed in the magic of the moment. And then, just as the night reached its peak, something extraordinary happened.

Zeek was lost in the rhythm of his performance, dancing across the stage with infectious energy. Suddenly, he lost his footing near the edge of the stage and began to fall off the stage. But Walter, ever vigilant, dashed forward, weaving past two startled young girls to catch Zeek just before disaster struck.

He would have really been seriously injured from the fall if it were not for Walter's quick actions. With a steady hand, Walter helped him to the ground, checking in with genuine concern.

"Are you okay?"

Zeek beamed up at him, "My dear man, I can't thank you enough. I am fine. I must finish the show for my fans, but will you meet me in my dressing room after the show?"

Walter nodded enthusiastically.

Zeek steadied himself and spoke to his staff. He pointed to Walter as Walter was now hugging Janet to reassure her that Zeek was ok.

Returning to the spotlight, Zeek took the microphone with a confident grin. "Sorry, folks, I slipped. I am fine, thanks to this man who has the speed of a gazelle and the agility of a white tail-ed deer."

The audience erupted in applause, the energy soaring as the performance and applause reached a triumphant crescendo. Walter and Janet were guided to a side door, traversing a long hallway until they reached a vibrant red door. Janet buzzed with excitement as they knocked and were invited in.

Inside, a delightful spread awaited them, filled with tables adorned with an array of sandwiches, a tempting cheese platter, juices, and bottled water. Groups chatted comfortably, some engaging with representatives from the venue. The atmosphere felt light and inviting.

In the corner, a purple couch caught their attention. There sat Zeek, diligently signing papers for a few people. Upon noticing Walter and Janet, his face lit up, and he beckoned them over.

"Come, have a seat," he urged with warmth.

Janet plopped down beside him, her eyes sparkling like full moons. Walter settled in at the edge, feeling a swell of gratitude. "Thanks for a fantastic performance," he said. "I hadn't heard your music before today." He explained how he had simply been helping a good neighbor. Janet beamed and gave Walter a supportive hug.

Suddenly, something caught Walter's eye—a simple lamp alongside a hand-drawn black and white sketch on the table. Intrigued, he asked, "Where did this come from?"

"It's a cherished gift from a fan," Zeek replied cheerfully. "I encouraged them to share their favorite nature scenes with me. This one touched my heart deeply, so I gifted the artist two tickets to the show."

Walter inspected the sketch closely, skepticism flickering. "This looks just like my garden."

Both men exclaimed in unison, "Who drew this?"

With a playful grin, Janet raised her hand. "That would be me."

Laughter erupted as they shared stories. Zeek expressed how the cheerful image of a man waving in a beautiful garden resonated deeply with him. He articulated how nature profoundly influenced his music and how this sketch helped bridge his thoughts to his melodies.

"Would it be possible for me to visit your garden?" Zeek asked eagerly.

"Of course," Walter replied, a smile spreading across his face. In that moment, they planted the seeds of a promising friendship, bound by creativity and shared passion.

Zeek did visit Walter in his yard. They had a long talk and ignited a beautiful friendship. Their long talks bloomed into heartfelt conversations that flowed through texts, calls, and postcards, each exchange weaving them closer together. Zeek asked Janet to create a new sketch, capturing a tender moment of him and Walter in the garden. The artwork became the cover of his next album, and its success was monumental as the music resonated with people far and wide, soaring to the top of the charts.

Recognizing the burden of Janet's father's financial struggles, Zeek stepped in with generosity, ensuring she could pursue her college dreams. Janet blossomed into a remarkable artist, and with her newfound success, she lovingly supported her father. Their bond with Zeek and Walter grew deeper, and they remained each other's greatest friends through thick and thin.

At every concert, Zeek honored their friendship by showcasing Janet's artwork. Whether it was on album covers, as vibrant backdrops, or framed in his dressing room, constantly reminding him of their shared journey.

This powerful legacy of creativity and camaraderie continued to inspire not only them but everyone around them, proving that genuine connections can light the way to success and happiness.

161. Crunch, Crunch, Crunch As I Walk Along.

Crunch, crunch, crunch as I walk along.

Red, orange, yellow, brown.

Nature paints its picture in **autumn's** glory.

From a distance, its colors blend in bright brilliance.

Up close, the details become fragmented and pixelated.

Falling leaves are bringing an end.

Old man, **winter** is around the corner.

He seeks out those not prepared for him.

I become tired more quickly in the **cold** and **darkness.**

I try to admire the colors before they are all gone.

While the **wind** will replace the **leaves,** the **cold** will replace the warmth.

Crunch, crunch, crunch as I walk along.

162. I Walked In The Rain Today

I walked in the rain today, and it was not bad.

The rain and the wind did not make me sad.

I looked at the wet leaves that I walked across.

The time that I had with nature was not a loss.

A rain jacket and waterproof shoes was all I needed.

The sense of fall had been seeded.

163. The Morning Wave

Every morning, as I step out into the fresh air, I find myself crossing paths with familiar faces. A simple wave, a warm smile, or a cheerful "good morning" becomes my daily ritual. Often, I don't receive a greeting back. Maybe they are lost in thought or simply caught up in their routine. Yet, I believe that a little gesture can make a big difference.

Imagine the power of that fleeting moment, a shared connection that briefly lightens their day. Even if my greeting doesn't spark an immediate response, it may inspire them to pass on the kindness to someone else.

We all carry the potential to spread joy in small ways. If each of us commits to those little acts of friendliness, we can create a ripple effect, transforming our world into a brighter, more uplifting place.

Keep waving, smiling, and saying hello. Who knows? That morning wave might just change someone's day, and the world, one friendly gesture at a time.

164. Merry Christmas, Mr. Lawrence

I often find myself captivated by new discoveries. When I stumble upon something intriguing, my curiosity sparks a deeper exploration, drawing me further into a fascinating world. One year, while searching for new music, I encountered a soft, enchanting melody played on an instrument that felt both familiar and foreign. I wondered if it was a xylophone or perhaps chimes. My investigation led me to the song's title: "Carrying You." It struck a chord of nostalgia as I realized I had heard it before.

As it turned out, my son and I adore the artistic magic of Studio Ghibli films, renowned for their stunning animation and rich storylines. "Carrying You" belongs to "Castle in the Sky," one of those beloved creations.

I started exploring various renditions of the song, captivated by a choir's harmony and a delicate piano arrangement. But then, I stumbled upon the enchanting sounds of a steel tongue drum and kalimba. This was the sound that first had drawn me in. It was pure magic, and I couldn't get enough. I decided to invest in a few compact steel tongue drums as gifts for friends and family, while also treating myself. The kalimba, with its wooden body and playful metal strips, beckoned to me, so I grabbed one for my son as well. Learning to play that song was a delightful adventure, and perfection did not matter to me. What truly filled me with joy was the serene calm that washed over me each time I played.

As I continued my kalimba journey, I searched for easy Christmas songs and stumbled upon "Merry Christmas Mr. Lawrence." Intrigued, I wondered what this song was all about. The first time I played it, I was captivated; the music transported me somewhere else entirely.

That year, I played it a few times during Christmas, content to know it featured David Bowie in its film. The following year, while creating my Christmas playlists for my car, the song resurfaced, prompting me to dig deeper. I discovered it was linked to two novels: The Seed and the Sower and The Night of the New Moon. I learned the song's true title was "Forbidden Colours," composed by the talented Ryuichi Sakamoto, who not only scored the film but also starred in it.

Sadly, Ryuichi had passed away the year before I began this exploration, along with Bowie a few years before that, yet my curiosity only grew. I watched various performances, including one featuring a piano that survived the Hiroshima bombings, a Hibaku piano. This particular piano had a heartbreaking history, owned by a 16-year-old girl who perished a day after the bombing. Her parents, forever changed, never played it again. These pianos now serve as powerful symbols of peace and resilience.

I finally watched the film on a really poor free version with subtitles, assisting my understanding. My son, seeing my frustration, found it on Blu-ray for me, making it much more pleasing to watch. My son also gifted me the two books, which I read for an even greater understanding of it all. While I won't spoil the plot, I came away realizing that in war, there are no winners, only shared sorrow.

I recently learned that Tom Conti, another actor from the movie, has a daughter named Nina Conti. She's an incredibly talented ventriloquist and comedian whom I enjoy watching on YouTube. It is amazing how interconnected our world is.

As I explored more captivating music, I stumbled upon "Holiday for Strings," a charming piece from 1944 by David Rose. My curiosity only deepened when I discovered he also composed "The Stripper" in 1962. It is a striking contrast between a Christmas classic and a song often heard at weddings and strip clubs.

Delving into his life, I learned he had brief marriages to Martha Raye and Judy Garland, the star from "The Wizard of Oz," who faced tremendous challenges during their union. He later married Betty Bartholomew and welcomed two daughters. Beyond his musical legacy, Rose was a passionate live steam hobbyist, with a delightful backyard railroad that sparked my imagination.

It inspired me to dream about creating a train display for my neighbors this Christmas. While I may only have a modest budget for lights and decorations, the thought of a whimsical train winding through the yard brings joy to my heart.

All of this inspiration stemmed from a single song I heard. It opened the door to a world of ideas, insights, and new discoveries.

165. It Could All Be Gone Tomorrow

Take a walk with nature today, for

It could all be gone tomorrow.

Take the chance to see and experience new things in life, for

It could all be gone tomorrow.

Do not procrastinate with mundane things that prevent you from doing great things, for

It could all be gone tomorrow.

Create something grand today, for

It could all be gone tomorrow.

See the sun, the ocean. Hear the wind, the birds. Feel the breeze, the snow, and the rain, for

It could all be gone tomorrow.

Tell that special someone you love them, for

It could be all gone tomorrow.

166. Boom, I Am Back At The Time Clock

Boom, I am back at the time clock.

I recognize that aging brings inevitable changes. Recently, I was standing at the time clock waiting to punch in. It hit me hard all at once. It seemed like I had just been there an hour ago. As I get older, time moves much faster. I do the same routine pretty much every day. It sometimes feels like I am in a loop. There just seems to be never enough time to do the extra things you wish to accomplish in the day. I try to do one little additional thing out of the normal routine, but it still seems I can never fully finish it in time.

Boom, I am back at the time clock. I try to get extra sleep, go to bed early, and find myself waking up early. There I am getting ready for the day.

Boom, I am back at the time clock. How do we slow time? Do we engage ourselves in something that takes our mind off our routine? Do we sleep more? Do we spend more time with friends and family?

Boom, I am back at the time clock. Time may not really change. I shall try to find something pleasant and cheerful to take my mind off the time.

Boom, I am back at the time clock.

167. The Stick-Shift Adventure For A Live Christmas Tree

When I was quite young, and before I learned of the dangers of a live Christmas tree, I wanted to get my own live Christmas tree. Normally, I would trudge off with my father and sometimes my brother to a tree farm out away from the city. I was always crunched in the middle of the seat, and it was always uncomfortable.

My father wanted to pick the first tree he saw, have someone cut it, throw it in the back of the truck, and head home. My brother and I took our time. We bypassed all other types of trees and only looked at Scotch pines. Next, we looked for the right height. Then we looked for a tree that seemed to have three good sides. The most important part we considered was the stump. It had to be fairly straight. We could always see ourselves cutting away and refining it once we were home to get it just right.

At some tree farms, you would find a shaker that vibrated the trees, shaking off the dead needles. But even with this helpful machine, it might feel like those pesky pine needles stuck around forever, lingering on the carpet for days.

Once, while at work, a guy offered me a deal on a Christmas tree from his second job at a tree stand. We couldn't resist and bought one. However, it wilted within a week, despite our diligent watering, shedding its needles all over the carpet.

Feeling a bit defeated, I decided to embark on my own adventure that year. I set out to find the perfect tree for my parents and one for my cozy apartment.

I was going to use my father's pick-up truck. It was a stick-shift. When one does not normally drive a stick shift, it can be quite interesting. The start is always the most "fun" as you slowly release the clutch and press the accelerator at the right pressure. It was always a delicate dance with your feet. If you do not do it right, it can stall out. My biggest concern was stopping at a busy intersection of the dreaded hill. It may not have been fear at the time, but it sure was some great apprehension I felt.

As I left my parents' home, I chose the back roads, gaining confidence with each turn. When I finally faced a bustling highway intersection, I took a deep breath. To my relief, the coast was clear, and I smoothly navigated through without stalling.

My confidence was grand, and I made it to the tree farm. I was able to secure two trees that day. I remember that I paid top dollar for what would probably be the last time I would ever buy a live Christmas Tree. I think it was a whopping $13.00 each. As of now, though, I see the prices are averaging between $80 to $100. That is quite a difference over the years. They were both in the bed of the truck, and I was on my way back home. I was alone, but brimming with joy. I was proud of myself for overcoming my fear, and I had the biggest smile on my face as I played Christmas songs on the radio, filling me with holiday cheer.

I made it back to my parents' home and pulled in the driveway. I think my parents were relieved I didn't crash. They were pleased with the tree I got them, and I set it right up.

Then I had to set oof across town to take my tree to my apartment. I soon found myself stopped on a hill. A car meandered by while another inched ever so close behind me. Panic flickered through my mind as I feared I might roll back into that waiting vehicle.

Then, I took a deep breath and focused on mastering the clutch and gas. With determination and poise, I regained control and moved forward, surviving once again.

The tree was put up, and the truck was taken back. I still remember the smell of a fresh-cut Christmas tree. I remember as well all the pine needles to sweep up and the inevitable task of hauling the tree outside when the season ended.

Joining the fire department opened my eyes to the hidden dangers of a live Christmas tree and how quickly it can turn into a raging fire.

That realization changed my holiday traditions for good. Yet, I cherish the memory of my last solo journey in the truck during Christmas. It filled me with a sense of adventure and joy.

168. The Bench

Sebastian loved to walk around the lake when he had the opportunity. The shimmering water, the chirping birds, the sturdy trees, the sunlight in the open blue skies, and the winding path all gave him a sense of blissful calmness.

On one of these strolls, he noticed an elder man in a sharp black suit and tie with a black hat, sitting upon a bench. Sebastian had passed this bench several times and never gave it a second thought.

But today, something pulled him to look at the man and the bench. He felt something inside him to turn towards the bench and the man sitting there.

The elderly man wore a warm, inviting smile that radiated joy, and in that moment, Sebastian felt a gentle nudge from within.

Compelled by curiosity and an instinctual pull, he decided to pause and take a seat beside the man, ready to discover what this unexpected encounter would bring.

 As Sebastian settled into the bench, the man beside him turned and said, "Hi, Sebastian, I'm Tony." A look of confusion crossed Sebastian's face as he wondered how this stranger knew his name.

A wave of uneasiness washed over him. "Don't worry," Tony reassured him. "You're sitting on a magical bench." Sebastian felt an odd sense of calm wash over him. There was an undeniable truth in Tony's words. The fear began to lift, replaced by a spark of curiosity about the wonders that lay ahead.

"Please explain," Sebastian asked, curiosity lighting up his eyes. Tony leaned closer; his voice was low but filled with excitement. "I was approached the same way," he began. "You'll have 24 hours to assist someone in need, and this bench will guide you to them." He pressed on, "You'll see when the time comes. We don't have much time left. Trust yourself, as you will know what to do and when it is right." Sebastian nodded, absorbing the weight of his words.

"When your time is up, return to this bench," Tony instructed. With a warm smile, he extended his hand. "Good luck, have fun, and enjoy this incredible gift." He gave Sebastian a reassuring pat on the shoulder before rising and walking away, leaving Sebastian charged with promise and possibility.

Sebastian watched as Tony disappeared around a bend in the path. Sitting on the magical bench, he felt a flurry of images dance before him. They were brief glimpses of all kinds of people.

At first, their faces eluded him, but soon the visions slowed, revealing a middle-aged man in a dark, hooded jacket. In that moment, clarity struck him, and he figured out that this was the person he was meant to help. Though uncertainty loomed about how to aid him, Sebastian locked onto the man's image in his mind.

Rising from the bench, he set off with purpose, the vision of the man by a tombstone guiding him. Recognition sparked him as he knew that cemetery well. With a quickened pace, he hurried in that direction, ready to be the light for someone in need.

It was not far from the lake, and Sebastian knew he could be there in no time. He entered the cemetery and was quickly drawn to an area he knew well. He then came across the man in his visions. He was getting up and touched his hand to his lips and back to the tombstone.

Just as he began to turn away, Sebastian approached him with a surge of clarity guiding his words. "Hello, Arthur, my name is Sebastian," he introduced himself with a friendly smile. Arthur squinted his eyes with a curious look. "Who are you? And how do you know my name?"

Sebastian leaned in slightly, his voice warm. "I am a friend, and I was given a special gift to help you."

Sebastian looked at Arthur, his expression filled with understanding. "I know how deeply you loved Abbey, and I can only imagine how difficult it is to accept her loss," he began gently. "But I truly believe she would want you to join the race tomorrow." It was a 5k run that supported cancer patients and their families. Sebastian continued, "She would have been thrilled to see you cross that finish line." He placed a reassuring hand on Arthur's shoulder. "I'll be right there with you, not just at the end, but running beside you, carrying her spirit in our hearts. Give me a moment to grab my things, and I'll be back at your home before you know it."

As Sebastian spoke, a sense of calm settled over Arthur, like a whisper in the wind, and it felt like a confirmation that this was the right path, and everything would be okay.

Sebastian raced home with his mind set on a singular purpose. He knew what to grab and soon found himself knocking on a door to a quaint home nearby.

Arthur welcomed him in, and then he began to share his beautiful story of his love for Abbey. They first met while running in 5k events, their bond blossoming alongside their shared passion.

They married, filled their lovely home with laughter, but then cancer cast a dark shadow over their lives. Tomorrow's race, once a celebration of their journey, now felt unbearably heavy without her. Abbey had planned to be at the finish line.

"I can't run anymore," Arthur said, his voice thick with deep sorrow.

Sebastian stepped closer, determination lighting his eyes, "Yes, you can. You will run and you will run for Abbey. Her spirit will be with you every step of the way, and I'll be right there by your side the whole way."

As the last rays of sunlight slipped away, they savored a simple pasta dinner, a meal that would fuel them up for the run tomorrow. As the evening settled in, Sebastian made his way to the couch. With a warm smile, Arthur gave him a blanket and said that it was Abbey's favorite.

As dawn broke the next morning, Arthur felt a flutter of nerves churning in his stomach. After sharing a simple breakfast filled with quiet anticipation, they laced up their shoes and stepped outside, ready for the walk to the race event. Side by side, Sebastian offered him a bright smile, his presence soothing his anxiety.

As they reached the starting line, Sebastian, having just secured a late entry, proudly flashed his running bib at Arthur. With a playful grin, he suddenly snatched Arthur's bib before he could fasten it and pulled a marker from his pocket. In bold letters, he wrote "For Abbey" on the corner. Arthur's eyes brightened at the sight, the simple message igniting a spark of motivation.

As the clock ticked down, a wave of runners surged around the starting line, their energy igniting the air with nervous excitement. Sebastian turned to Arthur, hope glimmering in his eyes.

"Do you feel her with us?" he asked. Arthur's smile widened, the warmth of a cherished memory touching his heart, as tears filled his eyes.

As the bell rang, a wave of excitement surged through the crowd, and runners took off, beaming with energy. Sebastian stayed right beside Arthur, pointing out heartfelt messages displayed on runners' shirts: "For Dawn," "For Mom," "Fight On," "Cancer Sucks," "Stay Brave," "Together We Can." With each phrase, Arthur felt a sense of camaraderie, realizing he wasn't alone in this battle.

The smiles and determination around him reminded him that every step was a tribute to resilience, hope, and the shared strength of all those fighting their own battles.

As they reached the halfway mark, a spectator's sign caught Arthur's eye—bold letters spelling out "LOVE." It was a simple yet profound message. With a bright smile, Arthur turned to Sebastian and gave him a thumbs-up. It was a small gesture, but it spoke volumes, reminding them both of the powerful support surrounding them. Together, they pressed onward, spirits lifted.

As they approached the imposing hill, exhaustion and fatigue hit Arthur like a brick wall. "I can't go on, it's too hard," Arthur said with a heavy voice. But Sebastian would not let him and replied, "You can do this, Arthur. I can almost hear her voice calling you from the top." Arthur pulled his head up and dug in. "Climb this hill for her," shouted Sebastian. As they reached the summit of the hill, a surge of energy rushed through Arthur, fueled by his love for Abbey. Peering ahead, he spotted the finish line glimmering in the distance. Sebastian slowed slightly, a grin spreading across his face. "Now it's your turn, Arthur. Run hard, finish strong. This time, do it for yourself."

Arthur crossed the finish line, a surge of happiness radiating through him as the adrenaline and endorphins from completing such a formidable challenge coursed through his veins.

He turned to Sebastian, gratitude lighting up his face. "Thank you, my friend. How long have you been running?"

"Never more than a block or two," Sebastian replied with a smile. "But somehow, I kept pace with you. I think something or someone guided me." With a serious yet warm tone, Sebastian added, "My time here is short, but remember this: live the rest of your life strong and hard, and you'll be just fine." They exchanged a firm handshake and phone numbers, their connection lingering in the air as they parted ways, each ready to chase their own paths forward.

Sebastian found himself back at the magical bench, his spirit soaring with the brightest smile he'd ever worn. Just then, a small elderly woman approached, her eyes filled with bewilderment as she settled beside him. He turned to greet her, catching sight of Tony in the distance, standing by a tree. With a beaming smile and thumbs-up, Tony tipped his hat, encouraging him on.

"Hello, Beatrice. My name is Sebastian," he said, and with that, the bench's magic continued.

The bench

169. A Series Of Hills Leading To The Pinnacle Of A Mountain

A man stood before a series of hills leading to the pinnacle of a mountain. Each one was marked by familiar words: obligations, responsibilities, work, family, friends, and finances. As he began his ascent, I noticed the signs of struggle etched on his weathered face, the winds of time whispering past him, and the rain of sorrow soaking his journey. Each step was heavy, the weight of the world resting upon his shoulders.

Yet, he pressed on. Along his path, he encountered obstacles. There were people who tried to push him back, but there were also those who offered a helping hand or a warm smile. His gaze remained fixed on a hill near the summit, boldly inscribed with the word "Hope."

I could see that deep within, he found it within himself to climb higher, to reach for the pinnacle of the mountain. I may never know if he reached his destination, but what truly matters is that he kept trying. In that moment, as I last looked upon him, he was still climbing. And so, too, can we all find the courage to keep moving forward in our own journeys.

170. "Ah, Go Fly A Kite"

When I was a kid, I often heard people say, "Go fly a kite," as a way of brushing someone off. But I always thought, why not? Flying a kite is a beautiful adventure. I remember the thrill of launching all sorts of kites.

Some were made of bright paper, brown shopping bags, and others of colorful plastic. The simpler ones needed a ragged tail to catch the wind just right. Starting the flight was always an escapade.

We didn't know about aerodynamics; we just chased the wind, running as fast as our little legs could carry us while the kite soared higher. Sometimes, we ventured too close to power lines and trees, but that only added to the excitement.

We would get our kites so high up in the air that we would attach fishing line to reel them back in. And those looping stunt kites? They usually met an early demise. My favorite was the box kite, as it flew effortlessly, needing no tail, capturing the wind and our imaginations.

Years later, on vacation in Myrtle Beach, I wandered into a kite shop. The kites were magnificent, but much more advanced than what I had as a child. Though the prices made me pause, the urge to reignite those carefree days lingered in my heart.

So, the next time you hear someone say, "Go fly a kite," take that as a reminder of the joy and freedom found in simplicity. Embrace your inner child. Go on, buy a kite and let it soar, and your spirit will soar with it.

171. The Skyro

I was never a Frisbee enthusiast, but I stumbled upon a unique version of one back in about 190. It was a Skyro frisbee. With my friends, we headed out to the open field behind our high school, or we would head over to the college and their open fields. We were eager to try out this disc that held the impressive world record of 242.5 yards, nearly two and a half football field lengths.

We started off close together, learning how to send it soaring straight. The key was to get a perfect spin, and if you nailed it, that disc would glide for what felt like forever. You either grabbed it as it came to you, or you ran your hand through the middle of it, as it was a very thin disc with a large open center. Chasing it down was the true workout, though.

As time passed, I noticed fewer young people enjoying such outdoor activities as this. It seems today's youth often trade the thrill of the chase of a frisbee for the comfort of screens. I can only imagine the spark of joy that could inspire them just as it did for us. That old Skyro might be long gone. Maybe it is a good thing, as this old body would have considerable difficulty chasing it down these days. Yet, the spirit of play is still timeless.

172. Still Thankful

I am thankful that I have learned to let go of the past, embracing its lessons instead. I look to the future with hope, driven by my goals that motivate me to push through all the negativity that comes my way.

Each moment today is precious, and though it will fade away, I choose to honor it with thankfulness, smiles, and laughter.

173. It Was Just A Hill

A young man embarked on a quest for answers, ascending a mountain in search of wisdom. At the base of the mountain, he looked up and discovered that the mountain was merely a large hill. "It's just a hill," he thought, yet curiosity propelled him forward.

At the summit of the hill, he spotted what looked like a towering tall, old figure of a wise man with a massive, long beard. As he approached, he realized it was merely the shadow of an old man sitting calmly, his beard draped across his lap. "It was just his shadow," he thought.

"I seek answers to life's questions," he said to the old man, who gestured towards an intimidating stack of books nearby. Panic momentarily gripped the young man at the thought of reading them all. Yet, instead of overwhelming him, the old man handed him a single, simple book. "It's just one book," he reassured himself, though doubt lingered.

Sensing his hesitation, the old man pointed to a feather marking a particular page. "It's only one page," the young man thought, a faint smile forming. The young man began to read aloud: "The greatest achievement comes when one learns to overcome daunting tasks by breaking them down into manageable steps. Upon a closer examination, one can reveal that even the most intimidating challenges can be simplified. Embrace the process, and the path will become clearer."

Reflecting on his climb, the young man realized, "I tackled each step one at a time. With every step, my perspective shifted, and I began to see what was really in front of me. It was just a hill."

The old man smiled and asked, "Who is the wise man now?"

174. It Wasn't Meant To Be

I ran a race and came in fourth. The guy right in front of me finished 3rd.

It wasn't meant to be.

That's ok, I ran well for not having run in a race in a long time. I didn't blow my knee out. He deserved the 3rd place finish.

I went to the casino, and the guy right next to me won a lot of money, and I did not.

It wasn't meant to be.

I looked at what the guy was betting per spin versus my bet and realized his big win may not have even covered what he put in the machines. I know my limits and how to have fun on my budget.

A car sped past me and made it through the traffic light, and I did not.

It wasn't meant to be.

I took my time and made it safely to my destination. I wonder if that car got in a wreck or got a speeding ticket. Is he full of anger and hate? Is he always in a hurry?

I was Christmas shopping and someone picked the last item I wanted before me.

It wasn't meant to be.

I can do without that gift. I will get something better.

I walked into the liquor section to seek a rare bottle of bourbon. A man in front of me grabbed the last collector's edition of a bottle I was about to grab.

It wasn't meant to be.

That's ok. We struck up a nice conversation, and I saved a few dollars for gifts for others.

We may not always get what we want, but we can always look to a better alternative.

175. Down Goes Frazier

I have this amusing habit of shouting "Down goes Frazier!" whenever someone takes a tumble. It's a nod to Howard Cosell's iconic call during the legendary boxing match when Muhammad Ali knocked down Joe Frazier. It usually brings a good laugh for both the person falling and me. A little laughter can lighten the mood in clumsy moments.

However, there was a winter hike in Hocking Hills where my brother slipped and fell just before we reached the end. Without thinking, I shouted my phrase before checking on him.

At that moment, he didn't find it funny, especially while in pain, and I feared he might need to be carried off the trail. Luckily, he managed to hobble to the finish.

Another time, someone took a spill in the bathtub, crying out for help. As I rushed in, I couldn't resist calling out my catchphrase before snapping a quick picture.

Those moments may seem silly, but they remind us that even in our falls, there's always room for a smile. I'll continue to use that phrase, "Down goes Frazier!", as it blends humor with support.

176. The Cold, Harsh Winter Wind

The cold, harsh winter wind cuts through me like a knife.

Aches and pains seem part of my life.

The cold dampness pierces my bones, muscles, and mind with dreaded gloom.

As the dreary site is set before me, I beg for a spray of white snow to cast a splash of color to wash away the gray doom.

I shall find the strength and stand resilient, I must add.

For now, I long for the comfort of a cozy blanket and the furnace turned up a tad.

Nothing warms one more than a warm conversation with friends and family.

This shall turn all gray days to one of happy glee.

177. Live Music Performances

I do not get to see too many live music performances. I'll take a quaint setting and a simple group, band, or solo artist. There is something magical about feeling the artist's emotions and energy wash over me as they perform.

The music resonates and rumbles deep within my soul, leaving a lasting impression upon me. Probably the best live performance is a group of friends just casually jamming on a front porch. Their raw expressions speak volumes about their passion.

I wish I had more time for these experiences because nothing connects me to music quite like seeing it live.

178. Some Songs In A Movie Actually Make The Movie

The soundtrack of a movie often defines its essence. Certain songs resonate so deeply that hearing them instantly transports us back to the film. Music has the incredible ability to evoke emotions, crafting the atmosphere that the director intends.

Imagine Star Wars without its iconic score. It is hard to see Darth Vader enter without his theme. Take Interstellar, where the rising melodies mirror the unfolding narrative, deepening our connection to the story. Each time I hear a note from Rocky, I'm swept into a montage of triumph and grit. Is it Rocky on his journey, or am I reflecting my own struggles and victories? Would Clint Eastwood's westerns be as enjoyable without the stirring music as they whisk us away riding our imaginary horse?

When music and film align perfectly, the experience is transformative. Conversely, a mismatched score can leave us feeling disconnected and disappointed. That's the power of sound; it can shape our perceptions and feelings, reminding us that no matter the obstacles, we can rise to the challenge. Let the music inspire you, acting as a companion to a good movie.

179. The Empty Box

Bob had grown weary of the predictable joy and disappointment that accompanied gift-giving. It was always the same. They either got what they wanted, or they had disappointment cast upon their face as they did not get what they wanted.

One Christmas, as his family was finishing the blazing rush of unwrapping their presents, he could see the familiar mix of delighted smiles and downturned faces.

With a glimmer of excitement and a hint of mischief, Bob presented one last gift to each of them. He handed each of them a simple square box that seemed extremely light. There was no wrapping paper. There were no bows. Each gift was just a simple colored gift box with a lid. Bob then asked them to open them up. As they opened their boxes, excitement, then confusion, clouded their faces as they found nothing but emptiness.

"What kind of gift is this? There is nothing in it. It's just a dumb empty box," his daughter exclaimed. Her voice was full of disbelief.

"Ah, but these boxes are not empty," Bob replied gently, his eyes sparkling with hope. He continued as each member of his family looked upon him with a puzzled looked. "Your box is not empty. Inside are many things. It is full of curiosity to the observer. Within each box lies the essence of life itself, pure air. It is an air filled with memories of joyful laughter ringing through open fields, the thrill of crossing rivers, the adventures that stretch our spirit, and the tears that held us together. It is each birthday candle blown out that breathes life into dreams we still pursue. This is new life. Life to be lived in abundance.

You can accept this gift with the memories of each exhilarating gift you have ever received from me, or you can take it to represent the things that were never fully completed but wished we could."

Slowly, realization dawned on them. His wife embraced him first, understanding the beauty of his words. Soon, his oldest daughter followed, remembering a cherished moment they'd shared.

One by one, his family's expressions transformed from bewilderment to understanding, and in that moment, Bob's seemingly empty boxes became the most precious gifts they had ever received.

180. Will You Walk With Me Under The Pouring Rain?

Will you walk with me under the pouring rain?

I will gladly join you if you hold my hand.

How about a stroll in the soft, falling snow?

I am in if you wrap me in a warm hug.

Will you brighten my day with a smile and rosy cheeks?

I will shine back if you give me a gentle kiss on my cheek.

Will you embrace me with your kind spirit?

I will open my heart wide if you fill it with love.

Together, we can weather any storm and celebrate every moment.

181. Don't Be Afraid To Chase Waterfalls.

Don't be afraid to chase waterfalls. Whenever time and resources permit, I wholeheartedly intend to seek new cascades. The thrill of discovering a hidden gem is unmatched. Whether it is the thunderous crashing sound of a grand falls, or the gentle murmur of a small stream or cascade, the beauty of flowing water speaks to my soul. I am always mesmerized by flowing water, and a waterfall is always the pinnacle of an adventure. Each waterfall, with its own distinct character, awakens my spirit and stirs my emotions. Whether you venture out alone, with friends, or alongside a loved one, chasing waterfalls is always a rewarding adventure. Don't be afraid to chase waterfalls.

Bushkill Falls, Pennsylvania

182. The Seed And The Sower

I dove into a few thought-provoking books and a related captivating movie that shifted my perspective. It struck me that each of us holds a unique responsibility. We can either plant seeds of possibility or become the Sower who nurtures them. Every action we take can blossom into something meaningful for ourselves and others.

I have often pondered my purpose in life, and I believe it may lie in planting seeds of wisdom in my son, letting him cultivate what I have shared with him. He is forging his own path, but I hope to have influenced his choices in a positive manner. At work, I strive to empower my colleagues to become more efficient; their growth inspires me in return.

Take a moment to reflect on the seeds planted within you. Embrace that growth and view the world through new lenses. If we all commit to sowing goodness, we will create a brighter future together. May we all keep planting the seeds and sowing the potential.

183. We Are Such Creatures Of Habit

We are all such creatures of habit that we have difficulty adapting to change. We feel secure in our daily routines. It can be as trivial as toothpaste refusing to cooperate, a slow driver in front of you, or a new, challenging project at work.

Maybe it is an unexpected power outage that interrupts your favorite TV program, or a loud noise like thunder that interrupts your sleep. Even something as small as a missed hug from a loved one. These can all lead to disruptions in our peace, leaving us feeling frustrated, anxious, and out of sync.

When a change occurs, it throws us off our rhythm, and we become upset, angry, nervous, overwhelmed, and even hateful.

Consider the fact that change is not a hurdle but, instead, a doorway to growth. Every disruption presents an opportunity to adapt and learn. Embrace the unpredictability.

Whether you choose to initiate a change, support someone else through it, or simply take a moment to pause and reflect, remember that through change we evolve. We then evolve as individuals, as communities, and as a world. The next time life throws you a curveball, take a breath and see if it is a stepping stone towards something wonderful.

184. What Type Of Goose Are You?

What type of goose are you? Perhaps you're the third one from the right, gliding gracefully in formation, or maybe you're the bold leader at the front, guiding your flock with confidence. Maybe you're the curious one left behind, exploring the cattails, savoring the beauty of your surroundings, even if it means a little solitude for now.

Are you the protective parent, hissing fiercely to defend your mate and the precious eggs, keeping a watchful eye as passersby navigate around your territory? Or could you be the goose destined for a family feast, embodying the spirit of nourishment and togetherness?

No matter what kind of goose you are, embrace your path with pride. Stay strong and true within your formation. Lead with courage, adapt with grace, and always nurture those you love.

If you happen to meet a fork in the road, remember that you have the power to make a positive impact (even if you are eaten, hopefully you will taste good). Fly high, stay true, and be the best goose you can be!

185. Upon Hearing A Last Name

It is quite remarkable how a single name can unlock a treasure trove of memories. Every last name carries with it a hint of nostalgia, evoking images of carefree summer days filled with laughter during backyard games and cherished moments on familiar streets.

Reflecting on those childhood neighbors and friends often reveals a deeper connection to our past than the names we encounter today. Each name, even after years of silence, can spark vivid memories of joy and friendship.

These ties remind us who we are and how they've shaped our lives, grounding us amid the changes that life brings. While some connections may fade, their essence lingers, encouraging us to keep alive the positivity and gratitude they inspire. Embrace those memories; they are a vital part of your story.

186. Dr. Killer Ken Crazy

Professional wrestling, especially in the WWE, is a breathtaking fusion of athleticism and storytelling. Each week, these dedicated athletes step into the ring not just to compete but to spark our imaginations with their larger-than-life personas.

With their meticulously sculpted physiques and dazzling moves, they embody the triumph of heroes and the cunning of villains, inviting us to cheer, gasp, and feel every twist in their narratives. Embrace the thrill of their journeys, as they remind us that passion, resilience, and creativity can transform the ordinary into the extraordinary.

Imagine a character like Dr. Killer Ken Crazy, an imposing figure standing nearly 7 feet tall, adorned in dazzling white sequined pants, with a bold pinstripe that shimmers under the arena lights. His plain white t-shirt and dramatic lab coat only enhance his intense, wild gaze. By his side is Nurse Goodbody, dressed in a crisp white nurse's uniform, with white stockings, white stilettoes, and a surgical mask. Her mask suggests a mysterious backstory about her disfigurement. Was she saved by Dr. Crazy or controlled by him? Clutching the doctor's black bag, she invites you into their captivating world of mystery and chaos.

As the heartbeat sound of a monitor fills the arena and transitions to a chilling flat line, fans erupt with anticipation. The announcer booms, "Dr. Killer Ken Crazy," as the screen shows a flat line monitor. Dr. Crazy, with Nurse Goodbody beside him, makes a formidable entrance. As he steps over the top rope with a commanding presence, the canvas vibrates beneath his feet. With a flair of dramatic elegance, he removes his lab coat and hands it off to Nurse Goodbody. He embraces the moment, ready to unleash his unpredictable force. The energy in the arena surges as fans revel in the anticipation of his wild antics. It is a moment to embrace the wildness and chaos that the genius Dr. Crazy embodies. It is showtime, and everyone is ready to see what havoc Dr. Crazy will unleash.

His regular moves, like the high leg kick and dramatic "scalpel cuts," which are sharp slaps across the chest, echo through the arena and captivate the audience. The crowd gasps in unison with each slap, an exhilarating "Oh!" echoing through the air. Nurse Goodbody provides sneaky moves herself, as she pulls a stethoscope out of the black bag and strangles the opponent, while the doctor is engaged with the referee. The announcer yells, "Is this some form of malpractice or what?" Together, they bring a thrilling twist to the competition, showing that creativity and teamwork can truly dazzle an audience.

His antics intensify as he makes a swipe with his thumb across his own neck. This symbolizes his request for a black surgical glove from Nurse Goodbody. The announcer exclaims, "Uh, Oh, he's calling for it." Nurse Goodbody then pulls one glove from the black bag and tosses it to him. As he puts the one glove on, the announcer screams, "He's going for it. It's the Kavorkian Death Claw." With a fierce expression, he lifts opponents effortlessly by the throat with the gloved hand, and his left hand lifts his body up, and then power slams him to the mat. "He should've called in sick today," the announcer chuckles in. As he gets up from his pin, he swipes his thumb once again across his own neck and makes a gesture of throwing blood at his finished opponent. He then crawls under the mat and pulls out a wooden stretcher and rolls his opponent on it, crafting a spectacle that's impossible to look away from. Then he picks up Nurse Goodbody and carries her away.

In interviews, Dr. Crazy maintains an air of mystery and menace, with Nurse Goodbody silently lurking, further tantalizing the audience's curiosity as reporters ask why she wears a mask. Her eyes enlarge with fear, but no answer is ever given, adding to the secrecy.

When the doctor is asked what he is a doctor of, he proclaims, "I am a doctor of love and destruction." Viewers can't help but be captivated.

The announcer's dry remark, "That's crazy," only adds to the allure.

187. I Saw A Tear Today On Someone's Face

I saw a tear today on someone's face. It was a tiny droplet full of a lifetime's worth of memories. It was clouded yet vibrant, carrying a blend of emotions.

Within its delicate form, I sensed pain, anguish, anger, and hate, but also joy, laughter, pride, and hope. At its tip lingered a profound slice of love. This tear, small and simple, was a reminder that even amidst turmoil, there's always room for hope and healing.

Embrace your emotions as they hold the power to transform and uplift you. Keep believing in the beauty that follows even the heaviest of moments.

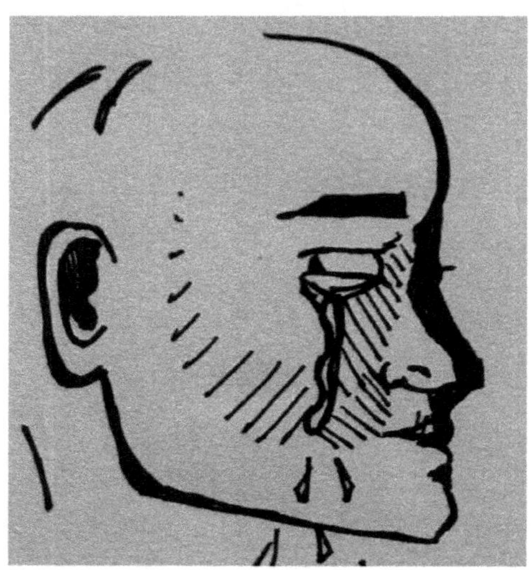

188. Mother Nature Seems Upset With The World

Mother Nature seems upset with the world. Natural disasters seem to be occurring with increased frequency and intensity these days. From raging wildfires to powerful earthquakes and volcanic eruptions, from devastating floods to formidable hurricanes, tsunamis, and tornadoes, Mother Nature showcases her fierce power.

The world is facing so much turmoil and challenges, with shadows of hate and conflict looming large. Political conflict and real wars seem to multiply, and crime is constantly rising. The negativity flooding our nightly news and social media can feel overwhelming, yet it ignites a fierce reaction from Mother Nature. As she weeps, perhaps her storms are not just chaos, but powerful lessons wrapped in the winds of change.

How do we calm her? Do we try to protect her? How do we stop the fighting, the hate, the evil? Maybe she tries to teach us a lesson after each disaster.

To calm her, we must first look inward and embrace compassion that encourages understanding over division and conflict. Each act of love and kindness creates a rippling effect that resonates far and wide, soothing the very fabric of our shared existence.

Protecting her means cherishing the beauty of the planet. We must plant trees, reduce waste, and advocate for sustainability. In doing so, we not only mend the Earth but also mend ourselves.

Let each disaster be a reminder of life's fragile beauty. Together, we can rebuild, rise stronger, and build connections that bind us instead of dividing us. Let's focus on what is truly important in life. If growth is the goal, why do we continue to provoke the very forces that shape us?

Perhaps she graces us with glimpses of greatness when we act with kindness. It could be a breathtaking sunrise following a fierce storm, or fresh life sprouting through the ashes after a forest fire. Maybe it's the warmth of laughter, smiles, and handshakes that bloom after a resolution is reached.

I would love to see more of this.

189. My Mom Out-Fished A Guy With Her Cane Pole

Once, when my mom was pregnant with me, my father and uncle decided to go fishing. With my mom being pregnant, they felt it best not to leave her home alone, so they decided to take her along.

When they parked the car at their favorite fishing spot, they quickly realized that it was not a good idea to just leave her in the car, so they took her with them to the water's edge. They gathered their gear and found their favorite spot on the pier.

Upon arrival, they realized they had no extra fishing pole for her. Undeterred, my uncle fashioned a simple cane pole, attaching a line, hook, and bobber.

As they settled in under the bright sun, their excitement was full. Another fisherman lounged nearby in a flashy chair with the finest equipment. With a sneer, he remarked, "You ain't gonna catch anything with that." But my mom just smiled, undaunted by his doubt.

Suddenly, the bobber dipped. With cheers from my father and uncle, she gave it a strong tug, reeling in one of the day's largest catches. The arrogant fisherman with eyes wide open, huffed in disbelief. He quickly gathered up all of his fishing equipment and chair as well. Before storming off, my mom exclaimed, "That'll teach ya, big boy!"

Gasping in the sun and the glory of showing the man up, she got a nasty sunburn that day. It was a small price to pay for a brilliant victory. It proved that it is not about the size or quality of your equipment and gear; instead, it is how you use it.

190. Different Laughs

Laughter comes in countless forms, and each person has their own delightful twist on it. It's a beautiful expression of joy that unites us, forging positive connections in our lives.

Isn't it amazing how, sometimes, you can identify someone just by their laugh? It's like a signature tune that tells you so much about their mood and spirit. Each laugh tells a unique story, and that is what makes them so special. Embrace your laughter and let it shine. It is a powerful way to spread joy to those around you.

Let's explore some of the different styles of laughter, each with its own charm:

- **The belly laugh** – A burst of deep, loud, hearty laughter that originates from the diaphragm. It involves loud, full-bodied laughter with deep and prolonged breaths. This laughter is considered the most honest type of laughter. It may also be the hardest type to experience. Why? Because we have to find something truly hilarious before we will go with the kind of laughter that has us clutching our bellies and gasping for air. It can be contagious to others.

- **The bray laugh** – A loud and harsh laugh.
- **The break-up or crack-up laugh** – An unrestrained, helpless laugh.
- **Contagious laughter** – This is when one person laughs and everyone else starts laughing as well.

- **The etiquette laughs or the Fake laugh** – A laugh you create when you think you are supposed to laugh, such as when someone tells a bad joke, but you laugh so it doesn't create an uncomfortable atmosphere. It refers to a laugh that is not heartfelt or genuine, often used to appear friendly or polite while concealing true feelings or nervousness.

- **The nervous laugh** – It is a laugh that is often considered fake. It is used in a subconscious attempt in high-stress and high-anxiety situations. Laughing like this can relieve some stress, but if developed into a habit, it can be found to be inappropriate and disapproved by others, making it even more stressful than before.

- **The silent laugh** – This occurs when someone laughs without making any sound. It is usually characterized by the shaking or convulsing of the body, facial expressions, and occasional breathless or wheezing sounds. Silent laughter is also practiced in laughter yoga and laughter therapy. It is often called the Joker's laugh, freezing your face into a smile like the Joker, then letting your belly do the work of pushing air in and out as if you are laughing out loud. A therapeutic clown even teaches sick kids the art of the silent laugh. The silent laugh has enabled kids to fall back asleep after they awake from bad dreams. The children get the calming benefits of the rhythmic exhalations without waking their roommates.

- **The pigeon laugh** – This is similar to the silent laugh. It involves laughing without opening your mouth. By keeping your lips sealed, the laughter produces a humming sound, much like the noise a pigeon makes. It is also compared to the humming of bees.

- **The snort** – This is a sudden and sharp sound made while laughing. It occurs when someone involuntarily inhales air through their nose. They often happen when something is unexpectedly funny or catches someone off guard. They say that 25% of women and 33% of men laugh through the nose. Some people find the snort very disrespectful. Men are more likely to grunt and snort, while women tend to giggle and chuckle.

- **Canned laughter** – This is another term for what is commonly referred to as the "laugh track". It is real laughter that is recorded and added to the soundtrack of a television show. It has been proven that it works. In a study, it was found that even the worst jokes got bigger laughs when they included canned laughter. This practice in sitcoms today, though, is phasing out.

- **The cruel, jeer, crow, or scoff laugh** - This laugh generally refers to a sarcastic laugh that is intended to be hurtful or malicious, often used to mock or demean someone. It is often associated with wickedness and cruelty.

- **The cachinnation or guffaw or cackling laugh** – This is a loud, unrestrained, and often boisterous and convulsive laugh. It is a more intense or exaggerated than a regular laugh. Cackling is a more repetitive laugh. It may sound like a hen laying an egg.

- **The chortle or chuckle** – A soft, partly suppressed, gentle, and low-level laugh, often accompanied by soft repetitive sounds. It is a combination of a chuckle and a snort. It is a mix of laughter and breathy sounds, resulting in a distinctive and often whimsical laugh. It is often associated with finding something amusing or clever.

- **The giggle, titter, or twitter** – This is a foolish or nervous laugh. Giggles are light and high-pitched laughter characterized by short, repeated bursts. It is commonly associated with children or when something is perceived as cute, funny, or silly. Twitter is a means to chatter or to tremble as if agitated.

- **The haw-haw, hee-haw, and horselaugh** – This is a loud laugh that sounds like a horse neighing.

- **The howl and the roar** – These are unrestrained and hearty laughs.

- **The titter, snicker, and snigger** – Titter is a nervous, restrained laugh. The snicker is more disrespectful and similar to a cruel laugh. The snigger adds mischief to it.

- **The squeal** – It is a high-pitched and shrill sound that accompanies a laugh. It is often an expression of delight or extreme amusement. They can be spontaneous and occur when someone is particularly tickled or overwhelmed with joy.

- **The split** – This laugh is a laugh as if someone is going to split their insides open. It is to laugh convulsively, as if continuing to do so will cause one's body to rupture.

- **The frank** – This is an honest, genuine, and without anything hidden or fake.

- **The social laugh** – This is used primarily for social interaction and connection, rather than solely for personal amusement. It is a laugh that is used to build rapport, express agreement, or signal that someone is enjoying themselves and is engaged and comfortable in a group setting. It can ease tension in awkward and uncomfortable situations and can fill silences or transition between topics.

- **The inappropriate, inopportune, or ironic laugh** – This refers to a laugh that is out of sync with the context, emotional state, or situation. It can involve laughing at something that is not funny, laughing when it is not socially appropriate (such as at a funeral), or experiencing paroxysmal laughter (sudden, uncontrollable bursts of laughter).

- **The evil laugh or maniacal laughter** – This is a distinct laugh that is typically exhibited by villains in fiction, especially in the horror genre. It is used to convey a sinister or malicious intent. It can signal the villain's enjoyment of their wrongdoing or a sense of triumph over others. The laugh itself can be written out as "muahaha".

- **The tickle-induced laugh** – This laugh is divided into two types: knismesis, which is a light, feather-like tickle, and gargalesis, which is a heavier, laughter-inducing tickle. Tickle sensations are processed by the brain, which helps determine if the touch is harmful or playful. The brain's ability to anticipate and process self-touch differently from external touch is thought to be one reason why you cannot tickle yourself.

- **The substance-induced laugh** – This is an uncontrollable and inappropriate laugh or cry. It could be Pseudobulbar Affect (PBA), a condition where there are sudden episodes of excessive emotional expression, and can be caused by various neurological conditions, including those that damage or affect certain brain pathways.

A person can howl, roar, scream, shriek, snort, or whoop with laughter. One can also be said to burst or bust out laughing, to convulse with laughter, to die laughing, and to be helpless with laughter, as well as to roll in the aisles (as if unable to keep from falling into the aisle while seated at a humorous performance. Other idioms include "laugh your head off", "laugh yourself silly", and to be in stitches.)

Laughter likely began as a vital tool for building connections and communicating within our groups. It signals safety, camaraderie, and a shared understanding, much like many social animals do. This joyful sound serves as a reminder of our playful nature, from the carefree giggles of childhood to the fun-filled moments of adulthood, enhancing our overall happiness and nurturing positive social interactions.

Imagine laughter as an evolutionary gift, promoting play, cooperation, and unity. Each chuckle releases endorphins, your body's natural pain relievers, uplifting your mood and easing stress. It boosts your intake of oxygen, energizes your heart and muscles, encourages healthy circulation, and can lower blood pressure, all of which contribute to a sharper mind.

Beyond the surface, laughter works wonders for your physical, emotional, and mental well-being. It fosters feelings of relaxation and comfort, allowing you to release pent-up emotions, both joyful and otherwise. As you laugh, your mind clears, your worries fade, and you recharge your spirit, inviting more positivity into your life.

Men are often drawn to women who laugh genuinely, while women tend to appreciate men who possess a good sense of humor, even if they do not laugh frequently. Laughter serves as a powerful tool for alleviating fear and anxiety, helping us put situations into perspective and bolstering our resilience in the face of adversity.

Laughter also acts as a psychological defense mechanism, surfacing when we confront mental difficulties, easing our internal tension. It is important to acknowledge that laughter can sometimes take on a more aggressive tone when used to mock or demean others, as it can provide a false sense of superiority.

The benefits of laughter are indisputable. Children giggle an impressive 300-400 times a day, while adults typically only manage about 18-24 laughs. Embracing laughter can boost your immune system, lower stress levels, relax your muscles, improve your mood, and burn calories.

Everyone can benefit from a good laugh! Laughter isn't just a skill; it's a wonderful routine that anyone can adopt. Look for humor in those little daily mishaps—find the silver lining and chuckle it off. Don't wait for laughter to find you; sometimes, a little forced giggle can work wonders too.

Take a few moments each day to seek out something that tickles your funny bone—whether it's a silly video, a comedy show, or a chat with a friend. Laughter has a way of brightening our hearts!

Consider trying laughter yoga, an uplifting blend of movement and mirth that can really boost your spirits and help fend off the blues.

Remember, choosing laughter over frustration is a beautiful gift you can give yourself. Embrace it fully, and watch how it transforms your day and uplifts your life.

191. Dancing Flames

There is an undeniable charm of a cozy campfire, a crackling fireplace, or a small blaze flickering in the backyard. As the flames spring to life, I'm drawn in by their graceful dance, twisting and turning over the logs, shifting in color and shape. When a fire settles on a sturdy log, it becomes a living performance with each flicker a new expression of its energy.

The dynamic rhythm of air and gas transforms the flames into a mesmerizing spectacle, wrapping me in warmth and comfort. It's a wonderful escape, allowing my worries to fade as I lose myself in their hypnotic movements. Watching the flames is not just enchanting; it's a reminder of the beauty in simplicity.

As a retired firefighter, I appreciate the power that fire holds, but here, in this peaceful moment, I find a soothing allure. I embrace the fire's gentle dance, and I let it ease my mind and uplift my spirit.

192. Sunrise Vs Sunset

I pose this question to you: Do you prefer a sunrise or a sunset?

For me, it's the sunrise that captivates my heart. As the first light of day breaks, it fills me with strength and promise.

Sunrises are symbols of new beginnings, brimming with promise and the potential of what lies ahead. Each dawn paints the sky with fresh colors filled with opportunity and hope, inspiring us to rise and embrace the day's adventures.

 In contrast, sunsets often offer a chance for reflection and gratitude. To me, they bring a sense of sadness, serving as a reminder of the day's closure and the goals left unmet.

I will try not to end each night with regrets and sorrow, but instead cherish the moments that filled my heart throughout the day. The sunrise will always awaken me with a warm smile.

Every day is a chance to grow, learn, and fulfill your aspirations.

193. The Girl With The Blue Feather

He awoke once more, uncertainty swirling around him. "Why does it always feel like this?" he pondered, feeling disoriented and struggling to piece together his memories, which were only flashes of a few friends and a meal at a small, cozy café.

Suddenly, a spirited boy burst into the room. "Hurry, hurry, it's today," he exclaimed.

Confused, he asked, "What's today?"

The boy chuckled, "Don't be silly. The festival starts today, and you have to do the thing."

Sitting up, he queried, "What thing?"

The boy pointed playfully, "You're just joking. Get dressed, we have to leave soon."

With that, the boy dashed out, skipping and singing, a bright light beckoning him to join the excitement awaiting outside.

The man got dressed and joined the eager boy in the next room. Brimming with excitement, the boy stood by the door, ready to go. Together, they set off for the festival, and while a mix of uncertainty and curiosity churned in the man's chest, he couldn't help but feel a spark of anticipation for what may lay ahead.

They arrived at the festival, buzzing with energy and adorned with vibrant canopies, tables, and melodies. Spotting a vendor struggling with her canopy, the boy pointed it out. The man quickly noticed the issue and jumped in to help, freeing a snag on the leg. The young boy beamed at him and declared, "And so it begins." The man glanced at him, curiosity flickering in his eyes.

As they strolled along, they encountered a flower vendor. The man admired the vibrant hues but couldn't help noticing some colors clashed. Curious, he asked the vendor for permission to rearrange them. The vendor happily agreed. Once finished, the display radiated warmth and joy, like a sunbeam captured in petals. With a satisfied smile, the vendor handed him a bright sunflower.

Out of nowhere, a soft wail of a baby echoed behind them. He turned instinctively, offering the sunflower he held to the child. Instantly, the crying ceased, and a warm smile spread across the mother's face. In gratitude, she handed the man a vibrant piece of orange chalk. He glanced at the chalk in awe, then looked up to find the entire festival crowd focused on him, the music fading into silence. The boy pointed eagerly to a clear space on the stone pathway, inviting him to draw upon it.

He began to instinctively draw with the chalk a radiant sun, its rays stretching out to embrace everyone around him. It felt like the perfect symbol for the festival, one that would unit everyone in joy. Spotting more chalk, he keenly handed it out to all the children nearby. They animatedly joined in, creating connections between their drawings and the sun. In that moment, he witnessed a beautiful connection forming as people gathered, their hands intertwined around their children, fueling their creative spirits. The links between the radiant sun and the diverse drawings symbolized a shared unity, a gentle reminder that they all belonged to something much larger than themselves. What began as uncertainty blossomed into a profound sense of togetherness. He realized this was more than just a festival; it was a vibrant celebration of life, creativity, and community. He had the uncanny sensation that he had done something like this before. It once again felt strange to him.

He continued to walk amongst the crowd of people. The smiles around him shone even brighter than when he first arrived. When he looked at everything, he saw a different way to make it brighter and more colorful. He saw that the sunlight was their guide to life.

As he strolled past two tables, one brimming with refreshing lemonade and the other showcasing beautifully painted glassware, a spark of inspiration struck him. "Why not sell the lemonade in your gorgeous glassware?" he suggested, his eyes shining with enthusiasm. The vendors exchanged smiling glances, their faces lighting up with understanding, and with a joyful clink of their colorful creations, they toasted to the new idea. In the midst of it all, the man was given a glass for himself, ready to savor the delicious moment.

As he took a sip of his drink, he turned to find a girl sitting alone at a nearby table. Their eyes locked instantly, and he felt a spark of intrigue.

Unlike everyone else in their simple shorts and t-shirts, she wore a beautiful floral dress that seemed to dance with color. Her smooth complexion and bright blue eyes were captivating, drawing him in further. Her red hair, intricately braided, framed her face perfectly, but it was the striking blue feather tucked in her hair that truly captured his attention.

Just as he was about to approach her, the vendors beside him began expressing gratitude for his kindness. When he turned back, the enchanting girl had vanished into the crowd.

Throughout the day at the festival, he continued to offer his assistance to those in need. With a keen eye for solutions, he noticed countless challenges around him. One touching moment involved a vibrant blanket; he gently wrapped a baby in its soft embrace, bringing warmth and comfort not just to the little one but also to the mother, filling the air with a sense of security and love. He felt an inexplicable urge to cradle the baby in the blanket a little longer, as if the moment held a deeper significance he couldn't quite grasp.

The clouds began to fill the sky, and the boy who accompanied him said, "I think our time is coming to an end." The clouds quickly turned into a soft rain cascading down upon the festival and its people. The man and the boy made their way to leave, but the man turned one last time to see the chalk drawings slowly being washed away by the rain. He found himself looking at the table where the girl with the blue feather was. The rain began to cloud his view, and with a feeling of sorrow, he left with the boy.

For the next few days, he woke up early and found himself going back to the stone pathway and to the table the girl had once sat at. The drawings were all washed away, and there was no sign of the girl at all.

Then one day the young boy said to him, "I don't know why, but I think our time together is coming to an end." The man looked at him with another questioning look. The boy smiled and said, "It may have been short, but it has all been well worth it."

"I don't understand.", said the man.

The boy replied, "Hopefully, you will one day." The boy handed the man a piece of chalk. The man instantly headed for the stone walkway.

He drew another sunshine on the stone. He looked at it and asked the young boy for a piece of blue chalk. The boy handed him a small sliver of blue chalk. The man used the entire piece to draw a blue feather into the sun he had already drawn. The boy said to him, "That should work." They left once again, but a different feeling came over him. He thought it might be hope. He thought it might be thankfulness to the young boy. Yet, there were still many unanswered questions.

The next day, he went back to the stone walkway and to his drawing. When he looked down upon it, he found a real blue feather lying upon it. He reached down and picked the feather up.

In an instant, he was transported to an entirely new place, a different time, a captivating realm. The blue feather remained clutched in his hand. He sensed a presence behind him and turned around. There stood the girl once more, and their eyes once again locked together in a familiar embrace.

She had a different dress on, of a different floral pattern. The braided hair this time was free from the blue feather in it. Her stunning blue eyes sparkled with a knowing light. Cradled in her arms this time was a delicate blanket, and as she unveiled its contents, his breath caught in his throat. Inside lay a baby, an image of himself reflected back at him. He was overcome with emotions and questions.

She beckoned to him, "Come with me, and I will show you everything you need to know." They strolled to a bench perched at the edge. His gaze flickered between the girl, the baby, and the inviting seat. As he settled onto the bench, he peered over the ledge and gasped in awe. Before him lay a world beyond his wildest dreams. Enormous structures floated effortlessly in the air, and mysterious objects zipped between them. Colors burst into life all around him, vivid and captivating. There was no clear distinction between up and down; the sky was a brilliant blue, stretching endlessly, without a cloud in the sky. He turned his focus back to the girl and the baby, ready for the extraordinary path that lay ahead for him.

"Do you know why you are here?" she asked. "I'm not entirely certain, but I have a feeling, and a sense, that this is where I belong." She looked a bit relieved. "I have been following you for quite some time."

She began to unveil the secrets of this world before him, a realm that had withstood a devastating assault from another dimension. "Unlike other worlds governed by sun, air, and water, ours is ruled by the continuum," she explained, her voice steady yet gentle.

With a deep breath, she continued, "I regret to inform you that during the attack, your parents lost their lives. Your wife is gone too, but I have your baby, and I'm here as your sister."

Her eyes sparkled with hope. "You possess a unique gift; you see things differently. You have the power to mend what seems broken, often without even realizing it. You unravel intricate problems in our world, while in others, you discovered elegant and simple solutions. To protect you, we sent you away at the onset of the attack, altering your memory as you journeyed through various worlds. I watched over you, and once it was safe, I reached out. The feather was a vital link, a way for you to reconnect with this realm. You had to initiate that connection by touching something from home."

Encouragingly, she added, "As you spend time here, your memories will return. We've fought back the assault, but our continuum is faltering. This world needs you at this time. You must restore it before this world and all of us fade away."

He cradled the baby in his arms, gently kissed his sister on the forehead, and said, "Let's go. There seems to be little time left. Hold my hand as this is yet unfamiliar." As she took his hand, a shimmering silver sphere emerged above the ledge, revealing two seats facing each other. They climbed inside, and the sphere sealed itself, whisking them away to a new structure.

Once inside, they were surrounded by a bustling crowd and towering walls adorned with intricate formulas. Conversations buzzed around them, but as he took a step forward, everything fell silent, and all eyes turned to him. "Dear brother," a voice echoed, "it's time to embrace your destiny."

He studied the intricate formulas on the walls and pondered aloud, "What if we rearranged three of these walls from 1, 2, 3 to 1, 3, 2?"

With a confident gesture, he flipped some writings upside down and rotated a few characters in unexpected ways. "That should do it," he declared, satisfaction washing over him.

As the crowd watched in anticipation, an elderly man with wispy white hair approached. "Your parents would be proud," he said, a warm smile lighting up his face.

At that moment, the world began to realign, freed at last to move freely within the universe once more. He looked at his sister and then at his child. A tear formed upon his face. His sister wiped it away and said the child was his wife's greatest gift to him.

194. Orange Barrel Farm

Just as spring breathes life into gardens, the orange barrels spring forth with purpose, marking new beginnings on our roadways. They are like vibrant flowers, tucked away in their hidden farm, patiently waiting for the right moment to reveal their bright orange hues.

As the sun warms the earth, these barrels emerge from their slumber, ready to guide us through the transformational landscape of construction and renewal.

Embrace their presence as they progress, growth, and the promise of a better journey ahead. Full bloom is not far off. Watch as they inspire change right before your eyes.

195. My Thoughts Crackle Like An Electrifying Thunderstorm

On certain nights, when sleep eludes me, my thoughts crackle like an electrifying thunderstorm. Waves of ideas surge through my mind with an endless stream of worries, aspirations, and to-do lists. It sounds something like this: I need sleep. I'd love to watch that game a bit longer. Imagine sleeping in instead of heading to work. But I need to work. I have bills to pay. I keep trying to set aside money for that upcoming event. Oh, and that thing needs fixing. The yard could use some mowing, too, and I really want to sit outside. I need a deck, a patio, and some nice chairs.

Time is slipping away, and I need sleep. I need to help my family and friends with those things and that stuff. I should read more, do more crafts, and listen to more music. That song I heard today was fantastic, and I spotted an unusual bird. Is that a strange noise outside? Am I hot or cold? I am quite thirsty. I need to go to the bathroom. My knee is bothering me. I need to exercise more. Will I ever lose some weight? I need to write more. I want to go on an adventure. Why do I fall asleep on the couch, but now I am wide awake? I need to sleep.

Sleep is a precious thing. I know some who can sleep without any interruptions. Others live off of only a few hours of sleep. Some sleep with a ton of covers, while others barely with a sheet. I know of people who have to have it pitch black and wear a mask. A few can sleep on the floor, or on a couch in the brightest of days, or during a tornado or a bad storm. I just want to sleep.

196. Bounce From Cloud To Cloud

If you could bounce from cloud to cloud and slide down sun ray slides?

If you could fly away with dandelion seeds in the bright blue sky?

If you could dance under the pale moonlight to an unknown melody with radiant fireflies blinking to the beat of the music?

If you could ride a powerful ocean wave with the spirit of jumping dolphins?

If you could float from the peak of a snow-topped mountain, kissed by the wind, to the tip of someone's nose as a snowflake?

If you could ride on a small brown leaf, down a gently flowing stream?

Would you, could you, do it with me?

197. If The Trees Could Talk

If the trees could talk to the rocks, what would they say?

Maybe they would say, "Don't be so hard on yourself, you are strong and steadfast. Your strength is your beauty."

And if the rocks could converse with the waves, what would they say?

Maybe they would say, "Embrace your rhythm as your dance brings life and joy powerfully and gracefully."

Should the waves whisper to the wind, what would they say?

Maybe they would say, "Stay calm, my friend, as your breath guides us all. Your whispers carry our stories across the world."

If the wind could share thoughts with the sun, what would it say?

Maybe it would say, "Have confidence as your radiant light warms our hearts with hope."

And if the sun called upon you, what would they say?

Maybe it would say, "Live without fear. Embrace each day with open arms as you let your heart shine brightly. Love is the flame that dispels darkness and lets the light of love within you guide you on your journey."

198. The Ocean Waves Cast Their Music Before Me

The ocean waves cast their music before me. The waves offer a symphony around me, each one with its own distinct song. Some crash with bold tempo and volume, while others whisper softly.

Each melody is a unique tale, with some lingering longer than others. They dance and sway along the spectrum of the water's essence, rising and falling along a scale with a captivating, unique rhythm of the ocean. They rise and fall, ebbs and flows, and I embrace this fluid melody as it inspires and encourages me to flow with life's ups and downs. Each note resonates with the beauty of nature, reminding us of the ever-changing landscape around us.

As each tune ends as it reaches my feet, I listen and search for the next song. I hear the percussion of another wave taking its turn. These endless harmonies continue to flow on, each note a different, beautiful riff. The music never stops.

The performance concludes as I turn towards the sunrise, basking in its glorious colors. It is a promise of new beginnings, just as each wave will cast its own song. It is a perfect encore to a mesmerizing performance.

199. The Stress, The Massage, The Relief, The Realization To Change

After a long drive and a tiring timeshare presentation topped off with an extravagant meal, I decided to treat myself to a massage during my vacation. I found a nearby spa and, surprisingly, it had an opening for an hour-long session. I expressed my concerns about my shoulders and knees and mentioned my interest in hot stone therapy.

Upon arrival, the therapist, attentive to my needs, inquired if I'd like a deep tissue massage. Perhaps it was the tone in my voice on the phone and when I arrived, or the weariness etched on my face that prompted her suggestion.

I was ushered into room 2 without much time to unwind, but I went with the flow. As I settled face down on the towel and pillow, I was ready to embrace the relaxation ahead. Some might view this as pure pain, but I was ready to confront the tension embedded in my muscles.

As she began kneading my shoulders, we both swiftly recognized the weight of stress I was carrying. I had experienced deep tissue massages before, but nothing compared to the intensity she wielded.

With one elbow pressing into my tense muscles while her other hand steadied herself and pulled away from the tightness, she expertly uncovered numerous knots, each a testament to my buried tension and stress.

Her focus shifted from a full-body treatment to a dedicated effort on my shoulders and back, where she offered unyielding attention. "Your shoulders and back are a mess," she remarked, and I could only agree.

For 45 minutes, she persisted, addressing not just my shoulders and back, but also a few tight spots in my arms and hips. Unfortunately, the time raced by, leaving my legs and knees untouched. I never even rolled to my backside the entire time.

I was face down the entire session, surrendering to her mission to release the knots. While it may have been an intense experience, it was also a reminder of the healing power of persistence and self-care. I quickly learned to regulate my breathing to match the intensity of her work.

When she asked if I was okay, I assured her I was just focusing on my breaths. She chuckled as she noticed the beads of sweat forming, telling me it was my body's reaction to the pressure on those tight, stressed areas.

A few times, I involuntarily jumped at the sensation, and we shared a laugh as she reminded me to breathe. Together, we felt the tightness in my muscles begin to melt away. She offered a hot towel to my back that worked just as well as hot stones. Not all tightness was gone, and not all areas were addressed in the time provided, but it was progress.

When it was finally over, I dressed and stepped into the world again, only to realize I must have looked bewildered and like someone emerging from a deep slumber or even a fight. Her immediate response was to hand me two bottles of water, insisting I hydrate and take a hot shower. After paying and leaving a tip, I reflected on the experience. As I left, I couldn't help but feel lighter, reassured that the journey to relief had just begun.

It's amazing how stress can show up in our bodies. This massage revealed the much-needed changes I must make to handle stress more effectively.

While I appreciated the relief this deep tissue session brought, I recognize it's not for everyone, nor is it a solution for every time stress rears its head. I savored the discomfort and am now committed to exploring new ways to manage my stress moving forward.

200. I Am Just A Single Pea In A Pea Pod

I am just a single pea in a pea pod. Yet, the pod itself is me cherishing those who closely love me, and I them. The pea pod itself is part of a stalk. Together, the stalk is my close friends and other family members standing resiliently as a unit, sheltered by the sturdy stalk of friendship and family. The row of stalks is my community. It is a collective strength, nurturing each one of us as we grow. The field it lays in is my country. A vast number of communities were forged into one.

I worry about the uncertainty that what forces of nature may strike upon me and my pea pod. I worry if someone or something will trample everything away.

I question every day if I, as a small pea in a pea pod, can still make a difference in the world. Even the smallest pea can create ripples in the soil around it. Every kind word, every act of love, can inspire change and cultivate a garden of hope.

I may feel small, but I hope my impact can be boundless. I am truly different and unique, for it is exactly what the world needs. I will stand tall, even as a little pea.

About The Author:

Pauley lives in Oberlin, OH, with his significant other, Debbie. Besides writing, Pauley likes to watch birds, play board games with his friends, and review beers on his Untapped page. Rising at the unconventional hour of 4:30 am, Pauley hears the chatter of early-rising birds at his backyard feeders, claiming it's the best time for creative sparks. By 7:00 pm, when most are winding down, he's already tucked in, dreaming of new stories.

Pauley loves exploring local trails and dreaming up stories under the Ohio sky. He crafts stories inspired by the world around him and the human connections he has made over the course of years.

- Spencer Pauley – son, Journalist in Seattle, Washington.

I would like to thank the following:

My son, Spencer Pauley, did some massive editing, critiquing, and offered endless suggestions. He encouraged me to continue when others laughed at my work.

Deborah Huston-Robertson, for listening endlessly to my re-writes and various thoughts and ideas.

Sketches by Arianna Ambrosio